Penguin Book 2803
The Anti-Death League

Kingsley Amis, who was born at Clapham in 1922, was educated at the City of London School and St John's College, Oxford. At the age of eleven he embarked on a blank-verse miniature epic at the instigation of a preparatory school master, and he has been writing verse ever since. Until the age of twenty-four, however, he remarks: 'I was in all departments of writing *abnormally unpromising.*' With James Michie he edited *Oxford Poetry 1949*. Until 1963 he was a university teacher of English; he is a keen science-fiction addict, an admirer of 'white jazz' of the thirties, and the author of frequent articles and reviews in most of the leading papers and periodicals. His novels include *Lucky Jim*, *That Uncertain Feeling*, *I Like it Here*, *Take a Girl Like You*, *My Enemy's Enemy* (short stories), and *One Fat Englishman*. *A Frame of Mind* and *A Case of Samples* are the titles of his books of poetry, and *New Maps of Hell* is a survey of science fiction. His latest works are *The James Bond Dossier*, a novel, *The Egyptologists*, written in collaboration with Robert Conquest, and *The Anti-Death League*. Kingsley Amis has two sons and a daughter.

Kingsley Amis

The Anti-Death League

Penguin Books

Penguin Books Ltd, Harmondsworth, Middlesex, England
Penguin Books Australia Ltd, Ringwood, Victoria, Australia

First published by Victor Gollancz 1966
Published in Penguin Books 1968
Copyright © Kingsley Amis, 1966

Made and printed in Great Britain by
Hazell Watson & Viney Ltd, Aylesbury, Bucks
Set in Linotype Granjon

To Colin

Contents

Part 1

The Edge of a Node

A girl and an older woman were walking along a metalled pathway. To their left, beyond a strip of grass, was the front of a large high building in grey stone. Reaching its corner, at which there was a pointed turret, brought them a view of a square of grass on which stood a tower-like structure supported by stone pillars. The afternoon sun was shining brightly and the space under the main part of the tower was in deep shadow.

The girl halted. 'What's happening?' she asked.

'That's just the old cat,' said the other. 'He's spotted something under the tower there, I expect.'

A small black cat, crouching quite still, faced the shadow. After a moment, a bird with tapering wings flew out, dipped towards the cat, gave two brief twitters and wheeled back to where it had come from. The girl went on watching.

'Oh, you know what that is,' said the older woman. 'She'll have got a nest under there, the bird, and she's trying to keep the cat away from it. Trying to give him a scare, you see.'

As she spoke, three uniformed men came into sight round the corner of the block beyond the tower and walked along the path towards the women. At the same time, a large aircraft, flying low, moved into earshot.

The bird made its circuit exactly as before. 'Why doesn't he move?' asked the girl. 'Can't he see the bird?'

'Oh, you bet he can. He's not missing anything, that old cat. He's got his eye on her all right. But he's not going to move and give the game away. Now we'll just watch them the once more and then we'll be getting on, shall we?'

The three in uniform came up. One of them, a tall fair-complexioned young man, slowed in his walk and stopped. 'Look at this,' he said. 'Did you ever see anything like it?'

'Like what?' asked the older of the two with him.

'That tower.'

'Just a water-tower they thought they might as well do in the same style. A bit sinister, I agree.'

The sound of the aircraft grew in volume sharply. The cat ran off towards a tree growing beside the path. Just when the girl turned and looked at the tall young man it was as if the sun went out for an instant. He flinched and drew in his breath almost with a cry.

'God, did you feel that?'

'I'll say I did. I thought I'd had a stroke or something.'

'It was like the passing of the shadow of death,' said the third man.

'But what it really was was the passing of the shadow of a passenger aircraft. Look, it'll cross that slope in a second. There.'

'Thank Christ for that,' said the tall young man. 'I really felt like, you know, a fly when the swatter comes down. Gave me quite a turn.'

He looked again at the girl, who was not looking at him. The older woman, however, was, and unamiably.

'Come along, Mrs Casement,' she said with an abruptness she had not shown earlier. 'We haven't got all night, dear. You're not the only one, you know.'

The two groups diverged.

'I never took our James for a student of architecture, did you, Moti?' asked the senior of the three officers, a gaunt man wearing a major's crowns and a clergyman's collar and silk.

'Ah, there you have his well-known subtlety, padre. He was really admiring something far more worth a young man's while than cold stones, am I right, James?'

'Well, yes. I thought she was wonderful, didn't you? Extraordinary eyes. But sort of blank and frightened.'

'Probably the shadow of that plane,' said the clergyman. 'It is scaring if you don't know what it is. It even got me until I remembered. I was quite used to it at one time.'

'I should have said she was frightened already. But then who wouldn't be in a bloody place like this?'

The clergyman frowned. 'It's got a pretty good reputation. I'm sure they all do what they can.'

'By putting up this sort of thing, for instance?'

The pathway had broadened to a circle. In the middle was an ornamental pond, its stonework discoloured and scabbed with moss, and in the centre of this a plinth on which crouched a stone creature somewhat resembling a lion. Each of its claws became a thin stem ending in a flower shaped like a flattened bell, from which in turn protruded a kind of tongue with three points. The thin tail appeared to have been broken off short and the break filed smooth. From the smiling mouth there curled upwards a triple tongue with a small object, not certainly identifiable, at each point. Every inch of the surface had at one time been enamelled with minute designs, but these were largely weathered away.

'A nice welcoming sort of chap to run into on your way in here,' said the young man addressed as James. 'I dreamt about him the other night.'

'Good for you.' The clergyman took him by the arm and drew him off towards a flight of stone steps that led up to the entrance of the building. 'Is there anything like that in your part of the world, Moti?'

'Not that I know of, I'm thankful to say. We're a pretty morbid lot in our own fashion, but rather more direct. We leave that kind of thing to our yellow brethren. In fact I seem to remember seeing a photo of a gentleman somewhat resembling our friend, though minus the horticulture, standing in a palace at Peking or one of those places. An interesting sidelight.'

They reached a panelled vestibule with notices on every hand, some pinned to the woodwork, others on small stands. *Pre-Raphaelite Exhibition All This Month in Lecture Room B*, said one. *Coach Excursion to St Jerome's Priory: Names to Office by Friday Please*, said another.

'What used to be at the end of his tail, do you think?'

The clergyman glared. 'Come off it, James, for heaven's sake. What's the matter with you today? I could give you my theory about that, and back it up, but it wouldn't go too well with my cloth. And what do you care?'

'Oh, the respected cloth.'

'Yes, the respected cloth. I know it's a bit threadbare in places, but it's all I've got. Now chin in, shoulders back, arms swung as high as the waist-belt to front and rear and get set to cheer him up. That reminds me – give me that cake.'

A small parcel was passed from hand to hand as they walked down the dip of a corridor that rose again out of sight.

'Intimations of infinity,' said the officer called Moti, taking in this effect. 'Highly therapeutic.'

'Oh, look at this,' said the clergyman after a moment. 'The Army's here. I detect the hand of Captain Leonard. Applied, as you might expect, a little late in the day.'

They approached a recessed double door outside which a young N C O was rising to his feet from a folding chair. Before him was a card-table on which lay an open foolscap notebook and a couple of technical manuals.

'Good afternoon, gentlemen,' he said, coming smartly to attention. 'You wish to visit Captain Hunter, I take it?'

'Yes, if the Army Council has no objection. What the devil are you doing here? I mean it's nice to see you, Fawkes, but what are you in aid of?'

The N C O grinned. 'Security, Major Ayscue.'

'I thought it might be that. Captain Leonard's inspiration?'

'His orders, sir. Everybody who comes and goes has to have his or her full name written down here, plus the time he or she came and went. Very vital information, those times. Captain Leonard was most insistent about them. Oh, and it might interest you to know, sir, that all visitors have got to go down in the book whether it's Captain Hunter they've come to see or not. You never know whether a North Korean mightn't worm himself in with a tape-recorder, you see.'

'There wasn't anyone here when I came last week.'

'No doubt, Mr Churchill, but that was last week. And this week we're making a special effort, because Captain Hunter might be coming out in a few days and we're only on the second page of the book. Now let's see' – he began writing – 'Fifteen forty-four hours ... Major ... Ayscue ... Captain ... Naidu ...'

'Is it all right for us to go in now, Fawkes?' asked Ayscue.

'Oh, I think so, sir. Captain Leonard did tell me not to let anyone by until I'd written them down, but I think I can hold Mr Churchill's name in my head for a few more seconds. You'll find Captain Hunter very cheerful, by the way. Quite his old self.'

'Thank you, Corporal Fawkes,' said Naidu. 'I take it I shan't be required to furnish a photostat of my commission to the Minister of Defence?'

'No, sir. Captain Leonard didn't say anything about that.'

The three officers entered a long airy room with sunlight beating through the windows. More light was reflected from the glossy walls and from the glass of the many pictures hanging on these. Down the middle ran a trestle table that bore dozens of vases of flowers and plants in pots. Thick streamers of greenery curled down from wire baskets attached to the ceiling.

A figure sitting up in bed at the far end of the room raised an arm and the visitors approached. On either side, also in bed, were men reading, men apparently asleep, men lying down but not asleep. One man was looking carefully round the room, as if for the first time, while another man in white trousers and tee-shirt watched him as carefully from a nearby chair. Yet another man, with irregular patches of grey hair on a grey scalp, got up from a bench by the window and moved away, keeping track of the arrivals out of the corner of his eye.

The man who was putting the Army to so much trouble seemed very much at home. He was lying back against advantageously arranged pillows within reach of various comforts: non-glossy illustrated magazines, paperback novels on the covers of which well-developed girls cringed or sneered, a comparatively hardback work on how to win at poker, a couple of newspapers folded so as to reveal half-completed crossword puzzles, a tin jug containing a cloudy greyish fluid, packets of French cigarettes and an open box of chocolates. Captain Hunter, a thin pale man of twenty-eight with a thin black moustache, smiled and extended his hand.

'Hullo, boys,' he said, and offered cigarettes which Ayscue and Churchill accepted. 'I'm afraid I can't give you a light.

15

You're not allowed to have matches and stuff in here because you might start burning the place down. Almost certainly would, in fact. Oh, thank you, James. Is that parcel for me? What's in it?'

'A cake,' said Ayscue. 'But don't go cutting it now.'

'My dear Willie, I couldn't if I wanted to. No knives like no matches. But the nice nurse comes on at six and he might see his way to lending me one.'

'Well, mind he isn't about when you start slicing.'

'What . . . ? I suppose there's a file and a rope-ladder in it.'

'Not exactly.' Naidu spoke with some disapproval. 'A different mode of escape.'

'You don't mean . . . ?'

'Yes,' said Churchill. 'Three quarter-bottles of White Horse. Corporal Beavis baked the thing up in the Mess kitchen. Sorry we couldn't get any more in.'

'Quite enough for a man in my condition. Thank you all most awfully.'

'How is your condition, Max?' asked Ayscue.

'Oh, splendid. Dr Best is very pleased with me. He says he's been able to explain to me just why I got myself into the state I did and so I shouldn't have any more trouble. He's letting me out on probation next Wednesday.'

Churchill said diffidently, 'What was the explanation he gave you? If you want to talk about it, of course.'

'I haven't the remotest notion, dear boy. I'm only telling you what he says he's done. He likes doing all the talking himself. It must come from being supposed to ask so many questions. I just let him get on with it.'

'It's bound to be a difficult task, giving it up,' said Naidu. 'But you can rely on us three to give you all the support and encouragement in the world.'

'Whatever is possessing you, Moti? Nobody said anything about giving it up. Any fool can give it up. I'm going to do something much more worthwhile than that – ditching alcoholism and taking up very heavy drinking. Talking of drinking, I'll have to watch that Scotch. Too much at one go and I'll start acting sober, and that'd be suspicious. You see, these pills they give you, when they really get hold of you you start acting pissed all the time. That's how they know when you're taking a turn for the better.'

'You're not acting pissed,' said Churchill.

'I'd like to think I've always known how to hold my liquor.'

'You weren't holding it too well the night we brought you here.'

'No gentleman can or should be always a gentleman. Some get more ungentlemanly than others, though. You see that white-haired old buffer down by the door? Last Saturday he was let out on a week's probation. Very early indeed on Tuesday morning they carted him back in, pissed. The "they" included a small detachment of police as well as a crying wife. There was no end of a to-do, I can assure you. I haven't heard such language since that last Sergeants' Mess party. At lunch-time today he fell out of bed. What do you think of that? Just try to imagine how he must have attacked the stuff to be still pissed after four and a half days. And he only had two days and a bit to fill his tanks. You know, I can't help finding that rather disturbing? It seems to flout some basic law. Oh, if you can't manage another cake by say Monday, do you think you could send me a book about drinks, cocktail recipes or what-not? There's a lot to be said for pornography in the absence of the real thing. Ask anybody.'

'You'd better be careful with those empties,' said Ayscue.

'Oh, no problem. I shall just heave them out of the loo window. There's a sort of cairn of broken bottles in the bushes by that corner. I found it on one of my rambles through the extensive grounds when, disinclined to trudge all the way back indoors for the purpose, I was looking for a place to pee. That wasn't all I found, either. In a brief circuit of fifty yards or so I came across no fewer than three very amorous couples, and that was without trying to come across them. Quite the contrary. I was virtually threading my way. I get the impression everybody's at it all the time. It's no more than you'd expect in an environment like this.'

Churchill ground out his cigarette. 'Not everybody, surely.'

'I was speaking figuratively. Not everybody, no. I question

whether the catatonics do much in that way, and no doubt the senility wards have a stainless record. Dr Best took me round them the other afternoon. Nothing personal about it – it's a standard trip, all part of the service. I was expecting him to take the opportunity to deliver a little lecture on the perils of self-abuse, but for once he let things speak for themselves.'

When none of the other three said anything, Hunter went on, 'I had our old buddy Brian Leonard round here a couple of days ago. He'd really come to keep Fawkes up to the mark, he told me, but having come so far he saw nothing against walking the few extra yards to my bedside. He wasn't entirely happy, he said. He seemed to think that a dipsomaniac in charge of the administration of a secret-weapons training unit represented some kind of danger to security. I did what I could to reassure him. I pointed out that if the worst threat of that sort came from the odd dipsomaniac then he hadn't much to worry about. He agreed with that, and said that anyway he was satisfied I didn't know enough to be a menace.'

Naidu had thrown off the slight uneasiness he had been betraying in the previous few minutes. 'If that is so,' he said accusingly, 'how does brother Leonard justify this quite ridiculous fandango with the unfortunate Corporal Fawkes at the door like the recording angel?'

Hunter did his silent laugh. 'We went into that. He was very man-to-man about it – I've never felt so close to him before. He was sure I'd agree that one had to go through the motions in matters of this sort. He never knew when his master in White-hall mightn't want to know what was being done to stop this dipso admin officer's mouth, in the talking sense, that is, and the Fawkes arrangement would cover him. I asked him whether in that case a sentry in radiation battle order mightn't be even more impressive, and he said he could tell I was joking and clapped me on the back and we had a jolly good laugh together. You know, I must introduce Brian to Dr Best one of these days. They'd get on like a house on fire.'

'Did Leonard say anything about this spy idea of his?' asked Naidu.

'Only that he was more convinced than ever that there was

one, at least one, somewhere in the unit. In fact he said he now had positive proof – he wouldn't tell me what sort. But he still had very little idea of who the spy might be, except that he'd now more or less ruled out the high-security people, plus me and the Colonel and you, Willie. I put it to him that any proof of a thing like there being a spy in a place ought to throw a good deal of light on who the spy was or else it was a pretty odd sort of proof. He turned all bland and mysterious and said yes, it was.'

'Very helpful indeed.' Naidu stood with his hand behind his back, evidently pondering. 'Did he voice any particular suspicions?'

'Not really. All these Indians and Pakistanis coming into the unit made his job frightfully tricky – I'm just telling you what he told me, Moti. He saw that they had to come, but he wasn't happy about the efficiency of their Governments' screening systems. His master in Whitehall is going to have a word with someone about it.'

After more thought, Naidu said, 'He seems most curiously ready to discuss the problem, even if he doesn't give much away. I ask myself why this should be. Would it not seem that a prerequisite of catching a spy would be to avoid putting him on his guard by letting it be known that his presence is suspected?'

'I asked him that very question. Apparently what's called the philosophy of phylactology – spy-catching to you – has been transformed. Keeping dead mum until the final pounce is old hat now. You go round saying how near you're getting and wait for somebody along the line to get anxious enough to show a break in their behaviour-pattern. The new method works better except with very brave spies and there are figures to prove that only nine per cent or something are that. Anyway, no more about Security. It's a subject for fools and madmen, as my chat with Brian Leonard might well suggest to you. But like everything else it has its compensations. One or two of Fawkes's mates have turned up to see him when they're off duty and they tend to look in on me as well. Somebody called Signalman Pearce, who works on the camp telephone exchange, appeared this very morning and discussed jazz and popular music with me for over half an hour. A most charming lad. Which somehow reminds me to tell you the only really interesting thing Dr Best had to say about my difficulties. According to him I'm probably a repressed homosexual.'

All four men burst into laughter.

*

'These repressed lesbian tendencies of yours,' said Dr Best, smiling. 'If it's all right with you I want to go into them rather more deeply than we had time for last week. Do you agree that we should?'

'Yes,' said Catharine. 'If you want to.'

'It isn't what I want, Mrs Casement, it's what you want. And I ask you whether you want to because, as I've warned you several times before, whenever we go down at all deep we're virtually certain to find something rather unpleasant waiting for us. Do you follow? Something that must be pretty shocking or it wouldn't be hiding away from us like that.'

'Just carry on, doctor. Another shock or two won't make much odds to me.'

Dr Best chuckled and shook his head in a kind of admiration. 'You're incorrigible, Mrs Casement. The very first time you were able to talk to me intelligibly, just after Christmas, you made exactly the same point, and I told you then what I see I must tell you again now, that a mere *unpleasant experience*, however much it may happen to distress you, does not in itself constitute a *shock* in the scientific, psychoanalytic sense. Let me tell you a couple of typical stories, both relating to patients that have been through my hands in the past year, which I hope will make the distinction clear to you.'

The doctor's manner became even more relaxed than hitherto, if that were possible, and there was a note of affectionate reminiscence in his voice when he continued, 'A little girl, ten years of age, is going home from school through a public park. It's a winter evening and dusk is falling, but it isn't dark yet, the park is only a few hundred yards across, and at this time there are usually plenty of people about – but not, unfortunately, on the evening in question. A man springs out on her, drags her into the bushes and rapes her, very thoroughly. After a time she makes her way home and is naturally taken to hospital.

'Today that child is happily watching television and playing her gramophone records just as before. Even her work at school has shown no significant decline in quality. It's true that there are gynaecological complications which may affect her ovulatory capacity, but emotionally and mentally she's quite untouched. What happened to her, you see, was an *unpleasant experience*.

'The picture's very different, I'm sorry to say, with the second case. Here we have a young man of twenty-five – which leads me to make an important secondary point. I say "a young man of twenty-five" because this is how we customarily refer to persons of that age-group. But in psychoanalytic terms that man is no longer young. This is very far from being a technical quibble, Mrs Casement. All our experience shows that the psychoanalytically young are far better equipped to resist both unpleasant experiences – as we saw with the little girl – and shocks in comparison with, let's say, the psychoanalytically non-young. Of which group you yourself are a member. (Indeed, at thirty-two you are hardly young in any sense.) I mention this distinction by way of reinforcing my warning to you about the dangers of beginning to go down deep.

'But to resume my story. Our young man, or man, was in the cinema one evening when the man in the next seat made a sexual assault on him. This probably amounted to no more than a hand laid on the knee or thigh. We can virtually rule out the idea of any genital contact, even through clothing. But I suppose we can never be quite sure, because ... Because that young man, after a short period of violent mania, is now in a state of deep and perhaps irreversible depressive withdrawal. He, you see, had had a *shock*, the shock, I have no doubt, of finding that something buried in him was deeply responsive to the assault. The sudden flash of insight into his own unconscious homosexual tendencies was too much for his sanity. Which brings us, Mrs Casement, to the point we reached five minutes ago.'

Catharine had started trying not to listen as soon as she realized the sort of thing that was going to happen to the child in Dr Best's first story, but she had to go on looking at him, because whenever you looked away from him he stopped talking, waited for you to look at him again and went back to the beginning of his last sentence but one. Going on looking at him made it harder not to listen to him, and it was not until she had heard what happened in the park that she was able to push the meaning out of his voice by hearing it as a flow of little cries and moans separated by puffs and clicks.

To keep this going, she had to push the meaning out of the doctor's face in the same sort of way. At the start, it was more of a face than most people's: a glossy pink bald crown with a patch of thick curly hair above each ear, wide and shining blue eyes, a nose that seemed too big for its nostrils, a band of broken veins across each cheekbone, lips of which only the lower one did any work, a bottom row of narrow black-edged teeth. As she concentrated on it, all this turned into shapes and colours, some parts moving, others not, as important and as unimportant as the whites and pale greens and lines and corners that were the papers on the desk, the dark greens and ovals and pinks of the flowers, the rectangles and dark blue and dark reds along the wall, or best of all the bands of light and shade everywhere. This was the method of dealing with things that she had learnt very quickly six months earlier, just after finding out that there was nothing about her life that she liked.

Making it so that either everything she saw and heard was important, or nothing but unimportant things were anywhere, had helped a lot at first. But as soon as she was really good at it, and could keep it up most of the day, she had begun having trouble with sizes and distances. It was about that time that her sister and brother-in-law had got Dr Best to look after her.

The trouble began again now. What was the doctor's face must be an ordinary size and an ordinary distance away. But, as she looked at it, it suddenly grew and receded at the same time, so that very soon it was, or seemed as if it was, yards across and yards and yards away, like a mountain miles off, a cloud in the sky. Then, with an invisible flick that she always expected but could never time, it was very small and near, the size of a penny at arm's length, a pinhead so close that she would brush it with her eyelash if she blinked.

Hardly frightened at all, Catharine said to herself, meaning it very sincerely, that what she was looking at was Dr Best's face, attached to the rest of him behind the desk in his office, surrounded by papers and all those flowers and the books, with bars of sunlight from the venetian blind falling on the walls and floor and furniture. And after only a few seconds everything was back as it should have been. Now she knew she was getting better.

Just then the doctor stopped talking. She felt so cheerful that she smiled at him and asked casually, 'What happened to the man? Did they catch him?'

'What man?'

'The man in the park. The one that raped the little girl.'

He clicked his tongue, thrusting out his lower lip. 'I don't know – that's none of my concern. Really, Mrs Casement, I do beg you most seriously not to identify yourself with other victim-figures in this way. It's childish, childish in the technical psycho-analytic sense as well as the semantic.'

'I was only asking. I wasn't identifying. I wasn't raped.'

'No no no, I meant . . . Let it pass, let it pass. We've wasted quite enough time already. Now. You agree you've been warned that investigating your lesbian tendencies may lead to your suffering a shock?'

'If you like to put that in writing I'll sign it.'

'That won't be necessary. Your oral consent is sufficient. Very well. You appreciate that unless you answer my questions fully and to the best of your knowledge and ability honestly there is no point in my putting them to you?'

'Yes, all right.'

'Good. Now just running over what you told me last time . . . You've never taken part in any overt sexual activity with another member of your sex, never so much as embraced passionately with another girl or woman, never made a sexual approach to one or had one made to you by one, never entertained any romantic sentiment toward one. Do you agree?'

'Agree? Of course I agree. It's what I said myself, isn't it?'

'I merely wondered if you'd had any second thoughts on the

23

matter. I'm particularly interested in your friendship with this . . . Lady Hazell. Would you care to tell me something about that?'

'It's just a friendship, doctor. There are such things, you know. Lucy is a widow and very rich and I met her through my first husband. When I left my second husband she said I could come and stay with her until I got myself sorted out. Only as you know I didn't get myself sorted out. But I must have told you this when I first came here.'

'In a rather different way. Do go on.'

'Well, that's all there is. She's been very kind to me and she makes me laugh and I'm fond of her.'

'What does she think of you?'

'I don't know. I suppose she's sorry for me. I suppose she likes me.'

'Is she ever . . . physically affectionate, does she put her arm round you, hug you and the like? For instance, does she ever dance with you?'

Catharine laughed heartily. '*Dance* with me? No. She doesn't ever dance with me. She's got quite enough male dancing partners.'

'So I confess I rather assumed,' said the doctor, hissing slightly. 'Oh yes, she came to see me after visiting you last week. Without an appointment, I may say. In fact she didn't even knock at that door. Fortunately I was disengaged. She said I wasn't giving you the right treatment and became abusive on the point.'

'I'm sorry, Dr Best. I didn't know she was going to do that.'

He gave a brief snorting laugh, probably to show how trifling had been the effect upon him of Lady Hazell's intrusion. 'Yes. She runs a sort of permanent salon for young men, doesn't she, at that grand house of hers? Officers from the camp and such? Parties and the rest of it till all hours?'

'She gives parties, yes.'

'A curious environment, it must have been, for a woman undergoing a breakdown. Did you join in the parties when you were there?'

'I just gave people drinks sometimes.'

Dr Best said suddenly, 'A very attractive person, I mean physically, wouldn't you say?'

'Yes, clearly. But if you mean have I ever wanted to go to bed with her the answer's no.'

'Living in that house you must often have seen her naked or semi-naked, in the bathroom and the bedroom and elsewhere. Have you ever experienced sexual excitement at such times?'

'No.'

'You haven't been aware of your nipples hardening or any genital phenomena?'

'Christ, certainly not. I told you I get little enough of that with men.'

'We'll come to that later. Meanwhile I can't help being struck by the extreme emphasis of your denial, Mrs Casement. Over-stressed reactions to such inquiries always tend to suggest that the subject is concealing an opposite reaction. So please think carefully. You have never in any way been sexually attracted toward Lady Hazell or any other girl or woman as far as you are aware, is that correct?'

'Yes,' said Catharine in a tone heavy with moderation.

At this assurance Dr Best's cordiality, which had been falling off ever since he ended his pair of anecdotes, vanished altogether. He curled his lower lip over his upper one, then drew it away with a plop. 'It's clear that these tendencies of yours are buried more deeply than I suspected. We must try another line of attack.'

'May I ask a question?'

He sniffed and shrugged. 'If you wish.'

'I know I'm very ignorant about all this, but me not ever feeling attracted to girls, mightn't that just mean I wasn't attracted to them? I don't see how –'

The doctor's good will was immediately restored. 'As you say, you're ignorant. That's natural enough. But there's nothing mysterious about this. Tell me. What do you think is the reason for your prolonged history of . . . let's call it failure with men?'

'Well, I suppose some of it's bad luck.'

'There's no such thing as luck in this field, I'm afraid. What else?'

'I told you I sometimes feel a bit afraid of them. There was that man early on who pulled the knife on me, you remember.'

'Yes, very good, that's certainly relevant, though its real meaning is rather different from the one you appear to attribute to it. You'll agree that threatening somebody with a lethal weapon is a manifestation of aggression? Yes, now what's the most probable *exterior* cause of aggression, not coming from *inside* the person who becomes aggressive but from *outside*?'

'Something you don't like?'

'Very nearly. *Something that doesn't like you.* Somebody else's aggression. Do you follow?'

Catharine considered. 'You mean I didn't like him? But I spent all my time thinking how nice he was. I wanted to –'

'That was what you thought consciously, Mrs Casement. All this is buried very deep, you know. Just look at your sexual career. Over the last months I've accumulated something like thirty pages of notes on it. And what does it amount to?' The doctor picked up the file in front of him and threw it a few inches further away on his desk, then, slowly folding his hands, laid them on his crossed legs. 'Nothing very hard to interpret. Two broken marriages. Literally dozens of affairs, starting at an unusually –'

'They weren't what you could call affairs, most of them, they didn't last any time at all. I kept wanting them to last when they started, but they kept going wrong and I couldn't make them last.'

'Because of your deep ... unconscious ... aggression ... toward ... men. Oh, it's a familiar pattern. You betray unconscious hostility, the man unconsciously senses it and begins to react overtly, you retreat, he responds to the primitive flight-situation with more hostility and so on. All of which increases your latent hostility yet further and makes the next failure that much more inevitable. Your course was set a long time ago. Originally, probably, your attitude to your father was what –'

'I loved my father.'

'No doubt, no doubt. I'm not a Freudian, so we can safely leave all that on one side. I'm not interested in the semi-mystical origins of mental disease. I'm a doctor, not a theologian.'

Dr Best ran his tongue to and fro behind his lower lip. 'Anyway, in case you're still unconvinced, let me if I may draw attention to your physical type. Your shape, Mrs Casement. Would you mind standing up for a moment? Thank you. Oh yes. Oh yes, it's all there. Tall ... shoulders tending to be broad ... small breasts ... rather narrow hips ... long legs. Turn around, would you? Quite so. You can sit down now. Quite typical semi-androgynous characteristics. You belong to –'

'I know, that means man-plus-woman, doesn't it? Well, if you think I'm not properly a woman or something you're wrong. All my men, all the men I've ever had anything to do with were always complaining about the very opposite. I couldn't do a thing without them all saying it was just like a woman. Bloody woman. Pull yourself together and stop acting like a bloody woman. And there was nothing wrong with my shape according to them. Whenever they weren't angry with me they were always going on about my shape, all of them. And my face. If you think I've got a face like a man all I can say is you've seen some pretty queer men.'

'Oh, I have, Mrs Casement, I have.' Dr Best seemed delighted. 'Some very queer men indeed. Including a number who were unaware of their condition until I pointed it out to them. Why, only yesterday I was talking to a young fellow under treatment here for alcoholism, an Army officer from the camp. Well educated, highly intelligent, you'd have said quite worldly and sophisticated. And yet when I suggested what was patently obvious, that he was drinking himself to death in order to conceal from himself his unconscious homosexual tendencies, he told me with evident sincerity that the idea had never crossed his mind. He meant his conscious mind, of course. In his case there was the fact that his appearance and demeanour and so on were those of a normal male, which in his uninstructed way he seemed to take as some sort of evidence of his basic heterosexuality. I lost no time in exposing the fallaciousness of that view.

'Yes yes yes,' the doctor went on with momentary petulance, perhaps repressing a negative reaction from the depths of his unconscious, 'the world is full of male counterparts of yourself,

Mrs Casement. Undoubtedly the men you attract are of this type. The self-hatred engendered by their hidden recognition of this is what leads them to react so aggressively to your own aggressions. It's hardly surprising that the outcome should be unfortunate on both sides. Such men would do well to recognize their homosexual psyche and set about coming to terms with it, as I told our young friend.'

Dr Best gave a bright nod by way of conclusion and reached for a vase of wallflowers, the scent of which he inhaled with a clear nasal whistle.

Catharine said, 'You're advising me to start sleeping with women, are you?'

'My dear Mrs Casement, men in my position never advise anything, any more than we condemn anything. All we try to do is explain. And the explanation I offer you is that all your difficulties spring from an unconscious preference for your own sex. In other words, you are a lesbian.'

He put so much into this last sentence that Catharine tried quite hard to respond with appropriate indignation or concern. But perhaps she had taken too much to heart his repeated warnings against giving him the kind of answers she thought would please him. Anyhow, the best she could do was to ask in an interested tone, 'Do you really think so?'

The doctor put the flowers down firmly but quietly. More thoroughly than before, he searched his mouth with his tongue. 'You seem unaware of the seriousness of your position. You became a patient in a *lunatic asylum* because you *went mad*. I've never gone in for sentimental euphemisms about mental hospitals and psychologically disturbed and the rest of it and I'm not going to start on your account. One of the marks of your condition is a fear of insight, understandable enough in view of what that insight would entail. But what I find far less ... explicable is your obstinacy. An individual personality defect. You are of your own free will resisting that recognition of the truth, that *shock* which alone will enable you to undergo what's known as a psychic shift and reveal the true nature of your disorder. Very evidently, nothing I can do here will bring that about. Very well then. We'll see how you get on in a rather less cosy and warm and safe environment. I've feather-bedded you against reality for too long.'

He reached for a pad of pink paper and began writing on it, his head swaying like a violinist's.

'What are you going to do with me?'

When he had finished writing, the doctor said, 'I'm putting you out on *probation*, Mrs Casement. For twenty-eight days in the first instance. You leave this asylum next Wednesday. That will give you time to make arrangements.'

He had, at last, succeeded in disconcerting her. Without any effort on her part, a sense of what it was like outside came upon her: railway stations, drinks, shopping, laughter, traffic, tele-phones, men. Catharine hugged her hands between her knees. 'Where shall I live? What am I going to do?'

'Your room at Lady Hazell's establishment is ready for you any time you care to go there. She was most definite on that point. I gather you're not in any financial difficulties. So you should manage perfectly well.'

Dr Best prodded a bell-push on his desk, smiled distantly and went on, 'You'll be back where you started from. The re-sults of this little experiment should be interesting. To both of us.'

*

'We'll give it to you in the arm today, Maxie, as a special con-cession,' said the nurse. 'Seeing as how there are gentlemen present.'

'We'd better be getting along,' said Ayscue.

'This is the main event of the afternoon,' said Hunter, un-buttoning his pyjama jacket. 'It would be insensitive of you to go now.' He swallowed quickly twice and licked his lips.

Churchill, about to follow Ayscue's lead, noticed this. He fancied too that a couple of paler patches had appeared on Hunter's pale face. 'It'll do us good to watch – might make us go a bit steadier with the pink gins tonight. What are you getting?'

'Little multi-vitamin shot,' answered the nurse, a muscular man in his thirties with one of the smallest noses Churchill had ever seen. 'All our thirsty friends start missing out on their carrots and liver after a bit. This will make our Maxie a healthy boy as well as a good boy.'

The nurse had placed a round metal tray at the foot of the bed. He took from it a small glass phial with a narrow neck which he nipped with a pincer-like instrument. Next he carefully filled a syringe with the dark amber-coloured liquid in the phial and then picked up an antiseptic pad.

'Is this all he gets?' asked Churchill, meaning only to break the silence as the man worked.

'Oh no, soldier.' The nurse began swabbing a patch of skin on the inside of Hunter's upper arm. 'There's the little blue sausages that make Maxie go bye-byes, and the weeny round orange jokers that cheer him up when he's feeling sad. Right. Now just relax, will you? Relaxie, Maxie. Good . . .'

'Incredible taste you get at the back of your throat with these vitamin shots,' said Hunter, looking past them at the wall. 'I don't think I shall ever be able to drink barley water with the same relish after this. Not that it does much to take the taste away. I think perhaps . . . a couple of nice solid sandpaper sandwiches might help. But they don't provide those here.'

'Good boy, Maxie.' The nurse patted Hunter lightly on the top of the head. 'You'll be able to see in the dark now. Just what you could do with, eh? You know, you blokes don't want to take your old pal's troubles too seriously. He's just a bit of a boozer, is our Maxie. Nothing compared to some we got here.'

He took a cigarette from Hunter's bedside table, lit it with a lighter from a pocket in his white knee-length coat, blew out a shred of tobacco and continued to talk, slowly stroking his forehead with the fingers of the hand that held the cigarette.

'That geezer over there, now. Fellow with my colleague in attendance.' Although the nurse did not drop his voice at all, the man who had been carefully examining the room went on doing so without any sign of having heard. 'Keen as mustard. In love with the stuff. This conditioned reflex treatment, now that's no buggy-ride, I can tell you. It's this idea where they start off by giving you a bomb that makes you throw up. Strychnine was what they used to use, but as the years rolled by they got to notice that it had, uh, undesirable side-effects. You know, like death.' The nurse gave a long chuckle, bowing deeply once like an actor taking a curtain call. 'All that's been ironed out. Anyway, you know the form, I dare say: fill him full of emetine hydrochloride and the rest of it and let the old tachycardia and sweating and vertigo soften him up a bit. Then the technique is to slip him a glass of Scotch or whatever he's hooked on about half a minute before the emetine makes him spew his ring. It's an art, really. If you do it right you get to where just the Scotch'll make him throw up. Our brother got that far and it's only about twenty-five per cent that do. Then the big white chief sends him out on probation – great on timing, the old chief. Comes a fortnight later and our brother's back in. Acute exhaustion and malnutrition. What he'd been doing, he'd been knocking back the Scotch and spewing his bloody guts out and then knocking back the Scotch. And so on. You see what I mean. There's a geezer who really cares about drink. It's what I said, our little Maxie's still in the kindergarten.'

'Well, I'll be getting along.' The nurse picked up his tray and shook his head philosophically. 'Oh, you get some peculiar buggers in here,' he added, seemingly by way of introduction to further material.

'Don't let us keep you,' said Naidu.

'Not on your life, General. And you'd better not stay around too long either. We don't want our Maxie getting over-excited and tossing and turning all night. He's being tapered off on the sodium amytol, see. Well, so long, my trusty lads. Fix bayonets and charge the old bomb, eh? That's the style.'

The man walked smartly away.

Naidu said, 'I'd be happy to go straight to whoever's in charge here and lodge a complaint in person. You've only to say the word, Max.'

'Oh, Moti, where's your sense of humour? He's really a very nice lad. In his way. He's as gentle as a child. When another child's trying to take its toy railway train off it. No, that's not quite fair.'

'Is he the one you call the nice nurse?' asked Churchill. 'Because I'd hate to –'

'No, the nice nurse is truly and demonstrably nice. He says I need looking after. He's promised to sit next to me on the coach trip to St Jerome's Priory on Sunday.'

Ayscue grinned. 'What are you going to do there?'

'Look at it, I suppose, and then come back. It'll make a break.'

A minute later the three visitors had taken their leave and were walking back along the corridor. Churchill was brooding. He said in a strained voice,

'Why does this sort of thing have to happen? A chap like Max in that horrible situation. It isn't right.'

'He's being made well,' said Naidu. 'It's necessary, James. I didn't like that swine of a nurse any better than you did, but you may be sure that if he over-stepped the mark in a big way then the authorities would get to hear of it and take necessary action. You know that. You must be reasonable.'

'I'm trying to be. I'm trying to see the reason in it. It isn't the nurse so much. I don't want there to be people like that but I'm not against the idea of it. What I'm against is it being possible for a man like Max being able to damage himself in that way. A man like anybody, come to that.'

They emerged into the brilliant sunshine. Naidu said earnestly,

'Man has free will. He has the things of this world before him and it's up to him what he does with them. That we must all recognize. There is such a thing as alcohol and if a man indulges in it to an excess then he has only himself to blame. I trust I'm not sounding censorious towards our good friend when I say that, you understand.'

Averting his eyes from the stone figure of the lion-like creature, which they were now passing, Churchill looked at Naidu. The small neat handsome face with its shapely bones and rich brown skin was troubled, but not unhappy. It was as if new reasons for envying him came up every day.

'I see that, Moti,' said Churchill. 'But why couldn't alcohol just have had good effects, or at least not have had such bad ones as it's had on the fellows in that ward? It could have been, you know, no worse than over-eating, making you fat or something if you went on with it. So why did it have to be so bad?'

'My dear James, why is there arsenic, why are there poisonous snakes, why is there cholera and bubonic plague and the other things of that sort? Come along, padre, you're the expert here. You must render me some assistance.'

'I'd be worse than useless, I'm afraid,' said Ayscue. 'I've been into this with James before, more than once. I just make him angry.'

Churchill flushed. 'Not angry, Willie, merely disturbed to find someone of your intelligence defending the indefensible.'

'Don't let's start.'

'All right. Sorry.'

As they drew level with the water-tower, a door in the adjacent building opened and the two women they had seen earlier came out. Churchill felt a shock, as if the aircraft had again passed between him and the sun. He realized that he had thought of the girl every couple of minutes since his first sight of her. He caught her glance now and held it until they passed. Immediately he was filled with shame at his own foolishness and lack of forethought in not having looked at the girl properly. She was thin and tall and perhaps had a slight stoop and her hair was neither light nor dark. Instead of noticing more he had just stared into her eyes, and after five seconds he could not even remember their colour. But he had a feeling he would know her again anywhere.

With no more said they rounded the corner and made for their car, one of the passé jeeps wished on the unit as a result of some turn of Captain Leonard's thought. Yellow lettering on its body said *6 HQ Adm Bn*, shorthand for the unit's cover name. Ayscue got into the driver's seat and they moved off.

'It's an exceedingly pleasant situation, you can say that much.' Naidu looked out at the grassy slopes, dotted with rhododendrons and azaleas, between which they were riding. 'Doesn't the whole place remind you of an English country house of the traditional sort?'

'It used to be just that,' said Ayscue. 'I was reading their pamphlet. Apparently the fellow who was squire here in Victorian times was a sort of pioneer in mental illness. Set up what amounted to a clinic, one of the first in the world. Then one of his successors handed it over to a trust, and there we are.'

'I can see there's been a lot of building since those days, but it still keeps its very charming historical appearance.'

Sitting behind them, Churchill heard little of this. He was trying to satisfy himself that there was nothing he could have done about the girl. Even if he had had the resource to give his two friends the slip and follow her back to her ward, he would probably not have been able to find out so much as her name. And her name alone would not have been much use – just a lot better than nothing at all. Why had he not been able to run after her, pretend he thought he knew her or something? Oh well, it was done now, or rather not done.

At the lodge, a thickset man in a blue suit peered at them through a sort of guichet, then waved them past impatiently.

'Rather lax security measures here,' said Naidu. 'How does that worthy fellow know we aren't three raving maniacs who have overpowered three unsuspecting Army types? He'd get short shrift from our gallant Captain Leonard.'

Churchill roused himself; he would think about the girl again later. 'Apart from the violent chaps, who never leave the ward, it's all open here, apparently. Max was telling me last week. The problem is keeping chaps who've been chucked out from worming their way back in.'

The traffic across their front was heavy. While they waited for a gap, a motor-cyclist in Army uniform drew over to the kerb near them, stopped his machine and pulled it on to its rest. As he approached, pushing his goggles up, they saw that he was a dispatch-rider of the Royal Corps of Signals. He crossed to Ayscue's side of the jeep, saluted with something of a flourish, and said,

'Excuse me, sir, but you seem to be part of the unit I'm trying to find, Sixth HQ Admin Battalion. Can you tell me where your place is? This is the second time I've been along this bit of road.'

'We're going there now, Corporal,' said Ayscue. 'Perhaps we can deliver your packet for you.'

'Not unless one of you gentlemen happens to be . . .' – the man referred to a typewritten instruction – 'Captain P. B. Leonard, 17th Dragoons? I've got to deliver to him personally and get his signature, you see. Thank you all the same, sir. Now if you could just give me an idea . . .'

Churchill half listened while Ayscue furnished directions. The dispatch-rider's head and shoulders were out of sight from the back seat of the jeep, and his voice was unremarkable. He was quite young : nothing more.

'You'll be there long before we are,' Ayscue was saying. 'By the way, I thought you fellows were all on four wheels these days.'

'We keep up a few of the bikes for special runs like this where there isn't a lot to carry. Better in traffic, too. And this weather, well, it's a treat to be in the saddle. Well, thanks again, sir. I'll probably pass you on my way back.'

In a few seconds he was off. Churchill fancied he waved as he went, but was not sure. By the time there was a gap in the stream of vehicles long enough to take the jeep, the dispatch-rider was out of sight ahead of them.

Naidu started a conversation with Ayscue about discipline, inspired, he said, by their brief exchange with Corporal Fawkes an hour earlier. Was that admittedly very pleasant young N C O not perhaps a trifle . . . free and easy? He, Naidu, ought not to have encouraged this spirit by offering even that very minor jest of his at the expense of Security and, by implication, of a brother officer. Or was he being over-scrupulous, too much the son of a subahdar-major father whose views on such matters were probably indistinguishable from those current in Victoria's Indian Army?

As Churchill had expected, Ayscue said more or less that everything was all right really. Saying that everything was all right really, however different it sometimes looked, earned Ayscue his living, of course, but at the moment none of his masters was in earshot. Surely he must forget himself sometimes? Never to do so would verge on the inhuman. Well : he was decent enough in other respects for it to be regrettable that he was a parson.

Churchill soon got tired of regretting this. Although he would not be able to think about the girl properly until after dark and when he was alone, he was encouraged to do so now by the stretch of country they were passing through, sunlit meadows on one side, shade over the road and on the other side, where there was also a stream splashing down among the rocks with ash and birch trees on the slopes and drifts of dead leaves seemingly undisturbed since autumn.

It was not that Churchill visualized himself walking among the trees with the girl, nor so much that he would have liked to be doing so. Instead, by a process familiar since childhood but never analysed, he used the thought of her to focus his attention on the scene, finding much more in it physically than he would otherwise have cared to, and taking its and her joint existence as a signal, almost a guarantee, that the real joyful life existed somewhere. Churchill was not an unhappy person, either by nature or by experience, but since leaving school five years ago he had several times been disconcerted by doubts about whether the joy of which he knew his heart was capable would ever find its occasion or its setting. Only sad or frightening things, like this afternoon's visit to Max Hunter, seemed to have the power that joy ought to have, and the necessity for getting through the ordinary day sometimes felt, late at night, as if it were detuning his heart, screening and muffling its capacities.

He could admit to himself now that it had been a relief to have been prevented by circumstances from pursuing the girl. Her apparent status as inmate of a mental hospital would certainly have raised unusual obstacles to his pursuit of her, but if he had managed to surmount these he would only have found himself committed to some variation on that repetitious and mechanical programme which had turned out to be the accepted way of dealing with women : telephone calls, restaurant dinners, car drives, seaside trips and attempted or actual seduction. He had been round this course a dozen times over the last few years and had got quite good at it, usually finishing successfully, always enjoying it after a fashion once he was off the mark, and hardly ever having to cheer himself up by reflecting that women who needed no pursuing were probably not much of a catch. But at times the whole thing would strike him as oddly out of touch with what it was supposed to be about. The proportions seemed wrong. He could only get them right in his thoughts.

'Hullo, what's up there?' said Naidu. 'An obstruction of some kind?'

'Looks like it.'

Ahead of them was a line of halted traffic. Ayscue drove up to the rear of it and stopped. A minute went by.

'Shall I walk on round the bend and have a look?' said Churchill. He wanted to be in the sun and alone, even if only momentarily.

'I think they're just starting to move now.'

After another minute they came to two stationary lorries almost side by side and blocking most of the roadway, an ambulance and a police car parked on the verge, and a small crowd just beginning to be dispersed by policemen. Churchill saw somebody's hand sticking out from under one of the lorries, just behind the front wheel. Two ambulance attendants and a man in plain clothes were kneeling nearby. The hand clenched, then opened again.

'It looks as if you may be needed here, padre,' said Naidu.

Ayscue drew into the nearside verge, stopped the jeep, got out and walked across the road. Churchill watched. Then he noticed a motor-bicycle lying on its side on the opposite verge. He had a view of its rear mudguard, across which were painted bands of blue and white, the insignia of the Royal Corps of Signals. He got out and went over.

As he approached, a police constable was saying to an Inspector, 'It's a ten-ton crane, sir. Should do the job all right.'

'Go and tell 'em to speed it up. Say it's a matter of minutes.' The Inspector turned and saw Churchill. 'He wouldn't be one of your lads, sir, would he?'

'No, but I can handle the Army side for you if you want.'

'I'd be most grateful if you would, sir.'

'We're about a mile down the road.' Churchill explained where. 'When you get his documents off him, have them delivered to the Adjutant. I'll warn the sentry on the gate. We'll see to it that the proper people are informed. Now there's the question of his dispatches. They'll be on his bike.'

The two men walked over to the machine, which had suffered no more than minor damage, and Churchill opened the dispatch-bag strapped to the carrier. There was only one packet inside, the one destined for Leonard. It was a fat foolscap envelope stamped *Top Secret*.

'I'll deliver this,' said Churchill, 'but I'd better give you my signature for it.' He wrote in the proffered notebook. 'What happened here?'

'He hit one truck and went under the other. Sounds like his own fault, but you can't tell at this stage.'

They were strolling back towards the two lorries.

'Has he got a chance?'

The Inspector shrugged. 'He had a wheel over him and must have got dragged a fair way before the driver could pull up. We can't get him out till the crane arrives. The doc's with him now.'

Ayscue was among those watching as the man in plain clothes, seen earlier by Churchill, bent forward with a hypodermic syringe. There was a gap in the passing traffic and a faint moan could be heard from under the lorry. The extended hand went limp.

'Coming, James?' said Ayscue.

Without answering Churchill turned back to the Inspector.

'One more point – if you'll just tell me where you can be got hold of I'll see that's passed on to his unit too.'

The Inspector gave the information and thanked him.

Ayscue was waiting a few yards off. The two walked back to the jeep in silence.

'It was that dispatch-rider we talked to just now outside the hospital,' Ayscue told Naidu.

'Oh. Is he dead?'

'Not yet. But he soon will be, I gathered.'

'Poor fellow,' said Naidu. 'Only a youngster, too.'

Standing on the verge, Churchill took out the packet addressed to Leonard and looked at it.

'Imagine dying delivering this. Whatever it is.'

Naidu looked at Ayscue for a moment, then said, 'He isn't dying delivering it, James. He was on his way to deliver it when something happened as a result of which he will presumably die.'

'Something happened. Why? Why did it have to happen?'

Again Naidu hesitated. 'If we must go into it now ... It's a question without an answer. And there is no question either. It didn't have to happen. It simply happened.'

'Come on, let's get going,' said Ayscue.

Churchill said loudly, 'Yes, let's do that. Why don't we do that? Chaps getting crushed under lorries, it's happening every day. Hardly worth stopping for. A bit uncomfortable for the chap under the lorry, but he was probably going too fast and this little experience'll see to it that he takes more care in future. And think of all those opportunities for spiritual growth on the part of the chap's girl, and his mates, and the chaps who were driving the lorries that knocked him off. All that fortitude and resignation and what-not that they'd have had to do without otherwise. The Lord giveth and by Christ the Lord taketh away. Oh, it isn't only all right really, it's better than all right, eh, Willie?'

'James.' Ayscue faced Churchill across the bonnet of the jeep. 'Please don't talk in that accusing tone. I can't think of anybody who'd try to justify this thing here. Surely you must know I wouldn't. Can't you see that Moti and I feel just as badly about it as you do?'

'I don't know where Moti fits in,' said Churchill as before, throwing away the cigarette he had been trying to light, 'but as regards you, Willie, no, I can't, I don't think you do feel as badly as I do. If you did, you wouldn't be over here, getting ready to drive off to the Mess and have tea, you're supposed to be a bloody parson, you'd have crawled under that bloody lorry and be doing your best to comfort that poor sod, instead of –'

Ayscue had walked round the front of the jeep and now put his face close to Churchill's.

'How?' he said. 'Comfort him how?'

'Don't ask me, that's your department, I only –'

'Stop trying to set up a monopoly in feeling. The first thing I could make out over there was that the doctor was preparing to give the man an injection that would make him unconscious in seconds. He gave him it. There was nothing I could do after that, because he'll probably never recover consciousness, and if he does it's unlikely he'd be able to take in what I said or even what I was.'

'But he might.'

Naidu got out of the passenger's seat and walked past them up the road away from the accident.

'Exactly,' said Ayscue to Churchill, 'and that above all is why I'm over here instead of over there. What's he going to think if he wakes up and sees me? Use your imagination, James. How would you feel if you came to yourself in a hospital bed with a man in a dog-collar bending over you and telling you to be of good cheer? You'd know where you were due next all right. Agreed?'

Churchill nodded.

'If I had any reason to suppose that that boy believed in God then I wouldn't have come away. But these days the chances are very much against any such thing. And I couldn't ask him. I just couldn't risk it, James. You see that, don't you?'

Churchill nodded again.

'Come on.'

'I'm sorry, Willie,' said Churchill as they drove away.

'That's all right. We'd better both apologize to Moti. I'm afraid we may have shocked him a little.'

'Because of what?'

'Inappropriate behaviour.'

They picked up Naidu and a few minutes later turned right towards the camp, first pausing to allow a heavy mobile crane to pass in the opposite direction.

*

Captain Leonard put on his mess-jacket and stood while Deering, his batman, fastened the buttons, using a thin cloth so as not to spoil the polish on the brass.

The jacket was of an unusual deep ultramarine, the mark of an honour awarded to the 17th Dragoons, Leonard's regiment, as a result of an incident in the Peninsular War when a squadron of them had been able to take an enemy force in the rear by swimming, horses and all, across an arm of the Mediterranean. The regiment was colloquially known as the Sailors in consequence. Nowadays it was a reconnaissance unit equipped with scout cars and light tanks, but had remained, as far as its officers were concerned, an abode of the landowning families. It was for this reason that Leonard's masters in Whitehall had chosen it as his cover, explaining rather offensively that nobody would suspect an officer in the Sailors of being anything but what he seemed. In a different mood, those masters had undone a fair part of this precaution by advising Leonard to divulge strong periodic hints about his real job, on the new-found principle – recently advertised to Hunter – that a security system works best when the opposition knows it to be at work and may react significantly to that knowledge. Many of the officers and men in the camp had heard that Leonard was not really a soldier at all but some sort of agent of military counter-intelligence assigned to prevent anyone outside from learning what No. 6 Headquarters Administration Battalion was actually up to.

Although he had never trained or served with the Sailors, had never been near them except to be given dinner and shown round once at their depot, Leonard's attention to his turn-out as one of them would have been judged adequate even by the Vice-President of their Mess. He pointed out various imperfections – a protruding thread at the edge of the revers, a fleck of dried metal-polish near a buttonhole – which Deering went some way towards repairing. Then, with the care of a cadet about to go on guard-mounting, Leonard examined himself in the full-length triple-panelled tailor's glass he took wherever his masters sent him.

The man inside the jacket and the close-fitting scarlet trousers with ultramarine stripe was forty years old. He had retreating black hair that was still thick at the sides and back, and a sallow complexion darkened round the mouth by a beard showing under the skin. When he spoke, it was with a perpetual air of urgency stemming in part from the guttural sound he regularly substituted for the letter R. He said urgently now,

'Brush.'

Deering walked not very slowly round his officer dabbing at his jacket with a clothes-brush, dislodging a few of the fallen hairs and specks of lint but merely changing the position of most.

'Sticky tape's the thing really.'

'You should have thought of that before.'

'Yes, sir.'

With a forgiving smile, Leonard crossed to the rosewood dressing-table that he had not had to bring with him. Such pieces as this and the imposing mahogany tallboy, tall enough almost to touch the beams overhead, harked back to the days when the Mess had functioned as a farmhouse. The place was large enough to accommodate all the unit's officers above the rank of captain, plus a few deemed to qualify for comfort on special grounds : the Adjutant, Hunter, as administration officer, Leonard himself, who had explained that he needed to be at the centre of things. Had he not thought to do so he might have found himself bedding down in an outhouse with a couple of subalterns, or even trying to live in one of the box-shaped, pastel-coloured huts that had recently been run up in a nearby meadow and rang with portable radios eighteen hours a day.

He now picked up a red leather spectacle-case, quickly removed the horn-rimmed glasses he was wearing, substituted a pair of pince-nez, and closed the case with a loud snap, his eyes steadily on Deering throughout. The effect of the change was to replace the semblance of an ambitious schoolmaster with that of a minor Slavic bureaucrat.

'Well, Deering, any news?'

This was the signal for the daily report on gossip and rumour within the camp. Only a short acquaintance with the Army had been needed to teach Leonard the usefulness of batmen as confidants, eavesdroppers and innocent overhearers. He had seen exceptional intelligence-value of this sort in Deering as soon as the Mess Sergeant recommended him, and that value had proved itself ever since. There was something about the man that he sympathized with more personally, too. Untidy and casual and sometimes faintly impertinent he might be, but his contempt for the politicians supposedly in charge of national security, combined with his respect for those few who (like Leonard) were really doing something about it, was as proper as it was rare, and would have been totally admirable if expressed in a better accent.

Losing no time in displaying his less attractive side, Deering took half a cigarette from his trouser pocket and lit it. He sniffed twice and said,

'The padre's been on the prowl again.'

'Are you sure?'

'See how it strikes you. About two a.m. Coates is parked in the forecourt waiting to take the Colonel's guest home when he sees someone creeping across that bit of meadow towards the huts. Whoever it is goes into one of the ones near the far end – Coates can't be sure which one, but that's where Ayscue's hut is. It was him all right, no doubt about it.'

'What do you mean, no doubt about it?' Leonard spoke sharply. A conversation about the work of the unit he had had with Ayscue the previous week had convinced him that no suspicion of spying could be attached here, and the idea of having to reopen a closed file was disagreeable to him. 'A couple of the Indians have got huts down that end. It might have been one of them, or Churchill, or almost anybody.'

'Churchill and the Indians don't keep dogs. Ayscue does. If it had been anyone else but him, that bloody Alsatian bitch of his would have cracked on like it does whenever you go near it. But there wasn't a peep out of the pooch, I asked Coates particularly. That proves it, see. I remember reading a story about that somewhere, you know, the case of the dog that didn't bark.'

The power of reasoning shown here impressed Leonard, but it would not do to let Deering see this. 'All right, suppose it was Ayscue, where does that get us? He might have all sorts of reasons for slipping out of camp for a few hours.'

'Like what? Going on the piss? He shifts a few here in the Mess when he feels like it, and he keeps a bottle in his hut, too, Evans says. Nothing there. Out on the ram? Can you see our respected spiritual counsellor engaging in amatory pursuits? He wouldn't touch a woman with yours. No, he's up to something. Why does he live in one of those bloody pencil-boxes when as a major he's entitled to a room here? So's he can keep a fatherly eye on his flock, I suppose?'

'Well, yes – from what I hear he does spend a lot of time talking to the lads.'

'Yes, in a very nasty nosey way, too. Always on at them to let him know if there's anything they're afraid of and whether they're happy. Happy! What business is it of his? And these

43

gramophone recitals and chamber concerts and what-not. It's not natural. Never trust a parson and you won't go far wrong. Say one thing and do another. Politicians who haven't been able to make the grade.'

For once, Leonard felt he could do without Deering's support. 'Is that all you've got?'

'Not quite. That cupboard of his, the one he keeps locked. Evans says he's done everything he can think of to get a look inside and he's got nowhere at all. How do we know he hasn't got a short-wave radio tucked away in there?'

'Nonsense, there'd be no –'

'It could be something like tit pictures, of course, but he'd only need a drawer for those. It'd pay you to have a dekko at that cupboard, I bet you.'

Wearily, but silently, Leonard agreed that he could not afford not to. He had recently been shown a training film about techniques of concealment in which great play had been made with double bluffs, dummy strong-boxes being hidden in the rafters or magnetically attached to the underside of bed-springs while the real one sat in view on the table, and so on. Leonard himself had followed this principle by setting a permanent guard on his office and stowing his most secret documents in a suitcase, which he kept under his bed. Its unusually complex lock, however, incorporated a fine wire which any attempts at forcing would rupture, thus triggering off an alarm circuit.

A trained spy might well have camouflaged the hiding-place of his tools after the same reasoning. Could Evans be bribed into doping Ayscue's whisky-bottle as preliminary to getting hold of his keys? Non-minimal risk-potential would be the verdict of the manual – which, however, would be sure to offer helpful alternatives. He must consult it, but not now.

'I think I'll be getting down to the ante-room,' he said.

'Funny, that dispatch-rider getting chopped just up the road from here. It was an accident, I suppose?'

'No doubt about it. I was at the inquest. Nothing wrong with him the smash wouldn't account for, or his bike, or the road. Why?'

'That packet he was bringing must have been pretty important, to send a special with it like that, and the regular D R run coming in at eight the next morning.'

'It duplicated stuff I've had for nearly a fortnight,' said Leonard, lying with his usual ease. 'You don't know the Ministry.'

'Some of the lads were saying the date of Operation Apollo's been brought forward. I don't know where they got that from.'

Leonard felt as if a hot sponge had been pressed against the back of his neck. The information mentioned, together with the many detailed changes of plan necessitated, was what the special packet had contained. 'I wish they'd tell me these things now and then,' he said, exactly as easily as before. 'Funny my chief didn't think to mention it when he had me on the scrambler that night.'

'I told them it was all rubbish. Thought you ought to know, though. I could probably get their names if you want.'

'Don't bother. You get this sort of thing all the time. Well, I must be off. Gloves.'

Deering went to the tallboy and produced a pair of white cotton gloves ironed as thin as wafers. He handed them to his master, who made no attempt to put them on. This was sensible of him, for their evolution resembled that of the sleeves of a hussar's dolman, and no hand bigger than an eight-year-old child's could have entered them. Leonard grasped them lightly in his fist.

'Hat.'

The scarlet-piped ultramarine forage cap was produced with similar formality, but proved to be designed to go on Leonard's long head, and to fit there well enough. He needed it and the gloves for the thirty-yard indoor walk to the ante-room.

'That's all, Deering, thank you.'

'Good night, sir. See you in the morning.'

Left alone, Leonard felt almost calm again. It had been a bad moment, but no more. Deering brought him rumours at the rate of a dozen a week, and only time had been needed for one of them to hit the mark by chance. Nobody but himself, he was certain, had seen the contents of that packet.

To restore his morale finally, he turned and gazed at a large oil painting which, like the tailor's glass, he had started to take with him everywhere. Partly illuminated by the late sun, it made a handsome and cheering sight. The plate at the top described the subject as Uniforms of His Majesty's 17th Regiment of Horse, the Duke of Staffordshire's Dragoons ('The Sailors'). The picture showed five men on mounts in varying stages of hysteria. The lower plate identified the riders as Trooper: 1810 – Lieutenant: 1856 – Trumpeter: Field Service Order: 1901 – Corporal of Horse: Service Dress: 1915 – Major: Full Dress: 1929.

Leonard's attention fixed, as usual, on the last-named. This was a slim, youngish figure, clean-shaven, gazing – unlike the others – directly at the observer with just discernibly blue eyes. His real-life analogue would have seen action in the last year or two of the first war, might well have commanded a brigade or a division in the second, would by now, if tradition held, be fretting at his uselessness in a south-coast resort or spa. In Leonard's fancy, this predecessor of his in the Sailors was saying to him, I did what I could in my way: I enjoin you to do what you can in yours.

There had been a lot of opposition when Leonard, coming across the picture in the Sailors' regimental museum during his sole visit to them, had set about acquiring it for the duration of his Army or pseudo-Army career. His insistence that it was vital to his cover as a serving officer had finally turned the wheels that secured it for him, but it had been a near thing. If the Commandant of the Sailors had behaved more tactfully at his interview with the relevant Minister, had as much as refrained from calling him a grubby little upstart, the issue might well have gone the other way.

To learn of this would have surprised Leonard. He had guaranteed in writing that, as soon as his job was done, the picture would be returned to its owners, and this, he would have thought, was enough. Now, drawing himself up, he snapped a salute to the blue-eyed major and left the room.

*

'Ah, here's our spy-catcher. What are you drinking, Brian? Spot of pink gin?'

46

'Dry sherry, please, sir,' said Leonard.

'Of course, should have remembered, never touch the hard stuff, do you? Quite right for a man in your position. Can't have you getting tight and blabbing secrets all round the place. What about you, Willie? More of the same, or are you going to take a leaf out of Brian's book?'

'Not this time,' said Ayscue. 'I'll have another whisky, if I may.'

'Let it be so. Anybody else? Oh, come on.'

Colonel White had been selected as Commanding Officer of the unit on several grounds. His standing as a reliable, orthodox professional soldier fitted him for a post where above all, it had been felt, nothing fancy was needed. It had been further felt that he would guard the secrets put in his charge as closely as, by purely military means, they could be guarded, nor would he be concerned to know himself just what these secrets were. Service psychologists had recommended a personality of his outgoing, socially oriented type to preside at a Mess where various tensions could be expected to emerge. And a man in the Ministry who had been with him in North Africa had thought that old Chalky White, whom a German mine had deprived of half his left foot and thereby of most of his chances of promotion, could do with a full colonelcy and its extra pay.

At the moment, the Colonel was displaying his psychological qualifications for his post. Leonard's isolation from most of the other members of the Mess had not escaped him, and he lost no opportunity of throwing conversational bridges across this gap, of inviting the majority to see that even a Security man was a man and his job a job. White now took up the job half of this task.

'Well, Brian,' he said, when the Mess waiter had brought the drinks and retired, 'how goes the great work?'

'Oh, not too –'

'I must say I wouldn't care to be up to what you're up to, would you, Willie?'

'It must be rather like my line of country, only more taxing.'

'Not being able to relax for a moment. On duty twenty-four hours a day. Your head the one that rolls if the opposition gets on to anything. Tell me, Brian, are you any nearer your man yet?'

'Yes, I think so. One works by elimination, of course. I was able to rule out the s 1 people more or less from the start.'

Leonard referred to those in Security Grade 1, the six British, four Indian and two Pakistani officers undergoing training for Operation Apollo, and their two Instructors, both British. Nobody else in the unit, apart from Leonard himself, was permitted full knowledge of the nature of the Operation. Grade 2, or s 2, consisted only of the Briefing Group, two British officers and one Indian – Naidu – whose duties were to provide certain ancillary information. s 3 comprised the Colonel, the Adjutant, the Medical Officer, Hunter, and Ayscue.

The Colonel laughed, knuckling his moustache. 'That brings us pretty near home, Brian. Leaves you with what? Half a dozen people?'

'Eight, as regards officers. I've been working on them pretty hard over the last ten days. They're down to four now.'

'Is it,' asked the Colonel, 'is it in order for me to inquire whether I am one of the possibly guilty four or one of the innocent four?'

'Oh yes, sir. You're clear. So are Hunter and the M O and captain Naidu.'

'Then I'm not clear,' said Ayscue.

'Now you're not to take this sort of thing in the wrong way, Willie,' said the Colonel, 'Brian's simply doing his job. And one of the ways we can help him is by forcing ourselves to put up with things we might think it was wrong to put up with in other circumstances. You're not accusing anybody, are you, Brian?'

Ayscue nodded. 'Oh, fair enough. But what interests me isn't so much the fact that tomorrow morning I may find myself arrested for passing secrets to the enemy—though it's an interesting enough fact in its way. Just for the moment I'm looking at it from Brian's point of view and wondering how he manages to stay alive at all without any human relationships. Not many people could stand being driven back inside their own mind the whole time.'

'You're diving a dit deep for me there, Willie,' said the Colonel.

'No, I see what he means, sir – he's quite right. You start living in a sort of dream world. You get worse at judging evidence, not better. When I started in this game I wondered why they gave us such long leaves. Well, it's only the last half of the time that's really like leave. You spend the first half gradually pushing yourself out of your shell.'

The Colonel was not certain what Ayscue's mild stare at Leonard meant. He said briskly, 'But of course one couldn't afford to rule out people outside the Mess, or even outside the unit, am I right, Brian? I must admit I've got a bit of a soft spot for the idea of a beautiful spy setting up shop in the village and trying to lure innocent young officers into her web, you know, the old Mata Hari touch. It'd brighten life up like anything.'

'That's unlikely, sir,' said Leonard carefully. 'Possible, but unlikely. The one bit of luck we've had does point pretty well unmistakably to the fellow we're after being somewhere in this camp. He could be – well, one of the sergeants, say, or even a guard, but that's rather unlikely too. I can't see any of the s 1 officers giving things away in that sort of direction. And the precautions you've taken, sir, have made it quite impossible for anyone to get at the secret stuff physically. No, I'm going to stick to my four candidates until I'm proved wrong.'

'I wish you'd tell us what this bit of luck of yours was,' said the Colonel. 'Why you think your man's someone inside this unit. How you can be so certain we're up against a spy at all, come to that. Can't do any harm to let it out, can it?'

Leonard made a decision. It would be useful to see whether, or how soon and in what form, this information would come back to him via Deering. 'The other week our people made an arrest in London. One of the things they picked up was a message reporting progress on penetrating Operation Apollo – nil, I'm glad to say. Well, there was something about that message, not its actual text, which established that it came from somebody serving in the Forces.'

'Kind of paper or something,' muttered the Colonel.

'And we learned something else, too. A man who leaves his tracks uncovered in that kind of way isn't a regular spy. He's what we call in the profession a neo-ideologue – an amateur, if you prefer it. That's a two-edged thing from our point of view. On the one hand it makes him more likely to give himself away through inexperience; on the other, he'll have had no previous contacts or history of any kind and there won't be a file on him. In that sense he might be anybody.'

What Leonard had been saying was full of interest for the Colonel, but it was time to draw Ayscue back into the conversation. 'Well, I'm sure we all hope you find him soon and we can breathe more easily. Are you a literary man, Brian?'

'I don't seem to get much time for reading.'

'No, I suppose not. Pity. I'm at it all the time myself. Of course, it's easy for me – I got my little machine in motion within twenty-four hours of arriving here, set up the guards and so forth, and now it's just a question of the odd time-table check. The rest of the time, when I'm not down here making sure you all get enough to eat and drink I'm ploughing through these French existentialist fellows. Bit arid, they strike me, but never mind. Anyway, I was just going to say that Willie here is thinking of starting some sort of magazine. I didn't give you a chance to tell me much about it, did I, Willie? What kind of thing have you in mind? Will you get enough contributions?'

'Well,' said Ayscue, rather unwillingly, 'there are twenty-three officers and a hundred and sixty-three other ranks inside this fence. Half the lads spend half their time hanging about waiting to go on guard duty in one form or another, and day passes are restricted to ten per cent of them. Quite a few of the others haven't a lot to do – the drivers and D Rs, for instance. I've asked around a bit, and my impression is that some of them might be fairly keen. I'll probably have to write a good deal of the thing myself, but then, I'm afraid I haven't much to do here either.'

'Sounds a good idea,' said Leonard. 'Very good idea.'

'Oh, then there'd be no objection from the security angle?'

'None at all. Quite the contrary. Excuse me.'

Leonard moved away down the room. This looked very much like the farmhouse sitting-room it had been forty years earlier, so much so that a mind inquisitive in other directions than Leonard's might have suspected a conscious attempt to preserve it.

From 1946 until three months ago the house had sheltered successive groups of officers on Intelligence courses, and it would have been some of these, or the President of their Mess, who had had the floor relaid without its ancient dips and slopes being corrected, the wide fireplace rebricked with the asymmetry of its flanking buttresses and low stub walls left as it was. Oak furniture predominated, including a rocking-chair with a vertical see-saw effect that nobody tried twice. Militarism appeared only in the dozen or so framed photographs, imported perhaps in a jeering spirit, showing officer-cadet classes now long since dead or pensioned off, groups of World War I generals and staff with moustaches and plumes, and a victory parade of the same era. The sole recent object was a large television set. Beside it, though not as if he were about to switch it on, stood the figure of the Chief Instructor.

From a distance this man evidently had no neck. Closer approach showed that there was a neck there after all, and a substantial one; its very thickness disguised it by blending it with the head. This was squat and heavy, with greying hair cut very short and a florid but small-featured face. The Chief Instructor was about fifty and getting fat, which his posture did nothing to hide. He was and looked a civilian in uniform. The uniform in this case, and on this occasion, was the Mess dress of the Army Information Corps, a dark-grey jacket and olive-green trousers. The olive-green revers of the jacket were covered with ash from the cigar its wearer was smoking. The Chief Instructor was called Major Venables. Nobody in the unit knew his christian name.

'Good evening, Leonard,' he said in his tight, groaning voice.

'Hullo, Major. I was –'

'Not Major. I have told you before. I am no more a major than you are a captain. Venables is my name.'

'Sorry . . . Do you mind a bit of shop?'

'I welcome it, even your sort of shop. It is considerably more appealing than what passes for conversation among these fusiliers and dragoons. Well?'

Leonard dropped his voice. 'The revised schedule.'

Venables maintained his. 'I told you there would be no difficulty and there has not been. The persons who control our destinies were aware of their ignorance for once and allotted an over-generous period for the completion of training. Terminating the course two weeks sooner than originally planned will entail nothing more than some intensified homework on the part of my pupils. I cannot speak for the so-called Briefing Group. From what I see of them in this social slum I would judge that they would find it difficult to pass on accurately the words of "Mad Dogs and Englishmen" within any fixed period of time.'

Leonard looked nervously about. 'Ssshh,' he said.

Venables laughed. It was like his voice talking without words. 'If a remark of that sort gives you cause for concern, you must find your duties very onerous. You should learn to take things more lightly.'

'Yes. I'm glad you feel you can manage all right in the shorter period. You've reported to that effect, of course.'

There was a pause. Venables's mouth gathered round his cigar, which was of square cross-section. A cube of ash fell on to his jacket. 'Are you not invading my province and exceeding your authority? Provided my contacts with my superiors are secure they are no concern of yours. And if these trinkets they gave us to wear on our clothing mean anything you are debarred from giving me orders. And allow me to say that I very much resent first learning of this change of date through you rather than in due form from my superiors.'

'I'm sorry ... Venables. I wasn't trying to order you about, honestly. It's just that my people seem to think I ought to know everything all the time. It gets difficult not to pry. As regards me getting the news first, that's just, well, inter-departmental rivalry. Showing how quick off the mark they are.'

'Yes. Why inform you by dispatch-rider instead of the equally secure and, as it proved, less unreliable method of scrambler telephone?'

Leonard shrugged. 'Well, there was a lot of detail. And I suppose it made somebody feel more important, sending for a D R. You know what they're like.'

'I am beginning to.'

'There's just one more point.'

'Oh dear. Yes?'

'Small but important.' Leonard reminded himself whose uniform he was wearing and faced Venables more squarely. 'You remember that you were not to divulge the bringing forward of the Operation until midnight tomorrow at the earliest.'

'Yes, yes.'

'This has now been amended. You are not to divulge it until what is in your opinion the last possible moment, and you are to give in writing forty-eight hours' notice of that moment. And that's an order. You see, you weren't quite accurate just now when you said I wasn't to give you orders. In all Security matters you do as I tell you.'

Venables threw his cigar-butt into the fireplace. 'Mm. Shall I not be informed of this by my own superiors? The matter of the giving of notice and so on?'

'No doubt. I was told to pass you your instructions as soon as possible.'

'Very well. I bow to your authority.'

The look Venables gave with this was unfamiliar. Perhaps he was respecting Leonard for having stood up to him, in the way that tyrants, martinets and so on were always supposed to. In Leonard's experience, this sort of respect was never hard to conceal behind a mask of increased tyranny or redoubled martinet-type behaviour, but Venables might be different. He was a man full of differences from other people. Leonard tried to imagine him in the act of giving some of the instruction he had been sent here to give, and soon stopped.

At this point the Mess Sergeant announced dinner, removing Venables from Leonard's thoughts as well as from his side.

Colonel White led the way across the cobbled hall and into the dining-room. The floor here was of marble, in squares of black and white. This was not an original installation, but one voted in key with the rest of the house when, a dozen years earlier, a programme of reconstruction at the county mental hospital had led to various furnishings and fittings there being advertised for sale. The then Mess Secretary had taken a truck over to collect the tiles and had been entertained to tea by Dr Best's predecessor.

On this distinctive foundation stood a pair of refectory tables, their surfaces polished to a high gloss by generations of batmen and defaulters, and on the bare wood was disposed a great deal of Victorian plate and silver and glass. All this, together with a large selection of wines, Hunter had bought off the previous owners at a price that had made them slightly angry.

As always the Colonel sat down at the further table, choosing a random point along the side facing the window. This policy ruled out any traditionally undemocratic nonsense of a regular place or chair for the CO while giving him the outdoor view he enjoyed. The main buildings of the camp were out of sight from here, but he could see the drill square and transport sheds, the clothing store, the concrete bungalow that housed the telephone exchange and the emergency wireless station, a couple of sleeping-huts. It was all quite deserted, apart from four or five men in khaki slowly making their way up the main track. They had the lethargic air of underworked troops drifting along to the canteen and its television room or poker schools. But down at the gate stood the two necessary figures with steel helmets, respirators in the alert position and machine-pistols slung across their shoulders. Then the grandfather clock behind the Colonel struck the hour of eight and within seconds, as he watched, three more men emerged from a nearby hut and marched formally towards the gate : the Sergeant of the Guard and the two relieving sentries. The exchange was carried out with exemplary smartness. The Colonel felt relieved. What really counted was being done.

He picked up the menu. The meal was to open with a choice of avocado pear and eggs Benedict, followed by cold salmon, roast duckling with cherry sauce and fresh peas, and ice-cream pudding with hot chocolate sauce (one of Corporal Beavis's specialities). A Kreuznacher St Martin 1959 and a Clos de Vougeot 1957 were offered.

The Colonel asked for avocado pear and it was immediately brought. Although of good colour, it resisted his spoon in parts. He mentioned the fact to the fattish mournful-looking young officer sitting on his left. This was his Adjutant, Captain Ross-Donaldson.

'Should have been held back another day or two,' said the Colonel. 'You have to keep these fellows up to the mark all the time. Good thing for us all when Max Hunter gets back from his rest cure. When's that going to be, Alastair, by the way?'

'Excuse me a moment, sir.' Ross-Donaldson turned to his other neighbour and repeated the question. 'Churchill thinks to-morrow, sir.'

'Not a moment too soon. Oh, I was just speaking about Max ...'

When the Colonel had shifted his attention to the Medical Officer, who was on his right, Ross-Donaldson went on with what he had been saying to Churchill earlier.

'This whole concept of denial is losing its meaning,' he said. 'And of course I don't just mean that ground is three-dimensional. In fact, to insist on that has become rather immature, now that delivery can be made along virtually any parabola one chooses. No, the moment one abandons the front philosophy one's logically forced to part with direction except purely locally, and when that's gone, denial's whole *raison de se battre* is in peril, though no doubt it'll continue to colour unfriendly thought, vestigially at any rate. In my mind there's no question but that prenodalization must be the working principle.'

'You mean you stay where you are and fight whatever you see,' said Churchill.

'Have some hock. Well yes, though that denigrates some of the subtleties. You ought to read the chap's article in the *Military Quarterly*. It's called, um . . . "Node and Anti-Node : Tomorrow's Denial?" You know. With a question-mark.'

'Sounds fascinating.'

'It's the most adult piece of thinking I've seen for a long time. Since the van Gelder-Hernandez-Funck mobility equations came out in '62, probably. Do you feel like a bit of fun this evening?' added Ross-Donaldson in the same tone.

'Yes. What sort of fun?'

'Let's look up Lucy. You know her, don't you? Lady Hazell? Oh, you must meet her. She'd like you. I suppose one might call it a slight Bacchante complex in her case, with possible Jocastan undertones. We'll drive over after dinner.'

When the meal ended, Churchill and Ross-Donaldson returned to the ante-room, where they soon put down a cup of coffee and a glass of Cockburn 1945. Taking their leave presented no difficulty, for Colonel White had abjured formal dessert except on the weekly guest night. In the hall, Ross-Donaldson stopped and turned to Churchill.

'I'd better just look in at the Command Post,' he said. 'Coming?'

They went to the rear of the hall and stood for a moment in front of the door of what had been the morning-room. Then the door slid aside and they entered.

A sergeant and a corporal were facing them at attention. Ross-Donaldson told them to sit down. Immediately beneath the beams of the ceiling were television screens giving views of the main gate and, from various angles, a long low building surrounded by a barbed-wire fence and a concrete pathway. As Churchill glanced up at these a soldier with a slung machine-pistol moved slowly and silently across one and out of shot. Elsewhere there was a telephone direct to the civilian exchange, another telephone and a remote-control unit connected by underground cable to the camp exchange and wireless station respectively, and a large red button marked GENERAL ALARM.

'Hullo, Fawkes,' said Churchill to the corporal. 'I thought you were spending all your time over at the hospital keeping the Viet Cong from getting together with Captain Hunter.'

'That packed up yesterday, sir,' said Fawkes. 'I think Captain Leonard reckoned the Reds would have lost heart by then. I arrived back just in time to get on the roster for this lot. Captain Hunter's coming out tomorrow anyway, I hear.'

Although he spoke with his usual cheerfulness, Fawkes did not look well. His face was pale and there was sweat on his upper lip.

'Are you all right, Fawkes?' asked Churchill. 'Feeling rough?'

'I have got a bit of a head, but it's nothing really.'

'Would you like me to get you anything? I can fix up a relief for you if you want.'

'No, I'll be okay, honest. Thanks very much all the same, Mr Churchill.'

A buzzer sounded. The sergeant got up and went and looked through the thick panel of one-way glass in the door.

'It's the bloke with our tea, sir,' he said. 'Can I go ahead?'

'Certainly,' said Ross-Donaldson.

The sergeant pressed a stud and the door slid back. A well-built young man of perhaps twenty came in carrying two pint china mugs. At the sight of the two officers he straightened his back. Without looking ridiculous he managed to hand over the teas in a sort of posture of attention, then turned and saluted Ross-Donaldson.

'Signalman Pearce, sir,' said Fawkes.

'Good evening, Pearce,' said Ross-Donaldson. 'Do please carry on.'

Churchill remembered hearing the name from Hunter. He was struck by the healthy look of the young man's complexion and eyes and by the extreme smartness of his turnout. He would have made a good model for a recruiting poster, thought Churchill, had it not been for his air of intelligence.

The sergeant and Ross-Donaldson began discussing an arms inspection due to take place the following morning. Churchill turned towards them. He heard Pearce talking in an undertone.

'These were all I could get. I should take three now and another couple about one a.m. Remember I'll be on the switchboard at ten so you can give me a buzz there if you want anything.'

'Thanks, Andy. Don't worry about me.'

The internal telephone rang.

'Command Post, Corporal Fawkes speaking. Right. Go ahead in five minutes, at . . . twenty-one twenty-five hours. Okay. Cheers.' Fawkes turned to Ross-Donaldson. 'Just the floodlight check, sir.'

'Thank you, Fawkes . . . Well, I'm afraid they're going to have to turn up whether they've been up all night or not, Sergeant. I'm not going to lay it on twice over. Anything else? Oh, who's Duty Officer?'

'Captain Leonard, sir.'

As the officer directly responsible to the Colonel for the discipline of the unit, Ross-Donaldson evidently felt that it would be unsafe to react to this name in almost any way at all. He inclined his head about an inch without looking at anybody, said good night and left.

Churchill followed. In the hall again, the two entered their names in the Sign Out book that lay on a handsome gate-leg table. After writing down a local telephone number in the Location column and bracketing it against both names, Ross-Donaldson hesitated.

'I'd better just ring and make sure,' he said. 'You go on.'

Lighting a cigarette, Churchill strolled outside and moved towards the officers' car park. This brought him near Hut D 4.

*

D 4 was the long single-storey building Churchill had been looking at just now on the Command Post television screens. Its contents were the reason for the Colonel's carefully planned system of guards. Overhead lights illuminated it and the pathway round it, where Churchill could see the two sentries pacing. Further off, two other figures could be made out, members of the patrol that circuited the area at all times. They were passing the foot of the steel scaffolding that supported one of the permanently manned machine-gun posts. The other was in the roof of the farmhouse. The guns were heavy-calibre weapons mounted on tripods. The noise with which they fired their 12·75 mm. alloy-jacketed ammunition (as heard at a recent practice alarm) was immense. Such bullets would penetrate any vehicle which Colonel White considered at all likely to be used in an attempt to enter D 4. A mere armoured car would be riddled in seconds. In the event of a full-scale tank assault, agreed to be a remote possibility in peacetime, the Colonel was to call on a neighbouring R A F base for assistance.

Churchill contemplated D 4. The thought of what was inside it hardly weighed upon him. He had felt nothing but a remote excitement when, three weeks earlier, a pair of five-ton lorries escorted by a full platoon of motorized infantry had delivered there a number of large sealed boxes. What he disliked about the building tonight was its reminders of a world which had started to disappear almost as he was starting to walk and talk, but which he knew about from written and other records. Even this, however, was less unwelcome than the kind of future the sight of

D 4 seemed to promise. It felt to him like a personal rather than simply a general future. The memory of the dispatch-rider's death five days earlier came into his mind as he stood in the darkness waiting for Ross-Donaldson, that and the memory of the girl he had seen earlier on the afternoon in question.

Just then D 4 and its environs became in an instant totally bright as the floodlights round it were switched on. Churchill flinched, and could have sworn that the sentries on the path did the same, each seeming to check in his stride. Near the single gateway in the fence they crossed and diverged, then one after the other passed out of sight round the angles of the building. For a quarter of a minute nothing moved. At the end of that time the lights went off and their image shrank and swirled and grew again on Churchill's retinas. The check had been successfully completed.

Ross-Donaldson came up and said, 'I suppose in a way one wouldn't have expected it. Second-stage concealment theory in a non-hostility context. Somebody with old Chalky White's history would have been much more likely to keep the beams on all night long so that even a Russian on a moon-run could see D 4, let alone any inquisitive strangers in the village. I tried to get her but she was engaged both times.'

'Well, at least that means she's in,' said Churchill as they got into Ross-Donaldson's jeep.

'Not necessarily. The engaged signal is given whenever the connecting apparatus is engaged, which will be the case if another subscriber is attempting to raise the same number. And Lucy's number is one people are constantly attempting to raise. It's one of the things about her. And her number. Of course, I did get here a couple of weeks before you and the other S 1 chaps, so I've had longer to explore and a clearer field at the outset. But even so I am slightly astonished you haven't come across Lucy before, or she you. I thought that most of the Mess had been round at her place at one time or another, except for people like Leonard and Venables of course. And Willie Ayscue. And the Indians and Pakistanis. Yes, I suppose there are quite a few who haven't been, when you come to work it out carefully. Adjutant and Lieutenant Churchill. Recreational.'

This last was said to, and taken down in writing by, a corporal who emerged from the guard-hut by the gate. The gate itself, a massive affair of steel and concrete which it would have taken a fair-sized shell to knock off its hinges, was pushed open by one of the sentries, while the other peered vigilantly up the road, as if aware that this would be a good moment for an attack by hostile motor-cyclists, should one be in preparation.

They turned right into what was no more than a lane, and then immediately left. Fifty yards further on they crossed directly over a substantial trunk highway and travelled along a minor road with tall hedgerows on either side. Ross-Donaldson had at once taken up his own words to the guard corporal. 'Recreational. I suppose that is the way to describe it. Do you think it'll help Leonard to know that we've been recreating?'

'He has to keep a check, presumably. But I do wonder what he gets out of these guard reports. If you and I were spies going off to meet our contact we'd be unlikely to tell the guard so. And we'd vary the times and everything, so that –'

'An omnifariously randomized schedule indistinguishable from the genuinely random. Quite so. However, I'm sure this is at least as clear to Leonard as it is to us. From all points of view he must start by doing what's expected of him. It's only then that he can surprise people. Are you warm enough?'

The jeep had no side-screens, but the rush of air was no more than cool. It smelt vaguely of earth and vegetation. Except for their headlights it was quite dark. 'I'm fine,' said Churchill, then went on.

'Why don't the Indians and Pakistanis ever go and see this Lucy woman?'

'Oh, I'm sure they sense that they wouldn't get on together. They and she.'

'Doesn't she like non-Europeans?'

'I've no idea. Light me a cigarette, Churchill, would you? No, it's what they'd feel about it. Not what she'd feel about it, if I know her. One of them explained to me the other day that they all have very excellent, very loving wife in Bombay or Karachi. I think it was your friend Moti Naidu.'

'It doesn't sound like him.'

'I'm sorry, I know I'm not good at imitations. I must stop doing them.'

'Why does it matter if they have any sort of wife in Bombay?'

'Well, I don't care personally one way or the other.'

'No, I mean why should that stop them going to see Lucy?'

'Having a wife might not stop me, but people like Asians often hold these strict views about marital fidelity.'

'Are you trying to tell me that they couldn't go to see this woman without popping into bed with her?'

'It's unlikely. She might jib a bit at taking on old Chatterji.'

Churchill felt slightly alarmed. 'Christ, what sort of set-up has she got there?'

'It's what you might call a *maison à une fille*. She practises promiscuous polyandry. You'll see.'

'Christ.'

'I thought I'd conveyed that. Anyway, everything's very well handled. Only those with exceptionally low embarrassment thresholds would feel any discomfort.'

'How good-looking is she?'

'Quite sufficiently. She spends a lot of money on her clothes and jewellery and stuff of that kind. She's the widow of a man who became very rich as a result of making furniture, so rich that they had to give him a knighthood. They hadn't been married very long, and he'd been a knight an even shorter time, when he fell off his yacht in the Adriatic and was drowned. There are no children of the marriage.'

'What was she before she was married?'

'I don't know. She's never said and I've never thought to inquire. I don't even know how long she's been polyandrous. One would imagine quite a time, but it's probably the sort of activity in which a high pitch of expertness is soon reached.'

Anticipation and nervousness were mixed in Churchill. After thinking for a while he decided that, although he had very little idea of what he was in for and still wondered energetically how many other men might turn out to be looking up Lucy tonight, he would be disappointed rather than relieved if for any reason she proved unavailable. He cheered up a lot at this thought, and became impatient to arrive.

'How far now?' he asked.

'We're just coming up to half-way, which I take to be St Jerome's Priory. It's behind that peak on the left. You can't actually see it from the road. In fact the site's well concealed from most points along the natural approaches. It lies at the top of what looks like a perfect example of a mesa, though one would expect other such formations to be found in the area, and I haven't identified any. More probably it's the remains of an unusually broad band of vertical strata whose slopes have been subject to a lot of snow action, giving us a kind of eroded hog's back. Anyway, a useful spot for a place full of valuables that isn't allowed to defend itself.'

'It's pretty much of a ruin, isn't it?'

'The western end of the chapel and a corner of the refectory are relatively intact, but elsewhere there isn't much that's higher than a couple of feet. Cromwell slighted it so thoroughly that they probably couldn't face the thought of rebuilding. It must have cost the most appalling effort originally, with everything having to be brought up on pack-animals.'

After another twenty minutes or so they turned off the road through a stone gateway and drove up between two lines of trees to a substantial house. Churchill realized that their journey from the camp had brought them along the diagonal of a kind of flattened square, with the village and the mental hospital at the other two corners and the Priory somewhere in the middle. There were lights burning in the house, though dimly.

Ross-Donaldson parked the jeep next to two other cars. He got out and straightened his jacket.

'I'm getting fat,' he said morosely. 'It's all that eating and drinking we do. But what I can't see is why being fat isn't good for you. Surely you'd be much fitter, you'd get much more out of the exercise, give your muscles more work to do, sweat more and so on, if you walked and ran about the place wearing a special boiler-suit padded with thirty pounds or so of sand. But that's an exact equivalent of being thirty pounds overweight. And why doesn't being fat make you thin? The boiler-suit arrangement certainly would.'

'There must be a fallacy somewhere,' said Churchill as they waited in the extensive portico.

'No doubt. I suppose Lucy hasn't gone off to St Tropez and left the lights on. It would be in character. Ah, here we are.'

The door opened slightly. A man's voice said something brief.

'Good evening,' said Ross-Donaldson. 'We've come to see Lady Hazell.'

'Who are you?'

'A friend of hers. Who are you?'

Further indistinguishable words were said, this time in a grumbling tone, then the door was pulled wide. Following Ross-Donaldson in, Churchill looked about for the man who had opened to them, but he was nowhere to be seen. This would have been more surprising if the hall had been better lit. As it was the only illumination, wan and pinkish, came from a couple of bulbs on or near the staircase that mounted the far wall. Across this there hung a gigantic figure, a mythological personage or beast portrayed perhaps on a tapestry. Other beings looked down from elsewhere on the walls and stood about the place in three-dimensional form. Directly ahead was a doorway from which a slightly stronger light was shining. Churchill walked through it.

The room he entered was as full of pictures and statuary as the hall had been. This gave so strong an impression of over-crowding that it was some time before he was sure that there were only about four actual people present. Two or three men were calling to one another.

'Get her cage up here.'

'I'm not going to lift that thing.'

'Can't you see she's frightened? Leave her alone for a bit.'

'Go on, grab her and get it over.'

One of the men was standing on a chimneypiece, clinging with one hand to the corner of an ornate picture-frame while he lunged upwards and outwards with the other. A periwigged face stared past his hip.

'Gin and tonic,' he said coaxingly. 'Gin and tonic, gin and tonic, gin and tonic.'

'Gin and tonic,' said another, ghostly voice.

'Come here, you fool.'

The man made a quick snatching motion and overbalanced, sending the picture swinging to and fro on its nail. He fell noisily but, it soon proved, without hurting himself across a table, a chair and the corner of a large writing-desk. At the same moment a small dark shape detached itself from the picture-rail, where it had been practically invisible, and made with a beating of wings into the middle of the room. A grey parrot with a bald crown to its head settled neatly on Ross-Donaldson's right shoulder.

'Okay now, keep still and we've got her. Cage over here quick. You're all right, birdie – gin and tonic.'

'Gin and tonic.'

A half-full glass was proffered and the parrot seemed to drink.

'That's it, you love the stuff, don't you, you old soak?'

'Here we are. Come on, in you get, curse you.'

'She can't, she's got her foot caught in this wire or whatever it is on this chap's shoulder.'

'Chain mail,' said Ross-Donaldson. 'Quite customary.'

'Customary or not, let's get her perishing foot out. Now . . .'

'That's no good, somebody'll have to hold her.'

When no one else moved, Churchill clasped the bird with the palms of his hands over its wings. Its heart was beating very quickly. After a moment it struck down at his finger with its beak. He kept his hold, eased the parrot into its cage and sucked at the tear in his finger.

'Let me see that,' said Ross-Donaldson.

'Lucky she didn't get her beak round it or she'd have gone through it to the bone. They're very vicious, you know.'

Churchill was aware that the company had just increased by one, perhaps two. While Ross-Donaldson peered at the injured finger, a cloud of scent and a rustle of skirts approached from somewhere in the rear. The hand in question was gently grasped by another one, thin, cool and dry, the owner of which Churchill took in as of medium height, dark hair, pale complexion and no particular age. There was elaborately cut clothing and earrings and necklaces, too.

Ross-Donaldson said, 'Lucy, may I present a brother-officer

of mine, Lieutenant James Churchill of the Blue Howards?
Churchill, this is Lady Hazell.'

'How do you do, Mr Churchill.' Lady Hazell gave the hand
she was holding a couple of shakes and went on holding it. 'It's
not much use trying to see anything in here,' she added truth-
fully. 'Let me take you along to the bathroom.'

Still holding his hand, she led him to a far corner of the room
and up a narrow staircase with linoleum underfoot and crum-
bling plaster on the walls. On the next floor, in virtually complete darkness, she drew him across a couple of yards of what
felt and sounded like bare boards, then switched on a light so
comparatively bright that Churchill blinked.

They stood in what was indeed a bathroom, for it contained
a bath, and in addition a washbasin and w.c. But he found it
hard to imagine anyone bathing here willingly. A dank-looking
rug covered some of the floorboards, its design indistinguishable.
Two disused pots of paint stood in a corner beside an equally
disused lavatory brush, and along the sill below the uncurtained
window were half a dozen jam-pots, most of them empty, one
or two holding an inch of pale-brownish liquid. The light-bulb
was unshaded.

In the two seconds he spent in taking this in, Churchill felt,
Lady Hazell had been taking him in. She gave no sign of how
he had fared when she said pleasantly, in her faintly hoarse
voice,

'I'm afraid things are in rather a mess. We don't use this part
of the house a great deal. Now let me have a look. I must apologize for poor Sadie's behaviour. She'd been over-excited and I'm
afraid she rounded on you when you were being the only brave
and helpful person there. That's life. But this doesn't look too
bad, thank God. Does it hurt very much?'

Churchill had had much more than two seconds to take Lady
Hazell in. He found her a good deal better than he had expected,
in several respects. To begin with, she was no more than thirty-
five, if that; he had assumed that the onset of promiscuous polyandry could not be expected before the later forties. Then, she was
slightly above the quite sufficiently attractive level promised by
Ross-Donaldson; her complexion turned out to be white and

clear rather than pale, with strongly marked black eyebrows and abundant lashes. And although her figure was obscured by the various artifices of her clothes, neither it nor they seemed too bad. Best of all, her manner was quiet to the point of docility. He knew very well that this might easily change later, but he was glad that so far she had not sprung at him with the kind of erotic snarl he had imagined when Ross-Donaldson first started describing her.

'What? Oh. No, it's . . . fine, thank you.'

The blow had been right at the limit of the parrot's reach, and in fact most of the tear in the skin had already stopped bleeding.

'Good. But I think we ought to disinfect it, and bathe it and so on. Now . . .'

She opened a wall-cupboard, the glass of which was cracked and foxed, revealing a hundred or more unstoppered bottles, uncapped tubes and lidless tins. After a brief search she took out a small bottle of beetroot-coloured liquid.

'Mercurochrome. Just the thing. Let's wash the cut out first, though.'

Now she turned on one of the taps at the basin. A loud shuddering groan filled the room, dwindled to a whimper and was quiet. Water splashed, trickled, splashed again.

'It'll run hot eventually, you'll find. I expect you'd like me to leave you to yourself, Mr Churchill. I think there's some plaster in the cupboard. Be sure to help yourself to a drink, won't you?'

Before leaving, she gave him a glance that clearly meant something, though he could not have said what. Perhaps he had already failed some vital test and would never be allowed near her again. He put one of his uninjured fingers under the tap, which was now delivering a steady but cold flow, and considered. Had he been meant to set about pulling her dress off the moment they arrived up here? And if so, would that have been taken just as a required show of keenness, to be noted and taken up later, or would one thing have been allowed to lead to another? And if so, where? In here? Then keenness was hardly the word. Or had Ross-Donaldson been pulling his leg about the whole thing? One could never be sure with him.

And what was that about helping himself to a drink? Were

there some dregs of medicinal brandy somewhere in the cupboard? He looked, but soon gave up. The risk of toppling bottles into the basin was too great, and any dregs he might find in this context would be unappealing.

The water from the tap had settled into a state between cool and lukewarm. He washed his finger, working up a little lather from a sliver of household soap, and dried it on his handkerchief. After some thought he poured mercurochrome on to it. There was no special result apart from a bright red stain on the skin. The plaster he decided against. He used the w.c., smoothed his hair back in the mirror, lit a cigarette and slowly groped his way down the stairs.

The room he had left could never look quite empty, but within a few seconds he was sure there were no people in it. He listened. Immediately there was the sound of a car being started and driven away. It was not, as he feared just when it began, the sound of a jeep. He went quietly through the hall to the front door, opened it and looked out. The jeep was standing on its own where it had been left, and a tail-light was receding along the drive. He shut the door and listened again. There was an absolute silence. He walked across thick carpets to the foot of the stairs. From here it was quite plain that the figure on the tapestry he had noticed on arrival was human after all, a girl in a long white dress reclining at the edge of a pool or stream. Nothing was to be seen up the stairs.

Back where he had just come from, he heard the parrot stirring in its cage. On his way over to it he noticed a tray with bottles, glasses and an ice-bucket. He understood now about being told to be sure to help himself to a drink. Grinning, he mixed himself a gin and tonic with ice. What little he had gathered of the men here earlier had not appealed to him much. They had certainly been sent packing; even now it could not have been much more than five minutes since Lady Hazell had left him in the bathroom, which meant among other things that he could not have been inside the house more than a quarter of an hour. This seemed to him very surprising. However – how much longer was he going to be on his own, and how was he going to fill in the time?

He resumed his interrupted progress towards the parrot. Watching him, it used claws and beak to move itself ungracefully across the back of its cage. Then it forgot about him and clung there without stirring. After calling it by its name several times without any result, he moved away again and looked idly at some of the pictures. Most were portraits. Several of these, whether true likenesses or not, seemed in the half-light to show such an ugly face that it was hard to imagine how they had survived the death of the sitter at latest, unless by the intervention of some close relative. The one above the chimneypiece, rendering a man in middle-life whose pop-eyed petulance the artist had perhaps tried, not very hard, to represent as authority, was a case in point. It hung a little askew after being disturbed by the climber there and he straightened it. On the shelf below it he noticed a framed photograph. Although its tones were in over-violent contrast, he could make out enough of the face of the girl in it to be fairly sure it was better-looking than the surrounding average. Faintly and, he felt, untraceably, it reminded him of somebody. He put it down.

Suddenly Churchill felt sure he was going to have to hang about here all night, forgotten or ignored by Ross-Donaldson and Lady Hazell, with nothing whatever to do, nothing to read and in any case – he fiddled vainly with the switches beside the door – no light to read by. He drained his gin and tonic and poured another : much faster drinking than his normal tempo. But that tempo itself had recently been quickening, ever since, in fact, he and the other SI officers had been fully informed of the nature of Operation Apollo.

He did not want to think about this now. Carrying his fresh drink, he moved towards the hall, then changed his mind and walked to the far corner of the room. Here, next to the staircase, he found a door, then a dining-room with a long table but no chairs, then a kitchen. This had a normal light in it. It was clean and tidy, although thinly stocked with food and means of preparing it. The refrigerator contained nothing but a lot of ice-trays and seven or eight tins of tomato juice. Apart from this, it appeared that Lady Hazell lived on eggs, black coffee and various spices. The racing page of a newspaper was spread on the table.

Churchill stood reading this and sipping his drink for a few minutes. Then he heard Ross-Donaldson call his name from the drawing-room.

'You weren't very long,' said Churchill when he reached him.

'No,' said Ross-Donaldson. Looking just the same as usual, he was gazing at one picture or another. 'Where have you been?'

'In the kitchen. You know, hanging about.'

'Did you notice any coffee there?'

'As a matter of fact I did. Lots of it.'

'I think I could do with a cup. Would you like some?'

'Well yes, but . . .'

'Oh, sorry, of course. It's the second door on the left along the upstairs passage. And I would be really honestly grateful if you didn't prolong the after-play unduly. Don't feel you have to rush it, but it'll take us an hour to get back to camp and into bed and I've got this arms inspection at nine hundred hours. Have a good time.'

It was not until now that Churchill really believed that the expedition was going to have some point as far as he was concerned. Mounting the shadowy staircase he felt pleased and excited, confident that he could take in his stride any unfamiliarities or momentary enigmas presented by what was in store for him.

Lady Hazell was lying in the middle of a very large bed with the covers up to her chin. Under the usual dim glow, it looked as if everything in the room was made of silk or velvet, but before Churchill could check on this impression she spoke to him.

'The thing is,' she said, 'for you to take all your clothes off now and then come and get into bed. It's much the best way.'

He did as he was told. Once in bed he very soon found that she too had nothing on. Her body was delightfully warm, and also well shaped in detail, firm, carefully looked after, healthy : or just young. He remembered faintly that he had expected her to be beyond him in one way or another, responding far too much or not at all, but her movements were those of someone whose mind was effectively on what they were both doing.

It was fine; it was successful; it was over. Lady Hazell stroked the back of his neck and smiled at him. She said, 'Is it James or Jim or Jimmy or something quite different?'

'James.'

'I've suddenly come over terribly sleepy, James. It's only about eleven. Not my usual form, I can tell you. Would you think it was awful of me if I sort of threw you out?'

'Not in the least.'

He got out of bed.

'The bathroom's through there. You can talk to me from it.'

This bathroom was radically unlike the one he had been in earlier. There was a bright red carpet that his toes sank into and wallpaper depicting colonnades and ornamental fountains. The bath was made of a beautiful pale green marble. There were two different kinds of lavatory paper. He said over his shoulder, 'Do you live here on your own?'

'I have been for the last few months. I've been making do with Mrs Stoker. She lives just down the road. She comes up every morning and does my breakfast and washes up the glasses and tidies round, and then she goes back and does my lunch and Mr Stoker carries it up here on a tray. He cleans out Sadie's cage and things too. And in the evenings I have a few drinks and don't usually bother. But it'll be different after tomorrow.'

'Why, what's happening then?'

'Well, tomorrow my great friend comes back. She's called Cathy. She's been away being ill but she's all right again now. You must come over again and meet her.'

Churchill went back into the bedroom and started dressing. Lady Hazell had apparently fallen asleep. He wished that those men had not been in the house when he arrived, and that he had come on his own. At this stage it was clear to him that he would not be making another visit here. If he did, he would probably like it less. Or he might like it more, in which case he would mind about the other men more. Or, possibly, he might find himself eventually minding about them less. That was an unpleasant idea.

He finished dressing and went over to the bed. Lady Hazell lay on her back just as he had left her. He did not want to leave her without saying good night, but was not sure how to wake her. He pressed his hand gently on the pillow beside her head and she opened her eyes at once.

'You'd like her,' she said. 'She's very sweet. Oh, you're off now, are you?'

'Yes.'

'Say good night to Alastair for me. How old are you, James?'

'Twenty-four.'

'I suppose I must seem the most fearful old bag to you.'

'You don't at all.'

He kissed her.

'You see, I suddenly found out that this was the sort of life I liked. I know there must be a reason for it but I wouldn't know what it is, would I? Now you're not to feel you've got to hang about, because you've got a long drive back to camp. But you must come over again soon and meet Cathy.'

'Of course. Good night, Lucy.'

*

The village where the officers and men of the unit did their minor shopping and their extra-mural drinking appealed to them chiefly because of its relative closeness to the camp. The local trades, such as they were, had become depressed over the previous decades, and the region had never attracted promoters of industrial development. Consequently, the village had declined in numbers and acquired a drab, dilapidated look which did not invite the better-off people from the nearest town to consider settling there. Recently, however, quite a few such people had got into the habit of driving out on summer evenings to drink at the White Hart, the largest pub in the place and the only one with pretensions to comfort. Among the results of this new trade were a modernized interior with a small grill-room, a furnished garden and a fresh intake of barmaids, these of a type thought to be more attractive to visitors than the village girls who had formerly done the job.

Catharine Casement became a barmaid in the lounge of the White Hart two days after she was let out of the mental hospital. The idea, and the arrangements, had been Lucy Hazell's.

Dr Best had given his qualified approval at his last interview with Catharine.

'I suppose in some ways it's not a bad thing that you should go straight into some sort of work,' he had said, rather dispiritedly. 'You realize that you'll inevitably be brought into contact with men at this public house?'

'Yes. That's all right with me.'

The doctor had shown his lower teeth. 'You know my views on your feeling toward men, Mrs Casement. I don't intend to go into them again now. What I want to impress on you is that in these next weeks you must show boldness and courage. If you find that some situation or person disturbs or frightens you, that's a sign that you must move towards it or them, not retreat. This is necessary if your probation period is to prove truly therapeutic. Remember, you are in search of a *shock*.'

'I'll see what I can do for you.'

'It's not for me, Mrs Casement, it's for you. Well, we'll re-examine your case in four weeks' time. Meanwhile, I advise you not to get in touch with me. The more isolated you feel yourself to be, the better the chances that something will come of our experiment. Something favourable, I hope.' At this point he had smiled cordially. 'But I shall be keeping myself informed of your progress.'

'How?'

'Don't worry, I won't be obtrusive about it. You'll be left to yourself all right. Well, good-bye. For the time being. And good luck. With the experiment.'

She had decided to forget all about Dr Best and his instructions until she had got used to being out of hospital. The first couple of days of this, at any rate, had been unexpectedly easy: completely non-frightening. On the second evening, as arranged, Mr Stoker had driven Lucy and herself down to the White Hart so that she could be introduced to the landlord and the rest of the staff and have her duties explained to her. The landlord was a red-faced man of fifty called Eames. He wore a short brown beard, grown as a personal contribution to the modernizing of the premises. He had taken the two women into the snug and insisted on giving them champagne. What he said, plus his manner, suggested a thorough but selective briefing by Lucy earlier.

'I'm putting you in my lounge bar to start with, Mrs Casement, because the trade isn't very heavy there, except sometimes at weekends, and there'll be someone else on then as well to give you a hand. You get a very nice type of people in the lounge. Nice type of men particularly. But I want to impress on you that if by any remote chance anybody does get impertinent or anything, you come to me straight away and I'll deal with him, won't I, Lady Hazell? No, you won't have any trouble. As I say, they're a nice crowd. You get doctors and business men and officers from that camp up the road. They'll all be on your side.

'Now as regards the technical aspect, if you could get down here at say nine-thirty, I'll run over that with you before we open, though I gather from Lady Hazell here that you're used to the serving of drinks, so I may not have very much to teach you there. The difficulty you will undoubtedly find is with remembering prices, totalling orders and giving change. What I've done, I've had a full list typed out for you in my office. Here. The drinks and so on are down this side, and over here there's the prices. I'd advise you to just work away at that until you've got it off by heart. Get Lady Hazell to help you. You could reel off an order, Lady Hazell, and Mrs Casement could work out how much it would come to. The two of you could make a sort of game of it. You know ... "Two large gins and tonic, please, miss, pint and a half of best bitter, one light ale, pint of ordinary bitter, scrub the light ale, how much, please?"—"Eleven and four, please, sir, and would you like a slice of lemon in the gins?"'

It had not risen to anything like that pitch during lunch-time opening the next day. Trade was small and slow, confined to a few local tradespeople and one or two young couples. Catharine got the tables and her counter cleared as soon as the bar shut at half-past two. Then she was free until a quarter to seven. Eames explained that the girl in the saloon, which communicated, could easily deal with any early evening custom, adding that Catharine was not to overtax herself and that she was to tell him at once if there was anything she thought was not as it should be.

In the afternoon she slept for an hour or so. After that she got up and made a pot of tea and took it into Lucy's bedroom. They went over the price list together a final time. At the end of it Catharine was pretty confident about everything except the bottled beers and stouts.

'I'll never get all those lagers right,' she said.

'What does it matter? What's so awful about looking at a list? You can't expect to have it all off by heart the first evening. Anyway, I've just noticed they go in alphabetical order. The Esbjerg's most expensive, then the Gesundheit and then the Lyre. And the price goes down threepence between the first two and three-ha'pence between the second and third. Just half as much.'

'Good, that is a help.'

'I hope this won't turn out to be too much for you, Cathy. I've realized it's getting on for two hours' travel by car every day. But you're a good strong girl, and I thought after being cooped up in that disgusting place all those months you wouldn't mind rushing about a bit. Now we've got to decide what you're to wear. It's Mr Eames we have to consider really. Strike the happy medium between what he'd think was tarty and what he'd think was dowdy. It won't be quite plain sailing. I tell you what, I think I'd better have another little sleep. I was late last night and as far as I can remember I look like being late again tonight. You go and have a lovely bath and then bring all your best things in here and we'll go through them together.'

By six o'clock they had finally settled on a blue sleeveless linen jacket, a pleated skirt, sandals and gold earrings, and Catharine was arrayed in these as she sat and talked to Lucy, who in turn was in the bath. She looked at Lucy's body as its owner soaped it. It seemed to her a prettily moulded body with delicate skin, and touching it would not have revolted her, but she could not imagine what it would feel like to want to do so. At this distance Dr Best's ideas, whose unexpectedness and difficulty she had taken as an extra proof that they were right, struck her as amateurish and affected. He talked as if he had forgotten all about going to bed with people, if he had ever known. But how was he going to keep his eye on her?

'Are you all right, Cathy?'

'Yes, fine. A bit nervous. It's all so public, you see. I know I can look after myself with just one or two of them to deal with at a time, but it's probably not so easy when there's a whole crowd of others there listening and getting ready to laugh. You know what they're like; you've been in pubs.'

'Not for some time, actually, until the other day with you. But you're looking at things the wrong way. You should be expecting somebody marvellous to turn up. It's about due for that to happen to you, goodness knows.'

'Yes, I suppose it might happen.' The difficulty was in deciding whether somebody was really marvellous or would only go on seeming to be until it was too late. Catharine felt she was slightly worse at this now than she had been when fifteen.

'That's the spirit. When you get back you can sneak up to bed if you want, or come into the drawing-room and mingle with the throng. You wouldn't have to mingle too thoroughly, I'll see to that. I can always keep the wrong sort away from you, you remember, even if you can't. Mr Stoker should have you back here by quarter past eleven, so there'll be some of the evening left if you fancy it. That's him hooting now. Off you go, Cathy. Good luck with the lagers. Enjoy yourself.'

Catharine arrived at the White Hart in good time, hung up her coat in the alcove next to Eames's office and went into the saloon. There were half a dozen people drinking there, all of whom turned to stare at her. The barmaid already on duty, a round-faced nineteen-year-old called Anne, raised the leaf of the counter to let her through.

'Nothing very much for you next door, Cath. Couple of peasants on brown ales and four of those soldiers, three of them on large pink gins and the other on angostura and soda. Can't think what he gets out of it, can you? I've been charging him ninepence a go. You'll have it easy for a bit but it'll start filling up after seven. Give me a shout if you want me for anything.'

Catharine went through the communicating doorway into the lounge bar and came face to face with a young man in khaki standing on the other side of the counter. Immediately she remembered having seen him on her way to her last interview but one with Dr Best. She was startled and could tell that he was too. Neither spoke for a moment.

'I've seen you before,' he said in a clear voice. 'At the ...'

'Yes. At the mental hospital. I came out the day before yesterday.'

'I knew you straight away.'

She could not stop herself saying, 'And I knew you straight away.'

'I know.'

She noticed his finely shaped ears and square hands. 'You'd better tell me what you want to drink. We can still talk.'

'Yes. Three large pink gins and a dash of angostura bitters with soda. Friend of mine on the wagon. I'm called James Churchill.'

'Catharine Casement. Any particular kind of gin?'

'I think the Plymouth. That's a pretty name.'

'Half of it's not too bad. Would you like some ice?'

'Yes, please.'

'In all of them?'

'Yes, please. How do you mean?'

'The Casement's somebody else's name. But I never see him. But I don't seem to be able to divorce him. He's in London. I live about fifteen miles away.'

'You're not usually a barmaid, are you?'

'No, I'm not usually anything very much. This is my first day. That'll be seventeen and three altogether.'

While he was taking out his money, the street door opened and four or five men came in. They all gathered at the bar and started looking at her.

'Thank you,' said Churchill, not paying yet. 'Can I take you home after you finish here?'

The new arrivals grinned and nudged one another.

'Well, I've got a car coming for me.'

'What sort of car?'

'Well, it's a sort of taxi really, I suppose.'

'You could cancel it, then.'

'Yes, I suppose I could.'

'Right.' He handed over the money. 'Thank you.'

'Thank you, sir. Two and nine, one pound . . . Yes, sir?'

'You've got a moment to spare to get me something now, have you, love?' said the man she had addressed, grinning no longer. 'Or would you rather carry on chatting?'

'I beg your pardon, sir, I'll get whatever you ask for immediately, of course.'

'Oh. Well, uh, two gins and tonic and a pint of best bitter, one light ale, make those large gins . . .'

After staring at the speaker for some seconds, Churchill withdrew, a drink in each hand. When he came back for the other two drinks he told her he had to leave shortly but would be back later. Until he did leave she kept glancing over to the corner where he sat with his three companions, a pale man with a moustache, a man who looked like an Indian, an older man wearing a clerical collar. They talked animatedly now and then but kept falling silent. She missed their departure.

By closing-time Catharine was tired, but not too tired to be pleased with herself for not once having given wrong change. Through the open doorway she caught sight of Churchill waiting on the pavement. The unspoken questions she had thought she would never again put to herself about anybody formed in her mind. Is it now? Is it you?

When she came out he took her arm and walked her along to a small military car with a canvas roof but open sides.

'This was the best I could do at short notice,' he said. 'I'll get hold of something more suitable next time. Which way?'

She told him. There were cars backing and turning in the street ahead with a mixture of lights and shadows, and they had reached the last few houses of the village when he said,

'I've thought of you every day since I saw you.'

'I've thought of you too.' She knew now that she had, though until this evening she had not caught herself doing so.

'You looked frightened that first time. Were you?'

'Yes.' She explained about the cat and the bird.

'But why should that have frightened you?'

'It was something I didn't understand but looked as if it was

77

going to turn violent and horrible, and those two things together tend to frighten me.'

'What, violent and horrible?'

'Well, more violent-and-horrible and I-don't-understand-it, really.'

'Have lots of things like that happened to you?'

'There were quite a few at one stage.' Catharine paused. 'Just before I went into the asylum. About six months ago.'

'Were they to do with Mr Casement, the frightening things six months ago?'

'Yes. I'll tell you about them another time, but I will tell you.'

'I hated you being in that place.'

'So did I, but it was necessary, I suppose. Anyway, it must have done me some good, because here I am going about my own business like everybody else, not mad any more.'

'You'd probably have got better on your own.'

'Maybe. I doubt it, though. I wasn't in a good way at all. I couldn't carry on any more. I used to sit in my chair all the time because I was afraid I couldn't find my way back to it if I got up. It was like having something wrong with your eyes.'

She looked at the small farmhouse they were about to pass. It was solid like a building brick, pegged down immovably into the ground, staying exactly the same real size as they approached it, drew level and left it behind. Since they were moving, the fence that ran alongside the house could not do otherwise than seem to swing towards them and away again. On either side of them now were acres of uncultivated land, rising to low wooded hills that swept round in a semicircle ahead. If she could see them, these would appear small, because they were quite distant. Everything was as it should be, and so the loneliness round about did not matter.

'But it's all right now,' she went on. 'Which is much more interesting. I used to think that being mad might be rather fun. Inconvenient, of course, and awful, but quite exciting, with visions and things, and thinking the Russians were after you, and doing marvellous paintings. But it isn't at all really, not my sort anyway. Nothing ever happens and the other people are such bores. Those first . . . weeks I suppose they were, it was like being on holiday in a lousy hotel with it raining all the time and you can't speak the language and let's say you've lost your glasses and can't read.'

'Sounds a bit like the Army. I'm glad you're well now. And I'm very glad you got that job in the pub. If you hadn't, I might easily not have seen you again. You know, lots of times I wanted to go over to the hospital and try to find you.'

'How would you have set about it? You didn't know my name or anything.'

'That was what decided me against it. All I could have done was to walk round the place on the off-chance of seeing you.'

'Just as well you didn't. If you'd stuck at it at all our learned Dr Best would have clapped you inside.'

'Oh yes, of course, you must have known Dr Best.'

'Why, do you?'

'Not personally. I know a bit about him from the chap I was visiting when I saw you. Did you ever run into him there? Name of Hunter, Max Hunter. He wasn't mad, only drying out after too much whisky.'

'I may have done, I don't remember.'

'Of course, he was only in there a couple of weeks. Hey, I had him with me when I was in the pub earlier.'

'Which one was he?'

'Moustache. The one who wasn't with me the day I saw you.'

'I don't remember anybody being with you then.'

'That is flattering. I'm afraid I remember somebody being with you.'

'It's true, though.'

'I know. What did Dr Best say was basically the matter with you?'

'He kept telling me I subconsciously wanted to sleep with other girls.'

Churchill burst out laughing.

'I don't, though.'

'Of course you don't. I'm sorry, I was laughing because he told Max Hunter the same thing, that he was a repressed homosexual. If you knew Max ... But you will soon. When's your day off?'

'Monday.'

'That's too far ahead. I'm only going to be round here another five weeks or so.'

'That's not at all long, is it?'

'Then I'm being sent abroad, but only for a short time. I'll come and see you as soon as I get back.'

'You're not being sent to fight anybody, are you?'

'No. Not fight anybody. It isn't that sort of thing.'

'That's not too bad, then. But Monday's still a long way off. I'm free for bits of tomorrow, the first part of the morning and the afternoon.'

'I'm free in the afternoon. I'll come and fetch you and we'll drive somewhere. It's a pity you live so far away. Where is it exactly?'

She told him.

He drove on to a level piece of ground by the side of the road, stopped, and switched off the ignition. There was a faint sighing in the air which she thought at first was just the sound of silence, but then she felt a gentle breeze on her cheek. She started being afraid.

'What's the matter? Why have you stopped?'

'Cathy. So you're Lucy's friend.'

'Is that bad? Don't be angry with me.'

'I'm not angry with you. The other night one of the other chaps and I drove over to Lucy's place. He went up and went to bed with her and then I did the same.'

'I don't do that, though. I'm just her friend and I just live there. She's got them all organized so they don't even make passes at me. I just help her with the drinks when I'm there, that's all. I don't sleep with any of them. We're company for each other. I haven't got many friends in this country because I spent eight years in Australia when I was married to my first husband. When I left Casement she was the only person I could really go to. She doesn't try to make me go to bed with any of them. She helps me not to. I haven't been to bed with anybody since I went to live there. Honestly.'

'Don't you mind my having been to bed with her?'

'Are you in love with her and do you want to go to bed with her again?'

'No, neither of those.'

'Then I don't mind at all. Do you believe me?'

'About not going to bed with those chaps? Of course I do.'

'Well, in that case . . .'

'There doesn't seem to be anything for either of us to mind, does there?'

'No.'

Catharine was not afraid when he put one arm round her shoulders and the other hand on her breast and kissed her. It is now, she thought. It is you.

'I love you,' said Churchill.

'I'm going to love you too, probably by tomorrow. But I'll have to have just a little time. I thought I'd stopped, you see. Loving people. So it'll take me just a little time to start again. Is that all right?'

'Yes.'

He kissed her another once and then started the engine.

*

Churchill parked Ross-Donaldson's jeep in its space and made towards the front door of the Mess. One of the D4 sentries, grateful perhaps for the smallest novelty, turned towards him and came to attention. Acknowledging, Churchill wished him good night and went indoors.

Hunter's room was on the first floor. It had one very comfortable chair in it, the seat of most of the drinking-bout which had ended in his admission to hospital. He had adopted it after becoming dissatisfied with the more usual procedure of drinking in the ante-room downstairs. It had seemed to him uneconomic to keep a Mess waiter up until four a.m. serving him with whisky, and twice running he had found himself, a couple of hours after that time, lying in the grass somewhere near the house and resisting the efforts of a member of the camp patrol to pull him to his feet. Even the chair had finally proved inadequate by being too easy to fall out of, and he had had to take to his bed, where, after a twenty-four-hour absence from the general scene, he had been found by Churchill.

When Churchill entered, Hunter was sitting in his chair drinking a glass of soda-water. Naidu was sitting opposite him, on the edge of the bed, a heavily diluted whisky in his hand.

'Willie not back yet?' asked Churchill.

'No,' said Naidu.

'Pour yourself a whisky,' said Hunter. 'On the dressing-table. You'll notice the cap is off. Don't put it back. In fact throw it away. Having no cap saves time, the loss by evaporation is trifling, and there are probably figures to show that a bottle's more vulnerable to being spilt or dropped when the cap's being removed and replaced. Like aircraft when taking off and landing. I must get Ross-Donaldson to give me the statistical breakdown. Look, you need more whisky than you've got there if you're going to be a satisfactory drinking companion to a man who isn't drinking. Moti's hopeless at that. He only drinks to be sociable, which is no use to anybody.'

'It's the taste of the beastly stuff which is such a snag,' said Naidu.

'No, it's a blessing, we'd all be dead if it were palatable. At least James and I would be. And Willie. Well, you're back early. It's only twenty to one. What didn't keep you?'

Churchill had taken his place on a heavy wooden chair with a high back, moving a pile of motoring magazines to do so. He lit a cigarette. 'It was quite late,' he said. 'And she was tired.'

'So you cut short the final embraces. Very considerate of you.'

'There weren't any embraces to speak of.'

'I'm sorry to hear that. How hard did you try?'

'I didn't try at all. She's not the sort of girl you want to rush things with.'

'Every girl is that sort of girl.'

Naidu took a quick pull at his drink.

'You don't know anything about it, Max,' said Churchill.

'Oh yes I do, my dear boy. I could see the way you were looking at her in the pub, and the way you weren't looking at anything in particular for the rest of the evening, except at your watch every ten minutes or so. She's very beautiful and that's a danger in itself to somebody like you. Before you know where you are you'll be falling in love with her. If indeed you haven't already.'

'I can't see anything against that.'

'You will, James, you will. All emotional attachments are bad. Get what there is to be got out of somebody without undue effort and then pass on to the next. It's better for everyone that way.'

'If I may come butting in here,' said Naidu, 'I dislike hearing James's romantic sentiments trampled underfoot in this manner. It's right and proper that a young man should hold these views and be respectful towards womankind and so on. He should not be laughed at, Max.'

'I'm not laughing at him. I'm trying to warn him. It won't do any good, I suppose. Well, who is she, James? I haven't seen her behind the bar there before. Where does she come from?'

'You'd seen her before, Moti. That day at the hospital when we went to visit Max.'

'Of course. Standing on the path. I remember your being . . . struck by her then. But what a remarkable coincidence.'

'That's not good,' said Hunter. 'He'll start thinking it's fate and all the rest of the rigmarole. So she's another of Dr Best's clients. Did she say anything about him? What was his diagnosis of her?'

Churchill grinned. 'I'll give you one guess.'

'Oh, no. Not suppressed lesbianism? You know, there must have been something in that man's childhood that gave him a morbid dread of the obvious. Anyway, come on. You still haven't told us about her.'

'I don't know what you want to know. She's got a husband but he isn't around. She's staying with this Lady Hazell woman you've probably heard about. But she doesn't, my girl, she's called Catharine, she doesn't join in the orgies.'

Churchill looked defensively at Hunter, who made to speak but remained silent.

'Even so,' said Naidu, 'not a very salubrious environment, from all I gather.'

'Ross-Donaldson was telling me about that evening the two

of you were there,' said Hunter. 'It sounds fascinating. Why don't we all four drive over some time? You could call on your light of love, James, and you could inspect the architectural layout and grounds, Moti, and Willie – surely there must be something for Willie to look at.'

'There's a library nobody's been near for God knows how long, Catharine says.'

'The very thing. He could write an article about it for this newspaper of his or magazine or whatever. Has he had much stuff sent in, do you know?'

'It's early days yet.'

'I suppose so. You'll have to write him a sonnet to Catharine.'

'I wouldn't know how to start. What would you do over at Lucy's?'

'Me? Oh, I'd go to bed with her. What else? It would probably be an experience. And my sex-life hasn't been very full recently. I don't like that. A chap tends to brood, and that's unattractive. Look at poor Brian Leonard. He'd be so much better company if he could get his end in occasionally. And probably better at catching spies too. Oh. Now that is a thought.'

'What is?'

'The Colonel's always saying he's got his money on some local temptress-seductress type as the most likely sort of spy. Of course, the old devil's building up to going over to Lucy's himself and giving her an official inspection. But why can't we introduce the idea to Brian? All we need is one of her friends tipping him off that while reclining voluptuously on her divan she got curious about what's going on up here. Ross-Donaldson would do it if you won't.'

'What would be the point?'

'My vivid mental picture of Lady Hazell's set-up convinces me that it's the very place for Brian. It would do him good. I can just see him with a parrot stuck to his shoulder, cross-questioning Lucy about her political affiliations.'

A car could be heard approaching the Mess.

'This will be Willie now,' said Naidu.

No more was said while the car came nearer and stopped, footsteps sounded outside and the front door shut. Hunter frowned at his glass of soda-water and drained it. After a moment Ayscue came into the room. He looked tired.

'He's dying,' he said, and went to the dressing-table and helped himself to whisky. 'In fact it's quite possible he's dead already. They said it was just a matter of hours, if that. He's been in deep coma since this morning.'

'Have they decided what it is?' asked Hunter.

'They didn't seem too definite, no. Some type of meningitis. Not a type that responds to drugs, apparently. There was a specialist there of sorts. He told me he was satisfied they'd done all they could.'

'I.e. they'd put him to bed,' said Churchill.

He too went and poured a drink, glancing inquiringly at Naidu, who shook his head slightly.

'He looked like somebody sleeping,' Ayscue went on. 'Very flushed, that was about all. There was nothing I could do for him. Young Pearce said he wanted to stay, so I wrote him a twelve-hour pass. I'll square it with the Adjutant in the morning.'

'How was he taking it?' asked Hunter.

'Pearce? Very well indeed. He was refusing to break down and cry, though it was absolutely all he could do not to. It seemed the best thing to leave him so that he could cry all he wanted. I asked him if he thought I could be of any help to him, and he said very tactfully that he was afraid not. So I came away.'

'He's having a whale of a time round about now, isn't he?' said Churchill vivaciously. 'That dispatch-rider last week. Fawkes today. Shaping up nicely, don't you think?'

Ayscue said in a weary tone, 'Probably a million people have died all over the world in that period. There hasn't been any —'

'Oh sorry, I was overlooking that point. That makes it all right, of course.'

'James, I suggest you try to reconcile yourself to what can't be changed.'

'Why? Why should I? I can see no reason for ever stopping minding what's happening to Fawkes tonight. No good reason. Lots of bad ones. Laziness and cowardice. Inability to

85

concentrate on what's important. Vulgar and unthought-out ideas about everything surely having to make sense and be all right in the end. Because if it doesn't and won't be, where does that leave us?'

Naidu said tentatively, 'If you will allow a word from one of a different and, I think I'm right in saying, older religion than yours, I would suggest –'

'I have no religion,' said Churchill.

'Oh, but a moment ago you were referring to some person, a "he" who in your view was having a fine time with the deaths of certain people. I must confess I took this to refer to your God.'

'That was an anti-religious remark.'

'With the very greatest respect, James, it seems to me not suitable that you should be doing anything so trivial as attacking your religion at such a solemn time as this. The thought of the impending death of Corporal Fawkes should, I submit, be filling you with sorrow.'

'It does. But it fills me with anger too. Just this one thing is enough to show that we live in a bad world.'

'There are no bad things in the world.' Naidu got up from the bed. 'Even what might seem to us most horrible can be rendered endurable by wisdom.'

'With just as much respect, Moti, I think you're talking about sentimentality and the servile acceptance of a wish-fulfilling tradition. Not wisdom.'

'Perhaps I am. Wisdom is hard for most of us to obtain. If sentimentality and your servile acceptance will render endurable what seems horrible, let us by all means take recourse to them.'

'Yes,' said Ayscue violently. 'And lies too if necessary.'

Churchill rounded on him as violently. 'Well, you ought to know, Willie. That's what you trade in, isn't it?'

'I'm going to bed,' said Ayscue after a short pause. 'Coming, Moti?'

'Yes. Good night, James. Good night, Max. Thank you for the whisky.'

'Well, well, well,' said Hunter when he and Churchill were alone. 'You seem to be getting nasty in your drink these days.

It's a stage we all go through. The trick is to drink much faster, especially early in the evening. Then the stuff attacks your brain on a steeper acceleration. You become inarticulate with dignity. That's the state to aim for, dear boy.'

He rose thoughtfully and strolled, hands in pockets, towards the dressing-table. 'I seem to have been expressing myself too vividly for my own good. I've often suffered because of that. Anyway, self-converted or not, this is the moment when I fall off the wagon with a resounding crash.'

He picked up the whisky-bottle. Churchill went over and put his hand on Hunter's shoulder.

'Don't be silly, Max. It's too late for that tonight. You'll get no sleep if you start now. You'll still be at it at breakfast-time.'

'Oh, jolly good, I'll be able to pick up another bottle when the waiters arrive.'

Hunter had poured a third of a tumbler of whisky and added water. He held it close to his body untasted.

'Look, don't do it. Not now. You said you were going to stay off it altogether for a month after leaving that place. Till the end of your probation period. It's only been two days. Give yourself a chance. Take a pill and get into bed. I'll stay and chat to you for a bit.'

'I'd need so many pills I'd be falling about the place all day tomorrow. And I don't want to sleep, I want to be drunk. And it isn't really a sudden decision. When I promised everybody I wouldn't touch it for a month I put a little secret clause in the treaty. A mental reservation. It said that it would be all right for me to get drunk if a certain kind of thing went wrong. It has. So here I go.'

He drained his glass and refilled it, then refilled Churchill's. They went back to their chairs.

'Do you mean the Fawkes thing?' asked Churchill in a puzzled tone.

'Not as such, no. He's all right now. It's a matter of some delicacy, really. To put to someone like you, that is. From my point of view it's quite crude, in the sense that its impact on me is strong and unsubtle. But it does connect with Fawkes. As we heard just now, the Fawkes business is hitting Signalman

Pearce hard. For some time, understandably, he won't be able to pay a lot of attention to anything else. And I was beginning to hope quite seriously that I might get him to pay a certain amount of attention to me.'

'You were going to make advances to him, were you?'

'I'd already started. Well, let's call them approaches. Nothing overt. But I feel there's a fair chance he knows the sort of thing he's in for, or knew what he was in for I suppose it'll turn out to be now this has happened. Which made it slightly encouraging that he agreed to let me take him into town and give him dinner tomorrow night. But, you see, that'll all be off. Hence my alighting from the wagon.'

'He was probably just going to soak you for an expensive meal and lots of champagne and then turn all shocked or nasty when you showed what you were after.'

'There's nothing cynical or mean about Andy. At the very least he was looking forward to an evening out with a kind friend. He's a very nice, open-hearted, unassuming boy. You don't know him.'

'How do you know him? You sound as if you and he were old buddies.'

'We had no fewer than three chats when he came over to see Fawkes at the hospital. We got on absolutely splendidly, Andy and I.'

'I shouldn't have thought he was your type, Max. I ran into him the other day. He's a nice-looking kid, I can see that myself, but not in the least effeminate.'

'Oh, I don't like them when they're effeminate. There's a kind of delicate handsomeness and physical grace that's not the slightest bit pansified, but is only found in young men. It's all gone by the time they're about twenty-five. Andy's got a lot of it. Do you know what I'm talking about?'

'Yes, I think so. But somebody like that would be basically heterosexual, wouldn't he?'

'Basically, yes. But having that type of good looks often means that he'll have been got at a bit in adolescence, when he was going through the phase of being drawn in that direction or at any rate wasn't averse from a bit of experimenting. So he'll have some idea of what fun it can be. On the other hand, he's had girls in the meantime and he knows by now he's attractive to them. So he's not in any doubt about his masculinity. Then I come along and suggest in the nicest possible way that just one more spot of what he used to get up to with his mates at school won't do him any harm. In fact, I tell him, it'll be more of a treat than it was then, because it'll take place in luxurious hotel bedrooms and such instead of behind the gasworks. I make a great point of laying everything on in style. French meals under crystal chandeliers, drinks in exclusive bars, theatres, trips to socially okay sporting events, I thought you'd look nice in these shirts so I got you half a dozen, I'd noticed you'd broken your wrist-watch so please say you'll accept this one. Well then, when his successor appears we've both had a lovely time and he goes back to his girls with a light heart and an intensified awareness of the possibilities of human nature. More whisky?'

'I'm all right with this, thanks.'

'I think perhaps just a tiny spot for me, not more than a quarter of a pint.' As he stood at the dressing-table, Hunter said reflectively, 'You know, describing my methods to you like that makes me see how closely they resemble those of your school of thought. As you probably know, a lot of homos are keen on squalor. Or they're deliberately undiscriminating about who they go with. Or they enjoy paying for it or being paid. But with one important exception I'm just like you. I wonder whether Dr Best may not have got on to a sort of mirror-image of the truth about me. Could I be a repressed heterosexual, do you suppose?'

'Christ, how would I know?'

'It might explain my feelings about women.' Hunter sat down again. 'As far as going to bed with them is concerned – something I've been known to do between affairs – I've always found them surprisingly pleasant considering they're not boys. Less interesting anatomically, true, but the main outlines of their shape strike me as all right, if a bit eccentric. It's the details I can't really do with. I don't like the shape of their hands. Little narrow claws like that never did anything of importance. And those finger-nails. There's something precious about them. And when did you ever see a good-looking woman with a decent firm nose? Little puggy snouts. Well. Doesn't it strike you that I'm sort of cooking up excuses for objecting to them? I mean, if I were as dead against them as an honest-to-goodness, middle-of-the-road, God-fearing queer ought to be, what I'd be taking against would be things like their breasts. Which in fact I'm definitely for. Do you see what I'm driving at?'

'Yes. So much so that you must be on the wrong track. From what I know of Dr Best's line of things, if you were a repressed heterosexual things like breasts would be exactly what you would take against, so that you could go on concealing from yourself your basic heterosexuality.'

'Whereas if I were a repressed homosexual the reason I'd take against things like breasts would be that my concealed hatred of women was fastening on one of their most obvious womanly attributes. Yes, I see. I must say I really shall have to do something about Dr Best. I'm beginning to feel quite strongly on the point.'

'What sort of thing have you in mind for the doctor?'

'A nasty sort of thing. That's as far as I've got with the project at the moment. But I've plenty of time to map out a scheme before we all finish here and go our respective ways.'

Churchill said, 'I think I will have some more whisky after all.'

'Help yourself. You're a bit up and down tonight, aren't you?'

'Sorry.'

'Don't worry about Fawkes. I told you, he's better off than any of us.'

'It's not only that. It's . . . the Army.'

'Why, what's it been doing to you?'

'I seem to have got completely fed up with it. I don't believe in it any more.'

'Christ,' said Hunter, 'did you ever?'

'Oh yes. I thought it did very good and necessary things. That's why I joined.'

'My dear, you never cease to amaze me.'

'Well, why did you join?'

'Just the uniform. My favourite kind of young fellow looks

at his best in it. I'm told that opportunities for the side of life we've been discussing are better in the Navy, but they make the lower deck wear such silly trousers. Whereas khaki really brings out the ... I remember the very day I decided I must take the Queen's shilling. My parents had dragged me along to look at and be looked at by a new school, a thing I'm sorry to say they had to do at more than one juncture. We were wandering round some gloomy bloody cloister in the wake of the Head, when there appeared from nowhere the most theatrically gorgeous child you ever saw in your life – wearing his Training Corps uniform. That's for me, I said. To myself, of course.'

'And was it?'

'Oh yes, it was, any time I cared to ask. But it was also for about forty other people any time they cared to ask. Unfortunately.'

'That's good, though, isn't it, according to you? It ought to have taken care of preventing you getting emotionally involved.'

'Yes, indeed it ought, but it didn't work like that. I was still feeling my way in those days. I'm in no such danger now.'

Hunter stood up and slowly took off his jacket.

'What's this I'm in for?' asked Churchill. 'A demonstration?'

'That takes at least two, and besides myself there's only you present, and you're not my type, I'm sorry to say. You're too mature. In looks, that is. No, I'm getting ready for bed. And don't say how sensible that is of me or I'll drink the rest of that bottle to put you in your place.'

'I'll be off, then. See you in the morning.'

'You will. Good night, James. Thank you for listening.'

When Churchill had gone, Hunter sat down on his bed and looked jerkily about his room, like a man in search of something to smash.

*

'Now you're sure Evans knows which key it is?' asked Leonard.

Deering clicked his tongue and sighed. 'I told you,' he said. 'There's only just the four on the ring. One's the key of the room. Evans knows that one because Ayscue's lent it to him dozens of times so he can pick up his laundry and the rest of it.

Then there's one that must be the key of Ayscue's strong-box because it's too small to be anything else. Then there's a Yale key we don't know anything about, but it can't be the one we're after because the cupboard's not got a Yale lock. So the only other one must be the one. Okay?'

'And Evans can get it out of the room to you and get it back in again without being spotted?'

'Look,' said Deering, shutting his eyes for a moment. 'To start with he doesn't have to search high and low because Ayscue always puts his keys with his loose change and the rest of it on his dressing-table when he hangs up his pants at night. Now then. In comes Evans with the tea tomorrow morning, puts it down by the bed, picks up Ayscue's shoes and buggers off out again, whipping the keys as he goes. I'm standing by with my bit of wax and in ten seconds I've done my stuff and I'm on my way. Evans goes back with the shoes and dumps the keys before Ayscue's got his eyes open. Okay? If you can't trust me to take the impression properly you can go down to the huts and do it yourself.'

'I'd be noticed. Nobody pays much attention to a batman wherever he is.'

'Oh, thanks very much, I'm sure. Any other worries?'

'That's all, Deering, thank you.'

The batman came to something not unlike attention. 'Thank you, sir. Good night.'

Left alone, Leonard paced the uneven floor of his room. He was feeling mildly uncomfortable, tense, short of confidence, a state he was growing familiar with. His walk brought him face to face with the major in his picture. A slight further decrease in confidence made him avoid that blue-eyed stare. It seemed to him to hold disappointment, perhaps reproach.

He was as far as ever from unmasking his spy; further, actually. Regular and searching inquiry among the s 1 group showed that no officer still under suspicion had asked any of them anything whatever about Operation Apollo. Nor had anybody else, for that matter. A resolute incuriosity pervaded the camp. And the Asycue thing, he felt sure, was a false trail, merely something he must factually and officially satisfy himself about. Meanwhile there was no news from the London end. The spy's new contact there, replacing the man recently arrested, was still untraced.

Then there was this new lead. He ought, he supposed, to be grateful for the least ray of light. But what it seemed to illuminate was as repugnant to his theories as if it had been specially contrived as such. And, with a prescience unusual in him, he could guess already that following it up would take a lot out of him, personally rather than professionally. He knew he ought to think that the last bit made it better, not worse, but could not manage to.

A knock came at his door. It proved to be from the hand of Ross-Donaldson.

'Ready?' he asked.

'Yes.'

'Let's go.'

They left the building and got into Leonard's car. This was fitted with a two-way radio set tuned to the frequency of the Command Post and the emergency station. Leonard switched it on and picked up the microphone. Conscious of Ross-Donaldson looking uninterestedly at him, he said,

'Hullo, Control. Padlock here. Over.'

After some delay a north-country voice answered from the loudspeaker.

'Hullo, Padlock. Control receiving you. Over.'

'Am leaving area for short period. Test personal alarm.'

A puny buzz sounded from an instrument strapped to Leonard's right wrist.

'Hullo, Control. Okay. Out.'

'What's that thing for?' asked Ross-Donaldson as they rolled down towards the gate.

'It tells me when there's something for me on the radio link. I always carry it when I move out of telephonic communication.'

'There's a telephone where we're going.'

'It may be insecure.'

'Oh yes, of course it may. How silly of me to forget that.'

'Security Officer and Adjutant,' said Leonard to the guard corporal. 'Operational.'

'You must suffer a certain amount from training-action disparity,' said Ross-Donaldson a moment later. 'Especially in the absence of the usual action-surrogates.'

'What are you talking about?'

'Things like parades, exercises, guards. Organized games don't help much because they aren't derived from training.'

'I still can't understand a word you're saying.'

'You see the phenomenon most clearly, of course, in troops brought to a high pitch of training for some specialized operation which is then unexpectedly cancelled. Immediate plummeting of morale, indiscipline, drunkenness, petty crime, even medium-scale desertion. Not that I'm suggesting you'd go to those lengths. Tonight's expedition should help you a little to reduce tension.'

'I think I see what you mean now,' said Leonard. 'Roughly.'

After they had driven for some time he said,

'Don't introduce me as a Security man whatever you do.'

'That might ruin everything, I do see.'

'Just Captain Leonard of the Sailors.'

'Right.'

'If you could manage to mention casually that I'm on very secret work at the camp it might be very valuable.'

'I'll see what I can do. Go left here.'

'Wasn't that the Colonel's car that went by?' asked Leonard suddenly a little later still.

Ross-Donaldson rolled his window down and looked back the way they had come. 'I believe it was, yes.'

'Indicative. It would naturally be assumed that he knew more than his juniors.'

'Logic plus inaccuracy in the pre-informed phase.'

'That's right.' Leonard, who recognized the expression from one of his manuals, was delighted. 'I had no idea you were practised in phylactological thought.'

'I try to keep up with most things,' said Ross-Donaldson modestly. 'You can park next to these three.'

'Isn't that your jeep there?'

'Indeed it is. Churchill asked if he might borrow it.'

'Ah, there's no danger to be feared in that quarter. I wish everybody was like him.'

'So do I.'

Within another two minutes they were standing in a dimly lit room where a bald-headed man in his forties was reading a journal with the aid of a pencil-torch.

'Where's that man who let us in?' asked Leonard.

'Somewhere. It's often like that here.'

The bald man looked up at them from ten yards away. With a deliberate movement of his wrist alone he brought the light of his torch round so that it illuminated in turn each of the soldiers from head to foot and back again. Then abruptly he returned to his reading.

Leonard was rather disconcerted. 'Has that fellow been round the place before?' He spoke more quietly than usual, but just as thickly and urgently.

'I've never seen him. What about a drink?'

'I'd like some sherry if there is any.'

'There won't be. Gin and tonic or nothing.'

'Gin and tonic, then. Easy on the gin.'

'Right.' Ross-Donaldson raised his voice. 'Can I get you something?'

The bald man continued to read.

While Ross-Donaldson was preparing the drinks, Leonard strolled across the room. His training had stressed the importance of attending to hunch and instinct, especially in what he had learned to call under-facted situations, and there was no doubt that hunch and instinct were telling him something now, though he could not have said quite what.

'Good evening,' he said.

The bald man looked up again, but otherwise stayed as he was. Ten seconds later he said, 'Good evening.'

'Do you come here often?' asked Leonard helplessly.

'No. In fact this is my first visit.'

'Mine too. How did you come to hear about it?'

'Hear about it? The fact of its existence is well known. As is that of its owner.'

'Oh yes, of course, but I mean about what happens here.'

'I think it possible that the two of us may have come here for different purposes.'

'I think we probably have. What have you come for?'

The man raised the light of his torch briefly to Leonard's face, switched it off and put it in his pocket. 'Who are you?' he asked.

'I'm an Army officer. I'm stationed at the camp not far from here. I expect you know the place.'

'I know where it is.'

'I'm engaged on some extremely important and very secret work there.'

'Indeed?' said the man, becoming more friendly. 'It seems as if it may not go on being secret very much longer.'

'Oh? What makes you think that?'

'Logic. If those engaged on it go round telling total strangers they're on secret work, the secret itself is half-way toward being found out. Effective concealment conceals the fact of concealment.'

This was so like something out of his manuals that Leonard needed all his conditioning not to start or exclaim. He took his drink from Ross-Donaldson without looking at him and sipped it with careful slowness.

'That's interesting,' he said. 'What suggested that idea to you?'

'My work.'

'And what's your work, if you don't mind my –'

'Let's just say that it consists very largely of uncovering what people would rather keep hidden.'

'You make yourself sound like some kind of spy.'

'A spy?' said the bald man gently. 'Now what on earth can have put such a notion into your head?'

'Just the way you were talking. I hope I haven't offended you.'

What with his vocal predispositions and his present mental state, the lightness with which Leonard spoke was very creditable. The man had reacted to his suggestion abnormally, no doubt of that. And – the thought came in an instant – if this Lady Hazell was getting information out of people there would have to be somebody to pick it up from her. In the pause that now followed, Leonard turned his face away and slightly up, as if glancing idly round the room. Then he looked out of the corner of his eye at the bald man, who proved to be looking at him in the same fashion. He shifted his gaze abruptly and found it held, also askance, by that of a parrot that was clinging uncomfortably to the bars of its cage.

There was a longer pause, broken by the sound of voices. Leonard turned and recognized Hunter and Ayscue coming into the room with Ross-Donaldson. A car had presumably driven up and the front door been knocked at and opened, but Leonard had been too absorbed to notice.

Hunter approached and nodded to Leonard, then caught sight of the bald man.

'Well, this is a surprise,' he said, on a higher note than usual. 'Fancy running into you here. I see that you and Brian have got together already.'

'We haven't been introduced. I was sitting here reading when –'

'Well, I must remedy that right away, though neither of you are the type to stand on ceremony, I know. This is Dr Best, who runs the mental hospital down the road where I spent those few days recently – Captain Leonard.'

'You and I have spoken together on the telephone,' said Dr Best to Leonard. 'I thought I recognized your voice.'

'You two have got a lot in common,' began Hunter.

Leonard said quickly, 'Something important has come up which I must tell you about at once. Will you excuse us, Dr Best?'

'Certainly,' said the doctor amiably, watching him.

'Would you like a gin and tonic, Hunter?' called Ross-Donaldson.

'Just a tonic, if I may. Well, Brian, why all the mystery?'

'I stopped you because you were about to reveal that I'm a Security man. You are not to do that under any circumstances. That's an order, Max.'

'But you don't usually. .... You don't mean you think there are spies about or something, do you?'

'Just a routine precaution. Now I want to ask you something. That man, Dr Best, I suppose he must have questioned you pretty exhaustively when he was treating you, about your life and your job and so on. Think carefully before you answer. Did he show any interest in what's going on at the camp?'

Hunter seemed to think carefully. Then he said, 'Yes. Yes, he did. It struck me at the time, but so much else was happening that I haven't remembered until now. He must have asked me what the chaps were up to half a dozen times in different ways. Was it the sort of thing that could cause me anxiety, was I worried the programme wouldn't be finished in time, it would help him if he knew more about it. He really kept on at me. I just said I didn't know, which you'll agree is true. And now that I come to think of it, I'm jolly glad it is true.'

'Why?' Leonard's habitual urgency was redoubled.

'I'll tell you in a moment. . . . Thank you very much, Alastair. Do forgive Brian and me for being unsociable, but we have a certain rather urgent problem to solve.'

'Right,' said Ross-Donaldson. 'Don't hesitate to call on me if you think I can be of the slightest assistance.'

He went over to Ayscue. Leonard closed in on Hunter.

'Why? Why are you glad you don't know about Operation Apollo?'

Hunter looked about and lowered his voice. 'Because Dr Best questioned me under hypnosis,' he hissed.

'And you can't remember what questions he asked you?'

'No. But I have a sort of feeling that they were put very . . . persistently. On and on and on at the same point without getting anywhere. Of course, I suppose I could be wrong about that.'

'Mm. You've been most helpful, Max. Thank you.'

'It's a pleasure, believe me, Brian. Anything else I can do?'

'As a matter of fact there is. I'll have this man investigated and watched, naturally, but there's often something to be gained from a frontal approach. I wonder, if we go back to him now, could you suggest to me and him that I go over to the hospital and he shows me round?'

'Yes, okay, but why do you want to see the place, from his point of view?'

'Oh, I'm interested in techniques of questioning prisoners under drugs and so on. Leave that to me.'

But in the event this stratagem was not needed. Hunter had

barely finished making his suggestion before Dr Best was leafing through his pocket diary.

'Would eleven-thirty next Tuesday be convenient?' he asked. 'And afterwards I hope you'll allow me to give you lunch in my quarters.'

Leonard thanked him and moved over to the other group. He was later to explain to Hunter that this withdrawal was aimed at allowing the doctor to comment freely and perhaps significantly on his prospective guest (and that pretending to welcome inquisitiveness or inquiry was a device as old as espionage).

For the time being, Dr Best said nothing about Leonard. Instead, he asked Hunter how he had been and was feeling.

'Pretty fair, thank you.'

'I see that at the moment, at any rate, you're keeping off the drink.'

'As you observantly observe, at the moment, at any rate, I am.'

'But on the other hand . . . . Would you object if we resumed just temporarily, the doctor-patient relationship we recently conducted?'

'Say whatever you like, doctor.'

'Thank you, Captain Hunter. I was about to venture to suggest that, while it's heartening to find you refraining from alcohol, you're still evidently engaged in denying your true nature by the pursuit of women.'

'Old Lucy? Yes, I thought I might look in and make use of the facilities. Is that bad?'

'Let's call it unhelpful. It'll only produce further tension and anxiety.'

'I'll just have to learn to live with it. You're next, are you?'

'Next?'

'To make use of the facilities. Or did Brian and my other friend get here before you?'

'You should not assume that everybody is engaged in the same frantic and deeply disturbed and ultimately totally stultifying pursuit of mere physical release as yourself, Captain Hunter. I'm here for a quite different reason. It so happens that one of my patients is living in this house. She came out of hospital on probation the very same day as yourself. A case of cumulative psychic dystrophy which I think I've been fortunate enough to check and may even have partly reversed. I hope in due course to speak to Lady Hazell and find out something of how this woman's been getting on.'

'Wouldn't it be simpler to talk to her rather than Lucy?'

'It's desirable that I avoid direct contact with her. She must learn to manage her life on her own resources. I don't want her to count on being able to see friends she can tell her troubles to and generally lean on.'

'Friends like who?'

'Like myself.'

'I see. I hadn't looked at it like that. Aren't you drinking, doctor?'

'It doesn't greatly interest me in this form. I'm not an abstainer, however.'

'I suppose only suppressed alcoholics are that.'

'That's oversimplifying matters a good deal, but there is such a tendency, yes, speaking broadly. I enjoy a glass of wine with a meal, a good brandy after. In fact I've a small but not ill-chosen cellar in my quarters. Which reminds me. This young man I'm entertaining to lunch next week. Is he a friend of yours?'

'Well, none of us have known one another very long, but I've seen a good deal of him over the last month or so. Why?'

'He seems to me a little ... anxious. Does he strike you as a well-balanced, well-integrated personality? A lay opinion based on direct contact can be useful.'

Hunter said nothing for some seconds. Dr Best looked at him with a smile.

'Why are you hesitating, Captain Hunter?'

'I'm not hesitating, I'm trying to make sure I answer your question accurately.'

'As you may have heard, students of the human mind set most store by a spontaneous, top-of-the-head reaction, but now that the opportunity for this has been lost, you may as well take your time.'

'I've taken it now. My opinion, for what it's worth, is that Brian Leonard is a complete stable sort of chap. He likes his work and as far as I know he's good at it. Socially he's a little shy, perhaps, but gregarious enough. Not a drinker, not a solitary, not a depressive. If you're looking for a lunatic, Dr Best, you're wasting your time with Brian.'

'You speak with a good deal of warmth, Captain Hunter, more perhaps that the occasion would seem to warrant.'

'I don't know about that. I'm getting pretty tired of all this not being able to take anything at its face value and seeing everyone as a case of something or other.'

'Or could it be that your partisanship for Captain Leonard springs from some part of your mind that sees him as potentially ... more than a friend?'

At this Hunter laughed so much that he slopped his drink and had to cling to Dr Best's shoulder for support. He took out a handkerchief and wiped his eyes. When he spoke next it was with none of the suppressed or open animus towards the doctor he had shown so far.

'It's probably jolly sinister to laugh as much as that,' he said, 'but I simply couldn't help it. Well, that rounds things off nicely. Now I must insist that you break your rule just this once and take a drink. Come and join the others.'

Dr Best seemed quite touched at being thus invited. He allowed himself to be led across the room and given a gin and tonic – a weak one, as stipulated. He listened to the ensuing talk with great interest.

Using a rather peevish tone, Leonard was saying to Ross-Donaldson, 'Aren't we sort of hanging about a good deal? How long can Churchill have been ... upstairs by now? At this rate I'll be –'

'James isn't with Lucy, is he?' asked Hunter.

'He borrowed Alastair's jeep and it's outside now.'

'Oh, I see.'

'Even assuming he was commencing matters just as we arrived,' said Ross-Donaldson, looking at his watch, 'he's still about five minutes overdue already. But of course a margin like that isn't really significant.'

'What computation are you using?' asked Ayscue.

'Well, naturally it's all very approximate, but the expected positive correlation between age and duration has shown itself to be experimentally verifiable. The interesting thing is that, whereas some parabolic function would seem likely, what you in fact get is something pretty linear. My guess would be that, with a broadened sample, you'd get a concave asymptote as you moved further along the age axis, though a convex one at the other end strikes me as unlikely. Anyway, I don't suppose we'll be able to plot that in practice.'

'Who do those two other cars outside belong to?' asked Leonard.

'One would be mine, no doubt,' said Dr Best with a smile.

'And the other presumably belongs to whoever let us in,' said Ross-Donaldson.

'But where is he?' asked Leonard.

At this point two men in civilian clothes appeared at the threshold. 'Good night, all,' they said, and withdrew.

Ross-Donaldson half closed his eyes and did a couple of very slow nods.

'Well, what happens now?' asked Hunter.

'We hang on for a bit,' said Ross-Donaldson, again looking at his watch. 'This is still Phase 1, wherein Lucy makes periodic reappearances. In half an hour or so we get to Phase 2, wherein she doesn't.'

'In the meantime we'd better decide whose turn it is next,' said Hunter.

'Dr Best's, obviously,' said Ross-Donaldson. 'He was here before any of us.'

'I thought I'd made it clear that I was visiting Lady Hazell in my professional capacity and in no other.'

'You only made it clear to me,' said Hunter. 'Until this moment you hadn't a chance to make it clear to the rest of us.'

Ayscue said, 'I think I'd better make it clear too. I haven't come along for what I believe is the usual purpose either. Which I'm not criticizing for a moment, don't run away with that idea.'

'You surely don't think, padre, that Lucy would want to see you in your professional capacity, do you?' asked Ross-Donaldson.

'Padre?' said Dr Best. 'Padre?'

'Yes, believe it or not I'm a member of the Army Chaplains Department. I know I'm not dressed as one, if that's what's mystifying you. But wherever possible I believe in not bringing the cloth into disrepute. If there'd been a crowd here tonight, as I understand there sometimes is, I might not have been able to get round to everybody and explain that my mind was on higher things than theirs was. Hence the incognito, doctor.'

'May I ask what does bring you here?'

'I gather there's a room full of old books somewhere in this building. Stuff that hasn't been looked at for years. I thought I might make arrangements to spend a day or two over here seeing if there's anything interesting. I go for the eighteenth century mostly. You never know what you might pick up in that way.'

After a pause, Hunter said, 'That doesn't leave many of us who are here for the usual purpose, does it? Just Alastair and me, it looks like.'

'Quite so.'

'And me,' said Leonard.

'Oh yes, sorry, Brian. Anyway, how shall we sort it out? There are still five people to be accommodated in various ways.'

'It's perfectly simple,' said Ross-Donaldson. 'But before I indicate the lines to be followed I insist that we all have another drink. Hunter, would you give me a hand, please?'

'Sure.'

The two moved away to the drinks table. On the others a short silence fell.

Dr Best eventually said to Ayscue, 'You're a literary man, then.'

'Oh, not really. Just a dabbler. Music is more my line. Again, the eighteenth century is my thing on the whole.'

'I've always myself thought there was a certain amount to be said for Bach, though his hysterical emotionalism is a grave limitation.'

'I suppose you're talking about that stuffy old provincial four-in-a-bar organist. I must say I find his son Carl Philipp Emmanuel far better value. All those wonderful tunes you can't sing. Not that there isn't something in Johann Christian as well, in a sort of Mozart-for-the-kiddies way.'

'A deeply anxious mind. That of Mozart.'

'Yes. Good in other ways, too.'

'Do you play an instrument?' asked Dr Best.

'Not to much purpose these days. I was a fair hand at the fiddle in my youth.'

'And you, Captain Leonard. Are you of a musical cast of mind?'

'A what? Oh no. No, I'm afraid not. I don't seem to get much –'

'Here we are, chaps,' interrupted Hunter, handing glasses. His demeanour was more excited than just earlier. 'A weak one for you, Brian. There. Now everybody pay attention to Alastair. He's worked out the whole time-table.'

'The padre's problem can be settled in one minute flat after Lucy appears,' said Ross-Donaldson. 'So that's him out of the way. Then I think that, by rights, Dr Best should have the chance of seeing Lucy about whatever he wants to see her about, which leaves –'

'It's kind of you to be so careful of my interests,' broke in the doctor, 'but I'd prefer to talk to Lady Hazell after she's ... I mean I'd sooner have her undivided attention.'

'We'll put you last, then.'

'I don't mind waiting around a bit,' said Leonard. 'Put me next to last.'

'As you wish. You've made a good recovery from your recent fit of impatience. So now it's just you and I to sort out, Hunter.'

'You go first if you like. Of us two.'

'Right. So it's the padre, myself, Hunter, Leonard, the doctor. Everybody got that? Good. The only remaining question is the transition from Phase 1 to Phase 2, and I'll deal with that when I take my turn. Just remember that in Phase 2 it's the responsibility of the outgoing man to advise the next on the list that the position is vacant. A couple of minutes' interval is all that's necessary ... Ah, good evening, Lucy. I always admire your sense of timing. May I present Major William Ayscue of the Army Chaplains Department, Captain Maximilian Hunter of the Carabinier Guards, and Captain Brian Leonard of the Sailors? And uh, Dr Best. Gentlemen, this is Lady Hazell.'

*

'What can I do for you, doctor?' asked Lucy at once.

'It's a personal matter, Lady Hazell. I'd like to defer it a little while, if it's all the same to you.'

'It isn't quite. I'd like to get it over now.'

'I really think, giving my professional opinion, that in the interests of all concerned it would be better to approach the question in private.'

'If you say so, doctor ... Well, Major ... Ayscue. Do I understand that you're a chaplain? A clergyman?'

'Yes, you do, Lady Hazell, in sheep's clothing as I am, but let me explain why I've come to call on you.'

When Ayscue had finished, Lucy said, 'Well, of course, please look at anything you like. It's nice to have someone taking an interest in the stuff. You can have a sort of first go now if you feel like it. I'm afraid things are in rather a mess in there, but Mrs Stoker dusts round once in a way and there is a light. If you come with me I'll show you where it is.'

She took Ayscue's hand and led him away.

'What I don't understand,' said Leonard, 'is where Churchill is.'

Ross-Donaldson looked mildly surprised. 'He's clearly not around,' he said. 'He understands the rules of the house as well as anybody. Either he'd be in here, or he's not around. He's not in here so he's not around.'

'Well, where is he, then?'

'He's probably gone ages ago.'

'I didn't hear him drive away. I'm sure I would have done. I'm going to have a look out the front.'

'Is he always like this?' asked Dr Best.

'I think it's just that he feels there are large parts of the world he doesn't understand. He likes to reduce them whenever he gets a chance. I can see his point in a way. I think in his shoes I'd probably do much the same.'

'He suffers, then, from certain anxieties,' said the doctor with a glance at Hunter.

'I wouldn't know about that, I'm afraid,' said Ross-Donaldson. 'Not one of my fields, what people suffer from.'

Leonard came hurrying back. 'Your jeep's still there, Alastair.'

'I dare say it is.'

'Well then, where is he?'

'He may be in the lavatory, he may be making himself a cup of coffee, he may have gone for a walk. It isn't worth exerting oneself to find out which, because on one point we can be sure. He's not around. We know the answer to the only question the situation can possibly be taken to pose. Or rather,' – Ross-Donaldson frowned slightly – 'one of the only two questions.'

'What's the other?' asked Hunter.

'It's only come up in the last thirty or forty seconds. Where's Lucy?'

'Showing Willie the library, I understood.'

'The library opens off the far end of the hall, a round trip of perhaps fifty yards. Half a minute's march.' Ross-Donaldson looked at his watch.

'But they've only been gone about three minutes. She's probably showing him round a bit. Nothing wrong with that, is there?'

'You don't know Lucy. She doesn't show people round libraries.'

'You think they may be hopping into bed? You don't know Willie. Very chaste chap, Willie. He never stops setting an example.'

'Lucy's a very attractive woman. In fact she possesses to a very high degree the most attractive characteristic of all: availability.'

'You find that attractive, do you?'

'Don't you?'

'Not especially, no.'

'In that case what are you doing here?'

'Let's leave that,' said Hunter. 'Anyway, even if they have gone off for a little while, what do you care? It'll be your turn next.'

'Once made, arrangements should be adhered to. And I don't think Asycue really grasped my point about the onset of Phase 2.'

'Oh, surely he must have done. It sounded simplicity itself to me. Anyway, I see that the situation is restored at last.'

On his way to the threshold, where Lucy now stood, Ross-Donaldson said to Hunter, 'Wait for me here.'

'Right.'

'About that matter we were discussing,' said Leonard, urgently even for him. 'Will you excuse us again, Dr Best?'

'By all means.'

'Oh, for God's sake, Brian, what is it now?'

'Where's Churchill?'

'I can't think of any way of stopping you asking that except by either killing you or telling you, so I suppose I'd better tell you. But before I do, you answer me a question. Do you want to know where James is for Security reasons or do you just want to know?'

Leonard opened his mouth readily enough to reply, but slowly closed it again. Then he said, 'I'm not sure. A bit of both, most likely.'

'There are times, Brian, when I very nearly like you a great deal, though I'd better not say that in front of the good doctor. Now' – Hunter went straight on – 'at this moment Lieutenant Churchill is upstairs in the bedroom, and in all probability the bed, belonging to a certain Catharine Casement, a friend of Lucy Hazell's and like me an ex-patient, or a patient, of Dr bleeding Best, who, if he heard what was going on, would, I know jolly well, dash upstairs and pull them apart and start asking them whether they thought they were going the right way about bringing their repressed hatred of each other out into the open.'

'Oh, surely not. You must be exaggerating.'

'Well, whether I am or whether I'm not, I just don't want that bastard pawing and nosing and snuffling his way round those two. You see if you can use your imagination a little to think how unpleasant that would be. And if you can't, shut up about where Churchill is just the same.'

'Of course, I understand. I'm awfully sorry, Max; I didn't know, you see. I do hope I haven't put my foot in it or caused any –'

'No no, dear boy, that's perfectly all right, I assure you. I merely wanted to head you off. But there's a more important point. You shouldn't be wasting your time wondering about Churchill while Dr Best's around. Ask yourself this. If, as he says, he's only here to talk to Lucy about Catharine, why has he turned up now? Why not come during the day? Why pick a time when the place is full of other people? Including officers from the camp?'

Before Leonard could reply, Ayscue hurried into the room with a sheaf of papers in his hand. His face was less gaunt than usual.

'This is amazing,' he said loudly. 'Look at this, all of you. Found it stuffed between the pages of a Victorian biological encyclopedia, of all things. Must have been there for a hundred years.'

What he was displaying was a number of sheets of music, creased, yellow and spotted, but quite legible. Leonard caught the words *Vivace assai*.

'Does the name Thomas Roughead mean anything to you?'

Hunter and Leonard shook their heads. Dr Best said he was not sure.

'Late eighteenth-century chap. More or less the generation after Boyce. Chum of Jonathan Battishall. Organist at the Temple at one stage. And ... pupil of the very same Johann Bach you and I were discussing not half an hour ago, doctor. Absolutely fantastic!'

'What about this Roughead?' asked Hunter.

'I have discovered,' said Ayscue, 'what I bet you anything you like is the only surviving copy of Roughead's trio-sonata in B minor for flute, violin and clavier. Hitherto known only in a transcription for two pianos by that awful old ass Cipriani Potter. Plus a couple of pages of a rather dull organ piece by John Stanley. I say, I wonder how much Lady Hazell would want for the Roughead.'

'I should think she'd let you have it for what it's worth,' said Hunter. 'Viz, nothing.'

'Oh, surely it'd be worth quite a bit,' said Leonard. 'It's not as if it's by anybody famous, I know, but it is old. You know, like an old master. You don't have to know who the old master is.'

'This is music, you fool,' said Hunter in his ordinary tone. 'Worthless by definition. I remember sitting down to listen to a whole piece of it once. Somebody's symphony in four movements, it was. I couldn't make out what it was supposed to do for me. It seemed to be inviting me to run about, lie down and go to sleep, rush about, and then run about again. But I didn't want to do any of that.'

'You were using it for the wrong purpose,' said Dr Best. 'Except for martial airs and such, and in a rather different way music for dancing, the art is not concerned with action. It moves us to contemplation, which assists us in resolving our various conflicts. Through harmony we progress toward harmony.'

'Well, I didn't, the time I was telling you about. I progressed in the opposite direction, thank you. That's another thing I've got against it. It introduced me to conflicts I didn't even know I had.'

'Who was this monster?' asked Ayscue. 'He sounds to me rather like Sibelius.'

'No, he began with a B. But then most of them do, don't they?'

Hunter continued to disparage music in general, on grounds that became increasingly obscure, until Ross-Donaldson returned to the room.

'Phase 2,' he said to Hunter. 'I should go up in a couple of minutes.'

'Let's fill in the time together.'

They moved apart. Dr Best looked as if he had got used to people doing that. Ayscue offered the music sheets to Leonard, who took them and turned through them with pretended interest. He tried to think of any comment at all.

'Where's the telephone?' Hunter was asking Ross-Donaldson.

'By her bed, I'm afraid.'

'Not the only one?'

'Oh yes. There used to be one in here, she was telling me, but she got rid of it because she got fed up with having to come all the way downstairs to put it back on its hook after she'd left it off its hook while she went upstairs to take it in her bedroom.'

'Thanks for putting it so cogently. But it leaves the problem intact.'

'She'll cheerfully go into the bathroom if you tell her it's Army business.'

Ross-Donaldson turned out to be right. Hunter was alone when eventually he picked up the telephone and sat down on the bed. The time he had spent in it with Lucy seemed to him much longer ago than the just-now it must really have been. What had taken place had been all right, but rather like trying to quench thirst by drinking a liqueur. The main difficulty had been to avoid catching himself pretending or fancying that he was with somebody else. This would have been far from unpleasant in itself, but not enlivening either. He had managed to steer clear of it nearly all the time.

He finished his telephone call and went and tapped on the bathroom door. Lucy came out. She had no clothes on.

'I'm off now,' he said.

'Did you get through and everything?'

'Yes thank you. Sorry to have pushed you out like that.'

'I was going in there anyway. Who's next on the list?'

'Brian Leonard. Then Dr Best intends to have his word with you.'

'Oh dear. Tell me – Max? Max – is Mr Leonard sort of all right?'

'Captain Leonard. He'd mind dreadfully if you got that wrong. Yes, he's all right really. Treat him gently, won't you?'

'I treat everyone gently.'

'I suppose it's possible. Oh, Willie Ayscue found a bunch of old music in your library. He wants to buy it off you. He seems to think it may be valuable.'

'Tell him he can have it, but I'd like him to send some money to a charity I do things for. Tell him I'll ring him up about it.'

'I will. Good night, Lucy, and thank you very much.'

'It's a pleasure.'

He put his arms round her and kissed her, wishing slightly

that he could find this rather splendid, which it obviously was in fact, instead of just rather agreeable.

'Come and see me again.'

'I'd like to.'

*

Before Hunter had shut the door behind him Lucy was back in bed. She was sure that Captain Leonard would turn out to be all right really, but the qualification meant something like when you got to know him thoroughly or although there were hefty reasons for thinking him not all right. Something had seen to it so far that nobody who was not all right, even really, turned up at what she referred to, but did not think of, as her evening parties. One of her most faithful friends, a dentist who had motored up from the town every Monday and Thursday evening for two years, except when he was on holiday, had explained to her that the thing worked very much like a club. A new person was not invited along unless he was well known to the inviter and had been carefully considered in the two key aspects, as drinking-companion downstairs and, in so far as this could be estimated, as performer upstairs. It had all been a matter of making a sensible choice of people to start with, and this, no doubt mostly by luck, she must have managed to do.

She predicted to herself that, should Captain Leonard turn out to be not completely all right, this would take the form of his having too little of something or other rather than too much. Her brief look at him downstairs had been enough to suggest to her that there was nothing masterful about him. That could raise problems. The problems raised by over-masterful men were, in her experience, less troublesome. They were certainly less varied.

When, a couple of minutes later, Leonard knocked and came in, her prediction about him looked as if it was going to be justified. He kept fairly close to the wall, like a child at a new school. He smiled at her and said,

'Jolly nice room you've got here, haven't you?'

'The thing is,' she said, 'for you to take all your clothes off straight away and then come into bed. It's much easier like that.'

'Oh, couldn't we have a little chat first? After all, we've only just met. We don't know each other.'

'We soon will if you do as I say. And chatting afterwards is nicer.'

Paying no attention to this, he sat down on the far corner of the bed and began polishing his pince-nez on a blue silk handkerchief that, she noticed, exactly matched his jacket.

'It's a great relief,' he said, 'to be able to come here and relax after a day on the sort of job I'm doing now. You get all wound up when you're engaged on vitally important, really very very secret work.'

The degree of guttural emphasis he gave the last phrase, and the peering look at her that accompanied it, puzzled her faintly. But she said nothing.

'I can tell you,' he went on after a moment, 'that some of those gentlemen in the East and round the place generally would give their eye-teeth for just five minutes with some of the documents I was dealing with today.'

He gave her another look, this time through the pince-nez. She still said nothing, feeling a little unkind, but knowing that total silence on her part would either pull him the more quickly into bed or push him the more quickly out of the door.

'Some of these new weapons we have are really quite terrifying.'

Silence.

'They make the atomic bomb look like a firework.'

Silence.

'Absolutely revolutionary.'

Silence. After about forty seconds of it Leonard got to his feet and, with a faint but sharp sound, pulled the bow of his evening tie apart. Lucy relaxed. She knew where she was now. It was the ego build-up as preliminary. Even her dentist friend would still sometimes be telling her, at this stage, about his plans for the welfare of indigent ex-members of his profession, other people's plans for luring him back into teaching. It made no difference to what happened next.

When Leonard had nearly taken off his trousers a kind of metallic trickling noise began. Lucy could not make out where it came from and was startled. So was Leonard, clearly, but within a second he was pulling his trousers back up again.

'It's all right,' he said abstractedly. 'It's an emergency. But it may not be anything. Thing on my wrist tells me when they want to get through to me. Got to go and get through to them now. I hope I'll be able to come back, but if I can't I hope you'll understand. I did want to talk to you.'

He ran out, his jacket over his arm. Lucy turned on to her side. When the trickling noise started she had been very interested in where it came from, but already the question seemed boring. Forgetting Dr Best she thought it was probably the end of the evening and might as well be. She fell asleep, but soon woke up again two or three minutes later when Leonard ran back into the room and set about undressing as quickly as anybody she had ever met in her life.

'What was that funny noise that made you rush out in such a hurry?'

With a kind of plunging dance-step he trod off one shoe after the other.

'Was it a telephone sort of thing or something?'

The zip of his trousers whined briefly.

'But it's all right now, is it?'

A sound like the plucking of a very slack guitar-string came from the elastic waistband of his underpants.

'Oh.'

Almost immediately after that Captain P. B. Leonard of the Sailors was demonstrating beyond possibility of error that as regards one side of life at any rate he was not just all right really, but all right. He went on with the demonstration rather longer than Ross-Donaldson's findings might have indicated as likely or average for the relevant age-group.

'Wow,' said Lucy eventually.

'Did I do it properly?'

'Yes, you did. Very properly indeed.'

'Honestly?'

'Yes, absolutely honestly.'

'Good. I particularly wanted to do it properly because I think you're marvellous. You're so pretty. When Alastair told me about the set-up here it somehow never entered my head that you'd be pretty. And I certainly never dreamt for a minute that you'd be sweet as well. But you are. You're very sweet.'

'So are you.'

'But what I can't understand is this. Why, being so pretty and sweet, you have to go to bed with all these men one after the other when you can't really know any of them very well.'

Lucy broke her usual rule of not discussing this question, which everybody except Ross-Donaldson and one or two others got to sooner or later. 'I don't have to do it. I just like doing it. I don't say I like sex any more than the next person but this is the way I like it. I know it wouldn't do for everybody.'

'It certainly wouldn't for me – the corresponding business, I mean. But I don't want to sound as if . . . How did you get on to it, kind of thing?'

'Well, like everything else, you find you've started before you've noticed you've started. To begin with, I just got married in the ordinary way, and it was literally years before I found out that my husband was having a lot of other ladies while I was going out of my way to be an absolute model wife from that point of view. So then I just started not being a model wife on a very tiny scale and he got most frightfully cross about it. He kept saying that that wasn't the point and that wasn't the same and surely I could see that. So I said of course I could, and the next time I started I really went to town on seeing to it that he remained in blissful ignorance throughout. Which you'd have thought would have solved everything. But it didn't at all, because the other person got frightfully cross because I was still living with my husband and hating it all that much and not not sleeping with him into the bargain. Well then just for the sake of a quiet life I had a divorce, and then before I could turn round I was back in the same position, only it was much worse this time, because everybody knew what was going on. That wasn't my fault really. What happened was that my new other person got so cross with me for not hating my new husband that he rang up and told him what I was up to. So then both of them were cross. But soon after that my new husband, old Hazell, he got drowned in an accident, and I was free again. I didn't want to get married again straight off, and there was more crossness about that. So then I must have decided I'd just had enough of all that. I must have worked it out that if I started sleeping with everybody nobody could get enough of me to start wanting to have all of me and getting cross about not. But that's only me thinking things over afterwards. At the time all I noticed was that I'd started sleeping with everybody.'

Leonard had listened to this as conscientiously as if it had been a lecture on Chinese eavesdropping techniques. He said, 'Will you let me take you out to dinner one of these evenings?'

'I never go out in the evenings.'

'Couldn't you make an exception?'

'I've just been telling you why making exceptions is the one thing I absolutely don't do any more.'

'I know, but . . . I promise I wouldn't get cross.'

'That's what you all say, and then when you get cross and I remind you of your promise you say yes but that was only a promise not to get cross about unreasonable things, it wasn't meant to cover things like *this*.'

After a pause, Leonard said, 'Could I take you out to lunch, then?'

'That's no better from my point of view, and I'm always in bed at lunch-time anyway. On my own, I mean.'

'Could I stay the night, I don't mean necessarily tonight, but some night?'

'No you couldn't. I hate sleeping in the same bed as anyone. Please don't ask me. Why are you so set on this sort of thing, anyway?'

'I want to talk to you, that's all.'

'We've been chatting nineteen to the dozen for the last ten minutes.'

'But I want to get you on your own. Really on your own.'

'Ah, there you go. What do you want to talk to me about? Not all that stuff about how awfully secret what you're doing is?'

'No. I'm sorry about that, I was on the wrong . . . I don't know why I said that. No, it isn't that I want to discuss anything in particular, I just want to talk to a woman, because I haven't for some time.'

'Aren't you married?'

'No. I used to be. Well, technically I still am, but she went off about two years ago after we'd been married for six years. She just went off.'

'Why?'

'She didn't say. I asked her several times but she didn't say.'

'What sort of man did she go off with?'

'She didn't go off with any sort of man. She just went off.'

'Oh, well that is a bit . . .'

'I haven't got a girl friend at the moment either.'

'But of course you usually have one.'

'Well, fairly usually. There don't seem to be as many girls about who like talking as there were just after the war. I find it difficult to get them to open up these days. But I knew straight away that you and I could talk about anything. But we can't really now, because of that Dr Best fellow hanging about.'

'Keep him hanging. He won't come in while you're here. He'd better not try.'

'I know, but he might knock or . . . Just him being in the same house puts me off.'

'He's horrible, isn't he? I've only met him for five minutes before, but I could tell he was horrible.'

'He's . . .' Leonard stopped and looked for a phrase that did not contain the letter R. '. . . undoubtedly most unpleasant. But tell me – do any of your other friends know him? Particularly officers from the camp. Have any of them mentioned him to you?'

'I don't think so, no. Why?'

'I just wondered. Well no, it's more than that. It's my job to keep an eye on the contacts people have. It wouldn't do to have blokes on secret work being indiscreet in the wrong sort of company. So . . .'

'Wrong sort of company. So when you went into all that song and dance about how tremendously hush-hush what you were up to was you were seeing whether I was a spy or not, is that it?'

'Well yes, roughly,' said Leonard, as Lucy started laughing. Her shoulders shook against his side. Presently he joined in, though without carrying complete conviction.

'But you mean you think Dr Best might be a spy,' said Lucy finally.

'Yes. What do you think of that idea?'

'Well . . . if I could swallow the idea of there being spies at all then I wouldn't have any trouble with the idea of Dr Best being one. But as it is . . .'

'The spy is a uniquely characteristic and significant figure of our time,' said Leonard, quoting from the introduction of one of his manuals and trying to make it sound casually thrown off.

'Oh, I thought it was moulders of the communal mind by means of manipulation of the mass media who were meant to be that. So somebody was saying in the newspaper on Sunday, anyway.'

'I suppose it depends on how you look at it. After all, there's no reason why you shouldn't be able to have two characteristic and significant figures of our time at once. But we're getting off the point. Dr Best could be a spy easily. Oh, I don't mean a Russian in disguise – what we call a non-transvasive defector. That means a man who goes over to the other side without actually going there. Our psychologists have done quite a lot of work on the personality patterns of people like that, and even their physical characteristics. Dr Best corresponds pretty closely to one of them. To several of them, in fact,' he added after a moment's reflection.

'Would you like me to sort of keep my ears open when he comes to see me? Lead him on, kind of thing?'

'Yes, I think it might be a good idea.' Leonard got out of bed and began dressing in a preoccupied way. 'Then you could let me know how you get on when I come over again. Tomorrow, perhaps.'

'As soon as you like. Look, I've been dying to ask you. What was that noise that made you run out of the room earlier on?'

'This thing.' He held up his right wrist. 'It tells me when I'm wanted on the wireless.'

'Wanted on the wireless?'

'I've got a wireless set in my car so that the camp can get in touch with me if anything urgent comes up. But I can't be expected to sit by it all the time just in case, so they buzz me on this thing.'

'What did they want you for?'

'Nothing really. It was a mistake. The bloke at the camp said he fell against the thing that operates this thing. Skylarking about, I suppose. I'm going to give them a rocket for it in the morning.'

'It sounds rather like a joke to me.'

'A joke? I don't see any joke in it. Who would want to do a thing like that?'

'I don't know. No, it wouldn't be much of a joke, would it? I say, you have got dressed quickly.'

'It's one of the things you've got to learn how to do in this job. You have to be ready to go anywhere at a minute's notice.'

He finished tying his tie and came over to the bed.

'I'll see you tomorrow night, then. I do like you very much, Lucy. It's all right for me to call you Lucy, is it?'

'Oh yes, I think we know each other well enough now.'

'I wish you'd be my girl.'

'I am your girl.'

'No, I meant just my girl.'

'I'm sorry, Brian, but I explained to you about how I never be just somebody's girl. It isn't because it's you; I'd say the same to anybody.'

'I understand. You got my name and you can't have heard it more than once.'

'It's quite easy to get good at that if you get plenty of practice. You'd be surprised, honestly.'

'Mm. Well. Shall I tell Dr Best he can come up?'

'Tell him to give it five minutes. And tell him I'm tired and he's not to stay long.'

'I'll remember. Well. Good night, Lucy.'

'Aren't you going to give me a kiss?'

'Oh, sorry.'

'Good night, Brian.'

As soon as she was alone Lucy jumped out of bed and went into the bathroom. When she came back she put on a pair of silk pyjamas and a black satin bed-jacket with a scarlet lining and got back into bed. She wished Dr Best had chosen another time to come and see her; she was marvellously tired now and felt she could sleep the clock round. In fact she did fall asleep, in a half lying, half sitting position against the pillows, her arms spread out on the covers.

She could not have slept for more than a few minutes, because when she awoke it was to hear a car, presumably Leonard's, driving away from in front of the house, and Dr Best speaking to her from close by.

'A most interesting type. Not unfamiliar, but interesting.'

'What?' asked Lucy in a hoarser voice than usual.

'You needn't answer this, of course, but did he acquit himself satisfactorily?'

'Who? Do what?'

'Captain Leonard, who left you just now. Is he a person of average masculinity? I assure you most seriously I ask you purely in a scientific spirit.'

'I don't care what spirit you ask me purely in, I'm not answering. You can go and . . .' Lucy checked herself. 'Why do you want to know?'

'As I said, he interests me.'

Dr Best came forward and sat on the edge of the bed about where Lucy's knees were. She glimpsed a couple of inches of pale and apparently hairless leg between his trouser-cuff and the top of his sock.

'Did he say anything to you about this job of his that he evidently considers so secret?'

Without taking any decision whether Leonard's ideas about the doctor were fantastic or not, Lucy became alert. 'A little, yes,' she said.

'Did this little strike you as plausible? Or was he talking wildly? In your estimation, naturally.'

'He's on secret work all right.'

'Mm. Of what nature? – according to him.'

Lucy was unfamiliar with Dr Best's line of inquisitiveness. She said experimentally, 'He didn't say exactly, but I gathered it was something to do with nuclear war.'

'Oh.' The doctor seemed delighted. 'That has a very familiar ring. The number of people who believe themselves to be engaged on that type of activity would comprise a World War II division. Did he give any details?'

She remembered a phrase from a newspaper. 'Tactical atomic weapons.'

'Wonderful,' he said, positively laughing now. 'The technology of the unconscious is never less than a decade behind its frontiers in reality. All the people who were the victims of private poison-gas attacks in the era of the flying bomb. Any moment now the Red Chinese will have stolen one of those tactical atomic weapons and start boring holes in his brain with it.'

The general drift of this escaped Lucy, whose temporary alertness had passed. But she would remember enough to pass a version of it on to Leonard the following evening. 'I expect you're right,' she mumbled.

'I didn't come here to discuss that, however. In fact I didn't come here to discuss anything,' he said, throwing the bed covers aside and seizing her in his arms.

It was against Lucy's principles, or at any rate her practice, to refuse to accommodate any man who had been properly introduced to her, but this proviso did not apply to Dr Best. She was to work out later that only the depth of her unwillingness to think of him behaving like this had stopped her expecting him to. All she could think of for the moment was how much worse being in contact with his mouth was than just looking at it. She twisted her head aside.

'Get away from me,' she said loudly. 'Leave me alone.'

He held her legs down with his own and started trying to pull her bed-jacket off over her shoulders. While he did this he talked quickly and quietly.

'One can see now what your much-vaunted enthusiasm for men amounts to. Like everybody else who purports to have dealings with large numbers of individuals you actually live at a low level of sexuality. Those like yourself who are victims of the Messalina syndrome have to hold in their mind the notion of an endless string of partners in order to render themselves capable of sexual intercourse.'

'Get away. I don't want you. Leave me alone.'

'Evidently a straightforward approach of this kind is less acceptable to you than you would pretend. Is your basic erotic impulse so feeble that you're compelled to energize it with adventitious aids?'

'Stop it. You're hurting me. Let go.' Lucy was shouting now. The shoulders of the jacket were far enough down her arms to immobilize them partly. The doctor set about lifting her body in order to pull off her pyjama trousers, still talking.

'What do you need to experience before you're able to receive the male? Flagellation by one party or the other? Or something even less conventionally acceptable? Or does nothing actually take place in this room at all? Is there an agreement to stimulate a series of sexual encounters in order to raise the amatory status of those concerned? That would be . . . Ah.'

He stopped talking as he drew the pyjamas clear and flung them aside.

'James!' screamed Lucy. 'I'm being raped! James!'

Her thrusting foot caught Dr Best on the shoulder and sent him reeling sideways into the dressing-table. He slid along the front of this, dislodging several jars and pots, tripped over the wastepaper-basket and fell to one knee. In a few seconds he was up again and coming for her, but before he reached her the door was flung open and Churchill came in wearing a shirt and trousers. Dr Best halted and began adjusting his tie.

Churchill took in the scene. 'Out,' he said.

'When certain women find their advances rejected they frequently avenge their loss of self-respect by making accusations of rape or attempted rape. An obvious –'

'I'm sure you're right, but that's not what was happening here. Out. Who are you, anyway?'

'My name is Best. I –'

'Best? Best! Out at the double! Can you manage under your own steam? Or would you like some assistance?'

'Certainly not,' said the doctor in some indignation. 'I welcome the chance of departure. Good night, Lady Hazell.'

He left. Churchill picked up Lucy's pyjamas and gave them to her.

'Are you all right? Would you like me to fetch Catharine?'

'No, I'm fine now he's gone.'

'I'll just make sure he does.'

He went out again. Lucy put her pyjamas on. It was a hot night and she was sweating slightly. She went into the bathroom and, not looking in the mirror, sponged her face with cold water. She heard the front door slam.

*

Churchill watched Dr Best's tail-light disappear. He did not immediately go back into the house. The sky had more colour in it than any night sky he could remember and there were thousands of stars. The moon was nearly full. There were no other sources of light.

He went inside, shutting the door quietly, upstairs, and along the passage to a room diagonally opposite Lucy's which he entered with some slight unnecessary noise. Catharine was lying in bed with the light on.

'It's all right,' he said. 'Some chap Lucy found she didn't like and cut up when she told him so. He's gone now. I'll just make sure she's okay.'

'Don't be long.'

'I won't.'

Lucy was in bed too. Her hairline was damp from the water.

'I shouldn't have let him come up here,' she said.

'Why did you?'

'He said he wanted to talk to me about a personal matter, but he never got round to saying what it was. Something about his professional services or something. It must have been to see how Catharine was getting on, don't you think?'

Churchill looked to make sure the door was shut. 'Or that was just an excuse to come over here so as to get at you. By the way, we don't mention to Catharine that he was here, do we? It might worry her.'

'Agreed. Hey, though, the cheek of him when he left. Quite as if he'd been trying like anything to get away gracefully for hours.'

'He was just saving his face.'

'James, the Army wouldn't let you come and live here, I suppose, would it? It'd be such a nice arrangement.'

'I'd love to, but I'm afraid they wouldn't. I can spend a lot of time in the nights here, though.'

'Good. You're doing wonders for Cathy, you know.'

'I'm doing wonders for myself. If you're not sleepy I'll go and get her and we can all have a chat. You've only to say.'

'No, honestly, I'm feeling marvellous now. You go off – she's waiting for you.'

'If you're absolutely sure. Do you mind if I go in there?'

'Good God, help yourself. Good night, James, darling.'

'Good night, Lucy. See you tomorrow evening.'

He kissed her and went into the bathroom, where he used the w.c. As he did so he felt slightly sorry not to be using instead the one in the other and decrepit bathroom. Earlier that evening he had decided that the one he was in now, though very handily placed, had better be avoided. He had not wanted to run into the Colonel or Hunter, far less one of Lucy's civilian friends. The thought of tramping all the way across the house and back in the interests of discretion had not appealed to him. But in the event he had been fascinated by his walk. The outward journey, with carpet giving place to matting and then hence to bare boards, wall coverings declining and vanishing, had been like some symbolic progress from the corporeal to the spiritual. And the return trip had introduced him to romance and unreality in one, as it might be a film set of a modern Rapunzel's castle.

Back in Catharine's bedroom, he took off his clothes and got into bed. He put one arm between her neck and the pillow and the other across her hip. Immediately they took up again the gazing at each other that Lucy's shouts had interrupted. He noticed as if for the first time, though in reality it was for the hundredth time, that she had hazel eyes with more dark flecks in the right one than in the left, hair the colour of dark honey bleached in places by the sun and growing low down on a forehead which was not itself low, rounded and rather childish ears, square jaws, a fair complexion more white than red, a straight nose with a faint upward tilt, a straight mouth with a recess under the lower lip. He reviewed these facts for a period he could not have measured. Then he passed to others no less well known to him. Her cheeks were smooth with a tiny down on them, her hair at the hairline smelt of honey as well as being of its colour, her lips were smooth and dry. With the spread fingers and thumb of his left hand he found out, as often before, the gentle swell of her skull above the nape of her neck; with his right he relearnt the small firmness of her breast, the softness of her stomach and the incomparably greater softness between her thighs. When he moved above and into her he found the parts of his body not in contact with hers beginning to slip away from him, ceasing to exist. His thighs were nowhere except where they were between hers; his arms were only as real as their clasp of her sides and her back. All he could hear was her breathing and then her voice.

He felt the sheet on his back and the sheet under his forearms and knees and toes.

'I love you,' she said.

'I love you.'

'I know.'

'That's nice as "I love you" really, isn't it? As nice a thing to say and to have someone say to you as well. Nearly as nice, anyway.'

'Have you loved anyone before?' she asked.

'No. Only been fond of people.'

'I've loved other people. Is that all right? You don't mind?'

'There's nothing about you or that you've ever done that I could ever mind.'

'I know. But I could do things you would mind, couldn't I? I could stop loving you.'

'No you couldn't.'

'No, of course I couldn't.'

Churchill got out of bed, went over to the washhand-basin and came back with a small towel which he handed to Catharine. Then he got back into bed again and put his arms round her.

'I'm sorry my breasts aren't bigger for you.'

'That's just one of the things about you that I don't mind. I like them as they are. Anyway, I think they're bigger than they were when I first came across them.'

'What, in a week? They can't be . . . Perhaps they are a bit. This is their worst time of the month, too.'

He rested his head on the breasts under discussion.

'That's nice, like that. Little James. It's all right to say that, isn't it?'

'Yes. I'm big enough for it to be all right. Tall enough, I mean.'

'You're big James most of the time. It's funny, I've never met anyone who was as gentle as you are, and yet you're more of a man than anyone too. Well, when you think about it, perhaps it isn't so odd, the two things together. I love the way you always make a noise when you're coming into a room where I am, so as not to suddenly be there and frighten me. How did you manage to think of that?'

'It didn't take any thought at all.'

'Oh yes it did, it took a tremendous amount of thought. Or a tremendous kind of thought. Some people it simply wouldn't occur to, not in a thousand years.'

'Well, soon I shan't have to bother about that sort of thing, if you go on not being frightened the way you have the last few days. I'll creep up behind you instead and give a blood-curdling scream and spring at you.'

'You won't really, though. But it's quite true, I very nearly don't get frightened at all now.'

'I wish you'd tell me what happened to you that started you off being frightened. It would make it much easier for me to help you stop being completely.'

'I will tell you, my dearest love, but I don't want to tonight. We're having such a lovely time, and it wouldn't sort of re-frighten me to tell you about it, but I think it would depress me a bit. Let's leave it until we're both in the White Hart and I'm serving drinks and giving change in between. That's the best way to do it. You're not to think about it or worry because of it : it's nothing very horrible or unusual, really it isn't.'

He kissed her and said, 'All right, we'll do it like that.'

'I think I'd like to go to sleep now. I'm a bit tired. Mind you wake me up when you go. It was very nasty waking up the other morning and finding you not there.'

'I'll have to be away by a quarter past seven at the latest.'

'I don't care, you're to wake me. Good night, James. I love you.'

'I know. Good night, Catharine.'

She turned on her side and he turned with her. He put one arm round her waist and the hand on her breast; the other arm he had to fold up behind her shoulders. He felt her fall asleep. But for her breathing there was the absolute silence he had noticed on his first visit to the house and found vaguely disquieting. It did not disquiet him now. He thought of the dispatch-rider's death, Fawkes's death, Operation Apollo, and they did not seem terrible. He knew they were and tried to feel that they were, but they remained just facts, dead facts, infinitely distant.

Part 2

The Founding of the League

Straight after breakfast the next morning Willie Ayscue returned to his hut in the meadow and settled down at his piano. He always had one available, but instead of taking the same instrument round with him wherever he went, as Leonard would presumably have done, preferred to hire locally. In his present quarters he only had room for an upright, a Bechstein, though, and one with an outstandingly good treble. Better than the average grand, he had decided.

He removed from the lid his walking-out cane, which Evans, his batman, regularly placed there when he tidied up, as if under the impression that his master was in the habit of using it to conduct invisible orchestras from the keyboard. Glancing over at his Alsatian bitch Nancy, who was watching him expectantly from her basket by the door, he raised the lid of the piano and tinkled a few notes at random. The dog made a squeaking noise, got up and came to him with a partly sideways gait, wagging her tail in an unconvinced way.

'It's all right,' he said, stroking her head, 'nothing's going to go wrong. It isn't going to blow up or fall on me. That noise it makes is just it singing because it's happy. It isn't angry or frightened or in pain. It's just a piano, that's all. It can't hurt me. It's nice of you to worry about me but there's no need.'

Nancy gave the equivalent of a shrug and went back to her basket, casting herself down into it with a loud sigh. When he began to play she cowered a little and gave another squeak, but not much of a one.

He went slowly through the clavier part of the Roughead sonata, not looking at the quality of the music for now, only at its difficulty. After half an hour or so he relaxed, smiling, and lit a cigarette. There were a few turns and some shakes in the bass that not many amateurs could be expected to play well, but that was a detail. Within twenty miles there must be a dozen people capable of making that part sound quite good. A glance at the violin part had suggested that it would not tax his own technical abilities. He was virtually two-thirds of the way to realizing the project he had conceived in Lucy's library within five seconds of knowing what it was he had found. He would give the piece a public performance, almost certainly its first in the original form for more than a century and a half, and in so doing would have made a tiny but real contribution to the understanding of English music of the later eighteenth century. And Roughead himself would have moved a fraction nearer receiving his eventual due as one of the most attractive minor composers of his era, a man whose naivety and professionalism blended uncommonly well. Ayscue suppressed the ungrateful wish that he had discovered instead some of Roughead's church music. One or two of his extant anthems showed a depth of religious feeling not very easy to parallel outside the choral works of Mozart and Beethoven. The choir at the village church could probably be drilled into rendering one of these adequately, and the organist there was pretty competent and might be cajoled into tackling one of the Roughead sonatas or fantasias. An ecclesiastical venue for the concert would have the advantage of stressing the essential connexion between music and religion, but might rule out the idea of including a couple of the secular songs that were such an immediately accessible part of Roughead's work. That vicar was a stuffy old horror. Still, if . . .

Ayscue pulled himself up. Before drafting the entire supporting programme he had better face the question of somehow getting hold of a flautist for the trio-sonata. He could count on persuading any one of three or four to come down from London, but this would diminish the local, home-made flavour he wanted to give the enterprise. Was there a brass band in the district? Any other kind of band?

Suddenly excited, he got to his feet. He was nearly sure he remembered someone saying that young Pearce played the flute in the camp jazz group. And he seemed a pleasant, obliging lad. And an interest like this would be just the thing to take his mind off Fawkes's tragic death, which, it was understood, he had not yet recovered from.

Well, no time like the present. Ayscue went to the telephone and lifted it.

'Exchange here, sir.'

'Oh, is Signalman Pearce on duty?'

'No, he went off at oh-eight-hundred, sir, after the all-night shift. He'll be pounding his pillow now.'

'Never mind, then.'

'I could call the guard room if you like, sir, and get someone to go over to his billet.'

'No, I don't want to disturb him if he's got his head down. I'll see him later. Thanks all the same.'

He put the telephone down and thought for a moment. Then he took his violin out of its case and was just about to try the violin part of the sonata when Evans knocked and came in with a pair of shoes back from the camp cobbler.

'Oh, and these are for you, sir.'

Both the letters Evans handed him were internal to the unit. Ayscue opened the first one, but before he had started to read Evans spoke.

'Will you be taking Nancy for her walk as usual, sir?'

'Yes, about ten-thirty, I expect.'

'I thought I might give the room a real proper brush-up like.'

'Good idea.'

Evans left. Ayscue looked at the letter he was holding. Clipped to it was a covering note with a rubber-stamped heading that read, From *O. i/c Adm.* Underneath was written in pencil, *Willie: Can you cope? M.H.*

The letter itself was a sheet hastily torn from a pad. On it were a few ill-written lines in green ink. Without formality the writer announced that he had recently returned to England after some years in the United States and South America, would like to address the unit on the public image of the armed forces in the countries in question and hoped to have a lecture on the subject ready 'in due course'. He would be writing again 'before very long' and signed himself 'L. S. Caton'.

Ayscue smiled to himself. It was Hunter's custom to pass to

him any unit correspondence received that smacked even faintly of culture. The previous week he had found himself put on the distribution list of a new Army Council Instruction on the internal painting of sleeping-huts and asked for his comments. Today's letter was less easily dealt with. As things stood, almost any diversion was to be welcomed, but this Caton's suggestion, and the manner of it, sounded peculiar. Well, nothing could be lost by trying to find out more.

He sat down at his work table and wrote briefly to the effect that the proposed lecture did not quite fall within the unit's recreational programme, but that as and when further details were forthcoming an effort would be made to find a place for it. He added a covering note to Hunter reading simply, *Okay? W.A.* and that was that. Then he opened his second letter. It consisted of a sheet of single-spaced typescript that read,

TO A BABY BORN WITHOUT LIMBS

This is just to show you whose boss around here.
It'll keep you on your toes, so to speak,
Make you put your best foot forward, so to speak,
And give you something to turn your hand to, so to speak.
You can face up to it like a man,
Or snivvle and blubber like a baby.
That's up to you. Nothing to do with Me.
If you take it in the right spirit,
You can have a bloody marvelous life,
With the great rewards courage brings,
And the beauty of accepting your L O T.
And think how much good it'll do your Mum and Dad,
An your Grans and Gramps and the rest of the shower,
To be stopped being complacent.
Make sure they baptise you, though,
In case some murdering bastard
Decides to put you away quick,
Which would send you straight to L I M B-O, ha ha ha.
But just a word in your ear, if you've got one.
Mind you D O take this in the right spirit,
And keep a civil tongue in your head about Me.
Because if you D O N ' T,

I've got plenty of other stuff up My sleeve,
Such as Luekemia and polio,
(Which incidentally your welcome to any time,
Whatever spirit you take this in.)
I've given you one love-pat, right?
You don't want another.
So watch it, Jack.

There was no signature and no covering note.

Ayscue read it through three times. Then he went to his
wardrobe, a standard-issue affair in imitation walnut, and took
a bottle of Scotch out from among his footwear. He swallowed
half a tooth-glassful neat in two goes, the first drink he had had
before noon for over ten years. When he had stopped coughing
he sat down again, lit a cigarette and went carefully over the
physical appearance of what had been sent him.

The poem had been inexpertly typed on a sheet of the cheap
lined writing-paper on sale at the canteen. The envelope, simi-
larly typed, bore his rank, initials and name in their correct form
– as they were to be seen on dozens of notice-boards and lists
round the camp – and, in one corner, *For the magazine*. That
was all there was.

It seemed important to Ayscue that he should find out who
had written the poem. But for the moment he was too agitated
to think coolly about this. Experience had taught him that
attacks on God along these lines meant that the attacker was in
urgent need of help, lest he fall into the unforgivable sin of despair. He told himself that to let his own emotions dwell on this
outcome could only postpone the chance of averting it, and
forced his attention on to the task of drawing deductions from
the text.

He made an annotated list in his mind. Spelling excellent by
modern standards but with a few illiteracies. Could indicate
either a good education imperfectly absorbed or a bad one nearly
transcended. 'Grans and Gramps', and 'quick' used as an ad-
verb. A lower social stratum? Or suggesting that the writer was
aiming at this effect in order to sound down-to-earth and non-
literary? Too sophisticated an idea? Raises the question of poetic

approach. Somebody unused to verse? Or somebody used to it, but deciding that the theme ruled out what was conventionally poetical? No help anywhere along these lines.

Then anonymity. Again ambiguous. And the stationery. Either somebody who ...

Ayscue pulled up short. These were intellectualist evasions of the central question, which he despised himself briefly for not having at once identified, and at once answered. Who had recently had an experience which could have rendered him emotionally capable of writing that poem? Signalman Pearce.

His hand went out reflexively to the telephone, then dropped: Pearce was asleep. Well, no harm could come to him in that state. Ayscue looked at his watch. Three and a half hours at least before he could hope to get into contact with the boy. And even then how was it to be done?

After some disagreeable thought he picked up the telephone after all and asked the operator to see to it that Pearce was given a message at dinner-time to the effect that the padre would like him to come along that afternoon, if he were free, and have a chat about music. It was promised that this would be conveyed. A pity, Ayscue reflected idly as he rang off, that such a message from the padre, however unmilitary its phrasing, was a summons to the presence of an officer, and a chat with the padre, however informal, was something worse, an invasion of privacy. He had once contemplated sending the Chaplain-General a memorandum saying that military churchmen ought to serve in the ranks if they had any respect for Christian tradition and any desire to be listened to. He had been deterred by reasoning that the CG would take no notice of it, if indeed it ever reached him, and moreover that the prospect of curates in inferior uniforms peeling potatoes in the cookhouse and having sergeants swearing – or not swearing – at them was, however strong in appeal, far too funny to be worth pursuing. And further, it occurred to him now, by trying to alleviate one problem he would be exposing another and much more dismal one. It was not as officers that he and his colleagues intruded upon the men but, by and large, as parsons. Every year, it seemed almost every month, it became harder to ask the most innocent, unloaded questions without setting off the look in the eye that said, covertly or overtly, 'What's it to you?' If one were to take off one's badges of rank, that look would find words. He had joined the Army with the idea of bringing the message of Christ to those who might any day stand in special need of it. He had hoped to build something genuine and valuable on the foundation of regular spiritual communion and pastoral contact which the Army had always provided. What he had really been looking for, evidently, was a captive audience.

Self-accusation was a form of self-pity and as such to be avoided. Ayscue got up, put on his cap and made for the door. With a rolling noise midway between a growl and one of her squeaks, Nancy bounded out of her basket and followed him.

Tongue flapping, she rushed diagonally away across the meadow as if in pursuit of the most provocative cat of her life. Then, at some inaudible but equally urgent call, she thrashed and skidded to a halt on the slippery dry grass and was off again at right angles, doubling her speed with each of her first few strides and keeping her dilated light brown eye rolling at Ayscue as she crossed his path.

He took the main track that led down to the gate. The sun shone hard on the roofs of the camp buildings and the leaves of the trees, glancing off windows and the glass and metalwork of the vehicles in the transport park and stirring thick vibrant bars of heat above the roadway. A motionless veil of haze hung at the wooded horizon.

One of the D4 sentries, rounding the corner of his beat, gave Ayscue a shoddy eyes-left. He acknowledged, as usual, with his smartest salute. The man flushed and his bearing grew more soldierly for his next dozen paces. Then it relaxed again. To Ayscue the tiny incident expressed perfectly the boredom, depression and uneasiness which pervaded the camp more and more and which he had no idea how to dispel.

'Major Ayscue,' he said to the corporal of the gate guard. 'Oh ... fornicational, intoxicational, desperational. Sorry, I was thinking about something else. I meant recreational.'

He walked down the lane and reached the main highway, where Nancy was waiting for him. Man and dog stood there for half a minute while traffic rumbled and rattled its way in both directions across their front. All the drivers were in shirt-sleeves and had their windows down. They seemed united by some single purpose.

Suddenly Ayscue remembered that he had left the poem in full view on his table, where Evans, in the course of his proposed brushing-up operations, would be certain to see it. The thought of it being spelt through, wondered about, perhaps uncomprehendingly grinned and whistled over was immediately as intolerable as if he had written it himself. He turned and went back the way he had come.

Nancy had paused to investigate what might have been a molehill and Ayscue's feet made no sound on the grass of the meadow, so that his return would have taken by surprise any-one who had crept into his hut during his ten minutes' absence.

And someone had. Brian Leonard, wearing newly pressed khaki, stood leaning in a casual and stiff attitude against the wall by the window. At his side the door of the normally locked cupboard, pushed to a second earlier, swung slowly open again with a whining creak.

'Hullo, Willie,' he said. 'I was just going to . . .'

Ayscue went and shut the cupboard and locked it with his key. He stared at Leonard, whose face was shinier and sallower and darker with subcutaneous beard than he had ever seen it before. Nancy came in, halted and growled softly, but at a sign from Ayscue went to her basket, where she settled herself with a groan.

'What? What were you going to do?'

'I was . . . Do you mind if I sit down? Thanks. I may as well be frank with you.'

'I should. I don't think you can be anything else.'

'No. Well, in my capacity as Security Officer of this unit I've been conducting certain investigations.'

'So I see. In a rather reckless spirit. My batman or I or any-body might have caught you at it. And I have.'

'I got hold of your batman and sent him on an errand for me,' said Leonard in a short burst of complacency. 'And I saw you go out with your dog. One has to take chances in this job.'

'I can't see why. Anyway, what did you expect to find here?'

'One often can't say in advance what one's going to find.'

'Have you actually found anything that interests you in your capacity as Security Officer of this unit?'

'Not yet. I'd only just started looking.'

'What made you decide to look in my room rather than any-one else's?'

'I didn't. I mean, I do spot checks of everybody's quarters on a random basis. This is just your turn.'

'Oh, good. But why couldn't I have been present?'

'There wouldn't have been much sense in tipping you off I was coming.'

'Wouldn't there? I thought that was your number-one prin-ciple, letting everybody know what you were up to so that you could see how they reacted.'

To be thus held up to question on a phylactological point seemed to shake Leonard more than anything else so far. He said crossly, 'This was different.'

'Well, you'd know, I wouldn't. But I wasn't thinking in terms of tipping people off. I meant you could have come in any morning when I was here and searched the place there and then. Like that I wouldn't have had a chance to eat my instruc-tions from Tirana.'

'You're right. I never thought of that.'

Ayscue's manner relaxed momentarily. 'You need some leave, Brian. We all do.'

'I know. Sorry to have upset you. I'm only doing my job.'

'That's all right. How did you get that cupboard open, by the way?'

'I have skeleton keys,' said Leonard. He did not add that he had been unable to open so much as his own dressing-table drawer by their agency, and that after having had to leave snapped-off portions of half a dozen of them in various locks round the camp he had decided to use them no more. 'But they're tricky things to handle,' – his voice thickened sharply as this recurred to him – 'and I'd be very grateful if you'd open it again yourself.'

'Hadn't you seen inside?'

'I was just that moment going to when you walked in.'

'Oh. In that case there's some point in refusing to open it for you or to allow you to open it. Which I hereby do.'

Leonard got up from the bed, where he had been sitting, and approached Ayscue and the cupboard. 'This is a Security matter,' he said, 'which means it isn't your place to give or withhold permission. If I have to, I can have you put under arrest and shoot the lock off that door. I'm ordering you to open it.'

'It's private, what's in there.'

'If it is, the whole thing'll go no further.'

After hesitating briefly, Ayscue unlocked the cupboard.

Two minutes later, Leonard was saying, 'One suit, civilian, three shirts, civilian, three pairs socks, civilian, seven neckties, civilian. That seems to be the lot.'

'Aren't you going to look for secret drawers and sliding panels?'

'No. You'd have known you couldn't have installed them without attracting notice. Now. Where do you go when you've got these on?'

Ayscue nearly told him to bloody well find out, but that would not have done at all. 'I go into the town,' he said.

'What for? Whatever the reason is it's safe with me.'

'I can't tell you that.'

With what seemed a great effort, Leonard said, 'You must tell me, Willie.'

'I wish I could. I really can't. It's a Church matter.'

'Ah – will you swear by almighty God and our lord Jesus Christ and the Holy Ghost and on your honour as an anointed priest of the Church – you are anointed, aren't you? – that whatever you get up to in town wearing those civvies it's nothing to do with Security?'

'I so swear.'

'Thank Christ for that.'

'Amen.'

Leonard slumped back on to the bed. 'That ought to hold them,' he muttered. 'If I had to I could take this all the way up to the C G and the Archbishop of Canterbury too. That'd hold 'em.'

'What are you waffling about, Brian?'

'Look, Willie,' Leonard spoke earnestly as well as urgently. 'I know you're not a spy as well as you do. But my master's a fanatic for detail, for closing every avenue and leaving no stones unturned. In my reports I've had to say I've been keeping you under surveillance. Now I can say you've solemnly sworn by God and the rest of them that you're not doing anything we ought to know about. That'll hold him. We can both forget about you. Of course, if you turned out to be a spy after all, my head would roll and so would his. But since he knows as well as you and I do that that won't happen, this'll be the end of it. I hated doing all this. I apologize most humbly.'

'Don't give it another thought, my dear chap. Now if you'll excuse me . . .'

'Yes, I must be going.'

Leonard's way to the door took him past Ayscue's work table. He gestured at it with his head.

'Funny poem or whatever it is you've got there. Who wrote it?'

'What's that got to do with you?'

'Nothing. Nothing in my capacity as Security Officer, that is. But I'm not in that capacity all the time, you know, even though you probably think I am. I can take an interest in a poem and who wrote it without thinking it's a code message from the Kremlin.'

This was said reproachfully and with a flash of spectacles that could have betokened some sort of toss of the head. Ayscue found himself nearly grinning.

'Of course you can, Brian. I'm afraid I've no idea who wrote it. There's no signature or anything.'

When Leonard picked up the typescript and looked at it consideringly, his mouth pushed forward, Ayscue again felt the sense of ownership, almost of authorship, that had made him interrupt his walk. He wanted to snatch the poem from the other's hand and put it somewhere out of sight.

'So I see,' said Leonard. 'Mind you, I can't make much head or tail of it, but it seems rather morbid to me. We all know these things happen, but there's no point in dwelling on them like this, I'd have said myself. Still. The bit that really beats me is this thing here about . . . Limb-o. Can you throw any light on that?'

Ayscue shook his head emphatically. 'No,' he said.

'Mm. He does nice punctuation, though. Well, I mustn't take up any more of your time. Thank you for putting up with me.'

When he had watched Leonard march rather than walk to the edge of the meadow, his shoulders hunching and unhunching in turn as he swung his arms, Ayscue went back inside and sat down at his table. He glanced at the poem again, intending to re-read it, but decided not to do so and locked it away in his cash-box. Leonard had omitted to ask to see inside this, perhaps an odd omission, certainly a fortunate one. The merest look would have nullified all Ayscue's efforts to conceal the purpose of his expeditions in mufti.

With the poem out of sight, he opened the stout manuscript notebook in which he drafted his sermons and prayer-meeting addresses. Since his ordination he had filled more than twenty such books, destroying each in turn as soon as the contents of its last page had been delivered. He had never knowingly used the same material twice.

The current page ran,

Ideas of God. Traditional see as human. Primitive, attrib own weaknesses, angry need placating, drought, sacrifice. Even Gks. altho Æsch etc., Soc, A'totle, + Parth, lech, anger, revenge, favourite (Achill). Only Xtn, father. Anthropols say origin 1) tribal authy 2) father-fig Freud 3) relic fear + man − someone makes thunder. Ok interesting, not whole story. Only Xtn God *not* human weakness. U K courts best, but always innocent/guilty & vv. 'Only human.' God always 100% fair, unable not. Human father v often gd, loving, no favourite, all kids same, ugly = gd-looking, when we bad = when we good. But only human, even best tired, worried, busy, just not there. Only God always there, 100% loving.

Having read through the above, Ayscue replaced his pen unopened in his pocket and shut the notebook. He went and switched on his gramophone, a table model with a plug-in second loudspeaker for stereophonic reproduction. The record he chose was the *Magnificat* of C. P. E. Bach. The pealing of the trumpets in the orchestral prelude drew tears to his eyes.

Before the chorus had done more than enter with *magnificat anima mea Dominum* the telephone rang. He turned off the music and picked up the receiver.

'Ayscue here.'

'Hold on sir, call for you ... You're through, madam.'

'This is the secretary of the museum library,' said a voice Ayscue recognized.

'Oh, good morning, and what can I do for you?'

'On the question of that manuscript you were interested in, you remember, Major? I've had a word with my chief and he says it's all right for you to have it if you make a donation to a charity of which he's the chairman. Would ten guineas be reasonable, do you think?'

'Oh yes, I think that's a very fair sum. Can I take down the address?'

'I'll give it to you when I next see you – there's no urgency. As regards the other matter you were interested in ...'

'Yes?'

'As you know, my chief's very busy these days. But he says he can give you an interview this evening if it's convenient.'

'Splendid, this evening will do very well. What time shall I present myself?'

'Ten o'clock. If you arrive at exactly ten my chief will be able to fit you in without any fuss or bother. He understands completely about you not wanting to have to chat to other people in the waiting-room and so on.'

'He's a very considerate man, your chief.'

'Well, you know, he's had a lot of experience of people and their ways. Now, you just come to the side entrance of the museum at ten – it's very easy to find – and I'll be there myself to take you up to my chief's office.'

'Right, I've got all that, thank you.'

'My chief says he's very much looking forward to having a chat with you.'

*

'Have another.'

'Yes, please. It's terrific stuff. What is it?'

'It's called green Chartreuse. I'm glad you like it.'

'Won't it make me tight? It tastes terrifically strong.'

'What do you care? We're on the loose tonight.'

When this brought only a smile by way of reply, Hunter searched his mind for things he could say. There were plenty of things he wanted to say, but they would hardly have been sayable unless Signalman Pearce had been in his arms, instead of sitting very upright on the far side of a hotel restaurant dinner-table. This was a perennial difficulty. Only by having been to bed with somebody was it possible to attain the pitch of conversational intimacy that was needed as prelude to getting them into bed. So, at least, it often appeared to Hunter at this stage of the proceedings. From this point of view there was much to be said for the heterosexual scene, where any old gap could be effectively got over by inquiries whether anybody had ever said how beautiful the other person was, by statements about eyes being like stars, and even, perhaps best of all, by wordless and mindless graspings of the hand.

The waiter appeared before this particular gap had stretched too far. Hunter looked up at him with approval as well as relief. Although instantly recognizable as one of the boys, of the persuasion which invited pursuit rather than that which pursued, he had not once rolled either eye or hip in course of serving the meal. Such self-restraint, Hunter knew, was rare. It helped to make up for the restrained contempt and amusement in the head waiter's demeanour, and for the unmixed and unrestrained amusement of the two young businessmen and their women at the next table. Pearce had seemed not to be aware of all this, but it was Hunter's guess that he was.

'A large green Chartreuse here, please, some more coffee and the bill.'

'Certainly, sir.'

'What do you think of the padre, Max?' asked Pearce suddenly when the waiter had gone.

He had said 'Max' and not 'sir' every time since being asked to, as if it came naturally to him. Hunter did not bother to speculate how or why it should. He was just delighted.

'Old Willie Ayscue? Not a bad chap for a God-botherer.'

'Why do you say that?'

'Well, you know. Always suspect somebody who goes down on his knees in front of an instrument of torture, even if it is an out-of-date one. But never mind about that now. What made you think of Willie all of a sudden?'

'He asked me to go and see him this afternoon. About music, he said it was.'

'Well, wasn't it really?'

'It started off with that. He showed me a piece of music he said he'd found somewhere. A classical piece, it was.'

'Oh, I know. Thomas Shithead or some such name.'

'Roughead, that's right. He's an old-fashioned composer. This piece of his is a trio. There's a violin in it, which the padre said he reckoned he could tackle himself. There's a piano, and he reckons there he could easily get one of the locals to do it. And then there's a flute, and he asked me if I thought I could have a go at that. He'd heard from somebody that I double on flute in the group, you see.'

'That was probably me, I'm sorry to say. Anyway . . .'

'Well, what he's got in mind, he wants to put this piece on in a concert. I was just wondering what you thought of the idea.'

Hunter refrained from answering while the waiter came back with their order and the bill. He poured the coffee efficiently and unobtrusively. Lighting a cigarette, Hunter noticed the smooth firm line of his jaw, and vaguely contemplated a little luncheon-party à un at this table while he was still in the area. He counted out money for the bill, adding a tip that was just perceptibly more than one-eighth of the total. The waiter took this in and bowed.

'Thank you very much, sir,' he said politely. 'I hope everything was all right?'

Hunter gave a friendly smile. 'Better than all right. You were very nice to us.'

Only somebody who was watching for it would have seen the waiter's eyelid move.

'It's a pleasure, sir,' he said, and went away.

'Oh yes, about Willie's concert,' said Hunter. 'I should say from your point of view all you needed to know was how much practice and what-not you'd have to do.'

'I'd have thought you'd have been against it never mind how little practice there was to it.'

'Why should I be?'

'Well, it's music, isn't it?' Pearce grinned faintly. 'I'd have thought that'd be enough for you, that it's music. The first time I came and talked to you in the hospital you sounded off against music.'

'So I did. What a good memory you've got.'

It was unlikely, considered Hunter, that Pearce remembered that occasion as well as he did himself. He had looked up at the sound of Pearce's boots on the block floor of the ward and seen him approaching past the table with all the flowers on it, blushing a little at perhaps intruding upon an officer who had chatted to him casually two or three times only, everything about him full of sensuality, empty of lechery or coquetry. For the first time in Hunter's experience he had felt a sharp desire not to have a drink.

He went on now, 'You don't want to take me too seriously about that sort of thing. Did you look at the stuff? Can you play it?'

'I don't think there's a lot to it. It looked pretty simple, what I saw of it.'

There was a short struggle within Hunter between his opposition to serious music, which was perfectly sincere, and his fondness for the prospect of Pearce's developing an off-parade life into which he, Hunter, could plausibly wander from time to time. Principle lost.

'In that case why don't you have a crack at it? It might be quite fun.'

'I might as well.'

Pearce took a sudden swig of his Chartreuse and licked his upper lip with a darting movement of the point of his tongue. Hunter's lips opened slightly in turn.

'Anyway,' said Pearce, 'I told him I'd think about it, the padre, and then ... Well, he started off by asking me how I was feeling these days. He meant about ... you know.'

'Yes.'

'So I said I thought I was beginning to get over it a bit, during the days at least, but I couldn't really be sure. And he didn't say anything for a bit, but you could tell he was, you know, sympathizing. But he looked terrifically ill, Max. All haggard. Is he really ill?'

'I don't think so. He's looked like that ever since I've known him.'

'I see. Anyway, then he wanted to know if what had happened had made me angry. Angry with life, sort of. I said not particularly, just sorry. Was I sure I wasn't angry with God, he said. I had to tell him I didn't believe in God, so I couldn't very well be angry with him. By this time I was wondering what it was all about. The next thing he said really floored me, though. Had I ever written any poetry. What do you think of that?'

'He must have been out of his mind is what I think of it.'

'I thought the same for the moment. But then he explained that someone had sent him a poem for this magazine he's trying to run, and it had upset him a lot because it looked as if whoever wrote it was very unhappy and had it in for God, which according to him is very dangerous, so he's trying to find the author. Apparently the chap hadn't put his name on it or anything.'

'Did he show you this poem? Poem, Christ. I feel rather more strongly about poetry than about music. At least with music the general sense of uneasiness and misery isn't tied down to anything. Poetry's got messages in it. You know, about love and spring and getting into a state. It says you ought to notice things.'

'I don't see any harm in that.'

'I do. The best way of dealing with the problem would be to send any author to prison who wrote a book that sold less than a million copies. That would put paid to most of the stuff I'm against. Anyway, it's not important enough to go on about. This poem that's got Willie all of a twitter. Did you get a look at it?'

'No, he'd got it locked away somewhere. It wouldn't really do for people to see it, he said.'

Hunter laughed silently. 'So presumably the editor will very much regret being unable to find a place for the contribution. Good old Willie. I never realized he was such a loyal son of the Church. I wonder he didn't burn the thing on the spot.'

'No, but he really was upset, Max. He said now he knew it wasn't me who'd written it he didn't know what he was going to do about finding out who had. He was very low, honestly. You could tell.'

'Well, there's no need for you to start worrying. Old Willie gets these moods. They don't necessarily mean a hell of a lot. I'll have a word with him in the morning. Quite likely he'll have forgotten all about it by then.'

'I wish you would. Sorry, I'm holding you up.'

'You're not in the least. Take as long as you like.'

'No, I'll just . . .'

Half an inch of Chartreuse at once was too much for Pearce. He choked and coughed. Hunter got up and beat him heartily on the back. He saw that the four at the next table were watching, with half-smiles of different kinds but the same high level of offensiveness. Fixing on the younger of the men, a shop-soiled faun with a small mouth, he gave him his best public-lavatory leer over Pearce's shoulder. All four heads turned away as if twitched by the same string.

Pearce gave a final gasp. 'Really does the trick, doesn't it, thumping? Sorry about that.'

'So I should hope. After that exhibition the least we can do is leave quietly.'

They did so. Outside it was still light. Hunter explained that where they were going was only a few hundred yards away, so they might as well leave in the hotel car-park the pick-up truck in which they had driven over. The street they walked along was crowded, but on one side there was part of a canal with yards and warehouses that looked deserted. Twice Hunter's shoulders brushed Pearce's as they moved to avoid groups of passers-by.

'Here we are,' said Hunter.

They went into the entrance-hall of a small block of flats dating some thirty years back. There was no lift.

On the stairs Pearce said, 'Tell me again about this bloke.'

'He's called Vincent Lane. About thirty. Unmarried. Friend of my brother's. In the insurance business. He spends about half his time here and half in London. I don't know who else he's asked tonight. It should be quite fun.'

By this time they had reached the second floor. Hunter pressed a bell. They heard it ringing, but then nothing happened.

'Mm, this doesn't look too good,' said Hunter, ringing again.

More silence. Hunter stooped down and turned back a corner of the doormat to reveal a latchkey. He opened the door of the flat with it.

'What do you think's happened?' asked Pearce.

'He may have got held up. He wouldn't mind us letting ourselves in like this. Let's see if he's left a note.'

Off the tiny hall was a long, rather narrow sitting-room with faded rugs, leather armchairs and an expandable dining-table against one wall. On this table they saw a sheet of paper with typewriting on it. It read,

Sorry boys – called to London late this afternoon. Urgent (they say). Couldn't seem to get you at the camp, Max – left a message with some moron which if you're reading this you can't have got. Managed to put everybody else off. Insist you have a drink now you're here. As many as you like. Help yourselves. Feel free. Give me a ring next week, Max. Many apologies for dragging you all this way.

Then, in a shaky hand,   In haste,
                                                                    Vince

Pearce gave a quick glance at Hunter, walked down the room to the window and stood looking out.

'Can I get you a drink?' said Hunter to his back.

'No thank you.'

'Do you mind if I have one?'

'Of course not.'

Hunter hesitated for a few seconds, then joined Pearce at the window. From here the canal was in view. There was still nobody to be seen near it. After another pause, Hunter put his hand on Pearce's nearer shoulder. He did this not because he thought this was the right moment, but because he could think of nothing else to do and nothing whatever to say. With his heart seeming to shake his whole chest, he turned slowly and put his other hand on Pearce's other shoulder, noticing the coarseness of the cloth there. Pearce's eyes were shut.

'Oh, Andy,' said Hunter, calling him by his name for the first time.

He kissed Pearce gently on the cheek near the mouth and felt him grow tense. When he kissed him again, on the corner of the mouth, Pearce strained away slightly. For a moment neither moved. Then Pearce stepped back and Hunter's hands fell to his sides.

'I'm sorry, sir,' said Pearce in a trembling voice. 'It's not that I don't like you. I just can't do it after all. I thought I was going to be able to, if it came to it. I wanted to, at least I wanted to want to, because you've been terrifically kind to me and I like you very much. I'd have given anything to be able to.'

A tear fell out of Pearce's eye.

'Perhaps I might have been able to,' he went on, 'if we hadn't mentioned ... you know ... him. Not that there was anything ... He and I were friends. You know, nothing more. But it just set my thoughts going and I couldn't go on. I'm sorry.'

'That's all right,' said Hunter, looking out of the window. 'We can't have you apologizing. It was my fault. I should have known better.'

'I didn't mean to call you sir just now. It just slipped out.'

'Of course, I understand.'

'I've been very bad about this. Until you ... until just now I was telling myself some of the time I wasn't sure what you were after. But now I know. I knew all along. You've spent all this money on me and I haven't given you any return.'

'Oh yes you have. It's been marvellous just talking to you. You mustn't think of it in that way. I enjoyed your company. And I've got lots of money anyhow.'

'I won't tell anybody what happened.'

'I know. You're a thoroughly ... You wouldn't do a thing like that.'

'If I'd known earlier on I wasn't going to be able to do it I'd

148

have let you know somehow, I'd have got out of coming along here, I wouldn't have had to hurt your feelings like this.'

'You haven't. Don't you worry about any of that. Signalman Pearce, your conduct has been exemplary in every particular. Your superiors have no fault to find with you. And now ... let's have a drink. You can have one now, can't you?'

'Yes. Yes, Max. A drop of Scotch if there is any.'

'There is. I'll be back in a second.'

Out in the extensive and lofty cupboard which was the kitchen, Hunter leant forward, put his hands on the edge of the sink, and took half a dozen deep, slow, quiet breaths. After that he mixed a very strong Scotch and water and drank it, mixed another of the same and an ordinary Scotch and water, took both glasses into the sitting-room and gave the one with the ordinary drink in it to Pearce, who had sat down on the arm of one of the leather chairs.

'Cheers,' said Hunter, grinning. 'Very generous with his whisky, old Vince Lane. And very discreet too. You might call him the perfect host.'

'There isn't anybody called Vince Lane, is there?'

'There must be somewhere, but this particular one is a child of my ever-fertile imagination. I don't think I'd like him much if he existed. He'd be the sort of chap who's always known everything he wanted to know. Good fun, but with a serious side to him. I'm glad we missed his party. There'd have been terrible people at it. Men whose personality consists of being self-assured and peevish girls with tiny chins and pearl necklaces.'

'Have you never gone for girls?'

'Not very hard. I can see the point of them, though. They must make life much easier for a chap. Especially if he's got anything in the way of a sense of humour. However hilariously you may behave over a girl you always feel it could be all right for somebody else. I mean it's just that you yourself are too ugly for her or too old or too poor, too something anyway, or not something enough, and that's all that's ridiculous about the situation. Whereas consider what you're taking on when you get frightfully fond of the postman or the chap in the place where you get your hair cut or your old school chum's uncle.

There's no way at all for that not to be funny, whoever's doing it. Oh, you can't help admiring someone who's prepared to do his best to heave a respectable middle-aged merchant banker in black coat and sponge-bag trousers on to his lap and ask him to run away with him. Lots of guts there.'

'I can't quite see you in that position,' said Pearce, smiling.

'Thank God for that. Actually one can't complain. As far as I'm concerned, not being able to keep a straight face under certain conditions does sometimes work as a restraining influence. And if you somehow never find yourself being restrained by things like prudence or propriety or conscience you need all the help you can get, believe me. Now what I suggest is this. We choke these down now as fast as we can and go back along the road to a pub I know of where there's a garden you can sit in without the management seeming to mind much. What do you think?'

'I'm for that,' said Pearce, getting up briskly and draining his glass.

'Off we go, then.'

At the door of the flat Pearce looked at Hunter, hesitated, and said, 'Don't forget to thank your pal Vince Lane for his hospitality.'

'Not on your life. I'll drop him in a bottle of champagne from both of us.'

Hunter shut the door. They went down the stairs and into the street, where the pavements were less crowded than they had been fifteen minutes earlier. Two men were standing talking outside one of the sheds on the far side of the canal. Their voices, calm and businesslike, were just audible across the water.

When he and Pearce drew level with the hotel where they had dined, Hunter stopped.

'I think I must have left my lighter in here,' he said. 'If you could hang on a moment I'll just dash in and see.'

Inside the building he went to the doorway of the restaurant and hung about. Within half a minute the waiter he was looking for came hurrying over.

'Can I help you, sir?'

'I was hoping so. I very much enjoyed my meal this evening, thanks largely to you, and I was thinking of lunching here one day later this week. On my own this time. I wondered whether you could recommend a good day.'

'Now let me see, sir ... Would Thursday suit you?'

'Yes. Thursday would do very well.'

'The chef does a very nice steak-and-kidney pie on Thursdays which I can thoroughly recommend, sir. There's just one point, though, and that is I'd advise your coming in comparatively early, because some of the staff go off at two-thirty that afternoon. Including myself as a matter of fact.'

'I see. Well, would twelve-forty-five be early enough, do you think?'

'Twelve-forty-five would be fine, sir.' The waiter turned through a booking register that lay on a nearby table. 'Stationed in the town, are you, sir?' he asked conversationally.

'Not exactly. I've got a flat just down the road from here.'

'Very convenient, sir. Oh, what name is it, please?'

'Lane. Captain Vincent Lane.'

'Thank you, Captain Lane. I'll look forward to seeing you on Thursday, then. Good night, sir.'

'Good night.'

*

'Ah, now here's an interesting case which will round off our tour in an appropriate fashion.'

Dr Best took Leonard fraternally by the arm and led him down the steps in front of the main entrance of the mental hospital to where a man of about fifty was sitting in a slumped position on the mossy stone surround of the ornamental pond. Nearby stood a wheeled invalid-chair. The sunlight was very strong.

'This man is called Underwood,' said the doctor cheerfully. 'Insult him.'

'I beg your pardon?'

'You heard what I said. Insult him. Call him names. Abuse him. His hearing, by the way, is as good as yours or mine. Go on, Captain Leonard.'

Leonard swallowed and coughed. 'You swine,' he said indistinctly to the man.

'Oh, you can do better than that. Be offensive. Imagine that he's your lifelong enemy and you now have him helpless in your grasp without fear of retaliation. You hate him deeply. Try again.'

'You revolting ... sod. You unpleasant idiot. I hate you. You're the most, uh ...'

'No, no, no. Hopeless. Now listen to me.'

Dr Best faced the seated figure, which had not so much as blinked since their arrival, and crouched forward slightly.

'Underwood?' His voice was soft and level. 'You can hear me. I know that and you know I know. Now, how would you like me to bring you a nice boy? A nice boy with beautiful fair hair and lovely pink cheeks? So that you could undress him and play with him and do all the things you've always wanted to do? You'd like that, wouldn't you? *Yes.* What would you do to him first? Perhaps you'd –'

'Stop that,' said Leonard. 'You've gone far enough. Leave him alone, poor devil.'

'Captain, you're reacting quite inappropriately. This is a scientific experiment. I'm asking for your co-operation. I was indicating to you the lines on which you should proceed. I want you to accuse this subject of what in your view is the most heinous and disgraceful crime in the world. By so doing you'll have the opportunity of adding to knowledge.'

Leonard calmed down and thought for a moment. Then he said in measured tones, 'You traitor. You renegade. You Communist spy.'

While Underwood still took no notice, psychiatrist and Security man looked each other over carefully. Dr Best smiled. Leonard frowned. Each glanced away and back at the same instant. At last the doctor's manner grew professional again.

'Complete withdrawal. He's unreachable by any normal stimulus. Now let me show you a characteristic of this condition that may be new to you.'

Underwood's arms were hanging loosely by his sides. Dr Best took one of them by the wrist and lifted it until it was nearly horizontal, then turned the hand palm upwards. When he released the arm it stayed in the same position, as if the man were begging or testing for rain. Then the doctor raised one of Underwood's legs so that its heel was about eighteen inches off the ground. It too stayed where it was when released.

'This characteristic is known as waxy flexibility, found in cases of total withdrawal. A notable feature is that the subject will sustain the postures in which he has been placed long after a normal person would be forced by intense physical pain to adopt a more restful posture.'

'What a terrible thing.'

'Not at all. It makes him portable. He can be brought down here and enjoy the sun. Or rather his skin can benefit from exposure to its rays. A more satisfactory state of affairs than lying permanently on his back.'

Dr Best turned away and made as if to resume walking.

'You're not going to leave him like that, are you?' asked Leonard incredulously.

'I told you his reactions aren't those of a normal person.'

'But good God . . .'

'Oh, very well.'

With ill grace the doctor put Underwood back as he had been. Watching this, Leonard suddenly caught sight of the lion-like figure in the centre of the pond. He screwed up his eyes against the sun.

'What on earth is that thing?'

'Oh, our mascot.' The doctor seemed gratified. 'That was done by one of our paranoiacs, as occupational therapy originally. It worked very well from that point of view, in the sense that as soon as he'd finished it his personality suffered rapid and complete disintegration. We couldn't allow him anywhere near a chisel now. Well, I got the idea of having the carving set up where everybody could see it. There was a poor copy of a Romanesque statue there originally, some nymph or other, a piece of sentimental trash quite frankly. This thing is much more . . . arresting. And useful. We get quite a lot of people in here of whose condition one could say little more with any certainty than that they are *mad*, in a generic, undifferentiated sort of way – screaming and weeping and so on. Then, perhaps overnight, such a case will issue in a fully crystallized, distinctive, autonomous psychosis - anything from suicide attempts to unsocial behaviour with excrement. I've been interested to note how often, in this asylum, progressants of this type have indicated the experience of seeing our mascot as the one which triggered off their psychic shift. There was even one fascinating case last year of a woman who believed she had counterfeited violent mania in order to be confined in one of the closed wards and thus escape the sight of our mascot, which, as you'll have noticed, lies unavoidably in the path of anybody entering or leaving the main building. A delusion, of course – she was as mad as a hatter – but a significant one.

'Long before the human mind became an object of scientific study it was recognized that abnormal mental states were highly communicable, not to say contagious, and I've often admired the instinctive good sense of those early practitioners who, without any body of theory to assist them, knew empirically that, by throwing together raving lunatics and those who were merely disturbed – as in Bedlam and other such mad-houses – they were encouraging the latter type of patient to make his physic shift and bring the real nature of his illness into the open. This communicability is, as I say, notorious; but I don't think it's ever been adequately noted before that this can work via an outward symbol or artefact, so that state-of-mind produces object which in turn produces state-of-mind. There are obvious analogies here with aesthetic theory, in particular with Eliot's notion of the objective correlative.'

Dr Best had evidently ceased to notice that it was Leonard he was talking to. The sunlight was reflected from his spectacles in such a way that they seemed to flash and glisten with the disinterested love of his profession. Now, however, as the two men strolled past the water-tower towards the entrance to his quarters, the doctor paused in his discourse and glanced briefly at his companion.

'I noted just now,' he said, 'that when I invited you to accuse the man Underwood of the deadliest crime you could think of, you chose to accuse him of being a Communist spy. Why was that, Captain Leonard?'

'Because it is the deadliest crime I can think of. What other reason could I have?'

The doctor beamed. 'Deadlier than murder?'

'Of course. A successful spy is far more destructive than even a mass murderer.'

'Oh, do you think so? More repulsive, too? More horrifying?'

'You didn't ask me for that. Anyway, why did you choose to accuse him of those disgusting things, or at least of wanting to do them?'

'Because my experience tells me that such accusations are the likeliest to produce a reaction in withdrawn subjects.'

'He didn't react, though, did he?'

'No. I wasn't expecting him to. But you did.'

'Good God, that was just because I thought you were being unkind to the poor swine.'

'Weren't you being unkind by accusing him of what according to you is the worst crime in the world?'

'That was different, doctor. I knew he couldn't be a spy, but he might quite conceivably have had some sort of hankering after the things you mentioned to him.'

'Ah. You knew he couldn't be a spy, and yet you accused him of being one. Why?'

Leonard hesitated. 'It's the sort of accusation a lot of people might resent even if it was utterly untrue.'

'Or is this accusation the one you instinctively bring against people whatever the circumstances and whatever your reason tells you about its inapplicability? Aren't you perhaps in danger of seeing spies everywhere?'

'In the circumstances,' said Leonard with more than his habitual urgency, looking hard at Dr Best, 'it's necessary that I do see spies everywhere.'

This came just as the doctor was stepping aside to allow Leonard to precede him through the outside door of the staff block. He looked as if he had found himself stepping aside further than he had intended, perhaps at a convulsion of laughter.

'You really are a character, Captain Leonard, I do declare,' he said. 'Really quite a card in your way. Now, if you'd like to leave your things here . . . That's right, come along.'

Leonard arranged his cap and cane on a hallstand that sheltered an immense golf-bag. Then he followed Dr Best into what might have been the board room of a small but prosperous private company. There was shoulder-high oak panelling and the ceiling was buttressed in the same wood. On a handsome Jacobean sideboard was ranged a double row of bottles and cut-glass decanters and what looked like a silver-plated ice-bucket. Some elaborate lilies in elaborate bowls gave off a thick and rather nasty scent.

Two men in their thirties wearing dark suits and silk ties with transverse stripes came forward at their entry. One was very tall and very thin with ears at right angles to his skull. The other was just a man.

'Captain Leonard, may I introduce my assistants? Dr Minshull' – the very tall one – 'and Mr Mann' – the one who was just a man.

Leonard shook hands with each in turn. Minshull kept his gaze level, so that it went over the top of Leonard's head. Mann smiled and nodded.

'Now,' said Dr Best, 'what's it to be? Sherry or Martini?'

'Sherry, please,' said Leonard.

'Manzanilla, fino or amontillado?'

'Amontillado, please.'

'Pedro Domecq or Harvey's?'

'Harvey's, please.'

'A lot or a little?'

'A little, please.'

Dr Best gave Leonard what was certainly a little, reaching as it did less than halfway up a cylindrical glass with a bore of about an inch. He gave himself what was presumably a lot, something like two-thirds of a tumbler. He looked at the glasses in the hands of Minshull and Mann, each of which held some liquor, and said he saw that they were all right.

'Did you enjoy your tour, Captain Leonard?' asked Mann pleasantly.

'It was most interesting.'

A high, dry, crooning laugh broke from Minshull and went on for some seconds.

'Are you perhaps professionally concerned in these matters?' continued Mann, raising his voice slightly. 'I know the Army's very high-powered these days on psychological warfare and so forth.'

Leonard made his prepared reply to this question, which for the last hour and a half he had been vainly expecting Dr Best to ask. 'I am involved to some extent. We take an interest in probing the minds of prisoners and safeguarding our own people against it. But my main job is Security. I expect you've heard there are some rather secret goings-on over at the camp. I'm responsible for seeing that the wrong people don't get to hear about them.'

'And who would those wrong people be, Captain?' asked Dr Best.

'Ultimately, of course, the Russian or Chinese Communists.'

'Not immediately. That's to say you don't believe there are actual Russians and Chinese hanging about the place in disguise.'

'No, I don't. But I know there's at least one enemy agent in the area.'

'And what sort of person might he be, do you suppose?'

'He might well be highly respectable,' said Leonard. 'Somebody widely known and accepted in the neighbourhood. Holding the sort of position that enables him to move about freely and talk to anyone he may come across. Perhaps with a profession that enables him to ask all sorts of questions without arousing suspicion.'

'Somebody like me, do you mean?'

'Yes. He might easily be somebody very like you.'

There was a loud sucking sound as Minshull drained his glass. Dr Best turned to him and Mann, rubbing his hands together excitedly.

'Isn't that wonderful, gentlemen? Isn't that wonderful?'

'I don't see anything very wonderful about it, sir,' said Mann. 'Captain Leonard's reasoning strikes me as perfectly sound, speaking as a complete layman in his field. And even if we failed to follow his argument, we'd have to give him credit for knowing what he's about.'

Dr Best grew rigid. 'Haven't I always been good to you, Mann?' he asked.

'I don't know what you mean, sir.'

'Don't you think that, if you were being rational, you'd admit that the presence of a guest makes this an unsuitable moment to start uncovering your hidden aggressions?'

'I wasn't being aggressive, I assure you. I was simply giving an opinion.'

'We won't pursue the matter for the time being. Let's just say that it's surprising to find somebody of your qualifications evidently failing to identify one of the best-known types of proemial persecution-fantasy.'

'But, Dr Best,' said Mann, flushing, 'Captain Leonard is a Security officer. It's his business to look for spies. And who's behaving unsuitably in front of a guest now, may I ask?'

This defiance did not act as Leonard had expected and increase Dr Best's annoyance. Instead, he turned to Minshull and said in a jesting tone,

'Abercrombie and Kraft, July 1963.'

Minshull gave another laugh, this time with a keening rather than a crooning effect. Leonard looked wordlessly at Mann, whose flush had deepened.

'A well-known paper on the effects observable when a subject's fantasies seem to be confirmed by something in his experience,' said Mann. 'As when, let's say, a man with a neurotic fear of being poisoned by his wife finds real arsenic in his soup.'

'You mean he thinks I'm mad,' murmured Leonard.

'Loosely, yes.' Mann glanced over to where Dr Best was talking up into Minshull's face. 'But he's always . . . But you don't have to put up with this, you know. Say the word and I'll take you out to a pub.'

'Thank you, but I'll have to stay now. What we've just had isn't an unfamiliar line of defence, you know. Discrediting the motive of inquiry is always preferable to answering it.'

Mann drew in his breath slowly. Then he said, 'You mean you think he's a spy?'

'There are strong grounds for not ruling out the possibility. You said yourself you thought that was reasonable.'

'I merely said your theory of the –'

The rest of Mann's remark was drowned in the pealing of a large brass hand-bell at the hand of Dr Best, who spread his arms and urged the other three towards a table laid for lunch in the window alcove. Leonard found himself placed with his back to the window. He was thus in a good position to take in fully the entrance a moment later of two tall girls, a fair-haired one in a skin-tight suit of black leather and a dark one wearing a similar garment in white. The former approached and set down on its stand a silver ice-bucket with an open bottle of wine in it, the latter handed round plates of smoked salmon.

'They must find it very hot in those clothes,' said Leonard when the girls had retired. 'Especially this weather.'

'Oh yes, they do, very,' said Dr Best, evidently pleased that this substantial point had been grasped. 'They're always complaining. May I pour you some hock?'

'Why do they wear it, then? Thank you.'

'They asked to, and I saw no reason against it. Quite the contrary, in fact. It was perhaps something of a coincidence that their respective fantasies proved to be reconcilable in such totally complementary forms. At any rate, I took advantage of the situation to test the possibility that the opportunity to act out a fantasy without social or other penalty might not bring about an alleviation of the condition giving rise to the fantasy, or at least make them happier.'

'And has it?'

'No,' said Dr Best. 'But the clinical implications are of interest. Minshull here is writing up the experiment. This is a rather amiable wine, don't you agree? It's a 1963 Durkheimer Schenkenbohl. I prefer to drink it when it's young and fresh.'

When the girls returned at the summons of the hand-bell, they brought a 1959 Château La Bridane and a saddle of lamb with French beans and new potatoes. The blonde moved round to Leonard and poured him claret. A stitch or two had given in the seam at her hip, revealing a small patch of bare skin amidst the black leather. He felt proud of himself for noticing this, and grateful to Lucy for giving him back the capacity, on the decline in him over the last few years, for noticing it and things like it. In itself it could mean no more than that the blonde, and by inference her companion too, had found a simple way of not adding to the heat engendered by unventilated outer garments of leather. But it produced in him a firm resolve to ring Lucy up at the first opportunity and arrange to visit her. That, however, must wait. For the moment the matter to concentrate on was that of introducing plausibly the information he had come here to divulge.

He held back until Mann asked him a casual question about the amount of co-operation Security officers commonly got from those in their charge. Leonard made sure Dr Best was listening before he said,

'I've always found people very understanding. Especially when it comes to rising to any sort of occasion. For instance, on Friday the unit's putting on something called Exercise Nabob. It's not really an exercise in the full sense, not much more than a demonstration and practice in the use of certain new weapons, but it does entail cordoning off part of a valley and denying access and observation. That's a mere matter of mechanics – the tricky and bothersome part is setting up search procedures and snap checks to make sure nobody walks off with some vital . . . piece of wherewithal in his pocket, or a miniature camera full of film. When you start organizing that sort of thing, you might expect to find yourself coming up against the old Army mentality, red tape and obstructionism and all that. Not a bit of it. All possible facilities were immediately placed at my disposal. The Commanding Officer issued an order that any officer or other rank who failed to accept my recommendations on the spot would be responsible to him personally. The Adjutant himself accompanied me on my various rounds and visits whenever his other duties allowed. The officer in charge of –'

Dr Best interrupted this recital, which had been designed merely to put a bit of circumstantial flesh on the bare bones of the central facts Leonard wanted to convey. 'It must be agreeable to find oneself the centre of so much attention.'

'Oh, I don't know. You just take it as part of the job.'

'You must enjoy giving instructions to colonels and such and seeing them rushing off to carry them out.'

'That's where the regulations are so helpful. In Security matters the normal gradations of rank don't –'

'Would you say that the prime satisfaction of your post was the sense of sitting at the middle of a vast web or machine and manipulating people by pressing buttons?'

Aware now of where this was tending, Leonard drew in a lot of breath to pronounce a negative, but was again interrupted, this time by the radio-alarm buzzer on his wrist. He jumped to his feet. 'I'm wanted on the wireless,' he said, and hurried from the room, hearing Minshull's laugh behind him as he shut the door.

After a fifty-yard trot in the sun across the car-park, he was sweating rather and peering through misted glasses as he fumbled through his keys. At this moment a man in denim overalls came out from behind a bush and sidled up to him, spade in hand.

'Acting on your instructions, I –'

'Hold it, you fool,' snapped Leonard. 'Get back out of sight.'

The man retreated. Inside the car, Leonard switched the set on and sat chafing, unable to think, while he waited for it to warm up. When the loudspeaker began to hiss and crackle he went over to Send and spoke into the microphone.

'Hullo, Control, hullo, Control. Padlock listening. Over.'

Preceded by a couple of seconds of carrier wave, Ross-Donaldson's voice, sounding harsh and boxy, issued from the loudspeaker.

'Hullo, Padlock. Sunray Minor here. Something . . . well, something has come up you ought to know about. Over.'

'Is it urgent?' Leonard waited, then added peevishly, 'Over.'

'I don't see how it can be, and it probably isn't a Padlock matter at all, but if it is it may be important. That's as much as I can tell you. Over.'

'Will return at once. Over.'

'Roger. Out.'

Leonard switched off and got out of the car. Sweat was running down his face. He walked in a meditative manner towards the shrubbery from which the man with the spade had emerged.

'Have you anything to report?'

There was a rustle and the snapping of a twig. 'No, sir,' said a voice.

'Then watch harder. And you ought to know better than to approach me in the open like that. Stick to the telephone arrangement.'

'Sorry, sir.'

'I should hope so too.'

A minute later, Leonard was making his excuses and shaking hands with the three psychiatrists. Drs Best and Minshull seemed in high spirits, Mann a little subdued. Leonard returned to his car and drove furiously back to camp. He had not enjoyed the tour of the hospital or the lunch-party. Both had done something to strengthen his suspicions of Dr Best, but without furnishing evidence of the kind he could put in his report. Then there had been the ineptitude of the pretended gardener. The installation of such an agent was required by the regulations covering cases of this kind. Leonard would much rather have done without him, preferring to wait until Dr Best could be moved up from a green suspect to a blue suspect and so merit having his telephone tapped. But regulations were regulations, which was a pity. This particular set of them, not for the first time in Leonard's experience, was bringing about an impasse whereby the evidence necessary to prove a man guilty was unobtainable except by methods that were only to be used on men already proved guilty by other methods. A lecturer on one of the courses attended by Leonard had cited such situations as reflecting the immature, unfinished state of applied phylactology. Half an accreted tradition given the force of law, half an exact science, it afforded germane analogies (the lecturer had explained) with the condition of Greek medicine prior to the emergence of Hippocrates. To find this view supported by events, or as now by non-events, was depressing. Leonard rallied a little, however, at the thought that he had at any rate managed to set his trap for Dr Best with about the right mixture, he felt, of emphasis and unobtrusiveness.

He parked his car in its allotted space and crossed the drive to the Orderly Room. The sergeant there jumped to his feet and asked him to go straight into the inner office. He did so and saluted Ross-Donaldson smartly.

'I'm sorry to have dragged you away from your luncheon-party, Leonard, and you may be sorry too when you know more. My sergeant brought me this. He'd found it pinned to the recreational notice-board outside the canteen. Since then another copy's been found among the periodicals in the Sergeants' Mess. I've got a squad out now, seeing if they can turn up any more.'

He passed Leonard a sheet of Service stationery. It was a smudged but legible carbon typescript that read,

THE ANTI-DEATH LEAGUE
incorporating Human Beings Anonymous

It has been decided to form a branch of the above organization in this Unit. We want you to join us if you agree with our attitude. There is no other qualification for becoming a Member, no entrance fee or subscription, and any activities you may see fit to carry out on behalf of the League are entirely up to you. You will not be given orders of any kind.

We think that the attitude of the League is sufficiently expressed in its name, but should you be in any doubt we invite you to consider carefully the three following cases, all taken from newspaper items of the last few years.

Case No 1: A woman of about 30 years old was dishing up the family supper. She took a potato out of the dish and popped it in her mouth. It lodged in her throat and she died of asphixiation then and there, in front of her husband and 3 young children who were present at the time.

Case No. 2: A house was set on fire by lightning. A woman of about 25 threw her 18-month-old son down to neighbours standing on the pavement, but they failed to catch him and he was killed. She jumped and her fall was broken, but she lost the baby she was pregnant with.

Case No. 3: A boy of 15 had been blind since birth. He was operated on and his sight was given him. 5 days later he caught a little-known virus infection (nothing to do with the operation) and was dead in 24 hours.

If you are against what happened on these occasions, you are fully qualified to join the League. We invite you to attend an inaugural meeting in the Camp Theatre at 1900 hrs this coming Thursday.

Please tell everybody you can about the League and the time and place of the meeting. This notice is not likely to stay where it is for very long.

Issued by the Committee, 6 H Q Adm Bn Branch, Anti-Death League

Leonard was bewildered. He felt dimly that Security was involved here in some way, but could not have said in what way. His manuals were silent on situations like this, if indeed there were any other situations like this. He could think of nothing to say.

No such difficulty beset Ross-Donaldson. 'A little bit out of the usual run, isn't it?' he said. 'Even so, as I told you on the R/T, it doesn't seem a very pressing issue. I doubt whether I'd have had you buzzed if it had been left to me, but fortunately I was relieved of the onus of thought by the existence of your standing order about always letting you know at once of anything with any conceivable Security connexion. I've a feeling you should redraft that, by the way. I spent several minutes after I talked to you trying to think of something of which it could validly be said that a Security connexion was beyond the power of the human mind to conceive, and failed to come up with a single one. I got pretty close after a bit when I started wondering how an orderly reporting sick with toothache could have a Security bearing, but then I realized he might have a microfilm in his mouth for the dentist to take out and send to Peking. That rather discouraged me, getting as warm as that and then ignominiously failing. Of course, empirical semantics teaches us what "conceivable" is intended to convey, but we should always strive for intensified precision. I won't ask you to work out a synonym now, however. Come in.'

A corporal entered, saluted, and handed over two more copies of the notice.

'Where did you find these?'

'One in the O R's latrine, sir. The other pinned to a tree by the sleeping-huts.'

'Right. Have you covered the whole area yet?'

'No, sir, we're still working on it.'

'Do that. If one more of these comes to light after you've completed your search, I'll have you and all the other NCOs in the party up in front of the Colonel and I promise you I'll do my best to see you lose your stripes. Is that clear?'

'Yes, sir.'

'Off you go.'

The corporal saluted and left with enough of a clatter to bring Leonard halfway out of his daze.

'You were a bit hard on him, weren't you?' he said. 'Why all the flap? One copy of this thing is all we need.'

Ross-Donaldson had spoken to the corporal in his customary level tone. Now he stood up, his plump face flushed.

'It may be all you need,' he said very sharply. 'As far as I as Adjutant of this unit am concerned, need doesn't come into it. If it's possible to catch this man, which I doubt, I'm going to do it. And I'll make sure he goes to military prison. You can talk to him there if you want to.'

'There's no point in getting hot under the collar about it.'

'There's every point. This is an abnormal happening and there's no knowing where it may lead. A secret project like ours has got to keep all parts of its environment under control at all times. We can't afford to have fanatics or lunatics or jokers round the place.'

'I realize that, of course.'

'I hope you do. It's our job to be pro-death, Leonard, and don't you forget it.'

*

'Sixteen and nine, seventeen, seventeen and six, one pound. Thank you, sir.'

'Thank you, my dear.'

The man pocketed his change and went away with the drinks he had bought. Churchill, perched on a stool at the bar with a large gin and ginger beer before him, looked carefully at Catharine.

'Are you sure you'd rather do it like this?' he asked.

'Quite sure.'

'All right, then. Why did he marry you?'

'I think it must just have been that he wanted to be married. All his friends were, you see, the people he'd been in the Army with and so on. He never liked the idea of looking different.'

'When did you find that out?'

'I suppose I started realizing it after about two years. But it took a long time to dawn on me properly. I was very ignorant in those days. I was only nineteen, but I'd had so much sex already then that I thought I knew all about it. I thought I couldn't not know all about it. What I didn't know was what it was for. I was like someone who knows exactly how a railway engine's put together, and who can put his finger immediately on any part you care to name with his eyes shut, but who it's never occurred to that the point of the bloody thing is that it pulls trains. You do see what I mean, don't you? So I wasn't getting a great deal out of it at that stage, early on. That didn't worry me much, though. I thought that perhaps the people who said they got a lot out of it were natural exaggerators, or else that I was somebody it didn't happen to appeal to an awful lot. I thought that getting married and being with someone all the time would make it better. So you see I was to blame too for things going wrong.'

She was speaking quietly and calmly, but Churchill felt she should not go too far with her story too fast. 'Have a drink,' he said. 'You'll be wanting to wet your whistle with all this chattering you're doing.'

'Very kind of you, sir, just a half of bitter if I may.'

While she drew the beer, Churchill glanced round the bar. At this hour, shortly before closing-time in the middle of a week-day, the place was almost empty. Neither the red-faced man who had bought drinks a little earlier, nor his closely similar friend, nor the three younger men who might have been students on vacation, showed any interest in Catharine or himself. Eames, the landlord, had explained that it was a point of etiquette with many drinkers to leave a barmaid and her steady escort undisturbed as far as possible. 'If she's on her own she's likely to be considered fair game,' he had added, 'which is where you may get trouble. So I'm most happy that Mrs Casement should have taken a fancy to someone nice and quiet like yourself, Mr Churchill.'

At times like this, and even more when he was in bed with Catharine, it often seemed to Churchill that the whole thing would go on for ever. He knew that, through no fault of either of them, it could not. But he was getting very good at paying no attention to this a lot of the time. He smiled at her when she stared at him as she drank.

'That'll be one and a penny.'

'Oh, sorry. Wasn't it better at all when you got married?'
She rang up the money carefully.

'Oh yes. By the standards I had then it was marvellous. Not having to worry about it ending, and him not going away all the time. But after a bit it was no better than what had gone before. Especially sex. Sex was what you did in bed, and eating was what you did at table, and plays were what happened in theatres and so on. You know – "I think we've just got time for a quick one." Now you could make that funny and lovely, darling. But you ought to have heard the wonderful statesmanlike calculatingness he used to say it with. "I think ... I *think* ... if we're *reasonably* quick ..." His favourite moment for that was just before the evening drink or going out. He liked to get it out of the way, he said, so that he could look forward to settling down undisturbed to a good night's rest. So then I had a couple of lovers and he was very good about it. I don't know whether I'm saying that sarcastically or not. As long as I was happy, he said.'

'What about kids?'

'He was rather the same about them. If I wanted them then it was all right by him. So I didn't have any.'

'I don't quite see that.'

'It's like sex, James. It's no good if one of you just has no particular objection. I reckon that sort of thing undermines at least as many women as sex not being all right. Anyway ... then Casement turned up. Can I have a cigarette?'

He gave her one and lit it.

'Casement's line straight away was wanting me to let him take me away from all this. What there was of this, he meant. He was marvellous at first. My best before you. So then we got married. We were back in England by this time. I'd lived with him about eight months and thought I knew him.'

One of the students now came to the bar and ordered three halves of bitter. She served him before going on.

'The moment we got married he started being different. I don't like that, James, people being different all of a sudden. About three nights a week he'd get angry with me, usually when we'd had people to dinner or been out somewhere and he'd had some drinks. He'd wait until we were getting ready

167

for bed, and then he'd bring up something I'd said or done during the evening which had made him angry. It didn't matter much what. If I'd said I liked one of his friends, it proved I was a bitch because it meant I wanted to go to bed with him. And if I hadn't liked one of his friends, then that made me a bitch too because I was fed up because the chap hadn't made a pass at me. And so on. The next stage was him hitting me. Mainly punches in the stomach and slaps in the face. He was very careful not to bruise me where it showed. Then I'd cry, of course, and then he'd cry too and start comforting me, and then he'd end by fucking me. Then he'd be perfectly cordial and nice until the next time.'

She had said this as quietly as ever, but faster, and with an occasional quick deep breath between sentences. Churchill watched her. He thought she had better tell him everything now she had started.

'I kept trying to leave him, but he kept coming and bringing me back. He was good at that. He was so charming that nobody believed what I told them about him. I could hardly believe it myself when it wasn't happening. And I tried lawyers, but cruelty's very difficult to prove, and he always let up as soon as anything like that was in the wind. He stopped altogether when I had my sister to stay, so she went off thinking I was a hysterical liar. Then something happened that showed me what it was all about. I could have realized before, if I'd taken it in properly that he almost never fucked me except after he'd been hitting me.'

Catharine's shoulders were hunched. She pushed her hand towards Churchill along the top of the counter. He took it and squeezed it.

'I had terrible toothache and the dentist couldn't see me straight away and I was lying on my bed groaning, and when I went out to go to the bathroom there was Casement on the landing playing with himself because I'd been groaning. So he hit me worse than he'd ever done before and sort of raped me on the landing. After that I stopped being able to deal with my life at all, any of it.'

'Where is he now?' said Churchill quickly.

'Oh, he's off. He won't come near me now, not even near enough to have a divorce. Me going mad would be sure to come out and that would be very disgraceful. I think he's feeling a bit ashamed of himself, too. He's a very moral, respectable man.'

'Oh, for Christ's sake.'

She sighed very deeply, then smiled. 'You see? It was very nearly all right, telling you that. Not even very depressing. It'll have gone altogether soon. But listen, I meant what I said about Casement being moral and everything. That was the whole trouble with him. If he'd said, "Look, ducks, here's this whip. I'm going to give you a bloody good belting with it if you don't mind, because that's what I like doing. No hard feelings, eh? Then we'll make love and I'll take you out somewhere nice for dinner," if he'd said that, well, I'd have known where I was. I might even have co-operated. But that would never have done for Casement. That would have been immoral, you see. He had to have a reason. It took me about three months to work that out and when I had I started getting better straight away.'

Churchill leant over the bar and kissed her.

'You won't be different all of a sudden, will you?' she asked.

'Of course I won't.'

'My God, what's the time? Last orders, gentlemen,' she called. 'Last orders, please.'

'Was he religious?'

'Well, there was just a touch of that, I suppose. He didn't go to church, but he was always saying how grateful he was for his Nonconformist upbringing. He was very responsible in lots of ways. Good about money, paying bills as soon as they came in, not driving when he was drunk, saying he was bored by all the filth on the stage and in the cinema, all that kind of thing. Yes, sir, the same again?'

She started serving the last drinks. Churchill went round the lounge collecting the used glasses and ashtrays. Then he got a damp sponge from the sink behind the bar and cleaned up the tables. While he was drying the washed glasses Eames came in from the saloon.

'Everything shipshape here as usual? That's the way. Well, if you ever get sacked from the Army, Mr Churchill, there's a job waiting for you here as potboy. I was just wondering if I could tempt you two to a little cold beef and pickles in my parlour before you go off. No? Well, in that case I won't keep you. See you this evening.'

Churchill reflected momentarily on Eames and his offer as he stood outside in the sunshine and waited for Catharine to join him. The landlord was undoubtedly a nice enough man, but he could hardly be such a wonderful man as he, Churchill, had just caught himself supposing, and after only two large gins too, and gins blotted up in about twenty ham sandwiches at that. The same sort of thing had happened the previous evening when, without any gins inside him at all, he had suddenly been attacked by the wish that it was Brian Leonard's birthday so that he could give him a present. He jumped now to the conclusion that there must be less love than there ought to be in a world where so many people went on being nasty to and bored by one another. How many people had the good-nature to love everybody without loving somebody first?

Catharine came out of the pub. She looked so beautiful in her white dress and white shoes and white hair-band that Churchill had an instant of sincere puzzlement at the way the passers-by went on passing by, the farmer climbing into his estate wagon over the road failed to reverse the direction of his climb and come pounding across to cast himself at her feet, the man laying slates on the roof of the barber's shop managed to stay aloft. Churchill put his arms round Catharine and kissed her.

'Sorry,' he said when he let her go.

'That's all right.'

'I won't do it again.'

'Oh yes you will. You are to.'

The scene was roughly unchanged. A middle-aged woman wearing a hairnet had looked over her shoulder at them, and the farmer paused inquiringly in the act of switching on his ignition. Nothing else. They don't know what it is they're looking at, thought Churchill.

He and Catharine went round the corner into the yard and got into the jeep he had brought. It belonged to the dispatch-rider section, whose sergeant had turned out on investigation to be very fond of whisky and by nature inclined to return favours. The weather was so fine that Churchill had removed the over-head canopy and windscreen. They took the road that led to-wards Lucy's house. The rush of air was cool to the skin. It reminded him of how Catharine's upper arm felt when he put his hand or cheek against it.

Soon after they reached the beginning of the wooded, hilly region he found a place where the jeep could be parked off the road. They climbed between the wires of a fence and des-cended a gentle slope where the turf was thin and in places broken by the roots of the trees that grew there. This made the ground awkward for someone wearing high heels, and he took Catharine's hand. On the further side of the miniature valley the grass was thicker and the going easier, but he still kept hold of her hand. He watched how she moved her body as she walked, out of the corners of his eyes because if she knew she was being watched she did things just as beautifully but in a slightly different way. In a minute or two he would let her know he was looking and try her like that.

They reached the top of the short rise, where the trees grew closer together. He admired their olive-green polished trunks. It seemed that they did not drop dead wood at all freely and that this small upland was regularly scoured by the wind, because the ground was as clear of debris as if it had been swept that morning. Fifty yards ahead there was a false horizon. Churchill wondered what was beyond it. As they went in that direction, moving in and out of patches of shade between strides, they heard the sound of water.

In half a minute they were standing at the top of a cliff per-haps twenty feet high. At its base were irregular heaps of boulders and smaller stones, some of which had found their way to the banks and bed of a stream that might have been a couple of feet deep in wintertime, but was reduced now to inches. The rest of the view was made up of trees, younger ones near at hand, taller ones with spreading foliage further off, the whole belt stretching for a mile or more. They walked along the edge of the cliff and soon found a way down, the rocky course of a dried-up tributary of the stream.

'This is going to be hard on your shoes,' said Churchill. 'I'd better carry you.'

'But I'm so heavy. I'm heavier than I look. Or perhaps I look heavy. Anyway I am heavy.'

'But I'm very strong, you see.'

He picked her up and carried her the necessary twenty yards with little difficulty and no stumbling, setting her down on a patch of coarse grass beside the stream.

'My God, you are strong. That was big James all right.'

'You enjoyed it, didn't you?'

'Mm, you bet. It gave me a sexual thrill.'

'What doesn't nowadays?'

'You may well ask.'

A jump that was little more than an extra long stride took them to the far bank. A faintly marked path led upstream and they took it. After a while it curved aside and led across a corner of the woods. Away from the water the sound of insects and the beating of birds' wings could be heard. Churchill took Catharine's hand as they walked and looked at her and past her together, so that girl, trees and stream formed a unity. She turned her head and looked at him. He knew for certain that in some way this moment had become inevitable ever since that other moment the afternoon he first saw her when he had looked at a patch of country similar to this one and thought of her. He felt his heart lift. This had never happened to him before, and he was surprised at how physical the sensation was. He was filled with joy.

'I could never love anyone else in the way I love you,' he said, stopping and drawing her to a stop.

'Of course you couldn't.'

'Even if you were to suddenly vanish altogether.'

'I'm not going to, though. I haven't done any loving before worth talking about.'

'Everything's all right now, isn't it?'

'Yes, that's exactly what's all right,' she said. 'Everything.'

'I suppose I might get thumped on the head some day and lose my memory, or go completely senile, but that's the only kind of thing that would make me forget this afternoon.'

172

'I'd remind you in any case.'

They walked on. The path curved back towards the stream, then into the woods again deeper than before. The shadows under the trees were very strong. When they drew level with a grassy bank a few yards from the path in the opposite direction to the stream, Churchill halted again.

'This looks like a good place to sit down,' he said.

'I don't want to presume, but do you mean sit down or lie down?'

'It's funny you should say that, because it was lying down I had in mind.'

'In that case I think it would be easier for everybody if I took off my dress. Is that all right?'

'Yes.'

When she had hung her dress on a bush and kicked off her shoes, he ran his hand up her bare arm, finding it faintly warm between wrist and elbow, cool above the elbow like the flow of air during their drive, fully warm at the shoulder.

'The grass feels marvellous under your bare feet.'

'I dare say it does, but I can't really see there being any bare feet as far as I'm concerned. I'd have all that shoelace and sock business to contend with. We oughtn't really to take very long.'

'Well, your jacket can come off, anyway.'

'Yes. There's no point in your going on just wearing those, is there?'

'I suppose not.'

'This is quite good grass,' he said a moment later, stroking it, 'but the earth underneath feels pretty solid. I'm afraid your shoulders and so on are going to go through it a bit.'

'There's a way round that.'

'Is there? Oh yes. Oh, *yes*.'

They kept their eyes on each other. He watched the steady change in her expression as it grew wilder and at the same time more serene, more longing and more contented. At first he thought she was becoming less human, less the person who was Catharine, but then he saw that she was really more human, more Catharine than ever.

When they were lying side by side he slid his arm under her

neck and round her shoulders and put his hand on her breast.

After a moment he said, 'There's a lump here, I think. Yes. You feel.'

'Oh yes. What do you think it is?'

'Well, it's only very small. It's probably just a little cyst. I used to get them in the lobes of my ears when I was at school.'

'I suppose I'd better get it seen to.'

'I think it might be as well, yes. As soon as you can.'

They got dressed and prepared to move off.

'Let's go back now,' said Churchill. 'I'm going to get hold of a doctor and arrange for him to see you in the morning. We want to have that cyst cut out before it gets any bigger. I neglected the ones I had at school and they were a hell of a bore. I don't like making a fuss, but I'm the one who's looking after you now.'

*

'I suppose you'll be going along, will you, Brian?' asked Colonel White. 'Fellow might turn out to be this famous spy of yours, eh?'

'I doubt it, sir,' said Leonard. 'I think we're dealing with a lunatic.'

'Of course. Of course we are. I went over that notice thing rather carefully and had a good think about it. Chap seems to regard himself as unique. As if he's the only one who's ever noticed that decent people sometimes come to sticky ends. Or that all ends are sticky if you look at it in one way. Necessary, though. Anyway, there's precious little that's crazier than imagining you're on a private line to the truth. What about you, Willie?'

'You mean am I going to turn up at this meeting affair, sir? Yes, I think I might as well.'

'I think so, too. Rather comes into your field, doesn't it? Good deal of dissatisfaction with the grand design rolling about in our friend's noddle. Have to see if you can't straighten him out.'

'Yes, there is that,' said Ayscue.

'You surely do not seriously imagine that this man will appear?' asked Major Venables, slowly waving the spent match that had just lit his cigar. 'Or, more likely, men. To me, this farce has every appearance of having been contrived over pints of small beer in the White Hart by a group of clowns suffering from underwork.'

Hunter had been ordering drinks from a Mess waiter. He now said, 'In that case, part of the joke would be to see how many people fell for it and who they were. He, or they, would have to be frightfully aesthetic about things to stay away. I'm going along, anyhow. I scent fun of some kind.'

'You have curious notions of fun,' said Venables. 'And not you alone. At the last Mess night I witnessed five grown men, three of them of s1 rating and thus bearing a certain load of responsibility, climbing about this room on the furniture in an attempt, so it was represented to me, to make a complete circuit without putting foot to ground. It was strenuous, it was ungraceful, it was noisy, it was distracting, it was pointless.'

'No harm in that,' said the Colonel. 'In its being pointless. It's a tradition.'

'And then last night I endured part of a sort of collective recitation, or chant, involving words of infantile near-obscenity delivered with great emphasis and killing slowness. Sister's ... *my* sister's ... *up* my sister's ... *pudding* up my sister's ... *black* pudding up my sister's ... *strong* black pudding ... And so on. The proceeding seemed to me to be indefensible.'

Ayscue laughed. 'That's rather heavy, isn't it? I'd have thought it was a very innocent way for young men to let off steam.'

'The steam you refer to is accumulated largely in the process of becoming drunk,' said Venables in his groaning way. 'Which process has evidently become as much a part of unit routine as guard-mounting or vehicle maintenance. The whole situation in this place is beginning to disquiet me. Boredom is giving place to group hysteria.'

'You're exaggerating,' said Ayscue firmly. 'The people here are working under a considerable strain. In the circumstances they like to forget themselves when they're off duty. I think everybody's bearing up wonderfully.'

'Well spoken, Willie,' said the Colonel.

With an emphatic, reinforcing nod at Venables, Ayscue picked up the glass of whisky that had just arrived for him. There was pink gin for the Colonel, sherry for Leonard, bitters and soda for Hunter. Venables picked up the remaining glass.

'Wait a moment,' Hunter said to him, 'didn't you ask for French vermouth?'

'I did. What of it?'

'Well, what you've got' – Hunter bent and sniffed – 'is Italian vermouth. I'll tell –'

'Indeed? It will do very well, thank you.'

'But they're utterly different drinks.' Hunter sounded rather shocked.

'Without doubt. I take no note of such matters.'

'Well, you ought to. Don't you agree, chaps? Oughtn't he to take note of such matters as the difference between French and Italian vermouth?'

Ayscue nodded again, hardly less emphatically than before. Leonard looked blank. 'Up to him,' said the Colonel.

'*Je n'en vois pas la nécessité,*' groaned Venables. 'What, to resume, is this considerable strain you refer to? I feel myself under none, yet I bear the greater part of the responsibility for the success or failure of Operation Apollo in its entirety. The officers under instruction are each partly responsible for the success or failure of one-twelfth part of that Operation. Yet they, together with others who are not privy to anything of much importance, are held to be showing the effects of considerable strain. How can they be?'

'It was you who were saying a moment ago that we were all on the verge of mass hysteria,' said Leonard.

'Hysteria of this sort need not be, and in the present case demonstrably is not, the result of strain. Unless, which you well may, you count as a strain the experience of depending on the conversational and other social resources of one's fellows when none has any to speak of, as here.'

'How do you manage, then?' persisted Leonard.

Hunter and Ayscue exchanged a grin.

'I depend on nobody.'

'Well, that clears that up,' said the Colonel. 'I think, chaps, if we're going to this do we'd better knock these back and be getting along. Did you arrange about dinner, Max?'

'Yes, sir, I've put it back to eight o'clock. That ought to allow time for a full-dress meeting with election of officials and proposals for additions to the library. The people who aren't coming will just have to put in an extra half-hour's drinking, I'm afraid.'

'Right, then. I take it you won't be accompanying us, my dear fellow?' asked the Colonel, using his usual vocative for Venables, whose lack of christian name, like other things about him, made standard Mess informality a little more difficult.

Venables removed and looked at his cigar before answering. 'I will,' he said. 'I have just sufficient curiosity to satisfy myself that, in accordance with my prediction, the authors of this tomfoolery will not show themselves.'

'Wouldn't you be prepared to take our word for that, if that's the conclusion we all come to?' asked Leonard.

'No.'

Colonel White, Leonard and Venables left together. Hunter and Ayscue followed. Out in the evening sunshine they took the cinder path that led round and up towards the camp theatre.

'How did your evening with young Pearce go?'

'Oh, it was very enjoyable in some ways.'

'But not in the way that was intended to be the most important way?'

'Unfortunately not. However, the evening was far from wasted. We were served at dinner by the most charming and understanding waiter. I drove over and lunched there today under his auspices, and then he spent most of the afternoon under mine.'

'Good show.'

Hunter frowned and stroked his moustache. 'I hardly like bringing this up, Willie, but why don't you disapprove of me?'

'Oh, good God, Max, surely you know me better than to have to ask that. I disapprove of as little as possible on principle. I want to encourage people to go in the direction I think is best for them, not tell them they're too disgusting to deserve to be able to make a start. So I can't oblige you with any disapproval. Why are you so keen to get it, anyway?'

'My dear, I don't think this line of talk suits you at all. Still, if you insist ... Tell me, Major Ayscue, *what makes you think* I want to earn your disapproval?'

'The first chance you got you told me you were a practising homo and went into quite a bit of detail. In the White Hart, with James and Moti. You remember.'

'Just. Perhaps I did blab a bit, but I was pissed at the time.'

'You were pissed all the time in those days. It didn't make you blab to the Colonel or Brian Leonard as far as I know. I got the impression you were trying to pick a fight with me, Max.'

'I told you I was pissed. Look, what's all this about?'

'Admit you've got it in for the Church.'

'Oh, I see, I see. You're probing about that bloody poem, aren't you?'

'Who told you about that?'

'Andy did.'

Ayscue nodded. 'Oh. Yes. You know, at one time I thought it was possible he'd written the poem.'

'Did you?'

'I don't think so any more. But he did seem to have the strongest motive.'

'How do you mean?'

'For heaven's sake, Max. Fawkes was Pearce's friend and Fawkes died.'

'Oh yes, of course, sorry.'

'Still, he seems to be pretty well back on an even keel now, don't you agree?'

'Mm. Steady as a rock.'

'I'd like to think I've helped him a bit there by getting him interested in this Roughead sonata thing.'

'Oh, you've got him interested in that, have you? Well done.'

'We've had a few practices. For an amateur, you know, he's remarkably good technically. There's a lot of talent there, Max.'

'Yes, I thought so, too.'

They fell silent and entered the theatre. This was no more

than an oversized hut with a low stage at one end. The weekly cinema show took place in it, and it had also been used for a concert organized by the Sergeants' Mess, two thinly attended lectures arranged by Ayscue, and a couple of morale-building harangues by the Colonel. No play had been presented here during the unit's tenancy of the camp, but for a moment Hunter wondered whether some ambitiously unextravagant production might not be impending, or even in progress. The blinds had not been rolled up after Sunday's film, and the screen was still in position. On and near the stage a number of uniformed figures, under strong illumination, were sauntering or standing about. As he and Hunter made their way up the aisle, Ayscue said,

'I've got a feeling we may be going to meet the author of that poem quite soon.'

'Why should you feel that?'

'He's obviously the same as this Anti-Death League character.'

'This is all rather too deep for me, I'm happy to say.'

Ross-Donaldson held the stage. Plump but elegant, his face at least as expressionless as ever, his hands clasped behind his back, he strolled to and fro in a measured way, glancing every so often towards the door. Near the back wall there stood two members of the main camp guard in the at-ease position. Both men were armed, and both looked rather self-conscious. Venables, Leonard, and Colonel White were grouped round a battered piano beside the stage, the first two staring into space in different directions, the Colonel in the act of settling himself in the only nearby chair with a large album of community songs which he had presumably found on the spot. He was quietly humming a tune.

In the audience, six or seven men were sitting in ones and twos. Hunter picked out Ayscue's batman, Evans, and then, in the front row, Naidu chatting to a sergeant.

'Fancy seeing you here, Moti.'

'Good evening, gentlemen.' Naidu got up and swept a mock bow. 'And to what do we owe this pleasure?'

'Vulgar curiosity,' said Hunter, nodding to the sergeant. 'The best kind, in fact. That's on my part. Willie seems to think he may have a professional interest in this League business. Or at least the Colonel thinks so. Or said he thought so. But what about you, Moti? Your attendance at this sort of caper is far more extraordinary.'

'Oh, no. I'm Orderly Officer today.'

'And it's part of your rounds to look in at all meetings convened by anonymous fanatics. Quite so. Brian thinks of everything, doesn't he?'

'Max, you're incorrigible. The truth is far simpler. The Orderly Sergeant here and I have survived the grim rigours of guard-mounting, and we're now on our way to the next port of call in our laid-down duties. We decided to dodge in here and lie doggo for a while before having to endure being asked to give a ruling on the edibility or otherwise of the meat pies now being consumed in the canteen. So we're here for utilitarian reasons. But what of all these others?'

Hunter ran his eye over the small remainder of the audience. 'I don't know anything special about any of these chaps,' he said. 'As regards the officers, it's mostly official interest, I suppose.' He lowered his voice. 'You know, if Alastair really wants to catch this anti-death merchant he's going a funny way about it. If I were he, the merchant I mean, I'd have been standing about outside for a good half-hour, reading the notices on the board and taking careful heed of anyone coming in here. I think the sight of the Adjutant arriving with a couple of armed men would discourage me from putting in an appearance myself. Alastair ought to have given him time to come on the scene first. We might as well go back to the Mess.'

'Let's give it a few more minutes,' said Ayscue.

'Actually,' said Naidu, 'I did notice a couple of guards outside, at a respectful distance from the entrance. No doubt they're keeping an eye on anybody who may be keeping an eye, as it were, on the place. Let me ask you,' he went on without perceptible quickening of interest, 'what you take the culprit's motive to be. What has he in mind, would you say?'

Naidu's inquiring glance embraced the Orderly Sergeant, who moved up and joined the group.

'Ah, you get your crackpots in any shower, sir,' he said. 'Pacifists and Communists and vegetarians and the rest of them. We had a brotherly-love king down the depot when I was there. Nasty piece of work he was. He never washed, either. Led us no end of a dance before we got him downgraded psychopathic and discharged him.'

'Is this man who may still favour us with his presence a brotherly-love king?' asked Naidu in the same tone as before. 'I'm merely asking for information, you understand.'

'I think perhaps he is, in a tortuous and tortured sort of way,' said Ayscue. 'And that's what makes it so sad. There's a genuine sympathy and love for humanity working away there somewhere.'

Hunter lit a cigarette. 'How dull,' he said.

'To me it's unmistakable.'

'Ah, they're all the same, sir. Just calling attention to themselves. You know, like children. Showing off. Cutting a dash, like.'

'Why are we all whispering as if we were in church?' asked Hunter. 'Oh well, never mind. I see your batman is in attendance, Willie. Does that mean he's President of the League, do you think, or did you ask him along in case you needed a shoeshine all of a sudden?'

'You decide that for yourself, old boy. As far as I'm concerned it's about as likely that I told Evans to come while I was having a heroin bout as that he could be mixed up in any enterprise that involves reading and writing.'

'A little harsh, I think. And he's reading now. That's a magazine he's got there.'

'You know what I mean.'

Naidu looked at his watch. Ross-Donaldson made the same movement, turned in his walk and came forward to the front of the stage.

'May I have your attention, please?' he said. 'I'd like everybody up here who isn't present either on duty or as an official observer.'

'What are we present as, Willie?'

'Shut up, Max, and sit still.'

After some hesitation and shuffling of feet, five men moved up the aisle and formed into a rough line along the stage. The

Colonel, Venables and Leonard moved in the other direction and took seats in the front row.

'Stand easy, everybody,' said Ross-Donaldson, then continued in his flattest voice, 'Are any of you men connected in any way with the Anti-Death League?'

There was silence, during which a lance-corporal at the end of the line consulted the others by eye. Finally he came to attention.

'No, sir,' he said.

'Stand easy, corporal. I'd like to hear from each of you in turn.'

Ross-Donaldson, hands behind back, walked up and down the line a couple of times and gazed at one man after another. Coming to a halt, he suddenly said,

'You.'

'Sir.'

'Are you connected with the Anti-Death League?'

'No, sir.'

'Or with Human Beings Anonymous?'

'No, sir.'

Pausing at every turn, Ross-Donaldson asked the others the same question. They all answered no. At the end of this there was another and longer pause, and at the end of that Ross-Donaldson, facing the lance-corporal, spoke suddenly again.

'What do you think about death?'

'Death, sir?'

'Yes, death. What do you think about it?'

'I never think about it, sir.'

'Never?'

'No, sir.'

'Right. Next. What do you think about death?'

'It's nothing to do with me, sir.'

'In that case why are you here?'

'No reason in particular, sir. My mate and I thought there might be going to be some kind of show, so we turned up on the off-chance.'

'I see. Next. What do you think about death?'

'It's something we've got to think about, sir. It's a big problem. I've got a few ideas on the subject, nothing very original, I'm afraid. I came along to see whether it was intended to hold some kind of debate on the topic, some sort of profitable exchange of views that might help to clear up the question.'

'But you didn't put up those notices?'

'Oh no, sir. They didn't express my feelings about the matter at all.'

'Right. Next. What do you think about death?'

'It's a terrible thing, sir. Terrible. A scourge, that's what it is. Millions of people every year. And nothing's being done about it. I thought perhaps somebody was starting to at last, sir, so naturally I decided to attend, to hear what the person had in mind. But it looks as if I'm wasting my time, doesn't it, sir?'

'Yes. Next. What do you think about death?'

The next and last man in the line was Evans. He rubbed the side of his face, grinning, before he answered.

'Well, sir,' he said, 'I don't want to strike the wrong note or offend anybody's susceptibilities, but on the whole I'm rather in favour of it, actually. It strikes me there's a lot of people about who could do with a dose of that kind of thing. A notoriously underrated way of solving the world's problems, to my mind. Because, after all, what does it mean? Mere cessation of consciousness, as I understand it. Which most of us could do with anyway. And then there'd be a better kind of life for the rest of us. If any. That was why I joined the Army, as a matter of fact. And they put me on polishing shoes and pressing trousers —no disrespect to you, Major Ayscue, I assure you. Whereas what I was after was killing people, you see.'

Evans started laughing. The other men joined in and stood in more relaxed attitudes. Ross-Donaldson went on walking to and fro.

'Remarkable,' said Naidu to Hunter in a low voice. 'An extraordinary performance. I owe so much of what I am to your country that it ill becomes me even to seem to criticize. But this is a reversion to the primitive, my dear Max. Progress should at least bring it about that one manages not to fall back to the first notions. This amazing show. Thank you for having civilized us in the past; I must now take leave to say I don't understand you any more, however, much as I should like to. Are you ready, Sergeant?'

The Orderly Sergeant got to his feet. At the same moment Ross-Donaldson halted and said, more quietly than before,

'Thank you all very much for answering my questions. You may go now.'

The scene broke up. The guards asked permission to smoke and were granted it. Hunter and Ayscue went forward on to the stage and joined Ross-Donaldson, who stood as if awaiting congratulations for his performance.

'Great fun, Alastair,' said Hunter. 'In a rather limited way.'

'Thank you. I'm satisfied now that we shall hear no more of this matter.'

'Oh, don't say that, I should hate to think you were right.'

Hunter turned to Leonard, who had just come over.

'What do you say, Brian? Has the League packed up, do you think?'

'I wish I did. This is very frightening. The whole situation has changed in the last fifteen minutes.'

'What, because five yobs say they've nothing to do with it and are obviously telling the truth?'

'No. The sinister thing is the non-appearance of whoever put up those notices.'

'I don't follow you.'

'Can I talk to you about it for a moment? Will you excuse us?'

Ayscue and Ross-Donaldson said they would, and Leonard drew Hunter aside.

'Well?'

'Until just now there were two important alternatives as to what was in the mind of ... X. Either the thing was some sort of joke, or there was something behind it. Now I remember you telling me once that there was no hard-and-fast division between jokes and being serious, but in a case like –'

'I was joking when I told you that, dear boy. You shouldn't have taken me seriously.'

'Let's go into that another time, if you don't mind. I was going to say that it made sense to take these two alternatives about X in turn. All right, he's joking, or fooling or whatever you want to call it. He wants to cause a stir. Bother the authorities. Get me and Alastair and the Colonel worried. Well, I heard what you said to Venables earlier on about that. You were right and he was wrong. If it was any conceivable sort of joke X would show up to see how it went over, even if there were fifty armed guards round the place. A man who could turn out all those notices and post them round the camp without being discovered would have the wit to bluff his way through the sort of nothing-to-go-on questioning he'd come up against. But he doesn't turn up. So he isn't joking. Or, if you like, the posting of the notices was an end in itself. In other words they weren't really notices at all. They were copies of a manifesto.'

Behind them, they heard Venables do his talking-without-words laugh. He and the Colonel were making for the door. He stopped laughing long enough to say to them,

'You see? A fiasco. The case of the absent pranksters.'

Then he went on laughing and followed the Colonel. Ross-Donaldson and Ayscue were also on the move. Hunter and Leonard went back down the aisle. Leonard turned off the lights. Outdoors again, the two headed back towards the Mess.

'Well, you see where we've got to if I'm right,' pursued Leonard. 'X is making a protest. A protest about what? About the infliction of death on the innocent.'

'I thought it was the infliction of death on anybody that was getting him into a state.'

'All right, on anybody, then. And this is a military unit that exists for combatant purposes, i.e. the infliction of death.'

'Not only that, Brian. The infliction of lots and lots of lovely death. The unusually efficient infliction thereof.'

'You're not shaking me. I don't see why you or anyone else not in the secret shouldn't have got that far. Yes. Correct. So we're dealing with someone who knows what Operation Apollo's about and has become distressed enough at that knowledge to protest in a very eccentric way. Now can you see why I'm frightened?'

'You're wondering what he's going to do next.'

'Wondering pretty hard, yes. If he runs loose with some of the equipment we've got here I can't forsee the consequences. Or rather I can.'

'There's none missing, is there?'

'Not yet,' said Leonard.

'But that wouldn't fit in, would it, if he's against death? He'd be more likely to try to destroy it.'

'That's another danger. But we don't know what he'll do. We can't assume he'll stay logical. If he does, his classic course would be to let the enemy know what he knows. Which gives me the equivalent of two spies to take care of instead of one.'

'Mm. I suppose X can't be your original spy. Calling attention to himself like this. He couldn't be sure you wouldn't trace the typewriter he did the notice on.'

'Not quite.' Leonard looked gloomy. 'I've established three facts. It isn't any of the machines officially in the camp. There are scores of thousands of this particular kind in the country. And none was sold to a stranger by any of the shops in the town over the relevant period. X must have gone farther afield. I can't see myself ever finding out any more that way.'

'Really?'

They walked into the cobbled hall of the Mess. The Colonel's voice was audible from the ante-room, calling for drink.

'Would you like to come up to my room for a bit?' said Leonard. 'There's some time to go before dinner.'

'Fine, yes.'

Deering was in Leonard's room, standing by the window smoking. He glanced over his shoulder casually as the door opened, then came to what he seemed to think was attention at the sight of Hunter.

'Evening, sir.'

'Good evening, Deering. I shan't be wanting you now.'

'I just came along on the off-chance you might need me for something.'

'Thank you, but as I said there isn't anything.'

'Okay, then. Anybody turn up at that meeting?'

'Nobody to speak of, no.'

'Bloody fool.'

'Who are you talking about, Deering?'

'Fellow who wrote that perishing notice. Barmy. Off his rocker. Round the bend on a one-way ticket. By the way, nobody was talking about the business round the place. It took me all my time finding anyone who's even heard about it.'

'I see. That's all, Deering, thank you.'

'Good night, sir.'

Hunter had been examining Leonard's picture of the five antique Sailors. When the door was closing behind Deering he turned round and smiled.

'I rather like the look of these chaps. Where did you get hold of it?'

'They are quite fun, aren't they? Oh, I got to know a few of the Sailors at their Mess and they more or less insisted I borrowed it.'

'Nice of them to be so free with their regimental relics. I say, Brian, what a horrid little man that batman of yours is.'

'I don't care for him much either, but he's very useful for letting me know about camp rumours and so on.'

'How disagreeable. I hope there aren't any rumours about me.'

'If I ever heard anything to your discredit it would go no further, and I should tell Deering that there was no truth in it.'

'You do what you can, don't you, Brian?'

Hunter sat down in a chintz-covered armchair and Leonard on a leather hard chair.

'I was a bit puzzled,' said Hunter, 'at what you said about the typewriter business being a blind alley. Aren't you going to search the camp?'

'I shall have to eventually, but it won't do any good. X isn't the kind of man to leave evidence like that under his bed. The likeliest place, I would say, would be in a plastic bag under a bush somewhere. No fingerprints. There are lots of other things I shan't be able to avoid doing if the worst comes to the worst, like getting hold of every typewriter salesman within a hundred miles and putting the whole unit on an identity parade. That's a desperate measure, though.'

'It sounds like it, certainly. Have you anything else to go on?'

'I'm still trying to sort it out in my mind. As I see it, the most disturbing thing is that X must be one of the si officers. Nobody in the mental condition we've been talking about is going to be fit to carry out his part in Operation Apollo.'

'How damaging would that be?'

'I can't answer that, but it would be damaging. I'll have to start going over each of their files again to see if I can turn up some hint of instability. It's hardly possible I'll find anything after the screening they all went through in the first place. I'll have to watch them all, too, and hope to spot something that way. Do you think it could be Churchill?'

Hunter made a wincing sound. 'Why him?'

'He was looking very odd when I ran into him this morning. Sort of jittery. I've always thought he was a sensitive sort of lad.'

'I haven't seen him all day. Look, I know him pretty well. Would you like me to talk to him? I won't give anything away, I promise.'

'I'd be glad if you would, Max. And if you notice anything that might be relevant to this X business do let me know. I need help, and I know I can rely on you. I'm very grateful to you for putting me on to Dr Best.'

'Think nothing of it. How's that going, by the way?'

'Slow but sure. I hope. I still need a piece of solid evidence, but I'm convinced he's my man. He's ... I just know he is. He must have a contact in the camp somewhere, but for the time being I'm concentrating on him, Best. I'm expecting results in the next day or two.'

'Good. Brian, going back a bit, why are you so sure that X wasn't in the reading room this evening?'

'Because the only si officer present was Venables, and he's lived with Operation Apollo longer than anybody. In a sense it was his idea. I can't see him changing his mind about it now.'

'Or about anything. No, I see. There's one other point occurs to me, if you don't mind my ...'

'Go ahead. This is good for me. I don't get enough constructive criticism.'

'I only wondered. If Best has got a contact in the camp, as you say, wouldn't it have been possible for him to have written those notices and had them smuggled in and posted round the place?'

'No. That's to say he couldn't have written the notices.'

'Why not?'

'He's not against death, you see. Shall we go down to dinner now?'

*

Lucy tapped quietly at the door of Catharine's bedroom.

Churchill's voice called, 'Come in.'

He was sitting up in bed reading a paperback novel. Catharine was asleep.

'James, are you all right?'

'Yes, of course. Why?'

'You looked sort of startled. James, your nice friend Max Hunter is here. He says he'd like to talk to you. He was terrifically emphatic that it was nothing urgent and could perfectly well keep till the morning, but since he was here he just thought he might as well pass the word.'

Churchill got out of bed, put on a dressing-gown and slippers and followed Lucy out. She led him into her bedroom.

'Is she all right?' she asked.

'Yes. I made her take a sleeping-pill.'

'Have you taken one?'

'No, I don't like them. Where can I find Max?'

'I'm afraid I've put him in the library. It's rather nasty in there, but there are two almost possible chairs, and at least you won't have my dentist friend and his friends breathing down your neck. They seem to be very thick on the ground tonight for some reason.'

'Anybody I know, apart from Max?'

'There's your other nice friend, Captain Leonard. Brian, I mean. He won't go. He sort of keeps getting on the end of the queue again. Then I was half expecting Alastair, but it's getting a bit late for him now. Those are the only ones you know, I think. We may as well go down.'

They left the bedroom and moved along the passage.

'In fact,' Lucy went on, 'there are two of them in the drawing-room I don't know myself. They're somebody's friends, I gather. It's funny how the hot weather seems to bring them out.'

As they started descending the stairs, Churchill's eye was caught by the figure of the girl on the tapestry that hung there. There was something unnatural in its posture, a stiffness he had not noticed before. He saw too that parts of its dress were slightly discoloured, presumably by damp.

'Oh well, I suppose I'd better get ready for Brian,' said Lucy. 'His turn seems to come round quicker and quicker. You know, I wish he wouldn't go on so. I mean talking. But you can't help liking him, can you?'

'No. Thanks, Lucy. May see you later.'

'Now mind you don't sit up chatting all night.'

Until this evening Churchill had only seen the library by day. Most of it was in semi-darkness now, so that the books filling its walls looked even more unreadable. They had been crammed on the shelves anyhow, some in horizontal piles, others with their spines facing inwards. Among their bindings an antiquated dull red was most prominent. They gave off a strong whiff of other people's boredom. Here and there, mostly on the floor, were busts of varying sizes. Churchill had looked them over one afternoon and had come to the conclusion that, whatever connexion with literature any given one of the men represented might or might not have had, all of them were certainly dead.

An intense light, given as it proved by a bare bulb in a brass lamp, came from a shallow alcove in one corner of the room. Here Hunter was sitting by a bulky davenport in an attitude suggesting that he had that moment turned aside from some mighty creative task. Nothing else gave this impression. Apart from the lamp, the objects before him consisted only of a foot-high doll in tattered clothes that had a national or peasant air, a French sailor in mouldering papier-mâché under a glass dome, most of an ormolu clock, and a glass of liquor. He waved Churchill to a dining chair with burst seat-padding like the one on which he sat.

'Make yourself at home if you can,' he said. 'This may help.'

He handed over the glass, which contained a very strong whisky and water. Churchill drank a third of it in one.

'How long have you been sitting here?'

'Not more than twenty minutes. I haven't been idle, however. I've been pushing ahead with my smoking like billy-ho. Two Gauloises one after the other, just like that. Have one.'

'Thank you. I'm sorry I kept you waiting.'

'I expect Lucy did most of that. She's got a heavy back-log to work through tonight. So heavy I had to come out. A discussion on the shortcomings of Britain's youth seemed to be getting under way. Not that it's very nice in here, I must admit. Erudition in the raw.'

'Has Lucy worked through you yet?'

'Oh yes, I'm no problem. But it seemed rather early to be off home, so I thought if you weren't asleep I might get hold of you for a few minutes' chatter.'

Churchill drank again. 'I'm glad you did. Well, what's the news?'

'Nothing out of the way. The Anti-Death League held its inaugural meeting and nobody turned up. At least, quite a few people turned up, but none of them seemed to want to join the League. And the founder, or X, or whatever one's supposed to call him, didn't surface either. What we got was a series of anti-climaxes, good in themselves but not at all encouraging. I felt very let down, I can tell you. Poor old Brian Leonard felt a good deal worse than that. He brought all his phylactological expertise to bear and came up with the conclusion that X isn't the spy he's been after all these weeks, but another chap altogether. I couldn't follow half of it. Still, I do remember him saying he thought X must be half off his rocker and might do anything at any time, which was awfully frightening, he thought. I didn't think so. It cheered me up no end, after the way the meeting flopped. Then it crossed Brian's mind that you might be X.'

Churchill started violently. 'Why me?'

'It was all complicated in the extreme, as I said. He was pretty well convinced, evidently, that X must be one of the s1 people. The way he saw it, X has been sent all dithery by the notion of having to knock off so many chaps in Operation Apollo, and this League business is his method of dithering about it in public, so to speak. A bit fanciful, perhaps, but you know these technical wizards. Nowadays they take the whole human mind and heart as their special field.'

'I see why Brian thinks X is likely to be in s1, but not why he thinks it's me in particular. Why does he?'

'Well ...' Hunter made a quick but awkward gesture with his hand. 'Old Brian is a divine creature, but not greatly gifted in ordinary observation. He ran into you this morning, he said, and thought you looked odd in some way. Jittery was the word he used. I decided you must have had a hangover, but I didn't like to tell him that. He's such an idealist, isn't he?'

'Yes,' said Churchill, finishing his whisky. 'But whatever he is he wasn't far off the mark this time. I did feel jittery. I still do.'

'Do you want to tell me about it?'

'Yes.'

'You shall. But not without an essential preliminary. Give me that glass. No, on second thoughts there's a more intelligent way. I'll be back in a minute.'

The moment he was alone, Churchill got up and walked up and down the floor of the library, looking about for some object on which to fasten his attention. He had not yet found one when Hunter reappeared, carrying with some ingenuity but some strain a nearly full bottle of whisky, a milk-jug containing water, a pudding-basin with ice-cubes and a soup-spoon in it, and an empty glass. He set these down on the davenport, wincing a little with effort and concentration, and swiftly mixed two drinks.

'There,' he said. 'The securing of supplies is the first object of the administrative services.'

'Why are you drinking too?'

'I just fancied one. No, it's really that I've been getting less and less out of watching other people drinking. And quite right too. Voyeurism is damaging to self-respect. What's bothering you?'

'Is that why you wanted to talk to me, so that you could ask me that?'

'Oh, no. Not altogether by any means. I've had what for me has been an unusually successful and varied sexual day, and that sort of thing always tends to loosen my tongue. Plus the lack of anything approaching ordinary humanity in the drawing-room, apart from Brian, and I've had plenty of him this evening already.'

'I see. Anyway, I'm glad you asked me. To start with, I'm not X.'

'No.'

'But I see his point so clearly that I might easily have been him if I'd thought of it. I used not to be particularly against death, especially not for people who were trying to kill me or who'd got to the point of being able to kill lots of my friends and fellow-countrymen unless they were stopped. So when I was picked for Operation Apollo originally I didn't object. Rather the opposite if anything, because in this case the people who were going to be stopped really needed very much to be stopped. Then, after we'd had the geographical and strategical picture filled in for us, we were told how it was proposed to stop these people. That part of it worried me a bit, and I started drinking more than I usually do. At that stage what I didn't like was this method they've been explaining to us and training us in for stopping the enemy. It isn't so much a new method as a new twist on an old one. The point of it is the way it kills people. I can't go into it, but you can take it from me that it's objectionable. I still wouldn't have backed out of Apollo, though, even if I'd been able to (which wouldn't have been particularly easy), because it somehow didn't matter much that I was going to do something I objected to, because I didn't matter much.

'Then I met Catharine and it started to matter very much what I did and what I didn't do. I started to matter. So it got harder to go on agreeing to take part in Apollo. It wouldn't have been so bad if I'd been able to discuss the whole business with some of the other chaps who're being trained. But it turned out that was no good. They all said of course they agreed it was a terrible thing we were being got ready to do, but it was necessary and it was orders. I thought at first they said that because they were stupid or unfeeling or both. Then I realized there was no way of knowing whether they meant what they said or not, because we were talking about death, you see. As soon as you get on to that, people stop coming clean about what they feel, even if they're the sort of people who wouldn't hesitate to tell you all you wanted to know about their sex life and so on. So there was no help that way.

'Then something else happened. Catharine has a lump in her left breast which may turn out to be cancer. I've been so frightened about that I've hardly known what to do. And I don't know how frightened she is because she doesn't say and I can't ask her. Until this came up I knew her better than anyone in the world. I knew everything she was thinking. Now I don't any more. Because death has come up. I've been thinking about this. It hasn't been as difficult as you might imagine. The alternative of thinking about it is to panic, and I can't do that.

'At first I just got angry at the way good things are vulnerable to bad things, but bad things aren't vulnerable to good. You know: all the way up from toothache being more powerful than an orgasm. But I soon moved beyond that. I decided I was slightly more frightened than I had reason to be, while there was still nothing definite about Catharine's condition. I felt as if I knew she was going to turn out to have cancer and would die of it. That didn't take long to disentangle, either. I'd had the dispatch-rider and Fawkes at the back of my mind. So I was being superstitious, and having worked that out I could go back to feeling very shocked and concerned and apprehensive instead of full of dread. But I didn't. I worked on that. You don't have to believe in God or fate or the hidden powers of the mind to believe that there are such things as runs of bad luck. Well, I found that bad luck didn't quite cover what I felt was happening, and not altogether because it's a rather pale sort of phrase for the occasion. Something out of the tactical mumbo-jumbo they keep throwing at us fitted the situation better, I thought. You've probably heard of these things they call lethal nodes. You don't have battles or fronts any more, you have small key areas it's death to enter. Well, we're in a lethal node now, only it's one that works in time instead of space. A bit of life it's death to enter. The beginning, the edge of the node was when that motor-cycle thing happened. Fawkes was further in. This looks like being near the centre. We'll know it's passing over when somebody else goes, somebody we know as little as we knew that dispatch-rider. That'll be the farther edge. I know all this sounds a bit mad. I'm sorry.

'The background to the whole business is Operation Apollo. That's like the theatre of war in which this is one operation. Well, what am I going to do about it? Now that I know more about death than I used to, you'd think I'd have to make up my mind that it's something nobody could deserve, however it was administered. That would mean having to opt out of the Operation, and that would mean all sorts of stuff, up to and including court martial and imprisonment and perhaps being quietly knocked off by Brian Leonard's friends for knowing too much to be allowed to turn pacifist. I think I could take most of that if I had to. But I don't suppose I'll bother to go that far. I'll probably just follow the line of least resistance. If Catharine's going to die it'll never matter again what I do.'

'When will you know about her?'

'The day after tomorrow. They're doing a probe on her in the morning and then it'll take them twenty-four hours to run tests on what they find. It sounds as though time has become tremendously important. Especially since they told us yesterday that Apollo's been brought forward two weeks. You'd think that would really shake us all up, wouldn't you? It would have me, in any other conceivable similar situation. But it hasn't at all. In comparison. It's always the comparison that counts. Like, you know, unless you pay a debt by the end of the week you go to prison. Very bad. Only today your son had a road accident. You see, Max, I'd desert now if I could stay with her, but they wouldn't let me.'

Hunter gave out cigarettes and refilled both glasses.

'I understand what you mean about lethal nodes,' he said when he was sitting down again, 'though I don't say I agree with it. Where I can't follow you is on this point about Apollo being the background to it. I don't think there's an analogy there. You may feel there's a connexion, you may have had your attention drawn to death in the first place by way of Apollo, but that's different. What is obvious is that part of your feeling jittery comes from it. Not a very large part, perhaps, but at least

195

you can do something about it straight away. The rest of it has got to wait for thirty-six hours or so.'

'What do you suggest I do about Apollo?'

'It's nothing to do with Catharine or Fawkes or the dispatch-rider. It's detachable, so detach it. Tell me about it.'

'Why? What good would that do?'

'There's no guarantee, of course, but I might be able to help you to feel better about some of it, less guilty and so on. It's worth a try.'

'I can't do it. I promised not to tell anybody.'

'Break your promise. If you can seriously go on about deserting and being court-martialled and the rest of it, you've got beyond that sort of promise. I shan't tell anybody else. You trust me, don't you?'

'Yes.' Churchill swallowed whisky. 'But supposing I told you and then found it didn't help?'

'Then you're no worse off, are you?'

'A lot of lives are involved.'

'That makes it particularly important for me to keep my mouth shut, but I was going to do that anyway. You don't think I'm a spy, do you?'

'No.'

'Then tell me.'

Churchill told him.

*

By first light on the morning of Exercise Nabob a cordon of troops was in position along the perimeter of an area in the hills amounting to something over two square miles. Official signs diverting all civilian traffic had been set up on the relevant roads the previous evening. At 0800 hours a convoy of vehicles made its way out of the camp and headed for the cordoned area. It included two lorry-loads of infantry in full battle-order and two armoured carriers containing machine-gun crews and their weapons. An RAF helicopter flew at fifty feet above the head of the column while another shuttled back and forth along the route. A sweep programme had been arranged for the duration of the exercise to ensure continuous observation of the ground.

On arrival at the assembly point, the machine-guns were unloaded and set up on tripods so as to command the main approaches. The infantrymen took up defensive positions round the rim of the slight depression in which the exercise proper was to take place.

'I trust you've remembered to order the light cruiser squadron to prepare to receive cavalry, Brian,' said Hunter.

'It's all very well for you to laugh,' said Leonard, doing so himself. He was in unusually high spirits, as if feeling that this was his day. 'I can assure you that none of this is unnecessary.'

'Do you really think there's the slightest possibility of armed attack? Attack by whom, anyway? Perhaps war was declared while we were on our way up here.'

'I'd know about it if it had been. No, any form of physical intervention is in the highest degree unlikely – as things are. This show of preparedness has done a good deal to make it so.'

'You mean unless we'd rendered ourselves capable of delivering a million rounds a minute at any intruder we'd have had a Red Chinese parachute company on our necks? I think I see.'

'Stranger things have happened.'

'Very few. What precautions have you taken against high-altitude photography? It's a good day for it.'

They looked up into the cloudless, deep blue sky. One of the helicopters was rattling along almost overhead with its curious not-quite-head-foremost aerial gait. The two men were standing at the corner of a rough square of level grass where the transport had been parked. Nearby, the main stores vehicle was being unloaded under the supervision of Ross-Donaldson and a sergeant-major. A number of long narrow wooden boxes, about five feet by nine inches by six inches, were being carefully handed down from the interior of the truck and piled side by side on the turf. Now and then Hunter glanced interestedly over at this proceeding.

Leonard was saying something about conditions actually being unfavourable to air observation of the secret material and activity about to be exposed. These were on too small a scale physically, he explained, to be meaningful if photographed at normal spy-plane height with even the most mature apparatus known to be available. To fly at the comparatively low altitude demanded, in the present absence of cloud-cover, would be to approach maximal risk-potential. The equations and curves prepared in advance at the direction of Leonard's masters, which seemed to have taken into account a meteorological spectrum ranging from the existing bright sunshine to unforeseen solar eclipse, gave the probability of unauthorized penetration of the air-space above Exercise Nabob as approximately two centicents, or 0.02 of 1 per cent. These two chances in ten thousand were being taken care of by a system of coastal watch and patrol which Leonard did not see fit to go into at the present time.

By the end of his exposition three more officers had approached. They were Major Venables and two taciturn captains called O'Neill and Isaacs who had arrived at the unit two days previously. The pair had spent most of the intervening period in the Exercise area accompanied by a large working-party.

'Are you happy, Leonard?' asked Venables. 'I use the ridiculous but serviceable locution. Your emotional welfare is no concern of mine.'

'I understand, sir. Yes, my preparations are complete. I suggest you conduct your preliminaries now and go ahead in your own time with final briefing.'

'I can find no objection to that.'

'How long will you need?'

Venables looked at O'Neill, who said, 'Fifteen minutes should do it.'

'See to it, then,' said Venables.

O'Neill and his companion moved off towards the stores vehicle.

'Would anybody mind if I watched this part, Brian?' asked Hunter.

Leonard hesitated. 'No,' he said finally. 'Mere acquaintance with externals isn't inappropriate for an officer of your Security rating.... That's if you approve, sir.'

'Who, I?' Venables seemed astonished. 'I have no grounds for disapproval. Hunter may do as he pleases, short of inconveniencing me.'

'Okay, then, Max. See you later.'

The two captains had already begun their preliminaries when Hunter reached them. A party under a sergeant was carrying the boxes from their stack by the lorry over to a small but substantial earth and concrete bunker built during the past couple of days. It lay just short of the crest of a minor slope. From it, Hunter found he had an unimpeded view of half a mile or more across the floor of the valley. He caught a wink of metal up near the skyline as somebody in the defence detachment shifted his position. From near at hand he heard a fluctuating roar and a grinding of tracks from the small obsolete-looking tank that had come from a nearby armoured training unit to join the convoy earlier that morning, incidentally imposing a twenty-minute delay in starting. Now the tank began to move slowly away round the inner edge of the depression.

With a certain amount of ceremony, the locking bolts on one of the boxes were pulled aside and the lid raised. Inside, resting between padded clips, lay an object roughly resembling an elongated golf-bag in webbing with brass studs. At this point Isaacs stepped forward, opened this container and drew out a rifle with an unusually extended barrel, a conical projection at the muzzle, a small bipod forward of the point of balance and a drum-type magazine to the right of the breech. He laid the weapon down on one of several piles of sacking arranged along the parapet of the bunker. Meanwhile another box had been opened under the direction of O'Neill, and within a couple of minutes five rifles of the type described were lying on the parapet.

'Ammunition,' said O'Neill sharply.

Isaacs moved to a metal box with a double stripe of red and yellow round it. He tore off the Ministry of Defence seal on its fastening and opened it, revealing a row of elongated cartridges with red-painted cases. Inside the lid was printed in red, *Danger – Atomics – Arm by pressing base and giving half-turn to right – Not to be disturbed except on the orders of an officer*. While O'Neill watched, Isaacs took five rounds out of the box and carefully laid one down beside each of the rifles.

Just then Hunter caught sight of Churchill standing with a couple of other officers by the line of vehicles. He walked over and Churchill came forward to meet him.

'Quite a show they've evidently got lined up for us,' said Churchill. His eyes were half closed, as if the sunlight were too strong for them.

'I'm surprised they haven't brought Willie Ayscue along to bless the proceedings. Are you actually going to fire one of those things?'

'I may and I may not. We're going to sort of draw lots for it.'

'Why isn't everybody taking a turn?'

'I don't know. It could easily be a benign growth, not cancer at all. I hope it is. I wish I hadn't let her talk me out of being with her this morning. I should have insisted.' Churchill spoke flatly.

'Why did she talk you out of it?'

'I don't know. I think it's just part of the way everybody's tacitly agreed to behave as if there's nothing much at stake. But I don't know.'

'I see. When will you hear what they've found?'

'Any moment now. Lucy's going to telephone to the Command Post and they'll get on to Brian over the radio link. He set up the whole thing.'

'I see. I hope –'

'Assemble for briefing, please,' said Venables's amplified voice on a loud-hailer. 'All s1 officers to the firing-point for briefing.'

'That's me,' said Churchill. 'Max, if the message comes through while I'm down there would you take it? I've arranged it with Brian. They'll say they're calling Blacksmith, which is my code-name, and then they'll just say "Good news" or "Bad news".'

'I'll do that, of course.'

'Thanks. I'd like you to be the one to tell me. But of course it might not come until they've finished briefing. I'll go over to Brian's car as soon as they have. See you.'

Churchill went off after his companions. Colonel White got out of his car, where he had been sitting reading what looked like some learned journal ever since arriving at the assembly point, and limped off briskly in the same direction. Ross-Donaldson appeared and joined him. Hunter returned to where he had left Leonard, who at that moment ran the few yards to his car, got in and slammed the door. The window was open, however, and Hunter arrived in time to hear him say excitedly,

'Padlock here. Over.'

'Man in civilian clothes sighted approaching south-east corner,' said a voice over the loudspeaker. 'I've got the glasses on him but I can't tell whether it's Optimus or not. Could be. He's coming slow and cautious, trying to keep concealed as much as possible. No doubt about it, he's seen us and reckons we haven't seen him. Over.'

'You keep it that way,' said Leonard, picking up a map-case and a chinagraph pencil. 'Give map-reference of his present location and estimate his general direction. Over.'

Letters and figures followed. Leonard marked a cross in red on the talc over his map and an arrow pointing north-west. Then he studied the map for a moment and said,

'He seems to be making for that re-entrant or gully that runs into the ridge about eighty yards north-east of you. Do you agree? Over.'

'Could be, sir. Yes, there's fairish cover for him most of the way there and the gully itself's pretty well wooded. Yes, he's moving that way now. Oh, and I'm pretty sure it is Optimus. Over.'

'Good, splendid. Right, sergeant-major. Instruct your men on both sides of the gully to move away from it when the man approaches. Gradually, mind. Nothing obvious. Check back to me when you've done that. Over.'

'Roger, Padlock. Out.'

Leonard looked up, sweat glittering among the thin hair on the top of his head. 'Looks as if we've got him,' he said.

'Optimus equals Best.' Hunter too seemed excited. 'What a scholar you are, Brian. How do your fellows know what he looks like? Did you send them all on a tour of the hospital?'

'I had him photographed. Without his knowing it, of course.'

'Marvellous. And what's in store for him now?'

'When he's through the cordon I shall let him find his way along here. The defence detachments have orders to show themselves as much as possible. Then, as soon as I find out what route he's taking, I'll get them to withdraw laterally, like the cordon just now, and presumably he'll arrive somewhere up there' – Leonard gestured at the skyline with his head – 'and start taking photographs.'

'And then you grab him.'

'No, we want him to pass on the stuff so that we can grab the people on his line of communication as well. I'm putting him under continuous surveillance. He'll be allowed to leave the area in the same way as he entered it. With one of my men in close attendance.'

Hunter shook his head admiringly, 'Very neat. And frightfully energetic. All this show just put on for Best's benefit.'

'It's not just for his benefit at all,' said Leonard emphatically. 'I don't know what gave you that idea. It's a vitally important piece of training.'

'Oh, of course. I was really only thinking what an efficient spy-trap it is.'

'Actually,' and here Leonard's voice grew as confidential as it ever did, 'it isn't really training in the strict sense. More of a demonstration. These fellows all know their business backwards. But it's felt that seeing this thing in action will be psychologically beneficial. It'll make them believe in it, give them confidence, stop them thinking exclusively in terms of theory.'

'Good idea.'

The loudspeaker came to life. 'Hallo, Padlock. Are you receiving me? Over.'

'Padlock listening. Over.'

'Civilian now approaching mouth of gully. Definitely identifiable as Optimus. Men on both sides of gully moving off as ordered. Over.'

Hunter did not wait to hear Leonard's reply. He strolled over towards the bunker, where the briefing was evidently about to begin. His expression was puzzled.

'This is Captain O'Neill,' said Venables without preamble. 'You may have met him. He will tell you what it is necessary for you to know about this device.'

With that, Venables sat down on the grass. O'Neill came forward holding one of the rifles by the stock.

'This, gentlemen, is the N H W-17,' he said. 'Now I know you're all fully trained in the tactical handling of nuclear hand-weapons, their mode of operation, special problems of supply and so on. But you'll forgive me if I just run over a few salient points. The first thing to remember is that this is an ordinary rifle that uses extraordinary ammunition, and that even the ammunition's ordinary enough until it arrives at its target. You'll see that it resembles an ordinary rather old-fashioned Service rifle with a few luxuries thrown in: bipod for greater steadiness, lengthened barrel for increased accuracy, flash eliminator for concealment. Ordinary magazine and bolt action.' He demonstrated this. 'You'll get a chance to practise that later on, using dummy rounds. Now as to the serious ammunition, the punch is .085 T, which as you know is jargon for eighty-five thousandths of a metric ton of TNT, or simply eighty-five kilograms. Nothing very much, you may say. Certainly it's a mere teaspoonful compared with what some of the NTWS can deliver. The purpose of this weapon, though, involves not the size of the punch but the rapidity and selectivity with which it can be delivered. A platoon equipped with the NHW-17 combines the mobility and ground-covering capacity of an infantryman with the fire-power of something like three field batteries of artillery. Ideal for a war of movement over difficult terrain.

'The other technical consideration is that of fall-out. This in my hand is a very clean bullet indeed, to a revolutionary degree, in fact. We'll be taking all precautions today, of course, but you can rest assured that residual radioactivity is negligible. If it weren't for the heat factor, which I'll go into in a minute, ground cleared by the NHW-17 could be occupied virtually at once. There are special circumstances, however, in which the use of an altogether different type of bullet will be advantageous. For obvious reasons we shan't be firing this type today, here in the middle of the English countryside. But consider the case of an enemy centre of population within reach of airborne approach. You can see the implications there.'

At this point, Hunter heard Leonard calling his name from where he had left him. He turned at once and hurried to the car.

'Blacksmith,' said Leonard.

'Have they passed the message yet?'

'I'll tell them to now.'

Leonard said into his hand-microphone, 'Hullo, Control. Pass your message. Over.'

'Hullo, Padlock,' said a voice Hunter recognized as that of one of the regular Command Post operators. 'Message begins. Bad news. I say again, bad news. Message ends. Over.'

'Thank you, Control. Message received and understood. Out.'

Beyond the frying noise from the loudspeaker Hunter could hear O'Neill going on with his briefing, but too far off for words to be distinguishable. Then the clatter of a helicopter passing above the firing-point cut out all other sound. Hunter and Leonard looked away from each other as they waited for it to recede. It had become a faint murmur before either spoke.

'What a terrible thing,' said Leonard at last. 'That poor girl. And James not able to be with her.'

'I know. It's an unpleasant situation.'

'Of course, there is a lot they can do these days. You've got quite a good chance if you catch it early on like this.'

'Yes, there is that.'

'When are you going to tell him?'

'I'll wait till I see a moment.'

'I don't envy you, Max, having to do that. What on earth is there to say in this sort of situation? One feels so helpless.'

'One does indeed.'

'Hullo, Padlock,' came from the loudspeaker. 'Charlie here. Over.'

'Padlock listening. Over.'

'Optimus now inside cordon, still proceeding roughly north-west. He'll be out of sight in a minute or two. Any further instructions? Over.'

'No, that's fine. Keep him under observation as long as you can. Report his position when you finally lose contact. You can give your men a breather now. You've all done extremely well. Over.'

'Roger. Thank you, sir. Out.'

'Hullo, Fox. Hullo, Fox. Have you understood Charlie's information? Over.'

'Hullo, Padlock. Yes, Charlie's information received and understood. Over.'

'Very good. Keep strict watch for approach of Optimus and report as soon as sighted. Over.'

'Roger. Out.'

During this, Hunter had been leaning against the door-post of the vehicle drinking from his water-container, which did not contain only water. He picked out Churchill from the group of s 1 officers sitting in a semicircle on the grass by the bunker, and stared at the back of his neck for some time. Then he settled down in a comfortable hollow in the ground a few yards away and took a paperback novel from his haversack. He had difficulty in finding his place in this and in remembering the main trend of the plot. Finally he started again at the beginning, but after a few minutes put the book aside and picked up his water-container. He sat in the hollow slowly drinking this down and smoking while O'Neill talked on and Leonard kept quiet in his car.

Eventually the briefing ended and Isaacs went through some weapon drill with one of the rifles. Hunter took some of this in, but soon began to feel drowsy. He had not time to fall asleep, however, when the group at the bunker began to break up. He got to his feet.

Churchill saw him at once and the two hurried towards each other.

'It's come, has it?'

'Yes,' said Hunter. 'Bad news.'

Churchill's mouth opened a little and closed again. 'I see.'

'Would you like a drink?'

'Yes.'

He took the container from Hunter and drank what was there.

'Thanks.'

'What are you going to do now?'

'I'm going to see the Colonel and ask for a short pass on compassionate grounds. I told him a bit about this yesterday. Will you drive me to Lucy's?'

'Of course.'

'I'll see you at your jeep in a few minutes.'

As Hunter moved away, Leonard turned in the seat of his car and caught his eye.

'How's he taking it?'

'I don't know,' said Hunter. 'I can't tell.'

'I'm sure he's a good brave lad. It'll bring out the best in him.'

'I expect so. I hope it brings out the best in her too.'

'Hullo, Padlock. Fox calling. No sign of Optimus. I say again, no sign of Optimus. Over.'

'Hullo, Fox,' said Leonard into his microphone. 'Roger. Out.'

He looked up, knuckling the sweat off his dark upper lip. His earlier animation had departed.

'I can't think where he's got to,' he said accusingly. 'Has he stopped for a kip or what? The defence detachment ought to have spotted him fifteen or twenty minutes ago.'

'Don't worry, he'll turn up. I'll see you later.'

'Hullo, George,' Leonard was saying as Hunter left him.

'I'm sorry I've been so long, Max,' said Churchill when he appeared. 'I had to clear this with Venables as well. I've got until oh-nine-hundred hours tomorrow.'

'Good.'

Hunter reversed his jeep out of the line of vehicles and they moved slowly down the rough track up which the convoy had crawled a couple of hours earlier. At first the soil was covered only in thin grass, with outcroppings of grey rock here and there, but presently ferns and low bushes appeared, and by the time they had joined a metalled road, a single carriageway with passing places, they were in wooded country. The greens of the foliage were very brilliant and the undergrowth dense for England. At one point a small stream ran down among rocks. Churchill looked out of the window at it and said,

'I knew this was going to happen.'

'No you didn't, James. You thought it might happen and now it has. It's nothing to do with anything else that's happened. The fact that you know about some things can't cause other things to happen. Don't make patterns out of coincidences. All pattern-making is bad.'

'The other night you said you agreed with me. About the node.'

'I said I saw what you meant. I didn't want to argue with

you then. I don't now, either. I just think that reading significances into things makes them worse, not better.'

'I'd sooner do that than concentrate on ... And I'm not creating a pattern, I'm recognizing the pattern that's been there all along. The overall pattern. It's an evil one. It's got death in it, you see.'

'You mustn't talk like that. The whole thing is totally random. All chance. Nothing and nobody behind it or in it or anywhere at all.'

'I know there's nobody there. But there are such things as patterns, even when we know nobody willed them. Runs of bad luck, as I said. And a system that runs itself is still a system. You don't have to believe in a weather god to find a climate unbearable.'

'Your job is to find a way of making this bearable. Never mind about whether it ought to be bearable.'

'Yes, I'm going to try. I don't want to talk any more now.'

When they arrived, Lucy came out of the drawing-room and kissed them both. She had been crying.

'How is she?' asked Churchill.

'She's taking it very well. At least I think she is. She hasn't said anything. She's lying down at the moment.'

'Right. Thanks for the lift, Max.'

When Churchill had gone, Lucy said, 'Come and have a drink.'

'Thank you, I do rather fancy one.'

They sat down side by side on a couch in the drawing-room. Hunter had never seen the place before when it was not littered with bottles of gin, bottles of tonic, bowls of melting ice and overflowing ashtrays. With the sunlight slanting in and the furniture in slightly unfamiliar positions, the room looked as if it had turned over a new leaf. In view of what had happened, perhaps this might turn out to be so.

'How bad is the news? Are there any details?'

'It's cancer.' Lucy spoke more hoarsely than usual. 'That's as much as they say they know. She's to go in tomorrow to be operated on and to have treatment.'

'Good. They're getting on with it, then.'

'Max, what causes these things?'

'Nobody knows. There are plenty of theories.'

'Can it be caused by what happens to you? You know, the kind of life you have?'

'That's probably one of the theories.'

'She told me last night she thought it might be, if she turned out to have it, perhaps it was because of her life before she met James, and he came along just too late. Wouldn't that be awful?'

Her eyes filled with tears. Hunter put his arm round her.

'No more awful that what we know has happened,' he said.

'Why did it have to happen to her?'

'It happens to bad people too. It's pure luck of the draw, love.'

'What sort of chance do you think she's got?'

'Oh, pretty good, I should say, where she's got it. They can ...'

'Yes. Can you stay to lunch?'

'I'd like to, but I'll have to go back to this absurd exercise they're having. It'll be finished by this evening. I'll come over then if I can.'

'Do try. Nobody else is coming.'

They had another drink, in almost total silence, and then Hunter said he must go. With Lucy's permission he refilled most of his water-container from a nearby bottle and topped it up with a little water. He was going to turn down her offer of an unopened half-bottle in addition when he found that jettisoning his luncheon rations – sandwiches of smoked salmon and of chicken liver pâté – made just the right-shaped space in his haversack. On his way out he stopped at the foot of the stairs and listened. He could hear nothing.

When he was still three or four miles short of the assembly point on his way back, a monstrous vibrating clamour filled his ears and seemed to make his jeep tremble in sympathy. He looked out and up and saw that one of the helicopters was matching his speed and course at tree-top height. After half a minute or so, its crew presumably satisfied by a close inspection of the white cross painted on the bonnet – an emblem common to all vehicles on the exercise – the machine sheered off.

A little later, Hunter caught up with a file of men in battle order trudging ill-naturedly along the side of the road. He pulled up alongside the N C O at their head.

'What's going on, Sergeant?'

'Don't know, sir. Sergeant-major got a message over the walkie-talkie ... Okay, lads, take it easy a minute.'

Muttering, the men sat down on the verge or leaned against the grassy bank beyond it. It was clear that they had done a lot of swearing up until the moment of Hunter's arrival, and would do more as soon as he was gone, at the latest.

'But what's it all about?'

'Don't know, sir. We've got a rendezvous fixed somewhere in this wood along here. The sergeant-major said something about carrying out a sweep of the area. Looks like it'll take us all day, sir.'

'Whose orders are these?'

'Captain Leonard's, sir.'

The muttering swelled. Phrases became distinguishable.

'I see. Well, I'll make sure there's a hot meal laid on for everybody as soon as they get back to camp.'

'Thanks very much, sir.'

As Hunter drove on, his eyes, which had become rather glazed over in the preceding hour or two, brightened again. When he had put a few bends between himself and the party on foot, he stopped again and drank from his water-container. At the junction with the track that led up to the assembly point he was waved down by a corporal standing on the verge.

'You'd better not go all the way up, sir. They're shooting one of those things off in a minute. Everybody who's not offici-ally allowed in the bunker has got to keep this side of the ridge.'

'Thank you, I'll manage.'

Hunter took the jeep another couple of hundred yards until he reached a point where, by engaging four-wheel drive, he was able to move it off the track. He got out and clambered up between bushes to the lip of the depression in which the bunker lay. It was in fact almost immediately below him and quite near enough for him to make out Venables and Isaacs standing together at one end. The tank Hunter had noticed earlier was to be seen at the far end of the valley, presumably unoccupied.

In the bunker, matters seemed to be coming to a head. An officer stood on the fire-step in the aiming position. O'Neill appeared and took up a position beside him. Everybody became quite still. After some consideration, Hunter dropped down behind a hummock and peeered over the top of it. A moment later he heard O'Neill's voice, high-pitched and clear.

'Fire.'

There was the sharp knocking bang of an ordinary rifle cartridge, and then what might almost have been a small piece of the sun came into being across the valley where the tank was. During the instant it was there, everything in that direction went vague and overcast. A bolster of warmish air struck Hunter quite hard in the face. Finally a very low-pitched tearing noise, like a short extract from a peal of thunder, pressed against his ears, and a balloon of dark grey smoke expanded rapidly outwards and upwards from the target area.

Voices could be heard from the bunker. The officer who had fired ejected the spent round from the breech of his rifle. O'Neill started lecturing again. Hunter watched the smoke for a minute or two, during which time it grew only slightly thinner. Nothing of any substance seemed about to happen next. After his years of training, Hunter was able to recognize without difficulty the opening moments of one of those long delays, rendered absolutely featureless by the impossibility of forecasting how as well as when they will end, which make up so much of Service life. He waited until the smoke had cleared enough to give him a view of the blackish and reddish patch of earth where the tank had been, folded and furrowed as if an oversized plough with a very blunt coulter had been briefly at it. Then he went back down the ridge and got into his jeep and drove it to the assembly point.

Here there was a scene of some animation. One party of

men under a sergeant was arriving, another leaving. The morale of both parties seemed closely similar to that of the one Hunter had met on the road. Two walkie-talkie sets were in simultaneous operation; a third was being dismembered by a couple of signallers. A motor-cyclist was trying to start his machine. Somebody was backing his jeep out of the line of transport, hooting at a group who stood in his path. A helicopter rose from behind the ridge, where it had presumably been sheltering while the shot was taken, and began to approach. Another appeared farther off.

At the centre of all this was Leonard, sweating a great deal, talking to two NCOs in alternation, walking jerkily from one of the functioning walkie-talkies to the other, finally running to his car and shouting into his microphone.

When the helicopters had landed and things were a little calmer, Hunter went up to Ross-Donaldson, who looked interested but not involved.

'Whence all the panic?'

'It's an obvious case of group emotion and the force of the example of authority working in push-pull. The Services afford an almost uniquely favourable environment for this effect. Evidently, it's by no means confined to our own era. There's been a series on historic paraneurotic débâcles in the *Military Quarterly*, beginning with the failure of that Athenian night-operation on the heights above Syracuse.'

Hunter lit a cigarette. 'What went wrong this time?'

'Leonard was expecting this Best person to arrive in the vicinity for purposes of espionage, supposedly. I expect you know about that.'

'I did hear something, yes.'

'Everybody seems to have done. Well, Best hasn't arrived. According to Leonard he should have been spotted something like two hours ago. So he's got to be found, it appears. For which purpose men are being taken out of the cordon and the defence detachment and grouped for a sweep. A simple enough concept, you'd have thought, but unexpectedly intractable in practice.'

'I see he's getting the whirlybirds on to it,' said Hunter,

nodding in the direction of Leonard, who was talking and gesticulating to the helicopter pilots.

'Quite useless. Over most of the exercise area the cover's good enough for even an inexperienced solitary man to hide from the air. The only exception is this valley – which incidentally looks like an unfilled glacial lake, wouldn't you agree? – and its immediate approaches, and if he'd got so far he'd have been picked up by ground observation. Would you care for a hand of piquet?'

'Very much.'

They went over to Ross-Donaldson's jeep, which proved to be carrying a number of supernumerary stores. Within a short time two folding chairs in moss-coloured canvas and unvarnished wood, a small card-table and a green and white golfing umbrella with an extending shaft had been unloaded and erected. They took their seats. Ross-Donaldson brought out two new packs of cards from his haversack and unsealed them.

'This is nice,' said Hunter.

'I'm glad you like it. Champagne?'

'Thank you.'

At a nod from his master, Ross-Donaldson's batman went and fetched from the jeep a metal cylinder about the size of an eight-inch naval shell, and two silver tankards. The cylinder turned out to be a thermos container and to have in it a very well chilled magnum of Krug 1955. This was opened and poured.

'Mm,' said Ross-Donaldson, sipping. 'Perhaps a little too cold.'

'It seems just right to me.'

'Well, the situation will improve if we merely replace the lid lightly on it instead of clamping it down. Shall we just play a short game and then see how matters stand? I shouldn't like to predict how long it'll take Leonard and his comitadji to carry out their evolutions. Cut.'

'They've only got a bit over a mile to walk once they start, haven't they? It shouldn't take them all night. What do you think, a florin a point?'

'Right. It's rather broken country, though, and he hasn't

really got enough men for the job, so he'll have to zig-zag them. Leaving one.'

'If you ask me,' said Hunter abstractedly, 'Best has slipped back through the cordon. Or if he hasn't already, he won't have much trouble doing it now, with the cordon thinned down to give Leonard his sweep party. Point of five.'

'Not good. My feeling exactly. Do you think this Best really is a spy? You know him better than anybody, I suppose.'

'Tierce to a knave. I simply couldn't say. Brian certainly seems to think so.'

'Not good. How much is that worth, in your view?'

Hunter hesitated. 'Oh, quite a lot. He strikes me as pretty competent.'

'I've known you to treat him as if you thought he was a bit of a joke.'

'Only as a man. I don't expect a Security officer to make much of a score as regards ordinary intelligence and so on.'

'Don't you? I see. What else have you got?'

'Sorry. Three knaves. But I don't know much about Security.'

'Do you think most people around the place look on Leonard as pretty competent?'

'As far as I know, yes. What do you feel about him in that way?'

Another rifle-shot and summarized thunderclap made Hunter start violently, though without causing him to spill his drink. Ross-Donaldson remained unmoved.

'Have some more champagne,' he said when Hunter had recovered himself. 'Now where were we? Not good.'

'Oh dear. And now I suppose I've got to lead.'

At the end of the short game Hunter was just over four hundred points down.

'I don't believe you know the odds properly,' said Ross-Donaldson. 'And your memory, if I may say so, is appalling.'

'A great advantage in most of the dealings of life, though not, admittedly, at piquet. Shall we go on?'

Ross-Donaldson took a Service notebook from his top jacket pocket. 'That makes just . . . three hundred and forty-eight pounds eleven shillings you owe me so far this month. I think

I'll stroll over and see if anything's happening. Help yourself while I'm gone.'

The sun, the champagne, and the contents of his water-container had made Hunter agreeably muzzy. The game had bored him, though not actively. He wished he had made it a hundred pounds a point instead of a florin. Even that, however, might not have sharpened his interest by anything like one hundred thousand per cent. Pouring more champagne, he decided that life was divided into wishing something was at stake when nothing was and wishing nothing was when something was.

A quarter of an hour went by in this sort of way. Then Ross-Donaldson came back.

'No result as yet,' he said. 'They've finished one sweep and have started another at right angles to the first. Two more helicopters have arrived. There's an argument raging over the air because the pilots won't go as low as Leonard wants them to.'

'Where is he?'

'Out in the field at the head of his troops.'

'You know,' said Hunter thoughtfully, 'if Best is hiding there'd be one very effective way of bringing him into the open.'

'Going round firing off those rifles, you mean. That might blow him up instead.'

'Not firing them. Brandishing them. Shaping up to fire them.'

'There's something about that idea that doesn't feel right.'

'What's wrong with it?'

'I don't know. It just doesn't feel right.'

'It would have the merit of putting those bloody guns to some use.'

Ross-Donaldson looked severe. 'They've been put to use already,' he said.

'Have they? Two practice shots? It's a funny sort of exercise, this.'

'They're studying effect. There's nothing special to learn about the actual firing. What matters is what happens at the far end.'

'That's where Venables comes in, I suppose.'

'Shall we have another game? I think we've got time.'

'All right. I mean he didn't come in at all at the briefing. Venables didn't.'

'That was mere technics. He's a technologics man.'

'Cut.'

'Have some more champagne.'

In the second game Hunter did much better, being taken down for only a trifle over fifteen pounds. By the time Ross-Donaldson had finished writing in his notebook a runner had arrived with the message that the exercise had been completed. He had no information about the success or failure of Leonard's search.

'But we'd have heard soon enough if he'd caught him.'

'Agreed. I must go and supervise the loading. And there are warning notices to be posted round the target area.'

'What for? I thought the stuff was supposed to be more or less non-radioactive.'

'Regulations, Hunter. Thank you very much for the game. You really should set about training that memory of yours. It can be done, you know.'

'I dare say it can. I'll take you on at backgammon later.'

While the stores were being loaded, Leonard's car came bumping up the track and stopped near Hunter. Its owner got out slowly. There was a tear in his trousers large enough to show a knee smeared with dirt and a little dried blood, and his shirt was stained with dried sweat. He looked silently at Hunter.

'Don't worry, Brian. You've got enough on him now, haven't you?'

'Not for an arrest. Only to make him a red suspect.'

'Well, that sounds pretty good.'

'Not good enough. You don't happen to know if there's any sherry anywhere, do you?'

'Not for certain, but I very much doubt if there's any within reach. Try some of this.'

Hunter offered his water-container.

'What is it?'

'Never mind what it is. It's very good for you and that's all you need to know.'

'Mm. Thanks.' Leonard drank. 'My God, I hope it is good for me.'

'What's happened to Best, do you think?'

'Don't ask me. He must have gone to ground somewhere and then got out somehow.'

'I see. But he can't have walked all the way here from the asylum, can he? He must have driven part of the way. Why don't you put a watch on his car?'

'I would if I knew where it was. I've left a section out looking for it. I had a man detailed to follow him on a scooter, but the scooter had a flat tyre. I shall get a rocket from my master for that.'

'Make sure you accelerate it when you pass it on. Well, well. You don't strike it very lucky, do you, Brian?'

'Things are bound to turn my way soon. I just know they will.'

Eventually the convoy was ready. After an unaccountable delay of unexpectedly short duration it moved off. Hunter was driving behind the second of the two lorries full of infantrymen that enclosed the stores vehicle. At his side was the quartermaster-sergeant who worked under him. They had reached the point where the track joined the road and travelled a few hundred yards more when the lorry in front stopped suddenly. Hunter pulled up. After a few moments he heard shouting somewhere ahead.

'More fun and games,' said the Q M S.

'Let's see what's up. Come on, Q.'

The deep ditch on one side of the road and the bank on the other made it difficult to get round the lorry. When they managed it, they saw the stores vehicle leaning slightly over to one side with one front wheel overhanging the ditch and considerable flames coming out of its engine, the cover of which was raised. Half a dozen men ran about in the roadway calling to one another.

'Shut the bloody lid.'

'Bugger's stuck.'

216

'Where's that bloody fire-extinguisher?'

'Bugger's stuck.'

'Get the major out before she goes up.'

'Bugger won't move.'

The QMS turned and hurried towards the lorry behind. Hunter went to the cab of the burning vehicle, where Venables was sitting in the passenger's seat reading a sheaf of typescript.

'I think I must advise you to vacate your seat, Major. This truck is on fire.'

'So I see. But there are present a more than adequate number of persons well qualified to deal with the matter. Let them extinguish the flames.'

'The windscreen may shatter at any moment. You'd do better out here in the road.'

'I am unable to leave. The door on this side is jammed against the hedge.'

'Come out this way. Get a move on, Major.'

'My name is Venables. Oh, very well.'

By the time Hunter had got Venables out of the cab Leonard had appeared. Making his way to the scene must have cost him some effort. A button had come off his jacket and there was a fresh scratch on his cheek. He too had begun shouting.

'Get the stores off quick. Everybody on it. Unload the stores.'

The lane was now jammed with soldiery, but some response to Leonard's order was soon made. Two men let down the tailboard and began shifting the arms and ammunition, much less gently than at the original unloading that morning. The fire itself, though now firmly established in the fore part of the vehicle, attracted less interest. Two rifles and a box of ammunition were in the roadway before the QMS could push his way through with a fire-extinguisher and start playing it on the flames. They died down reluctantly at first, then, when a driver ran up and applied a second extinguisher, were rapidly quenched. A murmur of relief arose. At that moment Hunter, who had been gazing into the thick woods bordering the road, grabbed Leonard's arm.

'Brian – look. There. Did you see him?'

'Who? Where?'

'Best. By that tree with the ivy on it. He turned and ran when he saw me looking at him. I'm almost sure it was him.'

Leonard did not hesitate. He pulled a whistle from his pocket at the end of its lanyard and blew a great blast. Silence fell at once.

'Optimus is in this wood,' he yelled. 'I want him caught. Everybody on it. Move. At the double. I want the wood swept from end to end. Get going, everybody. And I mean everybody. Drivers, batmen, the lot. I said *move*.'

When the first group of men, swearing unfeignedly, had jumped the ditch and begun pushing through the undergrowth, Leonard turned to the Q M S.

'Well done, Q. Now I want you to go and take my car and drive up to the rest of the convoy and say what's happened. They're probably only a few hundred yards ahead. Report to the Adjutant. Quick about it.'

'Right, sir.'

The Q M S departed. Leonard leapt the ditch and crashed and shouted his way out of sight. Hunter looked round for Venables, who proved to be sitting in the remains of the cab of the vehicle reading his typescript. He looked up uninterestedly as Hunter crossed in front of him and entered the wood in his turn.

After half an hour or so Hunter decided he had had enough of dirtying his uniform and being bitten by insects. His head was aching. He had seen no sign of Best, nor even of Leonard. The only people he had found in the wood were two infantrymen having a quiet smoke in the middle of a particularly dense thicket. These he pretended not to have seen. He took his time about returning to the road.

Within another half-hour Leonard and his men had returned empty-handed, the stores had been reloaded and a tow fixed up for the stores vehicle, and the convoy was on the move again.

Dr Best watched it go.

Part 3

Operation Apollo

About nine hours later Churchill was lying awake in bed with one arm round Catharine's waist and the other behind her shoulders. Every minute or so he listened carefully to her breathing. It remained deep and steady, and she had not moved for what he thought was a long time, but he had no idea whether she was asleep or not. She had said she had taken a sleeping-pill. The bedside alarm-clock was set for seven-thirty, when the two of them would get up and dress, doing so together for the first time, and drive over to the hospital in the town. Here, after Catharine had been admitted, Churchill was to have an interview with the doctor in charge of her case, an arrangement made without reference to her. Then he would return to camp, arriving there an hour or more after his pass was due to expire. He felt this would not matter.

He turned his thoughts back to the previous evening, not because he hoped to establish anything about it, but because the unmistakable fact of its having taken place reassured him. Every so often, perhaps when he momentarily came closest to falling asleep, he was visited by the illusion that he and Catharine had moved off the track of ordinary existence into an autonomous, self-sealing pocket of fear and helplessness. Among the advancing and retreating blankets of colour which his eyes imposed on the darkness he had several times seen, or imagined he had seen, a geometrical replica of the lethal node he had described to Hunter. It was in the form of a broad horizontal disc, vague and granular at the periphery, thickening towards the middle. Through the exact centre a taut vertical thread ran both ways to mathematical infinity. You entered the node, or it moved across you, until you arrived at the thread. Thereafter, instead of moving or seeming to move on towards the farther edge of the disc, you could only move up or down the thread. Presumably if your motion across the disc were along a chord instead of along the diameter you could continue to travel laterally until you reached the far side of the circumference and emerged. Hunter, Ayscue, Naidu, Pearce, Lucy were travelling along chords at varying distances from the centre. But Catharine had been on the diameter and had reached the centre and the thread. And so he too, Churchill, Lieutenant James Churchill of the Blue Howards, was on the thread.

Hunter had arrived at the house just as Churchill, Catharine and Lucy were finishing, or abandoning, the meal of cold roast beef, pickles and potato salad that Mrs Stoker had prepared for them. There had been some talk of the later phases of Exercise Nabob and speculation about the role of Dr Best. Only when an account of the events in the lane came round for the second time in a quarter of an hour had it occurred to Churchill how drunk Hunter was. He was paler than Churchill had ever seen him before and was evidently unable to sit still, leaning forward in his chair and continually stroking and kneading the outsides of his thighs, jumping up from time to time and going over to tap without result at the bars of Sadie's cage. Nobody had taken up his suggestion of a round of whist and eventually he had fallen silent, except for an occasional muttered remark in praise of the drink he was drinking or of drink in general. But his presence had made the circle less totally withdrawn and chilly, less committed to, as it seemed, smoothing over some unforgivable lapse or sitting out an episode of supreme boredom.

Catharine had sat in a corner of the couch with her feet tucked up under her and her arms clasped round her knees, as if avoiding unnecessary movement. Her hair looked darker than usual. Every time she caught Churchill's eye, or Lucy's, she smiled briefly and drew her chin inwards. When she smiled a part of the inner surface of her lower lip became visible in a way he thought he had not seen before, although he was not certain. She had refused drinks and cigarettes, but had eaten a fair amount of the beef and pickles.

'How are you feeling?' he had asked her.

'Oh, not too bad. Except it's a shame I've got to be such a misery. You know, having to be sat with like somebody's mother-in-law. There doesn't seem to be any way of organizing this part. It'll be different tomorrow. Everything'll be done for me then. Not for you, though. I expect you'll find yourself doing a lot of drinking. But try not to do too much of it on your own. Try to stick to Max.'

'Yes. Would you like to go for a drive?'

'No thank you, darling. I think I'll do better here, where I can see you and the others. You have another drink now and keep Max company.'

'Are you sure you won't?'

'I seem to have lost the taste for it in a funny way. Just as well when you come to think of it. But then it never has done much for me, drink. It's a man's thing really, I expect.'

'I wish there were something I could get you.'

'I know you'd get it for me if there were. Darling, if you don't mind terribly I think I'll go to bed now. I'm a bit tired.'

'I'll come with you.'

'You're off, are you?' Hunter had risen to his feet with remarkable agility. 'Look after yourself, darling.'

He had kissed Catharine. Lucy had come forward.

'I'll see you off in the morning.'

'You're not to bother, love.'

'Cathy, it's no bother.'

'I'd sooner, honestly.'

'Well, if you're sure ...'

The two women had embraced and clung together for some moments.

'I'll be in to see you as soon as they'll let me.'

'Good night, my dear boy. You know where to find me when you get back to camp.'

'Good night, Max. Thanks for coming along this evening.'

Catharine and Churchill had gone up by the front stairs, past the tapestry and along the corridor to her bedroom. A half-filled suitcase had been standing open on the chest of drawers. Only a brush and comb had been lying on the dressing-table. When she left him to go to the bathroom, he had stood

223

at the window. A sky haze saw to it that there was almost nothing to see, and there was nothing to hear, whereas usually, at this time, hardly five minutes would have gone by without lights advancing or retreating along the drive, car engines being started or switched off, voices, footsteps on the gravel. He had wondered how long it would be before Lucy's visitors resumed their calls, and reflected that Ross-Donaldson would have known the answer to that; at least, would have had a firm answer ready, with reasons. How was he spending his evenings nowadays? Churchill had grinned briefly.

Two minutes later, he and Catharine had started undressing as hastily as they had ever done when impatient to make love, but this time they had not faced each other. He had been about to get into bed when she said his name. He had turned to her.

'Look at me,' she had said. 'You know, just in case.'

He had gone over to her and they had kissed. She had trembled for a moment, and when she stopped she had still been stiff in his arms.

'I love you,' he had said.

'I know. And I love you.'

They had stood together a little longer. Then she had said, 'Let's go to sleep now. You set the alarm.'

In bed she had turned away from him at once and he had been grateful, because he would not have been able to make love to her and had been dreading her expectation of it. About a quarter of an hour later they had heard Hunter drive away from the front of the house. Just after that she had asked for the light to be turned out, saying she thought she would sleep better in the dark.

Every time he reached this point in his thoughts, Churchill found it harder to begin again at Hunter's arrival. The body lying against his seemed to call more and more urgently for action on his part, but he could conceive of none that would be relevant. Love had turned out to be action in a way that had gone on surprising him: he had always assumed it to be a process followed by a state. But now, the very thing that made action so necessary made it impossible. On the thread in the centre of the node, nothing mattered but being on the thread, nothing else could be thought about except by a tiny, remote, artificially maintained corner of the mind. As soon as he had put matters to himself like this, that corner was overrun. What was in store for Catharine – not the hospital bed and the anaesthetics, not the trolley and the table and the surgeons, but the ultimate – became all that there was and was going to be.

He felt the bodily mechanism that controls respiration switch itself off like an electric light. It soon proved to be useless, indeed misleading, to go on trying to breathe according to that dimly remembered earlier rhythm. He took in air and exhaled it and let his lungs stay idle until they should need more. But after a long time they still seemed not to need any, and he thought he had better breathe in again. When he did, he found he had no idea when to stop. There was a kind of corner ahead beyond which he would be able to breathe out as when yawning or sighing. He had still not reached it when his lungs turned out to have no room for more air. When he had stayed like that for a while without any discomfort or particular impulse to breathe out, he voluntarily breathed out. He failed to recognize the point at which he usually stopped doing this. It was a slightly less warm night than of late, but he felt sweat break out on his chest. He tried vainly to keep still.

'Are you all right?' asked Catharine, speaking with an immediate clarity that showed him she had not been asleep.

Panting a little, he reached out of bed and switched on the light.

'We've got to talk,' he said.

'Good. I was afraid we were never going to. Can I have a cigarette?'

The act of producing and lighting one for each of them cheered him a little.

'I've been wanting to say things to you,' he said, 'but then I didn't want to, I didn't see how I could, apart from stuff that didn't count about how are you getting on and don't worry too much, because I didn't want to frighten you. But of course I suppose that was silly. But I couldn't think of a way of really saying anything at all that wouldn't be to do with frightening things.'

'You couldn't have thought of anything that would have made me more frightened than I have been or frightened in an extra way. I must have thought of more ways of being it than you have, because it's me it's happening to. There are ways I wouldn't know how to describe, not even to you. And that's saying something, isn't it? Really, I'd hardly have believed this, but I haven't been able to remember what they were, some of them, for whole parts of today. I've been sort of separating things out.'

'You mean you're not so frightened as you were?'

'Oh, I don't know about that. I can't tell, you see. I mean you can't tell. One can't. It's impossible to tell how the next thing that comes along is going to seem. There's much less to go on than you might think. Even about dying. I don't feel I know anything at all about that. I feel I used to know more and it's as if I've forgotten. About what you're going to feel when it's starting to happen, I mean. For most people there probably isn't a moment like that, when they know it's starting to happen. But that's a tremendous way off, anyway, as far as I'm concerned. Lots of things have got to happen first. They may be very unpleasant things but they aren't it, they won't be it. And I've got a very good chance of getting away with it. Don't let's forget that. We ought to try not to, anyway. And nothing terrible can happen for the moment, while we're here. There's a lot of time yet.'

She had been speaking rather in the way Churchill remembered from the time in the White Hart when she had told him her history, quickly but calmly, with every now and then a sharp intake of breath. For the most part she kept her eyes on her cigarette or somewhere about the foot of the bed, only glancing intermittently at him and away. Once she smoothed her hair back at the side of her head, exposing most of an ear. The sight of it seemed to concentrate his feelings of outrage. For an unimportant moment he thought of the Anti-Death League. He would have had a good reason for joining it now, if it had existed and if, had it existed, joining it would have had any meaning.

'I wish I could be with you all the time,' he said.

'But you can't be. There isn't any way that could happen. And you're only going to be away on this thing for ten days.'

'I can't not go. At least I could, but it wouldn't help. They'd keep me under lock and key at least as long, probably much longer.'

'I know, you told me. Don't worry about it, darling. You'll be about for the next six days, well, five days now, and nothing can really happen in the ten days after that. I shan't like it but I'll be able to stand it. I don't think I shall be too frightened. Not for a bit, anyway. You know, this morning, I mean yesterday morning, I thought completely about dying, sort of looked straight at it and tried to be logical. And just for a minute it didn't seem so frightening. When I was frightened of Casement it was because he was going to hurt me, perhaps in some way I hadn't thought of before. And when I went mad I was frightened of everything, because I thought everything might hurt me. That was sensible in a kind of way, being frightened of nasty things happening, nasty experiences, even when I wasn't a bit clear on what they might be. But dying isn't an experience at all. It's an event as far as other people are concerned, but not as far as you are, one is. Of course, one can't go on being frightfully detached and sensible for long. You soon slip back. But I've sort of lost interest in the frightening part of it for the time being, if that doesn't sound too silly. Hating it is what I'm on now more. Hating having the chance of having to go off and leave everything. Well, I don't really mean everything, I just mean you.'

She put out her cigarette and turned and faced him for the first time since she had begun to talk.

'Another thing I was thinking this morning,' she went on, speaking less quickly now, 'was that I could leave everything else like a shot if I could just keep you. I saw a play once where you spent all your time in a room with three other people and that was meant to be hell – you know, real hell, instead of flames. Well, if it was just you and me there I wouldn't mind it at all. Even if they arranged it so we couldn't make love. I wouldn't mind never going out and seeing the sun and the flowers and things, or reading a book or anything. That was what I thought, anyway. I was ridiculous really, I suppose. In a hundred years we'd run out of things to say.'

'We wouldn't.'

'Anyway, what I hate is the idea of having to go off and leave you. After we've been together for such a short time.'

'That's the really damnable thing,' said Churchill with difficulty.

'Perhaps it is. I'm not so sure. I just said about the short time thing without thinking. I think I'd mind the idea just as much if we'd been married for fifty years. I'd never get sick of you, would I?'

'I know. It's just death that's wrong.'

'It can't be put right. Don't get all angry about it, darling. You'll only end up upset. That's all.'

'Do you believe in God?'

'I'll have to think about that. I've never been able to understand what it means, you see. It's the most difficult idea I've ever heard about. And yet people seem to be able to get results by it all the time.'

Churchill said animatedly, 'Only people with no sense of right and wrong. No real sense of it. What would you have to be like to worship something that invented every bad thing we know or can imagine?' He looked away. 'Death in particular. If there were no such thing as death the whole human race could be happy.'

'Most of the bad things that happen are done by people. All the cruelty there is.'

'Human evil is just an instrument,' he went on in the same tone. 'It's not much more than incidental. I think Dr Best is probably about as bad as a man can get, but he didn't create his own material, did he? The wherewithal for him to be bad. Pain and madness were there already. And even more so, the first men found out that if you picked up a big rock and dropped it on somebody's head, then something very peculiar happened to him. And people had been using that effect on one another ever since, but it was all there waiting for them, before they found out about it. They didn't invent it. And if it had never existed, there'd be no point in treating people badly in other

228

ways. The point of sending a man to prison is to shorten the part of his life he can be free in, to bring his death nearer. If you couldn't do that, he wouldn't mind going to prison and you wouldn't bother to send him. So if there were no such thing as death we wouldn't all just be happy. We'd all be innocent too.'

There was a long and total silence. Catharine lit another cigarette and looked at Churchill's averted face.

'But we're not happy and we're not innocent,' she said. 'We might as well agree to start from there.'

'But that's just giving up. There must be something one can do.'

'What do you suggest?'

'If people could see what their real enemy was,' he said, frowning, 'they might start behaving differently. They might be nicer to one another. A lot nicer. There wouldn't be any religion to give them excuses for oppression and intolerance and pride and not helping.'

'Is that what you really want?' asked Catharine after another pause. 'Sort of brotherly love all round? It doesn't sound your style.'

He turned to her, saw her hazel eyes with the dark flecks in them gazing back at him, her mouth as straight as ever, and spoke with much hatred.

'No, it isn't. When I look at you and think of what may be going to happen to you, I want to do something that'll show –'

A diffused yellowish glare showed through the thin curtains like an instant of daylight. Almost immediately afterwards the windows rattled sharply and some object in another room fell to the floor. Then, several seconds later, they heard a thick, tearing, thundering noise, not long in itself but followed by dozens of echoes.

Catharine had her hand in Churchill's. 'What was that?' she asked.

'I don't know. Yes I do. You've heard it before too. This afternoon when we were having a cup of tea in the kitchen. It was one of those weapons they were firing on the exercise.'

'Has the war started?'

'No. Let's think. It can't be a night scheme or I'd have heard about it. And even if it'd been a snap do Max would have had time to let me know. I suppose the technical chaps might have fixed up a night firing test. I can't think what they'd hope to establish, though.'

He got out of bed and went to the window.

'Nothing to see. But there are probably too many hills in the way. I didn't think it sounded the same as this afternoon. Nearer this time. But these things can be deceptive at night.'

'Come back to bed, darling. You can find out about it tomorrow.'

'It's very strange.'

'If there's no danger or anything, can't we forget about it for now?'

'I'm sorry. Of course.'

He got in beside her again. She put her arms round him and drew him down on to the pillows.

'I want to ask you something. This thing you're going off on next week. I still don't know what it is and I know you wouldn't tell me anyway and that's all all right. But how dangerous is it? You can tell me that without giving anything away.'

'It isn't dangerous at all,' he lied.

'Are you sure?'

'Yes. It's just a trip. There and back. But it's one of those things that would be absolutely no good if the opposition got to hear about it.'

He and the other s 1 officers had been told that they had something like a seventy-five per cent chance of surviving Operation Apollo. A Pakistani colleague with whom he had been chatting recently had suggested that this was a deliberate deception, and that the planners of the Operation would not dare allow any of those who had taken part to survive it. Churchill was half convinced of this. It seemed appropriate to the nature of their task. He told himself now, as often before, that he must go through with the Operation, that he ought to want to unreservedly, because the people it was designed to stop just had to be stopped.

'You won't leave me, will you?' asked Catherine.

'How could I ever do that?'

'I don't know. It's just a nasty fancy I've just had. You sounded so much off on your own just now.'

'About that explosion? I was only –'

'No, I meant before that, when you were talking about people being happy and innocent. It was like you talking to yourself. As if you might forget about me one of these days. You won't, though. Will you? If I've got to lose you I'd rather do it by dying than any other way.'

Churchill held her very tight and pushed his face against hers.

'I won't do anything like that, honestly.'

'Promise? Promise faithfully you won't leave me?'

'I promise.'

*

Brian Leonard parked his car in its space below the Mess and sat for some moments accumulating the will to get out. It was just on eleven o'clock in the morning and he had spent the preceding six and a half hours either on his feet or behind the wheel. He had had no breakfast and was unshaven. As on the afternoon before, a bloody knee showed through a rent in his trousers, but this was the other knee and a fresh pair of trousers. Now that he was stationary the heat of the day began to close round him and so drive him into the open, much as he would have preferred to stay out of sight.

What roused him finally was the sound of a heavy lorry moving up in low gear from the main gate. In it were some of the soldiers who, after traversing nine or ten miles apiece during the closing stages and aftermath of Exercise Nabob, had been turned out of their beds two and a half hours before reveille and transported back to the hills for yet another sweep on foot. All this was on Leonard's order and they knew it. Their debussing point would be in sight of the car park and he had no desire to run the gauntlet of their swearing, with perhaps, given the speed at which their feelings had mounted the last time he was near them, a few bursts of machine-pistol fire thrown in. He got quickly out of his car and hurried up to the Mess building.

An armed sentry outside the ante-room door came to attention as he passed. He saluted with less than his usual punctilio and made his way to the door of the Command Post, which opened to him after a short interval.

'At ease, please,' he said uneasily to the sergeant-major and corporal who had risen to mark his entry. 'Anything new?'

'No, sir,' said the sergeant-major, 'not since the ten o'clock report, the one we passed –'

'Which you passed to me over the air, quite so.'

'He's due to check in again any minute, sir.'

'Oddly enough, that's why I'm here.'

'Find anything up there, sir?' asked the corporal.

'No. Nothing. Nothing at all.'

'Who do you reckon did it, sir?' persisted the corporal. 'This bloke you're having watched? Is he the same one as you were all looking for on the Exercise?'

'Yes. I shall know more very soon.'

'But how could he have got hold of one of those things?' The corporal did not notice a silencing glare from the sergeant-major. 'And what did he think he was playing at? That place isn't a military objective, is it?'

Before Leonard could order the sergeant-major to have the corporal put under close arrest and on punishment diet, the civilian telephone rang.

'Mr Lock's house,' said Leonard into it.

'Public library here.'

'Go ahead. Lock speaking.'

'I'm afraid there's still no sign of that book you wanted, sir. We've looked in just about all the usual places.'

'Start looking in the unusual places, then, and quick about it.'

'Yes, sir. The trouble is, there are one or two, uh, bookcases that we can't get into without a key.'

'Get into them just the same. Remember it's a very large book. It shouldn't be at all difficult to find. Now what about the chief librarian? What's he been up to?'

'Just going round the shelves as before in his usual routine, sir. But he certainly looks under the weather. One of us asked him what the bandage was in aid of and he said he had a fall. No details.'

'Mm. Any unusual visitors to the library?'

'No, sir.'

'Well, you go off and find that book or I'll report you to the Town Clerk.'

'Right, sir.'

Leonard rang off, then picked up the receiver again, dialled the exchange and asked to be connected to the special tests engineer. While he waited, he stared at the other two men in turn until they picked up the magazines they had been reading when he arrived. He had not minded the way they looked at him as much as the way they looked at each other. Eventually a voice spoke into his ear.

'Special tests here.'

'Lock speaking. The frequency of the day is five kilocycles. How's the equipment?'

'No faults have developed. We've had four more transmissions since you spoke to me earlier, three outgoing and one incoming, all of good quality.'

'Are you sure?'

'Of course I'm sure. The incoming was from a doctor in the town, the outgoing were to the local golf club, a drug company and a wine merchant. We tested as usual after each transmission, and the quality was undoubtedly good. It's all here on tape; you can check for yourself if you want.'

'Never mind. The moment you get a transmission with the slightest hint of bad quality I want to know about it at once, you understand?'

'Of course I understand. Is there anything else?'

'No. All right. Good-bye.'

Ringing off finally, Leonard frowned. The first man he had talked to had sounded satisfied, if not pleased, with having no information to impart; the second had sounded casual, towards the end almost impatient. The latter was the more annoying. This mere technician, this electrical eavesdropper, seemed to imagine he was on a level with a qualified phylactologist like himself. Leonard thought he understood how, thirty years ago, a master farrier of the Sailors would have felt on being hob-nobbed with by an armoured-car mechanic in oil-stained dungarees. The image of the Sailors swelled in his mind. Even more than a bath and a shave and a change and a meal, he needed something that would uplift his spirits as never before: taking the salute, perhaps, at a march-past of the whole strength of the Sailors in full ceremonials, preceded by their trumpet-and-drum band and regimental mascot – a bull seal on a trolley drawn by a colour-sergeant.

'I'll be in the ante-room if anyone wants me,' he said, and went there.

Colonel White sat at a card-table in the middle of the room with Major Venables at his side, a telephone at one elbow and a bottle of sherry and a glass at the other, having decided that the location and amenities of the Mess made it a more suitable temporary headquarters than his office. Leonard came to attention before him and, at his nod, lowered himself rather slowly into a chair at the table.

'You look as if you could do with a drink, Brian, among other things,' said the Colonel kindly.

'I'd love some of that sherry, sir.'

'Press the bell, then, will you?'

'And what have you discovered, Leonard?' asked Venables.

'Nothing. The area from which the rifle might have been fired is a comparatively small one and it isn't there. We've beaten a broad path from that area back to the road and it isn't there. The sides of the road are being swept up to a depth of a hundred yards – they should be completing that any moment. But I'm convinced it isn't there. It's somewhere in that mental hospital or its grounds. I just know it is. The place is being searched as we sit here, but I've only been able to infiltrate three men into it and they may take an hour or two yet.'

Venables gave a groaning cough. 'Why do you not simply move your soldiery into this establishment and have them rend brick from brick until they find the missing weapon?'

'There are several objections to that, the chief of which is that it would almost certainly serve Best's turn. Whatever the exact reasoning behind this performance of his, attracting publicity to this unit and its activities as a means of embarrassing Operation Apollo must be a main consideration. So we've got to move as surreptitiously as possible. When the time comes for us to make an arrest we must attract the minimum of attention, so that we can release our own story about what's happened to him. I've a plan for that. As soon as the rifle's found and I receive my authority from my master, I shall act.'

By now a glass had arrived for Leonard and he had emptied it one and a half times. He already felt much better, very nearly certain that the missing N H W-17 would be found as he had predicted.

'It was by almost unbelievable good fortune,' said Venables, lighting one of his square-section cigars, 'that Dr Best was near at hand during the only period, and that a short one, when the rifles were unguarded, by almost unbelievable skill in woodcraft that he was able to approach and depart unseen, and by almost unbelievable coolness of head that he managed to conceive and execute the stratagem of removing the weapon from its wooden container and placing a number of stones there in its stead, thus preventing immediate discovery of the theft. I would go further. I would say that what is almost unbelievable in three such radical aspects is quite unbelievable in aggregate.'

'There may be alternative suggestions about what happened in the lane, although I must confess I find it difficult to imagine one.' Leonard was rather tickled to find himself paying Venables back in his own coin. 'But the finding of the rifle where I expect it to be found will put an end to all speculation of that sort.'

Venables made a noise that seemed to have snarl as well as groan in it, but said no more for the moment.

The Colonel had entered the time of Leonard's return and as much as he had had to report in a large Service notebook with the words *Incident Brickbat* written on its covers in red ink. He now passed Leonard a sheaf of large photographs.

'These came through just after you'd gone out for the second time, Brian.'

They were views from various distances of perhaps half an

acre of torn-up ground, with a crater in the middle and large fragments of newly exposed rock flung here and there. The longer views showed the affected area to lie on an almost flat but slightly tilted plateau.

'They're very good,' said Leonard. 'Who took them?'

'O'Neill. I shouldn't have credited him with the imagination you need for a good photographer. Never can tell, though. Fantastic business up there. Did you take a close look?'

'No, sir. They were still checking for radioactivity when I had to organize my men for the sweeps programme.'

'Clean as a whistle, apparently, according to O'Neill's report.' The Colonel tapped a typewritten sheet clipped to a page of his notebook. 'Still, you did quite right to keep your distance without protective clothing. Well. That was St Jerome's Priory, that was. It seems' – he tapped a gazetteer lying open on the table – 'there's not been a lot left of the place for about three hundred years. Nothing whatever left of it now. Not so much as a flake of iron or a scrap of stone. Fellow Isaacs was highly delighted. Seems they haven't got as much detail as they'd like on what these atomic airgun slugs will do to buildings. Help him to fill in one or two gaps. Nice to think the business has been some practical use to somebody.'

'Because it can have been of very little to Dr Best, assuming momentarily that he is the author of this affair.' Venables turned his great head towards Leonard. 'The man supposedly wishes to publicize this unit's activities. He does so by bringing about an atomic explosion in a remote corner of the hills, far from any human habitation, indeed topographically isolated from all but its immediate environs. Would not a strike at the village, with its attendant loss of life, have been more to his purpose? Better still, a strike at this very camp? The building in which we sit is an excellent target from several surrounding points, even for a flat-trajectory projectile.'

Leonard drained his glass and filled it again. Venables's objection had already occurred to him. It shook him not at all, reasoning as he did that Best's action had been improvised, not carried out to order, and feeling that it fitted perfectly into the picture he had already formed of the man's psychological patterning. But before he could do more than start trying to explain this the telephone rang.

'White here. Thank you. Why don't you come over and join us? Expect you could do with a little something after all that exertion, eh? Good ... That was Max Hunter. The rifle isn't in the camp. Don't suppose anybody thought it was, but you can't afford not to confirm negatives, as they say these days. I asked him –'

The door opened and Leonard turned in his chair, half expecting to see Hunter already arrived, but even when invited to take a little something he could hardly have been expected to cover the couple of hundred yards from his office in something under a quarter of a minute. The new arrival was Ross-Donaldson, who disconcerted Leonard by staring grimly at him for a moment or two before facing the Colonel.

'Yes, Alastair.'

'Nothing else is missing from the stores, sir. One N H W-17 rifle, one round P6 are gone, the rest is as it should be down to the last cleaning-brush.'

'Good. Another negative confirmed. What are you drinking, Alastair?'

'I think a quarter of that rather uncompromising Bollinger, sir, if I may.'

'Press the bell, will you?'

Ross-Donaldson did as he was told, but drink was driven quite out of his head a few seconds later by the high continuous mooing of the alarm hooters situated at selected points round the camp.

'Is this a practice?' asked the Colonel as he got to his feet.

'No, sir,' said Ross-Donaldson, just beating Leonard to the door.

They clattered down the cobbled passage and were soon in the Command Post.

'Unidentified aircraft overhead, sir,' said the sergeant-major.

Pausing only to snatch a miniature transceiver radio from its shelf, Leonard ran back down the passage after Ross-Donaldson and out into the noonday sunshine. A group of swearing men, fumbling with machine-pistols and equipment, was forming up on the main track to their right. Ahead and to their left, they could see the machine-gun crews standing to their weapons. The camp patrol was concentrating near the far end of Hut D4.

'I can't see him,' said Leonard.

'Perhaps he's up in the sun.'

The Colonel came up with them. 'There he is,' he said, pointing.

'A helicopter,' said Ross-Donaldson. He sounded incredulous.

With parts of it appearing liquid or even gaseous in the strong light, the machine was beginning or continuing an arc that would bring it directly above their heads. It seemed rather higher in the air than would be normal for such aircraft and to be descending only slowly, if at all.

Leonard turned the switch of his radio.

'What are you going to do?' asked Ross-Donaldson.

'Call out the R A F.'

'Don't be a fool, Leonard. You've done enough harm as it is. Who do you think is up in that thing, Dr Best? Or a Chinese? Surely you can't seriously expect hostile action from a couple of chaps in the slowest and most conspicuous type of air vehicle under maximum visibility. You've got the imagination of a schoolboy. This is a training flight off course, or whoever should have given or taken official notice of it, forgot to, or the local Group Captain is paying us a visit.'

As he said this, the helicopter began to lose height quickly and almost vertically. It appeared to have standard civilian markings.

'If they try landing they'll have to be arrested,' said Leonard. 'This is Ministry property.'

'Give me that box, will you?' Ross-Donaldson took the transceiver from Leonard. 'Which is the P A channel?'

'This one. What are you going to –?'

Ross-Donaldson pressed the stud indicated and blew experimentally into the microphone. A sound like a brontosaurus clearing its nostrils came from loudspeakers mounted on poles here and there.

'This is the Adjutant speaking,' he said, and his voice rattled and echoed between the buildings. 'Do not fire at this helicopter. I say again, do not fire. Take no action, I say again, no action, except at my personal order.'

By now the helicopter was only a couple of hundred feet up and still descending. Ross-Donaldson handed the transceiver back to Leonard.

'They're coming down in the meadow. We may as well go and meet them.'

Leonard, falling into step beside Ross-Donaldson and the Colonel, said aggrievedly, 'You ought to have let me handle that, Alastair.'

'Yes, I'm sorry. I was just keen to hear the sound of my own voice on the speakers.'

'You might have waited till a less crucial moment.'

'Who the devil are these people, anyway?' said the Colonel. 'I agree with Brian, it's a bit casual of them. Treating us like a public park. Good mind to let them cool their heels in the guard-room for a bit.'

He had to shout the last sentence over the noise of the rotor, and no more was said until the machine had touched down on the thick grass of the meadow. As its blades whirred to a stand-still the man next to the pilot, a tall fat civilian with red hair and a hooked nose, pushed his door aside and clumsily got out. The pilot, also in civilian attire, stayed where he was. The red-haired man came up to the three officers.

'Jagger's the name,' he said in a provincial accent, seeming to think this the utmost that could be required of him.

'Who are you?' asked Leonard.

'I told you. Jagger.' The man looked puzzled.

'This is a military establishment. What are you doing here?'

'Are you Leonard?'

'Yes, but –'

'Dear old official channels. All clogged to buggery again. So either you've lost your mind or somebody took their time letting you know I was coming. With luck you'll get the signal about midnight. Here.'

He had effortlessly taken from an inside pocket, and now handed to Leonard, a battered card bearing his photograph and the Home Secretary's signature. Between these were a few printed lines saying that the bearer was to be afforded full co-operation by all civilian, military and legal authorities. They did not say who employed Jagger or what his status was, and indeed Leonard never found out.

While he examined the card, he saw that Jagger was taking in the machine-gun crews and the nearby groups of armed men. He grinned, to Leonard's mind offensively, showing a mouthful of strong yellowish teeth.

'Nice little reception committee you've got laid on. Did you think I was coming down to bomb you all? Still, with me not expected you had some call to get the wind up. I took the old chopper on account of the trains are so bloody awful. Now you'll be Colonel White. Pleased to meet you, Colonel. And this is . . .?'

'Captain Ross-Donaldson, my adjutant.'

'How do you do, Captain. Flaming hot, isn't it? I don't know what we've done to deserve all this good weather. I'll just get my bag out of the chopper, and then perhaps one of you'll be kind enough to show me where I can get a drink. It's thirsty work, you know, flying.'

He turned back to the helicopter. Meanwhile Leonard spoke into his microphone.

'This is Captain Leonard. Stand down, everybody. Stand down. Some of you could have been a little quicker, but not badly done on the whole. Thank you.'

Jagger rejoined them carrying a bulky suitcase in tartan cloth with sheets of transparent plastic on the larger surfaces.

'Now what about that drink?' he said as they moved off, 'and then you can fill me in on what's been happening. All I know is that Leonard here talked to our mutual friends in high places on the scrambler early this morning and said some genius had been skylarking about with an atomic rifle and what about some assistance. So here I am with the assistance, such as it is.'

'I didn't ask for any assistance,' said Leonard.

'You didn't? I'm sorry. I was clearly given to understand you did. Another little bit of official channelling, no doubt. Anyway, as I see it, there's some sense in you being lent a hand. You've got your regular job to do and that must be pretty taxing on its own, without this atomic carry-on to see to. I'm not here to give anybody orders, by the way. Just assistance, any assistance in my power.'

'Thank you,' said Leonard distantly. 'I'll rejoin you in just a moment.'

The effect of the sherry had not taken long to wear off. Its departure had been assisted, he felt, by Ross-Donaldson's inexplicable rudeness and, far more, the arrival of this Jagger. It was typical of authority to leave one alone at difficult times and then, when one's luck changed at last, send in a total stranger, inadequately briefed, of undefined standing and probably likely to try to steal some of the credit. And without so much as prior notice ...

He left the others at the ante-room door and went yet again to the Command Post, where, after replacing the transceiver on its shelf, he was handed the transcript of a wireless message announcing Jagger's arrival by helicopter at the exact moment when the machine could be heard taking off from the meadow. No further information was given. Leonard wasted a couple of minutes drafting a sarcastic reply, then gave it up, told the corporal to send an acknowledgement and returned to the ante-room as the Colonel was saying,

'And that's all we've got.'

Jagger, sitting in the largest armchair with the reports and photographs on his lap, nodded and sniffed.

'What's known of the mental condition of this fellow Best?' he asked.

Leonard hesitated. 'Nothing for certain,' he said.

'Surmised, then.'

'Well, I think he's unbalanced.'

'In what way?'

'He seems to me to suffer from delusions.'

'What sort of delusions?'

'Well ... he thinks I'm mad.'

At this, the Colonel frowned, Venables groaned, Ross-Donaldson started to speak and stopped. Only Jagger showed no reaction.

He said, 'Are you sure?'

'Yes, pretty sure. One of his colleagues said he thought so.

That he thought Best thought I was mad, I mean.'

'And what is it about you that makes him think you're mad?'

'Because I think there are spies about.'

'About where?'

'Just about. In general. He seemed to think that anybody who thinks that there really are such things as spies must be mad.'

'Persecution fantasies. I see. Ah.'

A silver tray bearing a pint glass nearly full of not very pellucid beer had been brought to Jagger by a Mess waiter.

'Sorry it's been so long, sir.'

'Better late than never.'

'We had to send up to the other-ranks' canteen for it, you see, sir. We don't get much call for draught beer in the Mess.'

'Well, my lad, I'm probably not going to be here very long, but while I am you're going to get a rare lot of call for it, so you just get hold of the biggest jug you can lay hands on and get it filled and bring it back here and pour me another pint, because I'll be ready for one by the time you've done that, and then find a nice bit of tile or stone to stand the jug on. Okay?'

'Yes, sir.'

'Right, hop it ... Mm. Not as bad as it looks, thank Christ. Now, Leonard. Just another point or two, old lad, if I may. You let Best know you were after spies, eh?'

'Well, yes.'

'Quite right, those were your instructions. Tell me, what did you make of it when this colleague fellow said he agreed with you in thinking Best thought you were mad?'

'It increased my suspicions.'

'Your suspicions that he was an enemy agent. Yes. Why?'

'Because it's an obvious defensive technique. If Best could talk another psycho doctor into signing a paper the two of them could have me put away, couldn't they?'

'He'd have his work cut out doing that, I reckon.'

'Not necessarily.' Leonard poured himself another glass of sherry. 'This fellow Dr Minshull I met when I lunched there seemed at least as cracked as Best himself.'

'And at the same time he tipped you off that Best thought you were cracked. This is getting –'

'No, that was another man. Name of Mann.'

'All right, I've got it now. Best cracked, Minshull cracked, Mann possibly sane. Back to Best just for a moment. This business of him thinking you're cracked and what we make of it. It suggests he's cracked himself, because presumably he has no reason to believe you are cracked. But it also suggests he's an agent, in which case he's only pretending to think you're cracked as a means of getting you out of the way, in which case he's not cracked, he's no worse than cunning. You see the difficulty?'

'I think it's more apparent than real.'

'You do,' said Jagger flatly, and drained his glass. 'I wonder if that lad's back from the canteen yet. Would you be kind enough to give that bell a press, Captain?'

Ross-Donaldson, who had been following the duologue with close attention, did as he was asked.

'Thank you ... Now, where were we? Oh yes. Best cracked and Best just dead cunning. You were saying it didn't make much odds which way on it was.'

'Not that exactly. I meant that both could be true. He could genuinely think I was mad and still be trying to protect himself by getting me certified.'

'Mm. I'll have to let that one soak in for a while.'

The door opened and Hunter came in.

'Ah, here's somebody who can tell you a good deal about Best, and from personal contact too,' said Leonard urgently. He had been made more and more uncomfortable by the forensic manner of Jagger's questioning, and until this moment had seen no way of diversion.

Introductions were made and Jagger's role described.

'To save Brian embarrassment,' said Hunter, 'let me explain that I got to know Dr Best during the ten days I spent as an inmate of the alcoholics' ward at his hospital. Which reminds me to get myself a drink without delay. Sergeants and people kept me in my office arguing, or I'd have been here much sooner.'

'A good man, that,' said Leonard. 'I've found him very helpful.'

'He looks in bloody awful shape.'

'Most of us have been up since four-thirty or five. He's been on his feet for God knows how long supervising the search of the camp.'

'No picnic, I agree. Look, Leonard, this place'll be filling up soon, I take it, when the fellows finish their lectures, and it's all a bit grand for me anyhow. Is there a quiet pub round here where we can have a pint and a sandwich and a real chat?'

'The White Hart in the village does quite decent snacks. Shall we ask Max Hunter along? He can tell you about Best, and I need him for my plan for pulling Best in. I still haven't had my authority for that, by the way, but as soon as –'

'Don't you worry, I've brought that with me.' Jagger patted his breast pocket. 'It's conditional on the rifle being found in his possession.'

'Of course, I wouldn't move until that happens.'

'That's the way to talk. Well yes, by all means get Hunter to come, then. We'll have to watch our tongues, though, won't we? Ah, you were right about him being a good lad. He's bringing my pint over.'

*

Half an hour later the three were at the counter of the saloon bar in the White Hart. Anne, the round-faced barmaid, was on duty.

'Isn't it shocking about poor Mrs Casement?' she asked Hunter.

'Yes, terrible. I'll have one of those ham sandwiches, please.'

'They're tongue, sir. It seems only yesterday she was in here behind the bar.'

'That'll do. Well, she's in good hands. Have you any mustard?'

'And three pints of keg,' said Jagger. 'That's if neither of you have got any other ideas.'

'I've got lots of other ideas,' said Hunter, 'but it'll be better for everybody if I keep them to myself. Incidentally I can recommend the pickled onions.'

'Good idea. I'll have six, please, miss.'

They settled themselves at a small oval table by the window.

The sun was streaming in and Leonard drew the heavy linen curtain before getting down to the first of two Scotch eggs. The room was not crowded and seemed pleasantly dark and cool. When he had disposed of a large pork pie and asked Leonard a few questions, Jagger said,

'So the way you look at it, it's all over bar the shouting. Once we've nabbed him, then it's money for jam picking up his contact inside the camp. I hope you're right.'

Leonard nearly finished a mouthful of Scotch egg, making disagreeing noises the while, and said, 'Not money for jam. No. Substantially easier, though. A man of Best's personality make-up might easily tell us everything we want to know with a little pressure, or even without any at all.'

'Mm. It's possible. You know, the more I think about that personality make-up of Best's the more interested I get.' Jagger sat in a hunched position on the padded window-seat, blinking his pale greenish eyes and licking fragments of pie off his teeth. He spoke slowly. 'If he's all we take him for, he's been given a highly specialized espionage job concerned with finding out and transmitting secrets. Just secrets. Then, on the spur of the moment and at great risk of immediate discovery, he pinches a rifle and goes straight off and shoots it at something. Whatever else that does, it advertises the fact that someone's got that rifle who shouldn't have. You see? The rifle's a secret. If a fellow gets hold of a secret, he ought to try to stop it leaking out that anybody's got hold of the secret, or the secret instantly becomes less valuable.'

'I told you he was unbalanced,' said Leonard. 'He could have suffered a sudden outburst of paranoia. We'll probably get the answer to that when we question him. Anyway, I was going to say that, failing any sort of complete confession from him, the spy in the camp will be cut off from his line of communication and so neutralized for the time being. Then we can set it up so that as soon as the opposition start trying to provide him with another outlet, or he starts looking for one, we'll have him. So far I've been working from hand to mouth on this job, but with Best captured I'll be able to get all the men and resources I care to ask for.'

'It's a pity in a way you've got to pull Best in,' said Hunter, stubbing out a cigarette on the considerable remains of his tongue sandwich. 'If you left him at liberty with a close watch on him, he might lead you to other people.'

Jagger sniffed. 'Can't be done, my lad,' he said. 'He can do a lot more harm with that thing in his possession. And we can hardly take it back off him and let him go on as usual. Even a fellow with his personality make-up would think there was something a bit fishy about that.'

'But what harm can he do? He's got no more ammunition.'

'No no, I mean he's got to get bits of the thing away somehow to be gone over by experts, plus photographs and so forth.'

'Can't you stop him?'

'We daren't risk it, bugger it,' said Jagger, suddenly irritated. 'There's a sight too much at stake, my lad. At the moment we don't know who his courier is or how he gets to him or anything. We're still very much in the dark about all that end of it.'

'I see. But there is just one thing I don't see.'

'Well?'

'This is where Max has been so useful,' put in Leonard. 'Constructive criticism.'

'I'm sure. Well, Hunter?'

'Now Best's got the rifle, what more does he want? What can his contact in the camp have to tell him? After he'd tipped him off about the Exercise, I should have thought his job was done.'

'No no no. There's lots of other stuff Best needs. Technical details, stuff about tactics, strategic plans, all that.'

'Perhaps he's already got it.'

'Impossible.' Leonard was emphatic. 'I'd have known.'

'But look. Don't you think he's behaving like somebody who's got all he needs?'

Leonard merely shook his head, but Jagger stiffened in his chair. Hunter looked at him for a moment, then lit another cigarette.

'Well, either way we'll have him in the bag soon,' said Jagger.

There was an uneasy silence. It was still unbroken when Eames, who had appeared behind the counter a moment earlier, caught sight of Hunter, lifted the flap and came over to the group.

'Everything all right, gentlemen?'

'Yes, thank you, landlord,' said Jagger. 'Very nice bit of pie indeed.'

'Thank you, sir.' Eames turned to Hunter. 'I don't suppose there'll be any recent news of Mrs Casement, will there, Captain?'

'Only that she went into hospital this morning.'

'Yes, I heard she was going. It'll be early days yet, then, to expect to hear anything. But what a shocking business. Out of a clear sky. Act of God, as you might say.'

'Yes,' said Hunter, 'you might well say that.'

'Just as she and Mr Churchill had become so attached. How is he, by the way?'

'I saw him for a moment this morning. He seems to be bearing up fairly well.'

'A fine young gentleman, that. Would you give him my very best wishes, Captain?'

'Indeed I will, Mr Eames, and thank you very much.'

'Well ...' Eames seemed to want to say more, but ducked his head, said quickly, 'Good afternoon, gentlemen,' and left them.

'It's the most awful thing,' said Leonard to Jagger. 'This Casement girl has just developed cancer, very young, not much more than thirty, and she's, uh, involved with young Churchill, one of the –'

'Of course, lieutenant, Blue Howards, that's right. The youngest on the team, as I remember. Friend of yours, is he, Hunter?'

'Yes.'

'Very sad. Tragic, in fact.'

'You know, Max,' said Leonard thoughtfully, 'it strikes me as rather the sort of thing our Anti-Death League friend might have included in that notice of his if it had come up by then and he'd known about it.'

'Exactly the sort of thing.'

Leonard turned to Jagger again. 'Some harmless nut put up a

lot of notices round the camp calling for a meeting of what he called the Anti-Death League. Nobody turned up; it was a complete wash-out. There was a poem too which got sent to the padre and might have been by the same chap. Nothing in it really, as it's turned out, but it got me quite worried at the time, I don't mind telling you.'

'You must let me have a look,' said Jagger. 'Especially the poem. I rather care for a bit of poetry, though I know it's not to everybody's taste.' He laughed.

The alarm buzzer on Leonard's wrist sounded. The three jumped up and ran out of the building into the yard, where Leonard's car was parked. He flung the door open, releasing a waft of heat, got behind the wheel, switched the radio on and spoke enthusiastically into the microphone.

'Hullo, Control. Padlock here. Over.'

A voice on the loudspeaker said, 'Hullo, Padlock. Message from public library. Book has been found. I say again, book has been found. Representative will meet you as arranged. Over.'

'Roger,' said Leonard in a trembling voice. 'Out.'

He sat still for a moment, then turned in his seat and looked at them.

'Well, gentlemen,' he said finally, 'shall we go and get him?'

The other two climbed in and Leonard drove off down the village street, narrowly missing a parked lorry full of some root crop. As they went he outlined his plan, which was simple but to all appearance workable. After that nobody spoke until they reached a point some two hundred yards from the main gate of the hospital. Here Leonard drew into the side and stopped.

'This is where I'm meeting my man,' he said, got out and urinated into the hedge, or pretended to.

There was silence apart from the feeble chirrup of a bird and the ticking of the engine as it lost heat. After a moment Jagger spoke suddenly and angrily from over Hunter's shoulder,

'Rifle, rifle, rifle,' he said. 'Rifle this, rifle that, rifle the other thing. Buggering rifle.'

'It has been a nuisance, certainly.'

'Bloody sight worse than that, old lad.'

Leonard got back in again and they moved away.

'It's in that big hallstand affair outside his room,' he said. 'Bold as brass.'

'What took the blind bastards so long to find it, then?' asked Jagger.

'He keeps a bag of golf-clubs there most of the time. They thought the rifle in its covering was another one, I gathered.'

Jagger gave a groan of Venables pitch. 'There's some heads'll roll when this little lot's over,' he said.

'All right, Jagger,' said Leonard. 'Out of sight now.'

With more groans, Jagger laboriously lowered himself to the floor behind the front seats. Leonard turned into the hospital drive and stopped again. Hunter, very pale, got out and hurried into the lodge. The thickset blue-suited man confronted him.

'What can I do for you, sir? Oh, it's Captain Hunter, isn't it?'

'Yes. I want to see Dr Best rather urgently. Is he free?'

'I don't know about that, sir.'

'But he always keeps this time open for people who want to talk to him.'

'Well, he may have someone with him already, you see.'

'I don't mind waiting. Could you telephone him and find out?'

'I could. Who's that in the car with you?'

'Just a friend who drove me over.'

'Mm. Wait a minute.'

Keeping his eyes on Hunter, the man went to a wall telephone and cranked its handle. After a minute he spoke.

'Johnson here, doctor, speaking from the lodge. I've got that Captain Hunter here, with a friend of his, he says. Wants to have a word with you ... All right, doctor.'

He rang off and turned to Hunter.

'You can go up,' he said grudgingly.

Hunter left without a word, grateful for not having had to use an alternative part of the plan whereby, should Best have refused to see him, he was to have seized the telephone off Johnson, done a bit of – almost certainly ineffective – pleading, and pretended to Johnson that he had been granted an interview after all.

'Okay?' Leonard asked him when he was back in the car.

'No trouble. He'll see us.'

Leonard nodded sharply once and let in the clutch. Viewed sidelong, his face looked tense and determined enough, with tightened mouth and the familiar trickle of sweat from under the khaki cap, but about the eye visible to Hunter there was something exultant, ardent, even awe-struck, such as might be seen (it occurred to Hunter) in a devout youth off to his first communion, or an elderly sexual deviate approaching the arena where every detail of his hitherto impracticable perversion had finally been marshalled. Hunter hoped that nothing would happen to spoil Leonard's imminent triumph.

At the edge of the car-park a man was on one knee doing something very trifling to a rose-bush. His posture was stylized, as if conservatively adapted from an illustration in a military text-book. As prearranged, it was his part to fetch the rifle from outside Best's room and get it into the car.

'You've got two minutes,' muttered Leonard as he and Hunter went by. Jagger was to stay in the car – though he had been given permission to resume his seat, provided he kept out of sight – and act as a mobile reserve.

Crossing the hall of the staff block, Leonard kept his eyes straight in front of him, but Hunter could not resist a glance over at the hallstand where, almost hidden by raincoats and the bulky golf-bag in rust-coloured canvas, the N H W-17 stood on end in its webbing cover.

Leonard knocked at a door.

'Come in, come in, come in,' called a loud and hearty voice.

They entered and Dr Best rose to greet them.

Hunter thought he had never seen the doctor in such good spirits. His blue eyes were wider and brighter than ever before, and his smile showed an unprecedented number of black-edged teeth. The bandage round his bald head was neat enough, and set sufficiently askew, to seem raffish or exotic rather than a sign of physical injury. He shook hands warmly with Hunter, at the same time holding out his left hand towards Leonard in the manner of some celebrated or ambitious actor. After a moment's hesitation Leonard reached awkwardly across his body and shook the hand.

What Leonard, perhaps typically, had not foreseen, or at any rate had not mentioned to Hunter as a possibility to be reckoned with, was the presence of Dr Minshull, who had also risen to his feet, if he had not been on them all along, and who now stood gazing over the heads of the new arrivals. He and Best were at either side of the dining-table, which was bare apart from a half-full decanter, two glasses, a brass hand-bell, and a printed document with handwritten insertions.

'Sit down, my dear fellows, sit down, sit down,' cried Dr Best. 'I hope you'll join us for coffee and brandy.'

In the absence of any lead from Leonard, Hunter did as he was told. He found himself in a very low armchair padded in yellow satin. Before he had done more than begin looking round the room, which he had passed through several times before now on his way to the adjacent consulting-room, Dr Best rang his hand-bell.

'Actually I can offer you a very nice Oporto-bottled Constantino 1935 which came my way recently,' he said, 'though do please take brandy if you prefer it.'

'I'd like some brandy, please,' said Hunter mechanically. He realized without much precision that, however free of Best he might have felt over the last weeks, returning to Best's home ground reawoke in him certain feelings of being trapped. They seemed reinforced by his present nearness to the floor. The smell of lilies was almost overpowering.

'Hine, Martell or Courvoisier?'

'Hine, please.'

'Three Star, V S O P or Antique?'

'Antique, please.'

'A lot or a little?'

'A lot, please.'

He was given a lot. Not having heard the door behind him open, he was surprised a moment later to find at his shoulder a dark-haired girl wearing a single garment of white leather that stopped only at neck and wrists. She was carrying a silver tray and, from where he was, looked very tall.

'Black, sir?' she asked.

'Oh. Yes. Thank you.'

She poured and handed him a cup of coffee and moved over to Leonard. A blonde girl in black leather took her place.

'Just sugar for you, sir?'

Hunter tried to dispel the disagreeable sense of unreality that had been growing on him since entering the room. 'No, I'll change my mind if I may,' he said. 'I think there's room there for just the tiniest spot of milk ... And the merest suspicion of sugar ... No no, that's splendid, that's quite perfect ... Many many thanks.'

He was still trying to think of something useful to think to himself about the girls when the door shut behind them and Dr Best said,

'Can I offer you a Romeo y Julieta?'

'A what?' said Leonard, speaking for the first time.

'Perhaps a Half Corona?'

'Oh. No thank you. Dr Best, I'd like to have a word with –'

'Well, this is a great day, a great day, my dear Captain Leonard. Here you are at last, eh?'

'At last?' Leonard seemed mystified.

'Oh yes, we've been expecting you. Haven't we, Minshull?'

The man addressed gave a long, ascending whinny of laughter.

'Well, I have been meaning for some time to return that very pleasant lunch you gave me here,' said Leonard bravely, 'by asking you over to our Mess. So when my colleague here mentioned to me that he –'

Here both doctors laughed.

'Oh, Captain Leonard,' said Dr Best, shaking his bandaged head, 'what a wag you are. So very droll after your own fashion. But let's be serious if we can. What is the real purpose of your visit here?'

'I was just going to explain that it was Captain Hunter who mentioned to me that he wanted to come and see you, and I simply –'

'Ah yes, of course, the liquor-loving Captain Hunter. How are you, sir? – but I can see how you are. In need of a further course of treatment. Well, it'll be a pleasure to furnish that.

Your probation isn't up for another ten days or so, but we can easily advance matters.'

'Dr Best,' said Hunter, 'what's the matter with your head?'

'It was rather annoying. I went on a little expedition into the country yesterday, a short drive followed by a ramble on foot. Much as one enjoys the society of one's fellow-creatures, there do come times when one prefers to be ... unencumbered. I'd noticed that one of the new gardeners here was taking a great interest in my activities, following me to the golf club and back and so on on his scooter, so before setting off yesterday morning I took the liberty of letting the air out of one of his tyres. What's that called in your parlance, Captain Leonard? – "shaking a tail" would it be, or is it "losing a tag"?'

Leonard said nothing. He was sitting quite still.

'Anyway, after this short drive of mine I parked my car in an inconspicuous place and set off across country. I must have gone about a mile and a half, I suppose, and was getting the full benefit of the sun and the fresh air, when I fell into a hole. It was so well camouflaged with ferns and other greenery as to be virtually undetectable. I hit my head on a stone and was rendered unconscious for what must have been several hours. When I came to myself the shadows were lengthening, and I was full of chagrin at the time to think that my expedition was wasted, that its purpose was unfulfilled. But it wasn't, was it, Captain Leonard? It very clearly was not.'

'I don't follow you.'

'Oh yes you do, my dear fellow. I succeeded in my aim, didn't I? Because here you are to arrest me for espionage. But I'm glad to say that there's some real hope for you. The rapidity and decisiveness with which you've made your psychic shift is prognostically highly favourable. Your illness now stands revealed, naked in all its ... majesty.'

Leonard rose shakily to his feet.

'I am a Security officer,' he said, 'with credentials from the Ministry of Defence, and with authority from the same body to compel you to accompany me before a tribunal, against the composition of which you will be at liberty to appeal in due time. I must ask you to accompany me now.'

'What are the charges against me, Captain Leonard?' asked Dr Best interestedly.

'Specifically, the theft of property lying under the Official Secrets Act and the unauthorized use of it in a manner calculated further to prejudice the safety of the realm. No doubt there'll also be a civil charge relating to conduct likely to lead to physical injury or loss of life.'

'That's not so good, is it, Minshull?' said Dr Best, grinning as broadly as when they had entered the room. 'I don't like that at all.'

With a despairing glance at Hunter, Leonard said, 'What do you mean, not so good?'

'What is this property and how am I supposed to have used it?'

'You know very well, Best,' shouted Leonard. 'You stole an atomic rifle and fired it off in the middle of the night.'

'Oh? And where is this rifle now?'

'Outside in your hallstand. At least it was. I've repossessed it.'

Both doctors laughed again.

'So it isn't there any more,' said Dr Best in childish tones. 'What a pity. If it was still there we could all have had a jolly game with it.'

'You're raving mad,' Leonard was shouting again. 'And let's have no more of this nonsense. You're coming with me.'

'Oh no, Captain Leonard,' said Dr Best cordially. 'I'm not mad. It's you who are mad. And I have a piece of paper to prove it. It's much more powerful than any piece of paper you can produce against me.'

He picked up the document from the table and flourished it.

'I have here an order committing you to an asylum under the Mental Health Act, 1959,' he went on. 'This asylum. It's signed by two doctors – I'm sure you can guess who they are – and it provides for a course of treatment lasting one year in the first instance. Which means that I shall not be coming with you. It's you who'll be coming with me. Not very far, of course, but far enough.'

Hunter too got up.

'We've a car outside,' he said. 'Either you go there voluntarily, or Leonard and I will take you.'

'You really shouldn't have had that brandy, Captain Hunter. I fear it's been too much for you. Neither of your alternatives is acceptable.'

Hunter and Leonard each took a step forward.

'Stay where you are, you lunatics. Nurse!'

Hunter turned and saw someone he recognized come through the doorway from the consulting room, a man of about thirty-five with an unusually small nose. He had discarded the white coat he usually wore and had on a white tee-shirt, under which his muscles were noticeable, and white drill trousers. In each hand he carried a large hypodermic syringe.

'Hullo, Maxie dear,' said the man. 'Long time no see, eh?'

'You'd better take them one at a time, nurse,' said Dr Best. He indicated Leonard. 'This man first, I think.'

The nurse placed one of the hypodermics carefully on the sideboard between two decanters and advanced on Leonard, who took a small automatic pistol from his pocket.

'Keep away,' he said more steadily than earlier, pointing the pistol at the nurse.

The nurse came on. 'Don't be silly, my old nut,' he said.

As soon as Leonard had snicked off his safety-catch Dr Best caught hold of his gun-arm. Hunter jumped forward and, though hampered by the intervening corner of the table, hit Dr Best hard enough on the cheekbone to send his glasses flying and perhaps make him loosen his hold. Anyway, Leonard shook it off, but was unable to turn before the nurse was on him. The two spun away, the left hand of each grasping the other's right wrist. At once Hunter was on Dr Best again and bent him backwards over the table. While they were struggling, Hunter heard Minshull's laughter and then a clattering sound which he interpreted correctly as that of Leonard's pistol falling to the floor. A moment later Dr Best got a hand to the decanter on the table and hit Hunter twice on the side of the head with it. This was not very painful, and quite soon Hunter had that wrist, so that when the stopper came jumping out of the decanter he was able to direct a stream of brandy into Dr Best's face. While he was doing this, he heard more noise behind him, this time a crashing and smashing which turned out later to have been caused by Leonard being hurled against the loaded sideboard. The brandy quietened Dr Best down a certain amount, so then it was not hard for Hunter to pull him upright by his lapels and give him a punch on the jaw that caused him to fall over immediately and decisively. Hunter now went for the nurse, who had transferred his hypodermic to his left hand and was repeatedly hitting Leonard with his right. He stopped this just for the instant required to bring his right elbow round and down into Hunter's stomach. Hunter dropped to hands and knees, from which position he was able clearly to see Jagger burst into the room and run up to the nurse, but not what it was which flung the nurse so hard against the oak-panelled wall that he slid quickly down it and finished up motionless.

'Dear oh dear,' said Jagger. 'Got yourselves into a right mess, didn't you? Good job I got bored with huddling up in that car and started wandering round outside here. Why didn't you yell when this lot got going?'

'We didn't think of it,' said Hunter. 'At first there was no need to, and then there was too much going on.'

'I gave you strict orders to stay in that car, Jagger. Where are my spectacles?'

Leonard spoke indistinctly. He was dabbing with a handkerchief at the blood trickling from his nose and from a cut at the corner of his mouth.

'Here,' said Jagger. The glasses were undamaged.

'A good thing for you he did disobey orders, or they'd have had you in a strait-jacket by now. Where's Minshull?'

'Eh?'

'There was another doctor in here. He must have slipped out. Didn't you see him?'

'Bugger him for a start; there's plenty here to keep us busy. What was that about a strait-jacket, Hunter? Are you serious?'

Hunter had poured himself another large glass of Dr Best's Hine Antique. He now retrieved the committal order and handed it over.

'They had something lined up for me as well. This chap was

going to inject both of us. There's my dose on the sideboard.'

'Now do you believe he's mad?' asked Leonard, who was carefully going through what bottles remained unbroken. 'Ah.' He picked out a bottle of brown sherry, uncorked it, and drank from its neck.

'Mm.' Jagger nodded and sniffed. 'A bit wild, certainly. But is he a spy?'

'I can answer that question,' said Dr Best from the floor behind the dining-table.

He got up without apparent difficulty and came over to them. His eyes looked a size larger without his glasses. When he spoke it was in a clipped, brisk tone that Hunter had never heard him use before.

'There must have been a leak,' he said. 'A big leak. Twelve of our key men had been pulled in. Nearly all the others blown. Throughout the country our spy network was in ruins. The chief was in despair. The biggest job of all time had come up and he had nobody to send. Nobody? There was Best. But would Best agree to go? Best's last exploit had saved the world from destruction by death-rays. Best had been decorated by fifty governments. Best had been given a hundred million in gold and everything he wanted and no questions asked. Best was dining in his villa. Best was being served incomparable food and wines by his staff of Greek boys. Best's eye ran lazily over their naked forms. Best was called to the telephone. Best was humbly begged to come to the chief's office. Best tried to refuse. "Best," said the chief, "the world is in danger of destruction by death-rays." Best said it was none of his affair. "Best, you're the only one who can save us." Best let himself be talked into it. Best went to see the chief. "Best, meet your assistant." Best was introduced to the most marvellous twenty-year-old. Best's eye ran lazily over his naked form. Best was called to the telephone. "Best," said the chief, "the world is in danger of destruction by death-rays." Best knew he was the only man who could save them. Best . . .'

By this time the nurse had joined Best's audience and Jagger had gone into the consulting-room next door, where he could be heard telephoning. When he came back, Best was still talking.

'They're all barmy here, you know,' said the nurse.

'He's no danger to us any more,' said Jagger. 'No use either.'

'That's the end of that,' said Leonard. 'Now we can go after the man in the camp.'

'It hasn't been as much fun as I thought it would be,' said Hunter.

Best went on talking while Mann arrived and, with the zealous assistance of the nurse, took him away.

*

'Very good,' said Ayscue, dropping his violin and bow on to his bed. 'Only a few minor points. Mr Townsend. In bars 24 to 27 . . .'

The curly-haired young man seated at the Bechstein flipped back to the place indicated. As the village church organist and choirmaster he had worked so hard preparing for the Roughead concert that Ayscue had not been able to avoid asking him to be the pianist in the trio-sonata. In this role he had proved musicianly enough, though inclined to overdo his interpretation of the figured bass.

'Yes, Major,' he said in his country voice.

'Where Andy and I are swapping those little phrases. I think unless you stick to a rigid four-in-a-bar there you may be in danger of . . .'

'Swamping you. Right, Major. Duly noted.'

'Fine.' Ayscue ran a handkerchief round his neck. 'Now, Andy. Just after that, in bar 28, that first note. It ought to have a good strong accent on it, I think, from both Mr Townsend and you.'

Pearce put his flute to his lips and produced a note with a good strong accent on it.

'Yes. Not sudden, of course, just the natural top of the crescendo. Oh, I wanted to ask you both . . . Going back to bars 17 and 18: would it be a good idea if I did a rather different sort of staccato bowing for the middle two quavers in each of those bars? The trouble is, if you're hopping downstairs like that, you've got the volume but it's difficult to get the tone. Anyway . . .'

When Ayscue had tried over the two bars in question, Pearce said tentatively,

'I don't know, sir, it sounds a bit fancy that way, somehow.'

'Well, it's not right for the period, is it?' said Townsend.

Ayscue pretended to consider. He had merely wanted Townsend to feel paid back in kind for being criticized on the figured-bass detail.

'No, it isn't. I see that now you mention it. I'll leave it, then. Well. That's all I've got, I think. Is there anything else?'

'Just the ending, sir,' said Pearce. 'Those last few bars — are we still supposed to be staccato there?'

'No, very much not. Four long accents to the bar, and as tight together as you can get them without actually phrasing them over.'

'Right, sir.'

There was a pause. Pearce played a short run rapidly, then slowly. Townsend looked up from the piano.

'Shall we run through it again, Major? I've got plenty of time myself.'

'No, I don't think so. Let's leave something in hand for the performance. Thank you both for coming. Now what time shall we say on Sunday? Two-thirty at the church? Can I give you a lift to the village, Mr Townsend? Sure? See you both on Sunday, then.'

Conscious of having bundled them out rather, Ayscue began wandering slowly round his hut, hands in pockets. A final play-over of the Roughead piece would not in fact have been wasted, but he had decided against it to make certain that his interest stayed alive, that the trio-sonata remained untouched by the mingled anxiety and boredom that had infiltrated other concerns of his. He had abandoned his scheme of a unit magazine. The only contribution of substance had been the anonymous poem. This, when asked for it by Leonard earlier that afternoon, he had handed over without question, without any of the personal concern he had felt on first reading it. Determining its author-ship and that of the poster about the Anti-Death League had begun to suffer the process, odiously familiar over the past few years, of ceasing to involve him and becoming something that merely nagged at him for a time, until he woke up one morning and added it to the list of his evasions. And when had he last thought about Pearce's situation? And then there was Churchill's news, reported by Hunter the previous evening. Ayscue knew he must work out some means of helping, but felt he had become unable to solve such problems. He was afraid that quite soon he would no longer be capable of any action.

There was a knock at the door. When it opened, Nancy rushed in as if she had spent the previous hour in a cage instead of running about the camp. She was followed by one Tighe, who had replaced Evans as Ayscue's batman at the first opportunity after the League meeting.

'All right, sir?' asked Tighe. 'Or do you want me to take her round again?'

'No, they've gone now, thank you. Here.'

Ayscue handed over five shillings.

'Have a drink with me, Tighe.'

'Thank you, sir.'

Was he really very much surprised and slightly puzzled, or only pretending to be? Ayscue gave it up. When Tighe had gone, he stooped down and took Nancy's head on to his knees.

'Would you like another little run?' he asked. 'Say if you're too tired.'

The telephone rang.

'Ayscue here.'

'Call for you, sir ... You're through to Major Ayscue.'

'This is the museum,' said Lucy's faintly hoarse voice. 'Could you come over, do you think?'

'I'm afraid this evening isn't very convenient. I have to take the chair at a lecture here.'

'A lecture?' She sounded puzzled, no doubt wondering if this was a code phrase she was expected to interpret on the spot.

'Yes, a lecture. By somebody called Caton. On American and South American armed forces and their public image. What you might call a very real lecture. An actual lecture, so to speak.'

'Oh. Oh. I see. But I wasn't thinking of this evening. I meant straight away.'

'Is it urgent? Is anything wrong?'

'I think it is rather. Urgent, I mean. It's . . . Mr James.'

'What's the trouble?' asked Ayscue, trying not to sound frightened.

'Well . . . he won't get up. He's gone to bed and he won't get up.'

'Is he ill?'

'Not exactly. He just won't get up.'

'You mean because of . . .'

'Yes.'

Ayscue hesitated. 'I don't think I'd be any good to him,' he said. 'Whenever we've talked about this sort of situation in the past, more or less in general, all I've done is make him angry.'

'Well, that would be better than nothing, honestly. Better than him being as he is. You don't know what he's like.'

'All right. I'll come over at once. Of course I will.'

When he had rung off, Ayscue sat for a time staring at the front page of the Roughead sonata. Then he got up, put on his jacket and cap, told Nancy she must stay where she was, and hurried across a corner of the meadow to a hut of the same pattern as his own.

Naidu was sitting on his bed in his shirtsleeves reading a lavishly illustrated work on Georgian furniture he had borrowed from the town library. He put it aside and stood up when Ayscue came in.

'Good afternoon, my dear Willie.'

'Hullo, Moti. Can I ask you a favour?'

'By all means, of course. Would you care for a glass of fresh lemonade?'

'No thanks. Look, Moti, it's about James Churchill. I've just had Lucy Hazell on the telephone and he's at her place now and as far as I can make out he seems to be suffering from . . . well, having some sort of breakdown. I'm going to drive over there and I wondered whether I could persuade you to come along too. He'll probably pay more attention to you than to me.'

'Oh, do you think so?' Naidu stood considering for a moment. 'I give a conversation class at five p.m.'

'That won't leave you any time. Can't you postpone it or something?'

'Naturally I can. I take your word for it it's necessary. Excuse me for two seconds while I telephone.'

They were soon on their way in Ayscue's pick-up truck. As they passed near the place where St Jerome's Priory had been, Naidu said,

'That proceeding last night carried an air of fantasy. What could anybody hope to gain from such a thing?'

'I don't know, Moti. And I don't really expect to. There's a lot going on in this part of the world that you and I have no idea of. Anyway, the Colonel told me before lunch that Brian Leonard expects to arrest that psychiatrist chap any moment.'

'I can shed no tears over that, can you? A man all of whose feelings are malevolent. From what Max and Brian have to say of him it's easy to form a picture of a man very hostile to his fellow-creatures. He wages war on them to the utmost of his ability.'

'Like a sort of super-Venables.'

'Oh, there I think, Willie, you're being rather unjust to the gallant major. He views human beings with nothing more than a weariness and contempt for not being the vessels of perfect reason he'd like them to be. This makes him an excellent choice to supervise the training for this highly destructive project, whatever it is, that the unit exists to further. A person of the type of Best would be excessively involved with the destruction. Whereas Venables is detached. As is our good friend Alastair Ross-Donaldson, who is, if you like, at a further stage. Mankind as such makes no appeal to him one way or the other. In his eyes we're all just a lot of little points on a graph.'

'Now who's being unfair? I've always found Alastair perfectly pleasant. He's certainly got very nice manners.'

'Oh, of course he has. I don't want to be harsh to him, Willie. He's a very nice chap indeed. But his manners, admirable as they are, are purely and simply the product of his training. The finest kind of English training.'

'Scottish, actually, I imagine. But I take your point. But I still think there's more to Alastair than just shows on the surface.'

'Which no doubt would only be revealed in certain situations. Until these things come along, I agree there's a lot we don't know about people, including ourselves.'

They said nothing for a time, each thinking of Churchill. Then, when they were nearing their destination, Naidu said,

'I've heard a good deal about Lady Hazell in the Mess, but some of it sounds wildly exaggerated. Is she as promiscuous as Alastair, for instance, gives one to understand? Whatever you say will of course go no further.'

'I don't really know the answer, Moti. I've just met her a couple of times over this piece of music I found in her library. She seems pretty decent to me. She's certainly been very kind to poor Catharine Casement.'

'Yes, a warm heart is known to accompany, what shall we say? – the free granting of sexual favours. I hope I didn't sound puritanical about that just now, by the way. At the least, Lady Hazell has helped several of the young men in our midst to remove their frustrations. Or would you feel bound to take a harsher view?'

'Good God, no, I've seen too much of life. There's nothing blessed about frustration.'

'I know that all too well.'

'Forgive me, Moti, believe me I'm not prying, it's just that I come across this a lot in my work, but how do you cope with that problem?'

'I just cope. Sometimes it gets very difficult, and then I think hard to myself about a lovely girl in Ujjain and a couple of young bairns, and it becomes not quite so difficult for a while.'

'It must be different when you've got someone.'

'You've never had a wife, have you, Willie?'

'Oh yes. Indeed I still have. It wasn't a success, though.'

'What went wrong?'

'Oh, it was all my fault.'

'I doubt that, knowing you. Is this the place? It looks rather grand, I must say. In what period was it built?'

'What you see dates from the eighteen-sixties, I'm told, though there are supposed to be some bits left over from Queen Anne or so. That's Lucy coming out now.'

'A striking-looking woman.'

'I agree.'

When they had got out, Naidu saluted Lucy, then swept off his hat and kissed her hand.

'This is Captain Naidu, Lucy. Moti, you've heard me speak of Lady Hazell. Moti's a friend of James's too.'

'How do you do, Moti. Let me take you up to James straight away, both of you. He won't get up, you know, Willie. He just lies there.'

'What does he say about it?'

'He just says he can't. Get up. When he says anything at all.'

They went into the house, where it seemed very dark in contrast to the sunlight.

'How long has he been here?' asked Ayscue.

'Three hours? I don't know. I went in and found him there. It scared the life out of me, honestly.'

'Has he had lunch?'

'He didn't say. You know he took Catharine to the hospital this morning and had a talk with the doctor in charge of her? Anyway, I don't think it's anything the doctor said to him. Nothing in particular, that is. They can't know anything yet. I think it's just the whole thing ... you know ...'

'Yes,' said Ayscue. 'In here?'

'Yes. Do your best for him, won't you? I know you will. I'll be downstairs.'

The two men entered the room formerly occupied by Catharine. Churchill was lying on his back in bed with the covers drawn up to his chin. His uniform jacket and trousers were neatly hung on the back of a chair and his shoes symmetrically arranged underneath it. He made no movement when they went and stood at the foot of the bed.

'Hullo, James. Moti and I thought we'd drop in and see you. How are you?'

Churchill went on looking at the ceiling, or into space.

'Tell us how you feel,' said Naidu. 'Describe it as exactly as you can. Then Willie and I will be able to help you.'

After a minute of silence, Ayscue started to speak again, but Naidu checked him with a hand on his arm. Perhaps another minute had gone by when Churchill spoke, in a faint and monotonous voice, as if very tired.

'I didn't want to stay in camp,' he said, 'and go to lectures. I came over here. It was so quiet. I thought it would be better if I got into her bed. I thought that was a good idea. There was nowhere else I wanted to be. I couldn't think of anywhere else I could be. But it's just as bad. There isn't anywhere to be.'

About this time they noticed tears beginning to flow steadily from his eyes. He himself seemed unaware that this was happening. His face did not become distorted in any way.

'It's worse,' he went on. 'It just shows me how much she isn't here. It isn't like the same bed or the same room. You can't remember it well enough. It wipes it all out. It stops it ever having happened. You're falling off a cliff and yesterday you saw something beautiful. Now you're falling off a cliff and so yesterday you didn't see something beautiful. She wasn't really here. Because she's gone.'

They waited, but there was evidently no more for the moment. Ayscue sat down on the bed, took out his handkerchief and wiped Churchill's eyes.

'There are things we've got to settle, James,' he said hesitantly. 'You'll have to get back to camp pretty soon or you'll be marked absent. And in a case like this, top secret and the rest of it, that's serious, James. If you don't look out you're going to get yourself arrested, and then you won't be able to see Catharine at all.'

'I don't mind what happens,' said Churchill almost at once.

'That's what you say now. You'll mind all right when you find they won't let you see Catharine.'

'That's already happened.'

'I mean at all. You told me yourself they'll put you away for God knows how long if you desert. Your only chance of going on seeing Catharine is to go on this Operation thing and then come back.'

'Oh, I'm not going on the Operation,' said Churchill, his tone betraying for the first time some slight emotion: surprise that Ayscue should need to be told anything so self-evident.

Ayscue was not speaking at all hesitantly now. 'You've got

to,' he said. 'You can't just lie there. Get up and I'll drive you back to camp.'

'I'm not coming.'

'You must! James, don't be a fool. There's no sense in this kind of behaviour. It just makes everything worse. Surely you can see that? Or are you trying not to? From every point of view it's your duty to get out of that bed and get your clothes on.'

'Don't tell me my duty,' said Churchill slowly.

'I'm not talking about your duty as a soldier. Not altogether, anyhow. Mostly not. You've got a duty as a man as well. That's much more important.'

'I don't want to hear about it. Not from you. Padre.'

'Forget the padre.'

'I can't forget. Or forgive. Go away. You love everything I hate. Go away. Leave me alone.'

'I won't.' Ayscue leant across and took Churchill by the shoulders. 'I know what you think. You think God's arranged all this. That's absurd. You must stop yourself thinking it. It's dangerous.'

'God doesn't exist.'

'I know that as well as you do. Better than you do. You're afraid he might exist. You've got to convince yourself absolutely that there's no such thing if you don't want to go mad.'

'But you're a parson.'

'What about it?'

Churchill tried feebly to disengage himself from Ayscue's grip.

'This is worse. Pretending to agree with me. It won't work.'

'Now you listen to me,' said Ayscue loudly. 'You're not quite as original as you think you are. To believe at all deeply in the Christian God, in any sort of benevolent deity, is a disgrace to human decency and intelligence. Of course it is. We can take that as read. I was so convinced of it when I was about your age that I saw the Church as the embodiment of the most effectively vicious lie ever told. I declared a personal war on it. That was why I joined – so as to be able to work against it more destructively from within. I used to have a lot of fun in those days with things like devising an order of service that would please God much more than merely grovelling and begging for mercy or praising him for his cruelty in the past and looking forward to seeing more of the same in the future. Selected members of the congregation getting their arms chopped off and/or their eyes put out as a warm-up. Then a canticle about his loving-kindness. Then some whips and scorpions treatment on children under sixteen, followed by a spot of disembowelling and perhaps a beheading or two at the discretion of the officiating priest, with the choir singing an anthem about the beauty of holiness. Then an address explaining about God's will and so on. Then a few crucifixions, bringing out the real meaning of the Christian symbol. Finally a blessing for the survivors, plus a friendly warning that it'll probably be their turn next. I used to think it was the Aztecs who came nearest to establishing the kingdom of God on earth. What was it they were notching up, a thousand human sacrifices a week? But then the Christians arrived and soon put them down. He's a jealous God.'

When he began this speech, the tone of emotion in Ayscue's voice had been partly synthetic. Now it was all genuine. He was conscious of this and of the silence when he paused. He let go of Churchill, who lay there as before. A glance showed that Naidu had turned his back and was looking out of the window.

Ayscue said, in a hurried, apologetic way, 'But I got converted. That's to say I realized that not wanting to see these things as they are, which most people don't, doesn't necessarily make them completely stupid or insensitive or not frightened of life and death. Christianity's just the thing for people like that. A conspiracy to pretend that God moves in such a mysterious way that asking questions about it is a waste of time and everything's all right really. I joined that conspiracy. As you know. The only awkward part is covering up one's sex activities and so on. One can't bring the cloth into disrepute because that would weaken the conspiracy. And then there are times like this.'

He felt he was on the threshold of an important point, of something that would resolve the current situation, but could not grasp what it was. Churchill had not moved. Ayscue got up from the bed.

'I'm afraid I haven't been any help at all,' he said.

'No,' said Naidu, turning. 'I'm afraid you haven't.'

'I didn't expect to be. Will you see what you can do?'

'Of course.'

Naidu walked briskly forward and sat down on the bed at a conversible distance from Churchill.

'My dear friend James,' he said. 'Let's please agree to omit God from our considerations. Your God, or indeed your no-God, or anybody's God. If you bother about such ideas, you'll have no time or attention to spare for how you should be behaving. If you make God responsible for situations, you're not responsible for how you should behave in them. But if you love even one other person you must be responsible for this. In your present state you're no use to Catharine at all. You're trying to be in her state. You're making an effort to take her place. Yes you are indeed. Now. However these events came, they're here and you must deal with them. And you can do this, because they're not unchangeable. Oh, nobody can work miracle cures, I don't mean any such thing. But you can modify these events, you can make them less bad. But to do that you must accept them first. You must forget hatred and all feelings of blame. Unless you do that you can do nothing.'

'Nobody can do anything,' said Churchill quite suddenly.

'Oh yes, my dear James, somebody can. You can. But not unless you want to. Now consider – consider with me, James, what we have. We have a chain of bad events. They're made much worse by your being afraid. And what you're afraid of is in the first place your own death. Not Catharine's.'

'No,' said Churchill. 'At least, I am afraid, I can be afraid. But not now.'

'Yes, now. And this is not intelligent of you. Death is not your enemy. Death's nobody's enemy. Your enemy's the same as everybody else's. Your enemy is fear, plus ill feelings, bad feelings of all descriptions. Such as selfishness, and not wanting to be deprived of what comforts you, and greed, and arrogance, and above all belief in your own uniqueness and your own importance. All these bad feelings come from considering yourself first. It's hard to say and I don't want to be a preacher, but if you could simply begin to love life in everything there is, then your bad feelings would start to diminish. You must make up your mind to love Catharine with all your heart, so that your heart has no room for the fear that you'll be deprived of her. You must cast out that fear, and then you'll have begun to cast out all fear. At the moment you're so afraid that you're pretending to be dead. Please stop, James, and begin to try. We must all try to become men.'

Five minutes later, Churchill said, 'There's nothing to say, except about this thing. And there's nothing to say about that.'

*

'What about cover?' asked Jagger.

Leonard fastened the flies of his scarlet dress trousers and examined their hang in his triple mirror. The disposal of Best had bred in him an unaccustomed kind of buoyant off-handedness.

'Everybody's used to comings and goings in this camp,' he said when he felt ready to. 'A special technical section can easily be posted in. The more unmilitary they are the better. I hope I get sent some good people, by the way. Those blokes they gave me to keep an eye on Best were very sub-standard. Perhaps you could have a word with our masters about that when you get back. Are you travelling by helicopter again?'

'No, I'll probably get the early train in the morning. I'll see what I can do for you about the extra lot of fellows.'

'With a small group under my personal orders,' said Leonard, with a judicial look at his reflection as he buttoned the ultra-marine jacket, 'I think I can promise to nail our man within the week. The moment he moves we'll have him ... Ah, here you are at last. What's been keeping you?'

Deering had shuffled his way in and now shuffled his heels nearly together as he handed his master a pair of white gloves.

'Sorry, sir, had to wait for a turn with the iron.'

Jagger glanced over from where he lay full length on Leonard's bed.

'What in hell's name are those things?'

'Ceremonial gloves.'

'Gloves? I'd like to see anything bigger than a whippet get its hand in there, old lad. Gloves!'

'You're not supposed to be able to get your hand in,' said Leonard in a cold tone. 'You just carry them. It's a tradition.'

'Lot of that around here, isn't there? And the bloody place has only been going a few weeks. Springs up like weeds after rain.'

'Any news, Deering?' asked Leonard, not expecting any much, but not wanting to have to defend Mess tradition to Jagger.

'Well, the blokes are bitching and binding like buggery about the way you've been messing them around,' said Deering contentedly. 'Up in the middle of the night, off into the wilds before they could –'

This evening, Leonard could have faced a mutiny single-handed. 'I'm not interested,' he said. 'Anything else?'

The telephone rang.

'Leonard here.'

'Have you any idea where I can reach Mr Jagger, sir? There's an outside call for him.'

'He's with me now . . . For you.'

At the second attempt Jagger heaved himself off the bed and took the receiver.

'Jagger.'

'Then this ragtime search,' went on Deering. 'Three hours of it and they come up with a couple of rusty shells that must have been around since the Boer War, a typewriter in a sack and a set of filthy pictures stowed away under one of the sleeping-huts. The padre's, I bet you what you like. Apparently they were really something. You know, people on the job. Who's got them now, do you know?'

'I do not. Is there anything else?'

'Yes, I want to apply for a transfer. I'm brassed off with this joint.'

'Talk to me about it in the morning.'

'All right, sir. Good night.'

Deering left. Leonard turned to Jagger, who had replaced

the receiver after a bare couple of assenting words and whose face was now thoughtful.

'Big news?' asked Leonard.

Jagger gave an instant impression of falsity. 'No,' he said. 'No, nothing in particular. Nothing to do with this job, anyway.'

'Oh. Are you ready to go down?'

'Christ, I've been lying about waiting.'

In front of the glass again, Leonard scrutinized the image of his face, which was looking a bit meaty after what Dr Best's nurse had done to it, then turned his attention to Jagger's reflected form, now peering indecisively at its original.

'Aren't you going to comb your hair?'

'All right, if it'll make you feel better. Have you got a comb to lend?'

'Well . . .'

'Look, me combing my hair was your idea. I'm not going all the way up to that attic they've put me in to fetch a bloody comb. If you want me to be a credit to you and the Service you've got to provide the wherewithal, right?'

'Oh, very well. Here you are.'

The comb slipped and tore jerkily through Jagger's fiery thatch in a way that suggested this was something he did every couple of years. His body was canted over to one side and he kept the operative elbow unhandily close to his chest. In the end most of his hair was horizontal, including some portions that would have done better to follow the curve of his skull.

'They'll have to take me as they find me,' he said, plucking the greater part of a ragged tuft of red hairs from the comb and handing it back. 'Now if there's any buggering protocol like kissing the Adjutant's bum or cheering whenever the Queen's mentioned you'd better fill me in right away.'

'Just do as I do and you'll be all right. Come on, we're late already.'

In the ante-room they were hailed by the Colonel.

'Ah, here are our spy-catchers,' he said. 'Magnificent job of work this afternoon, both of you. Congratulations. Settled that crazy fellow's hash in fine style. Great relief. Now, what are you drinking, Mr Jagger? Spot of pink gin?'

'I'd as soon just stick to my beer, thank you, Colonel. I took the liberty of laying on a supply with one of your waiters.'

'First-class idea. And sherry for you, eh, Brian? Ah, and Willie. You're looking a bit harassed, Willie. A drop of whisky will put you right.'

'Thank you, sir. Is there any sign of my guest, do you know?'

Ayscue, who had just hurried into the room, did look harassed, also more gaunt than usual. He was rubbing his eyes as if they itched intolerably.

'Oh, the fellow who's going to lecture us on our Patagonian opposite numbers. No, not a trace. Don't you worry, he'll be along soon.'

'I'm sure he will, yes. Could I have a word with you about Churchill, sir?'

'Of course, of course. I take it you've been over to see him. Tell me . . .'

The Colonel and Ayscue moved away. Hunter moved in from the other side.

'I wonder what's going to become of poor Dr Best,' he said.

'Well, he's not our pigeon any more,' said Jagger. 'No point in interrogating a lunatic, let alone bringing him to trial. If he ever recovers I suppose we might take an interest again.'

'Will he, do you think?'

'How would I know? You heard what Mann said. The quicker it comes on the less likely it is to go away. He's Secret Agent Best for evermore, I'd say. Good luck to him.'

'I wonder if that bang on the head he got had anything to do with it.'

'I'd say not, but Mann's sending me a complete report as soon as he can. I'll let you have a copy. Just out of interest.'

'Thanks. Anyway, you're satisfied you got the right man.'

'Oh, completely. Aren't you?'

'Of course, for what my views are worth.'

'. . . some time tomorrow at the latest,' said the Colonel, coming back into aural range. 'Otherwise I shall be forced to take a serious view. No joke when a fellow's missing vital training.'

'I'll do everything I can, sir,' said Ayscue.

An expression of horror appeared on Leonard's face.

'For Christ's sake,' said Jagger, 'what's the matter now?'

'My gloves,' muttered Leonard. 'I've left them in my room. I'll just slip up and get them.'

'Is everybody off their head around here? What good will they do you, old lad? You told me yourself all you do is carry the buggers. What's it all for?'

'You wouldn't understand. I'll be back in a minute.'

Leonard went out thoughtfully and rather sadly. What was saddening him was the realization that, with the end of his job here in sight, his service as a Sailor must also be drawing to its close. His next assignment, requiring him to impersonate a lounger in a Whitehall pub, perhaps, or a checker at a naval dockyard, would hardly allow him to appear in his present guise. Perhaps he could acquire some sort of honorary post in the regiment's Old Comrades' Association, keep up the connexion that way.

He opened the door of his room and had scarcely taken in the fact that Deering was already there before the man had sprung at him. For the second time in four hours, Leonard found himself involved in a severe and painful physical struggle. A fist caught him on the ear and sent him reeling against the bed, where, he noticed, the suitcase containing his secret files lay open and a copy of his preliminary report on the Best affair, completed that afternoon, had been unfolded. He threw himself forward and got in what he thought was going to be a punishing headbutt in Deering's stomach. That stomach proved to be a good deal harder than it had ever looked, and Leonard lost the initiative further when the edge of Deering's hand came down on the back of his neck, though without enough force to knock him over. The two closed and for a time grappled indecisively, banging into chairs, slamming into walls and then sliding along them, but the end of this phase came when Deering got a good grip on Leonard's throat and pushed him back against the rosewood dressing-table. Very soon it turned out to be impossible to loosen Deering's hands with his own, so Leonard started feeling about on the dressing-table top for possible weapons. He identified by touch an unopened carton of toothpaste, an empty sponge-bag, a plastic bottle of scalp tonic, finally, when his changes of ever drawing another breath seemed remote, a clothes-brush with a heavy wooden back. Hitting Deering on the head with this hard and repeatedly made him take one hand away and grab at it, upon which Leonard was able to gain some sort of footing and kick him on the shin. He released his hold and Leonard followed up, but too slowly or feebly, because Deering grabbed him by the arm and swung him forcefully into his triple mirror, which collapsed and shattered under him. He hit his head on something.

He rested on the floor for a few moments, wondering whether he had spent any time unconscious. There was some blood on the back of his hand, although the skin there seemed to be whole, and a lot of broken glass all about. He got carefully to his knees and looked down at himself in one of the larger fragments of mirror. The light was good enough to show that he was more or less undamaged apart from a long but evidently shallow cut on his forehead, the source of the blood on his hand. Up again at last, he lurched over to his painting of the five Sailors, knocked askew during the fight, and straightened it. Then, still panting pretty hard, but otherwise his own man once more, he hurried to the telephone.

'Command Post, quick ... Leonard here. General Alarm. Seal the gate. Private Deering is at large somewhere in the camp. He is an enemy agent. Arrest him. Get cracking. I'm coming along to you straight away.'

Before he had finished speaking the hooters had set up their steady high-pitched clamour, as at the sighting of Jagger's heli-copter that morning. Acting on a strong but vague impulse, Leonard snatched his raincoat from its hook behind the door and flung it over the mess of exposed secrets on his bed. That done, he ran out of the room and down the stairs.

The hall was full of colourfully attired officers shouting questions and speculations at one another. Leonard shouldered his way through and gained the Command Post. Jagger, Hunter and Ross-Donaldson followed him in.

'What happened?' everybody seemed to be asking him.

'It's Deering, my batman. I found him going through my

files in my room. I fought him but he escaped. He's our man all right. He can't get away.'

'Any idea where he is, sir?' asked the duty sergeant-major.

'I —'

The rapid battering of a heavy-calibre automatic weapon started up from somewhere above them. All present turned reflectively to the television screens on the walls. One of them showed considerable chips of concrete flying off part of the wall of Hut D4. On another, a sentry, half doubled up, was just running out of shot.

'Well, we know where he is now, don't we?' said Ross-Donaldson. 'He must have gone straight up to the roof. A good position for maximally destructive self-terminating improvization.'

Another burst sounded overhead, though without effect visible to those in the Command Post. Hunter started for the door.

'Where are you off to, old lad?' asked Jagger.

'Take a look out front. Can't see anything from here.'

With Ross-Donaldson close behind, Hunter ran down the hall to the front door. Here a group that included the Colonel and Ayscue was in rapid internal movement, some of those still inside the threshold pushing outwards, those beyond it halting or stepping back as the machine-gun started firing again. Hunter and Ross-Donaldson squeezed past and moved along the outside wall until they were almost directly beneath Deering's position. A familiar voice, the tension in it sounding through the amplification, bawled out over the public-address system.

'Leonard speaking. Keep down, everybody. Camp patrol to concentrate at northern gable end of farmhouse. Take your time. Don't expose yourselves unnecessarily.'

'That's sound enough, anyway,' said Ross-Donaldson. 'From the northern end they'll be able to move round and take him in the rear.'

'I liked the bit about exposure, too.'

Figures were moving among the huts beside the main track. A civilian vehicle of some sort was halted there, its windscreen reflecting the evening sun. The gun opened up, sounding shockingly loud and near to the two under the wall, and the reflection seemed to vanish. The figures went to ground.

'Somebody'll get killed if this goes on,' whispered Hunter when the gun had stopped. 'No doubt there's a silly little man down there thirsting for a decoration. Deering'll murder them if they get much nearer. Let's see ... Ah yes. Would you give me a hand up here?'

He indicated a nearby drainpipe, from the top of which a short crawl across sloping tiles would bring him to the machine-gun post.

'You'll get your head blown off,' said Ross-Donaldson.

'I think not. He won't be able to depress that thing far enough to bring it to bear, and it'll take him much too long to get it off its mounting, even if he knows how to. Come on, Alastair.'

Ross-Donaldson offered his shoulders and Hunter soon had his head above the level of the gutter. Deering was about fifteen feet above and to the right, blinking along the gun-barrel. A pair of boot-soles and an outflung arm presumably belonged to the man who had been on duty at the post. Hunter spread his hands on the gutter and set about heaving himself up. A part of the gutter gave with a creaking sound. Deering heard, looked and saw him. Without touching the machine-gun, the man reached behind him and picked up a machine-pistol, no doubt the property of the unconscious guard. Before he could swing its muzzle round Hunter was below the level of the gutter. He hung there, listening carefully. When he heard the scrape of metal or shoe-leather on the tiles above he dropped straight to the ground, shouting to Ross-Donaldson to run.

They both ran. There was no burst of machine-pistol fire from behind them. Instead they heard a machine-gun, though not from Deering's position. Without any clear idea of how they got there, they found themselves behind the lee of a corner of Hut D4, where a solitary corporal lay full length.

'That was kind of him,' shouted Hunter, indicating the machine-gun post aloft in the meadow. 'Saved our bacon.'

'What?' yelled Ross-Donaldson as the gun continued to fire.

Hunter flapped his hand and started crawling to the corner of the hut. As he did so the clamour of the heavy-calibre ammunition suddenly doubled. For a few intolerable seconds the two machine-guns continued to shoot it out, then the one in the meadow fell silent. Smoke and sparks and chips of flying stuff could be seen around it. After a moment, while Deering fired on, somebody started descending the steel ladder that led down to the meadow. Hunter turned quickly and snatched up the corporal's machine-pistol from where it lay beside him. The man's mouth started moving largely. Hunter moved round the hut into full view of Deering and fired a burst at him from the shoulder. He missed, but there was immediate silence as Deering shifted his sights to the new target. Hunter fired again and saw brickdust rising from the farmhouse roof. A moment later he was startled by the tremendous noise through the air about him made by what Deering was shooting. A moment later still a hand seized his arm and pulled him back into cover. The machine-gun stopped at once.

'No need to overdo it,' said Ross-Donaldson. 'That chap's down the ladder now and away. I must say he might have opened up in the first place a little sooner than he did. And why didn't he stick it out where he was?'

'We'll discuss it later,' said Hunter. 'I must say Deering's quite useful with that popper, isn't he? Perhaps they put him through a course in Moscow or Hanoi or one of those places.'

'There isn't very much to it, actually, at close range anyway. The impact on material is so tremendous that you can correct your aim by it. It takes a few seconds each time, of course, or you wouldn't be here now.'

'No, I don't suppose I would. What a blessing ... Would you reload your very handy gun for me, corporal? We might need it again soon.'

As he grudgingly obeyed, the corporal said, 'This wouldn't be one of that Captain Leonard's ideas, would it, sir?'

'Oh, I doubt it. The Ministry are very sticky about living-target practice shoots. They're still living in the nineteenth century in many ways. Ah, thank you.'

'What have you in mind now?' asked Ross-Donaldson.

'Just a little look. I won't go far.'

Hunter lay down and moved his face slowly round the corner. He instantly caught sight of Jagger's red hair shining in the late sun as its owner began to emerge from a window some twenty feet from Deering and on a level with him.

'Oh, Christ,' said Hunter.

'What's up?'

'Jagger's getting out on to the roof.'

'Good idea.'

'Not from his point of view. He probably doesn't know Deering's got that machine-pistol with him. He can knock Jagger off in a second.'

When Jagger was fully out of his window, Hunter took up his previous position and fired a burst at a chimney-pot fifteen feet away from Deering on the other side. The machine-gun started up after a couple of seconds. Hunter ran twenty yards, fired again, this time more or less into the sky, and ran on. The air in his path seemed to fill with invisible rushing metal, any piece of which, it occurred to him, would be fatal if it struck almost anywhere. He tried to make himself run straight on, could not, turned at a right angle, ran a few more paces, tripped over a tussock and fell. For a single second the sound of flying metal grew louder, then it and the sound of the gun ceased abruptly. The silence made him put his hands to his ears. When he looked up at the roof he saw Jagger's hand raised in a wave and at his feet a shape that must have been Deering.

*

The whole action, from when Deering fired his first round to when he fired his last, had taken six minutes. After another seven or eight, Hunter was lying in the best armchair in the ante-room drinking champagne out of a silver tankard. Discussion raged round him.

'First-class show, Max,' said the Colonel.

'Thank you, sir.'

'I'll see you get a gong for this.'

'That's frightfully kind of you, sir.'

'And of course it'll make all the difference to your career.'

'I'm glad you think so, sir.'

'No doubt about it . . . Yes, Alastair, what's the score?'

'Casualty report, sir. Two men superficially cut by flying splinters, otherwise nil. As regards this unit, that is. One civilian casualty.'

'How on earth did that come about?'

Ross-Donaldson accepted champagne from a proffered tray. 'The man concerned was to have lectured here tonight,' he said. 'Name of Caton, Dr L. S. Caton. It seems he arrived by taxi just before the alarm sounded. The gate guard admitted him according to arrangement, and presumably he'd just started being driven up to the Mess when the firing began. The driver pulled up, they hung on for a bit and a stray round came through the windscreen.'

'Mm. He's dead, I take it?'

'Oh yes, sir. Full in the face. I'm afraid he won't be easy to identify. Ayscue's down there now, taking care of things.'

'What about the taxi-driver?'

'Not a scratch. But he's naturally rather upset. His taxi's in a bit of a state. I had him taken to the Sergeants' Mess. I'll go over there and sort him out when I've drunk this. Oh, as regards the damage report, sir, will the morning be soon enough for that? There won't be much on it, apart from the second machine-gun.'

'Of course, Alastair, of course,' said the Colonel. 'Thank you. Spot more champagne all round, I think, before we go in to dinner.'

Hunter had more champagne. It made him feel tired, or he began to feel tired while he was drinking it. When the time came to move to the dining-room he excused himself, saying he thought he would finish his drink and take a sandwich up to his room. Left alone, he shut his eyes.

'Passing over,' he muttered. 'Somebody we don't know. The farther edge.'

He opened his eyes when the door opened and Jagger's gaudy head appeared round it.

'Hullo, Hunter. All on your tod, eh? Mind if I join you? I couldn't face it in there. Too much buggering protocol. I thought of slipping out to the pub and having another go at those pork pies of theirs. Perhaps you might feel like coming along too.'

'If you don't mind awfully I don't think I will. The notion of going to bed reasonably soon has begun to exercise a hypnotic spell over me.'

'Sure, you've had a long day. Well, in that case we'll just have a quiet noggin together and I'll toddle down there by myself. Can I get you something?'

'I don't think so,' said Hunter, indecisively. Then he added decisively, 'If there's a bottle of champagne already opened I don't mind helping to clear it up.'

'Okay, understood. Be back in a minute.'

Hunter shut his eyes again. When he opened them Jagger was settling himself at his side with a tankard of champagne, a pint glass and a large bedroom ewer that proved to be full of beer.

'Now we shan't be disturbed,' said Jagger, filling his glass. 'There are just one or two points you might fill in for me if you will.'

'Points about what?'

Jagger looked at Hunter for a few seconds without saying anything.

'I see.' Hunter lit a cigarette. 'What do you want to know?'

'The mechanics, first of all. How you managed to move in and out of here without notice being taken and the rest of it. There's a pretty tight guard on that gate.'

'Nothing to it. I drove out of camp after dinner in the ordinary way. I came back in after midnight on foot, having put my car in a field on the other side of the main road. The guard had changed by then and they don't keep a record of how you leave and return, only when and what for. Then I had a quiet lie-down for a couple of hours, after which I went out again by way of the fence. Easy enough for anyone who knows the ground and the habits of the patrol. Next, a pleasant drive to the target area via the place where I'd hidden the rifle, the destruction of St Jerome's Priory, and a much quicker run to the neighbourhood of the mental hospital, where, again, escaping notice was no problem if you knew the place. Dodging Leonard's men in the grounds and round the staff block was terrifyingly easy.

Finally, a swift belt back in this direction and participation in the general chaotic comings and goings which, as I reasoned correctly, everybody would be far too busy and bothered to keep a detailed check on.'

'That was a risk, that last part. Anybody might have started looking for you at any time, to give you a job to do or whatnot.'

'In which case I was somewhere else. In the Army, people are never where they're wanted. It's a condition of life. And the whole thing was a risk. I didn't mind. In fact that was almost the best part. Anyway, I had to go through with it. Things are going wrong for people all the time in such devious and complicated and unlikely ways that as soon as that lorry caught fire and the whole scheme occurred to me I was completely committed. Not to bet on things going unbelievably right for once would have been letting down everything I stand for. I don't know whether that makes any sense.'

'Oh yes. Quite a bit of sense. Well, that clears that up nicely. Mm. Another thing that bothered me was the typewriter. I can't figure out how you let it be found. You were in charge of the search of the camp, after all. It would have been dead easy for you to decide to be the one who searched C Company shithouse or wherever you'd hidden the bloody thing.'

'What put you on to that?'

'Plain as a pikestaff, old lad. I hadn't been here five minutes before I was quite clear in my own mind that the point of the priory being blown up was that it was a priory. Belonging to God the Father Almighty. So I was looking for somebody who didn't like God the Father Almighty. Then as soon as Leonard shows me that poster about the Anti-Death League and gets the poem off the parson and gives it to me I know I'm looking at more work by the same fellow. And I've narrowed the search down a lot, too. Here.'

Screwing up his face and making faint trumpeting noises, Jagger searched his pockets. Finally he produced the piece of paper in question and vainly tried to flatten it out on his thigh.

'Quite a nice piece,' he said, 'in a rather unshaped colloquial vein. But the unshaped part's deliberate, of course. How long did you spend on it?'

'About twenty minutes.'

'I'd have said longer. There's been pains taken, I can tell that. Still, what I'm on about is that, whereas there are a number of illiteracies in spelling, the punctuation is correct all through. Now that's odd, you see. For every twenty people who can spell there's hardly one who can punctuate. Pretty well everyone who can punctuate can spell as a matter of course. So our man isn't really semi-illiterate, he's just pretending to be. Why should he do that? To give the impression that any old potato-peeler or boot-polisher might have written the thing. Right. Now Leonard says he's certain the writer's one of the inner ring, the s i Group, who's got a fit of the horrors about what he's got to do in Operation Apollo. From some points of view that's a fair enough deduction. But it just struck me that it isn't a necessary one. If you base your reasoning on your subject-matter, your mode of approach and suchlike, you don't quite see what you'd expect to see. You'd expect a fellow who was against the Apollo caper to be going on about men. Generals. Politicians. Scientists. People, that's to say, not the Father Almighty. A bit subtle, that, perhaps, but after all we are dealing with poetry. So I'm looking for an educated man who quite likely isn't in the si Group. Then I hear friend Deering telling Leonard that the camp search party turned up a typewriter, and I recall you, as officer in charge, reporting that nothing significant was found, and the typewriter's obviously significant, whatever it was significant of, and I've got you. Mind you, there was plenty of other stuff – you were about when the rifle was pinched, you put Leonard on to Best, you don't like Best, et cetera. But the typewriter was what clinched it for me. Which reminds me. You still haven't said how you let the bloody thing get found.'

Hunter laughed silently. 'That's very straightforward,' he said. 'I was pissed when I hid it and I'd already forgotten where by the time I got into bed. Like wiping a slate.'

'Mm.' Jagger topped up his glass. 'The only other thing I'd like you to tell me, that's if you feel like it, is your motive. No. Not your motive. Scrub that. I know your motive. Your occasion. What started you off on your poem and your notes?'

There was a long and virtually total silence. Eventually Hunter said,

'I've never been particularly keen on having to think about things. And on things that make you think about things. You know, like music and all that. Love's another one. I joined the Army specially to get away from them. I will say it worked jolly well for a time. But then quite recently I suddenly found I'd fallen in love with somebody in a more completely disastrous fashion than ever before. At first sight, too. I got as drunk as I could to try to put it behind me. No good. Then the somebody's best friend went and died, and I decided I'd better cry out before I was hurt, when somebody else was hurt, in fact. Hence the poem. Then the love thing nearly turned out my way, but it didn't at all when it came to it, because the somebody was think-ing of the dead friend. That really got me down. Hence the Anti-Death League. Then a friend of mine fell in love and his girl got cancer, as you heard. That more or less finished me off. Hence the rifle and the priory. As a way of voicing some sort of objection. Plus a bit of revenge thrown in.'

'It wasn't very practical,' said Jagger. 'Any of it.'

'No, it wasn't. But sometimes you've got to be impractical and illogical and a bit useless, because the only alternative is to do nothing at all, and that would be simply offensive. You just can't let things like this go sliding past without any kind of re-mark, as if nobody noticed or cared. It won't do.'

After another silence, Jagger said,

'How do you feel about it now?'

'A good question. It embarrasses me slightly, I think. It didn't altogether work the way I'd expected it to. On me, that is. I keep feeling I've gone too far in some way.'

'Then you don't really see yourself rushing off some fine morning and dynamiting Westminster Abbey?'

'No, not really. Far too repetitive, for one thing.'

'See you stick to that. If you get up to any more of your tricks you might land me in some bad trouble.'

'Any ...'

'Yes,' said Jagger, nodding vigorously. 'That's right. You've got it. I'm not going to do anything about it. On account of

283

several considerations. Consideration one. You saved my life just now. I take very kindly to that type of thing. Consideration two. It just so happens I've got it in for God the Father Almighty a bit on my own account. He took my daughter off me the year before last. Thing called disseminated L.E. A disease of the connective tissue. There's not a lot to see, except a red rash on the face that gets worse in the light, so she couldn't go out in the sun. Twenty, she was. Engaged. All that. You know, Hunter, if you ever get round to properly setting up your League you could do worse than rope me in. You can always find me via the Ministry.'

'Are you serious?'

'As serious as you.'

'Yes. Are there any other considerations?'

'Yes, there's consideration three, which is much more important than the other two. The case is closed. It's better all round that it stays closed. Even if Best recovers we wouldn't bring any charge against him. He was mad at the time of what he's supposed to have done. The real thing, though, is that to have the whole business stirred up all over again might just conceivably interfere with the tremendous success we've had with Operation Apollo.'

'Had?' said Hunter. 'Aren't you being a bit previous?'

'Oh no. It's succeeded already old lad. I got the news about an hour ago, just before old Deering started cutting up. I'm afraid I can't say any more. You may find out what I'm talking about in due course. Anyway, we're all highly delighted at the way things have gone. Well. What are you going to do with yourself when this place packs up? I'll tell you what I think you ought to do. Do you mind? I think you ought to get out of the buggering Army and find yourself a nice, decent, steady young somebody and settle down with the somebody. It's been done before now.'

Hunter picked up the ewer and filled Jagger's glass.

'You know about style,' he said. 'But settle down? And throw away the marvellous career I've just opened up for myself? No. I'm going to decide on somewhere nasty, somewhere really very nasty indeed, and get myself sent there. It was being shot at like that that put the idea into my head. I didn't know what it was like before. I found it most interesting in some way I can't quite put my finger on for the moment.'

'Sooner you than me. I didn't enjoy myself on that roof one bit, I don't mind telling you. Well ...'

After a couple of abortive tries and a bit of shrieking Jagger heaved a loudly ticking watch out of his top pocket and looked at it, then glared at it. He urged himself to his feet.

'Christ,' he muttered, 'I'll have to run if I'm going to get fed.'

'Off tonight, are you?'

'No, I've got a date up at that loony place. It's quite a way, isn't it?'

'Forgive my curiosity, but who's your date with?'

'If anyone wants to know, that fellow Mann, to ask after Best, but really those two pieces in leather who served you your coffee. I ran into them on their way out. I'm afraid I must have spent a bit of time chatting them up when I should have been finding out if you and Leonard needed a hand inside there. Sorry.'

'That's all right. You should have an entertaining evening.'

'You never know. I suppose you wouldn't fancy changing your mind and coming along to make up the number?'

'No thanks. The setting would be wrong, somehow.'

'I see what you mean.' Jagger's face became animated. 'Here,' he said, tapping Hunter on the shoulder, 'imagine Leonard not telling us about those two when we were all discussing whether Best was mad or not. Any fellow who dresses women up in that rig-out must be off his trolley. Anyway, you'd think it worth a mention. But Leonard didn't, even though he told me later he had noticed them when he went up to the place for lunch the other day. I pressed him and got him to admit it did strike him at the time as a bit unusual.'

'I'm afraid he's rather uninstructed in some ways.'

'Now then, you let him be. He's one of the best, is Brian Leonard. He's got first-class stuff in him. The only trouble is, he doesn't seem to get much luck. And that reminds me, my old Max. In the next couple of days you've got the chance of being a real good pal to our Brian. He's going to need one.'

*

'How much do you know about the psychology of the Chinese?' asked Ross-Donaldson.

Leonard hesitated. He was still in a state of unrelieved gloom and foreboding at the ever-present thought of the way he had allowed Deering to steal secrets from under his nose. Bewilderment had been added when he arrived in response to Ross-Donaldson's unexpected summons to find that the latter had had his outer office cleared and an armed guard placed on its door. Leonard's breakfast of eggs *bonne femme* felt as if it had not quite completed its journey to his stomach.

'Only what I learnt in the basic training they give us,' he said finally. 'I've never done a course on it or anything.'

'No. Well, at the risk of covering familiar ground, let me just place the relevant point, which is that they suffer from an unusually wide schemata-data divergence. In practical terms, and as regards their attitudes to the West, this means that their ideology teaches them to despise us and think us stupid, while empirically they're forced into continual *ad hoc* respect for our efficiency and cunning. Consequently, any project aimed at deceiving them must contain elements of apparent stupidity and elements of apparent cunning in highly critical proportions delicately balanced. Let's just examine those set of elements in turn as they appear in the project you and I have been concerned with over the past weeks.

'First, the elements of apparent stupidity. At the outset, ostensibly in sole charge of Security arrangements for a uniquely secret Operation, we find you, an inexperienced officer working without assistants. When, later, assistants must obviously be furnished to watch Dr Best, they're men of tested and proven incompetence. The Chinese agent, Deering, finds no difficulty whatever in becoming your servant, in which position he has at least putative access to your secret files. Your training for this project, by stressing the importance of supposed subtlety and encouraging you to keep those files in the most exposed place possible, ensured that that putative access had the best chance of becoming actual. To a Chinese mind, of course, and to lots of others as well, that supposed subtlety would appear as real stupidity. It was hardly expected that you yourself would train

Deering in a highly unsophisticated method of getting at your files, but after some discussion it was agreed that this worked out substantially on the credit side. Finally, there was the almost unbelievable stroke of good fortune whereby you began to concentrate your efforts on Dr Best, a dangerous man, certainly, but one totally unconnected with the business in hand.

'So far, so incorrigibly, predictably, imperialistically stupid. Now as to ... You look tired, Leonard. Would you care for a cup of tea?'

Leonard thought of asking for sherry instead, then just nodded.

'Milk and sugar?'

'Milk. No sugar.'

Left alone, Leonard sat there without moving, hardly thinking. Until Ross-Donaldson came back he spent his time wanting to be with Lucy.

'What department do you belong to?' he asked without much curiosity.

'It's name would mean nothing to you. It was set in being for this project alone and will shortly be disbanded. I'd like to fill in the other side of the picture now if I may. I hope I'm not boring you.'

'No.'

'Right. We've covered satisfactorily the elements of apparent stupidity. Now as to the elements of apparent cunning. The prime concern here was lavishness, the unstinting expenditure of time, energy and money on the pretence that this unit was created as a training establishment and briefing centre for the use in war of tactical atomic weapons of a reasonably mature sort in unprecededly far-forward areas. Here, incidentally, we achieved a rather elegant bonus. It'll do the Chinese High Command quite a durable bit of good to believe, or at the lowest to wonder whether, the British Army can dispose of nuclear hand-guns at infantry-section level. In fact, of course, the so-called N H W-17, or rather its ammunition, is far too expensive and troublesome to produce for its warlike employment to be practicable.

'I was referring to lavishness in the expenditure of time,

energy and money. Of these, money was probably the most important as, in the Eastern mind, a guarantee of genuineness. You perhaps recall from your training a famous World War I case in which Turkish Intelligence, having had certain fake Allied battle plans put in their way, became convinced of their authenticity largely on the grounds that a considerable sum in current notes had fallen into their hands under the same cover. The cost of the physical Security arrangements here was immense by Chinese standards, from the building of Hut D4 to the installing of closed-circuit television. So much outlay on a cover, on a deception, plus our apparent willingness to sacrifice, if need be, the secrecy of the N H W-17, must convince them that what lay behind the cover was genuine. The depth of our cunning was underwritten by the costliness of our deception.'

Here the tea arrived, brought in by a corporal whom Leonard remembered as having done far more than his fair share of swearing on the day of Exercise Nabob. The man glanced at him several times with an incipient grin that told of vicarious triumph. Nobody outside could have known just what Leonard was going through, but anybody with more than a week's service would have known that he was going through something.

'Right,' said Ross-Donaldson when the door of the outer office had shut. 'All this means, in the simplest terms, that when the Chinese get the word from Deering that they stand to lose a million men in the third week of their invasion of the Indian sub-continent, and two and a half million in the fourth week, they're going to take him seriously. The peculiar horror of the weapon behind the cover, the weapon we were supposedly going to use on them as soon as they were over the Himalayas in substantial numbers, was an additional guarantee of authenticity: Western inhumanity, imperialist savagery and so forth. In fact, the horror was designed purely to horrify. Operation Apollo was impracticable from the start. Millions of non-combatants would have died in the sub-continent alone. But that was yet another guarantee of authenticity: capitalist indifference to Asian suffering.

'The aim of the project, as you must see by now, was to frighten them off. For which purpose, clearly, they had to know all about the weapon behind the cover. It was your job, Leonard, to be seen trying hard and in vain to prevent the escape of that information. You succeeded admirably. Twelve days ago sufficient details of the weapon behind the cover left England on their way to Peking. Earlier than we'd counted on. We were very pleased with ourselves. But recently a couple of snags developed.'

Ross-Donaldson paused and looked at Leonard for some moments as if he very much wanted to see him clearly. For the first time since Leonard had known him he seemed at something of a loss. At length he said,

'I suppose this must be something of a shock to you, Leonard. I'm sorry. I think too that to some extent you've suffered at my hands. In the general interest of distracting you from looking in the wrong, that's to say the right, direction I had to introduce you to a red herring or so. And I'm afraid I amused myself at your expense a couple of times. Perhaps you didn't notice. It seems to me now that I fell unduly under the sway of Hunter.'

'Max is a splendid officer.'

'Sufficiently gallant, it appears, but not a healthy influence, unfortunately. Would you like another cup of tea?'

'No, thank you. Tell me the rest. What were these snags you mentioned?'

'Two. One concerned the onward transmission of the information. We couldn't watch it all along the line for fear of being caught watching. It got as far as Albania and promptly vanished. You know what the Albanians are. If it had stuck there we were in trouble. We were still looking for evidence of its arrival in China when snag number two developed. The rifle. That disturbed me a great deal, I'm afraid. There were two possible deductions. One was that our screening processes were at fault and Best was an agent after all, which would have meant that the vital information had indeed got stuck somewhere and Peking was still interested in the rifle. At this late date that would have been nothing short of disastrous. Jagger was inclined to that explanation at one stage. I tended to take the other view, the one that turned out to be correct, that Best was just a lunatic set on some paranoiac form of self-expression. But that was hardly more comforting. From the Chinese point of view the incident would look very suspicious. It didn't fit into any pattern. God knows what sort of pattern they might have made it fit into, and how long it would have taken them. I was disturbed so severely that I had to send for Jagger. I owe you an apology, Leonard, for being rather short with you yesterday morning. I held you responsible. Not that you weren't.

'At any rate, things could have been worse. You and the others got rid of Best in good smart style. And any residual suspicions about the affair, if the opposition ever get to hear of it, will be more than offset by the splendid performance last evening, complete with fatal casualty, which they'll certainly get to hear of. Not even a Chinese could doubt that that was authentic.

Ross-Donaldson leant back in his chair, smoothed his paunch, and smiled. Then he turned authoritative.

'I can now inform you,' he said, dropping his voice, 'that the project has succeeded. The information went through after all. The invasion is cancelled. They're early signs, I gather, but unmistakable. We've won, Leonard. No Operation Apollo. No war. Well? Aren't you pleased?'

'I'm sure I will be. I can't take it in at the moment.'

'I understand. I felt like that too at first.'

After a short pause, Leonard said, 'What's going to happen to me?'

'Well, there I'm afraid we'll have to follow through rather. There'll be nothing too public. A court of inquiry that'll recommend your discharge with dishonour. Purely a formality, entirely for the benefit of the Chinese. Well, very largely for their benefit. We'll see it doesn't get to the Press or anything, so your chances in civilian life won't be affected. And ... you've a reward to come. As soon as it's safe, perhaps in eighteen months' time, a fictitious relative of yours is going to die and leave you about two thousand pounds. Net. After death duties.'

'That's quite generous, isn't it? Two thousand pounds for being the biggest bloody fool the Service could lay their hands on.'

'I shouldn't look at it like that if I were you. As I told you, you were selected for your inexperience. You were also isolated. Somebody had to do it. When the project first took shape there was a school of thought favouring the officer in your role being fully informed of the true state of events and aims, but I was able to argue successfully that the continuous deception called for would be an intolerable strain. The alternative was somebody of your general type – conscientious, not excessively imaginative, predictable – to be kept in ignorance. You were chosen. You did what was expected of you. You've nothing to be ashamed of.'

'I've everything to be ashamed of.'

Sighing, Ross-Donaldson stood up and settled his clothing into position. Leonard also rose.

'I think, if I may say so, Leonard, you'll quite likely do better outside the Service. I doubt if you'd ever have become a top-flight Security officer. You're too interested in people.'

'I don't know a thing about them,' said Leonard.

He put on his hat, saluted smartly and turned away. Ross-Donaldson shrugged his shoulders.

*

More than an hour went by before Leonard began to feel in the least degree better. On leaving Ross-Donaldson's office he decided that he needed sherry just as much as he needed Lucy, and sherry was nearer. But before entering the Mess doorway he stopped. It was only nine-fifty and he disliked the idea of being caught drinking at such an hour by a brother-officer, or indeed of being caught doing anything at any foreseeable hour by a brother-officer. After a moment's thought, he drove down to the village and bought a bottle of Murillo Hermanos' Manzanilla off Eames, who was just opening the White Hart. While he was waiting for it to be wrapped, Leonard got Anne to serve him with a glass of whatever was nearest. This proved to be a sweetish South African wine which vanished without trace before even getting as far as his breakfast had done.

His gloom persisted during his drive to Lucy's and changed direction slightly at the suspicious, even hostile, way she greeted him.

'What's the matter?' he asked as he stood in the portico. 'What have I done?'

She glared at him. 'What are you doing here? I told you not to come over.'

'I thought that only meant the evenings. I've just come to see you. I've got some free time. I'll go away if you like.'

Her glare lessened. 'You're not after James?'

'James? Why should I be after him? Is he here?'

'You're a sort of policeman, aren't you? Yes, he's upstairs.'

'What for? I don't understand.'

He understood better within about ten minutes, by which time he and Lucy were sitting in the shade of an oak-tree on the unkempt lawn outside the drawing-room. As she talked, she sipped a weak gin and tonic. He had two glasses of sherry inside him, a third in his hand, and the bottle beside his deck-chair. For one reason or another, he had forgotten about being gloomy.

'I should have been informed, really, I suppose,' he said at one point. 'But it doesn't matter now.'

'No, this whole business is much more important.'

'And he hasn't eaten or drunk a thing?' he asked when Lucy had finished her account.

'He won't eat. He doesn't even want to smoke. Willie's got him to drink a glass or two of water.'

'What about, you know, going to the lavatory?'

'Willie's taken him I think three times. The last time he had to more or less carry him. To the little lavatory, that is. He hasn't been to the big lavatory. He's sort of shutting down completely. Here's Willie.'

Ayscue came over to them across the sunlit grass. He nodded unsmilingly to Leonard, refused a drink, sat down in a third chair and began rubbing his eyes slowly. He was pale and un-shaven.

'Anything?' asked Lucy.

'No change. Except perhaps a little for the worse. It's getting harder to tell whether he's asleep or not.'

'You ought to get some sleep yourself.'

'I might as well. I'm not doing any good up there. You've come to take him back, I imagine,' he added accusingly to Leonard.

'No. Brian just wanted to see me. I've been telling him about it all. You want to help, don't you, Brian?'

'I don't see what I can do if you two can't do anything.'

'Brian,' said Ayscue. His manner had become more friendly. 'What will happen to him if you and I dress him and take him back? From the Security point of view, I mean.'

Leonard knew that the cancelling of Operation Apollo would not lead to any remission of the checks and restraints on those concerned in it, at any rate for some time. He guessed that his chiefs would not permit to be at large an individual in possession of such vital secrets who had clearly become unstable mentally.

'They'll lock him up,' he said.

'That's what I thought. Brian, I want to ask you something important. I think James has got more on his mind than he says. Than he said he had when he was still talking. I think it's this Operation Apollo. I think he can't face it. I know all war is dreadful, but whatever this is must be quite unusually dreadful. I want you to tell me if I'm right. Just that and no more.'

'Yes,' said Leonard. 'You're right.'

'Yes. He's fallen into a state of hating God, you see, Brian. That's bad enough. But I think he's lost faith in everything else too. In the world. He's against it all.'

'I think I understand. Will you excuse me? I'll be back later.'

He went off towards the house. Before going inside he looked round at the other two, Ayscue in his rumpled khaki, leaning back now as if asleep, Lucy in her spotless white dress that shone in the sun, sitting forward with her arms clasped round her knees. Then he entered and hurried upstairs to the room where Churchill was lying with his eyes shut. Leonard went and knelt by the bed.

'James. This is Brian Leonard. I know you're worrying about Operation Apollo. Well, you needn't any more. It's off. It's been cancelled. You haven't got to do it. You're free. It's all over. Operation Apollo has been cancelled.'

Churchill made no move. He hardly seemed to be breathing.

Leonard cleared his throat and said in a caricatured military tone, 'Official message for Lieutenant James Churchill, Blue Howards. Top secret. Operation Apollo is hereby cancelled, repeat cancelled, effective forthwith. Acknowledge. Message ends.'

This too had no effect. Leonard rose to his feet and stood thinking. After a short while he went out and downstairs, left the house by the front door, got into his car and drove away.

The two on the lawn heard him go. Ayscue stirred irritably.

'Where's he off to?' he said. 'Gone to turn out the Brigade of Guards, I expect, or something equally helpful.'

'That isn't very nice of you, Willie.'

'I'm sorry. He's a very decent man, I agree. But a very foolish one. He's never asked himself a serious question in his life. He knows no more about the way things work than he did when he was fourteen.'

'I don't think that's quite right either.'

'Perhaps not. I'm not really on form today. I think I'll go and have a lie-down on the sofa. Could you look in on James occasionally?'

'I'll sit by him, don't you worry.'

Lucy took an illustrated magazine to Churchill's bedside, but she too was underslept, and in a few minutes she nodded off, half awakening from time to time and changing position in her chair. She awoke completely when two vehicles began to pull up below the window. The first, she saw when she looked, was Leonard's car, and Leonard was getting out of it. The second was an ambulance. The driver got out and went to the rear door. Very soon Catharine appeared, followed by a bespectacled young man in a dark suit who was glancing impatiently about. Lucy hurried downstairs.

'Darling,' she said, embracing Catharine in the hall, 'what's happened? Are you out or what?'

'Only for an hour or two. This is Dr Galton, who's come to look after me.'

The young man nodded briefly and turned at once to Leonard.

'You can have forty minutes,' he said in a high-pitched but commanding voice, 'after which I shall see to it that Mrs Casement takes whatever suitable light refreshment is available here and then immediately returns to hospital.'

'Thank you,' said Leonard. 'That's quite acceptable.'

'It had better be. I hope you know what you're doing.'

'So you said earlier, doctor. You can rest assured that I do.'

'Can I see James?' asked Catharine.

'There isn't much time,' said Leonard. 'Seeing him may be more effective if you listen to what I have to tell you first. Let's go out on to the lawn. We can't be overheard there.'

They went, leaving the doctor pacing the hall.

'How are you, Cathy?' asked Lucy. 'How is everything?'

'Fine. No snags. Everything under control.'

'How did he get you out? Brian, how did you get her out?'

'Never mind that for now. The important thing is James.'

'He's not too bad, is he?' asked Catharine. 'He's not really so awfully bad, is he?'

'He's sort of withdrawn into himself,' said Leonard. 'But I think you'll be able to get him out of it. I've got no experience of these things, but from what I gather from Lucy here and Willie Ayscue part of why James is like this is because of what's been happening to you, Mrs Casement. I don't know how much –'

'Catharine.'

'Catharine. Well, that's part of it. The other part comes from this thing called Operation Apollo he was getting ready to be sent on. I'm going to tell you about that now. It won't take long.'

They reached the chairs under the oak-tree and sat down.

'This means I shall have to break the Official Secrets Act,' he went on. 'And if the information gets out there might be a war. So I want you both to promise me that you won't pass on what I'm going to tell you to a living soul.'

The two women looked at each other.

'But aren't you terribly risking we'll break our promise?' asked Lucy.

'No. I want you to hear this so you can help Catharine, and I know you're all right. And James loves you, Catharine, so you're all right too. So there isn't any risk. Do you both promise?'

'Yes,' they said.

He gave them a much edited account of his interview with Ross-Donaldson earlier that morning. At the end of it he studied

Catharine, whom he had seen for the first time an hour before. He could find no trace of illness, pain or fear about her, only of tension under control. He admired the straightness of her mouth. Leaning forward in his chair, he said emphatically, but he hoped not too loudly,

'So the big point is, Catharine, that James would never have had to go and make all those people die. But he still thinks he's got to. So do the other officers in his position, just for the time being. We're supposed to wait for orders saying it's all right to tell them. But when the others are told, they'll listen, they'll understand. But James has taken the whole idea of Operation Apollo much harder than they have, because of you. I suppose it's as if he can't see anything but death anywhere. I think in that state any of us might get withdrawn. Anyway, the result is it's no use telling James the show's been cancelled, because he won't listen. I've tried him. That's to say he won't listen to anybody ordinary. I think you're the only one he'll listen to, because he loves you. But if you're going to get through to him you've got to understand exactly what's in his mind, and that means you've got to hear exactly what he thinks he's going to have to do.

'Apollo was the Greek god of the sun, and of music, and of agriculture and other things. He was also the god of disease. The sender of plagues. I think calling the Operation after him was meant as some sort of twisted clue to the Chinese. What James and the others have been training to do was spreading a plague in the Chinese army, and probably in China too. Each man was going to be given a small party of local helpers and be stuck in a hideout near a Chinese line of communication. They were to wait until they could safely ambush just one Chinese soldier carrying mail, say, or a couple of chaps in a lorry, and knock them out with a gas that would keep them unconscious for three hours or so. Then they give them the plague and disappear. The Chinese blokes come to, feeling perfectly okay, and continue their journey to the fighting areas or back to their base. Nothing happens for about ten days, by which time scores of them have had the same treatment. Then they start their symptoms.

'It was decided that these symptoms ought to be as unpleasant as possible so as to have the maximum psychological effect. Ordinary plagues weren't good enough from that point of view. Fever, inflamed glands, delirium, difficulty in speaking and walking. Nothing much out of the way there. Our bacteriologists found they couldn't get as far as they wanted with just improving the existing plagues. But plagues are so handy, because they're so easily passed on. So they decided to start at the other end, with a more unpleasant disease that wasn't a plague that they'd tinker about with until it could be transmitted like a plague. Finally a scientist called Venables came up with something he'd managed to make just about as infectious as what's called pneumonic plague, and in the same way: in your breath, in droplets, like the common cold. They found this out two or three years ago, by the way, and kept it by them. It was all ready when they needed it.

'Well, what Venables had invented was a form of hydrophobia. That's what you get when a mad dog bites you. Only now you could get it off somebody's breath. Some people say it's the most extreme form of suffering. A man who's caught it starts off with feeling very depressed and frightened. There'd be plenty of that when you'd seen your friends die of it. Then the man gets very agitated and can't breathe properly. But the main point is that he gets very thirsty, only he chokes and has convulsions whenever he tries to drink. Or when he sees water, or hears it being poured, or thinks of it. Or when there's a draught or somebody touches him. Or a lot of other things. In between he breathes with a sort of barking sound and snaps his jaws. He has four or five days of that. Then he dies. It's an odd thing, but just before he dies he can breathe and drink and swallow perfectly well.

'Each detachment on Operation Apollo was to be issued with a number of small plastic tents just big enough for one person. The idea was that you put your unconscious Chinaman in there and sealed it up. Then you turned on a tank full of air which had water droplets in it, and the droplets had the hydrophobia virus in them. You gave the chap a couple of hours of it, took him out, stuck him back in the cab of his lorry, and

297

moved off to another area. The chances of him developing hydrophobia were better than ninety per cent. Oh, there is an antidote thing, but they'd never have been able to get it made and distributed in time to make any difference.

'Anway, that's what James thinks he's got to go and do.'

Catharine sat on for a few moments, then rose to her feet.

'I think I'll go and see James now,' she said, and went.

'I hope it works,' said Leonard.

'Brian, you didn't tell the people at the hospital any of that, did you?'

'Of course not. I got by on bluff and luck. I talked about international crises and secret weapons and spies. The luck came when they telephoned Whitehall and my master was out. There was only a junior on the desk and I soon settled him. Even then I don't think I'd have managed it if the doctor hadn't made the mistake of admitting that there wasn't any likelihood of Catharine's health suffering by this trip. I'm afraid she was very bewildered until I got a couple of minutes alone with her. What a marvellous girl she is. She'll bring it off if anyone can.'

'Brian, what will happen when your master finds out what you've been up to with the ambulance and everything?'

'He'll be so angry he won't be able to speak. For a minute or two. He'll speak then all right.'

'Don't you mind?'

'Well, it had to be done, hadn't it? And I've got the sack anyway. Already.'

Leonard picked up his sherry bottle and uncorked it.

'Brian.'

'Yes?'

'If you've got the sack, can you stay the night?'

'Oh yes, please, Lucy.'

By now Catharine was with Churchill. After some effort, she arranged things so that she was able to put her arms round him and take his head on her lap. Twice she raised him so that his face was near hers. Both times she looked into his face very longingly, though without managing to see in it more than she could have recognized at first glance. She felt not at all sure of being able to do what she had found she must do. When she spoke, she tried to use her mouth and lips so that they would put the words into exactly the right shape to penetrate the barrier of his hearing and reach him, reach the person she knew was there.

'Dearest James. I haven't got to tell you who this is, have I? Because all the most important part of you doesn't need to be told. It couldn't ever forget. Little James. We said it was all right to say that. You've always listened to everything I've ever said to you. You're to go on listening now.

'First there's me. I've had the operation. It all went off all right. Everybody's very pleased with me. I'm afraid there are bits of me missing now. But that's something you're not going to mind as much as all that. Not as much as you expected to. There's not everything gone from there. And they've promised me it isn't going to look horrible. I believe them, because they're very good. You don't know how good they are. Now they say I've got to have a lot of treatment which I shan't like at all. I'll have to keep going to hospital for a few weeks while I'm having it. But that's all right, because you'll be able to see me the rest of the time. Yes you will. You're going to. And they say I've got a good chance, because they took it so terrifically early. That's thanks to you, that they managed to do that. A good chance. You gave me a good chance.

'Now, darling. I know there's more to it than just me. And you're not to mind me knowing it and saying it. There are bound to be some things love doesn't reach as far as, however you look at it. It wouldn't be right any other way. There are things you can't ever do. Like giving people hydrophobia. I've just finished being told all about that. It was all right me hearing, because it's not going to happen. It never was going to. It was just a threat. I know exactly what you've been thinking, because I've been told. Sometimes you have to be told things. That man you were going to put into a little plastic bag and spray with stuff so that he couldn't swallow however thirsty he got. He's been let off. It's not going to be done to him. And that hasn't come about by chance. People have decided not to do it. They never even meant to.

'I remember you talking to me about God and how bad he was. I didn't feel as you did about it, but I saw what you meant. I can see how horrible it must be if you think that God's very cruel and then something comes up that makes you think people have started behaving like him. But when you told me that God had invented all the bad things, and so whenever anything bad happened it was really him who was doing it, you weren't talking to me. I thought you were going off on your own then and now you're trying to completely. You knew very well that it's up to people not to get on with the bad things God has invented for them. It's their job to show they're better than he is. Well, now here they are doing it.

'I know you think that bad things go together. All right, you had reason to. But this time it isn't going to happen like that. It isn't like you thought. There's just one bad thing on its own that you really mind about. What's been happening to me. And even that isn't a bad thing for certain. And if bad things can go together, so can good things. You and me ever meeting in the first place. Think what a good thing that was, and how unlikely. And then us falling in love and going to bed together and going on being in love. I'm not going to let you go mad. When I went mad I couldn't find any reason not to, and that was really why I did. You've got a reason not to. Me. And I know how hard it is not to go mad once you've sort of thought of it. But you're going to manage it, however hard it is even after what I've told you just now. You're going to dare to be sane, James, dearest James, little James. And big James. I love you.'

Churchill stirred, opened his eyes, and fixed them on Catharine.

'I know,' he said.

*

Ayscue stood at the lectern of the village church waiting for the end of the Thomas Roughead anthem, *Lord, Protect Thou Thy Servants*. He had agreed to deliver a short address from this position after the vicar had made it clear to him that, while the accommodation of visiting preachers in the pulpit was probably unavoidable in the course of a regular service, no such obligation existed when a house of worship was being made use of as a concert-hall. He was sitting now rather huddled up in a front corner pew staring at Ayscue, the expression of wondering outrage endemic to his face faintly intensified, it might be, by the memory of some of the verbal turns of phrase in Roughead's song, *Airs and Graces*, performed just before the anthem.

The concert was going at least as well as Ayscue had expected. Young Townsend had led off very creditably with the far from straightforward C major organ fantasia, and a slight raggedness among the choir altos, noticeable at the start of the first two extracts from the masque, *Hector and Andromache*, had quite soon cleared up. Ayscue thought it unlikely that anybody in the audience would have noticed, except no doubt the music critic whom a widely read and respected provincial newspaper had sent to report on the occasion. And this man, from a couple of minutes' chat in the church porch before the concert, had not only seemed pleasant and easy-going, unlikely to attend overmuch to foreseeable shortcomings of this kind, but had professed himself a devotee of eighteenth-century English music. Ayscue thought that if Townsend, Pearce and he could manage the trio-sonata, set down to follow the address, with as much accuracy and decent stylishness as they had shown at their final rehearsal, Thomas Roughead might indeed be launched on the modest posthumous career he deserved.

A moment in the closing pages of the anthem, two bars of contrary motion in the bass and tenor voices, caught Ayscue's ear. He remembered noticing it when glancing through the score with Townsend the previous week. Then he had passed it by as unremarkable, the taking of an obvious opportunity; now he caught his breath and felt himself shiver imperceptibly all over. Considering what he was about to say, it was mildly ironical that at this moment music should once more have revealed itself to him as the true embodiment of the unaided and self-constituted human spirit, the final proof of the non-existence of God.

As the series of florid, rather Handelian amens swung to

301

its close, he caught Churchill's eye and his sense of irony sharpened. But this was a faulty, outdated reflex. In the couple of days since his return to activity, Churchill seemed to have become quite at peace, no longer frowning or continually on the verge of protest or sarcasm. He gave a faint smile now and said something to Catharine at his side. Lucy Hazell leant over to hear it too, but Brian Leonard next to her still stared to his front, his look of puzzlement unaltered since the first chord of the fantasia. Even so, it was heartening to see him there. Apart from a squad of nominated volunteers from among the men off duty, and a few of Pearce's mates, the attendance from the camp was not strikingly good. The Colonel, Ross-Donaldson and Venables (not that the latter had been seriously expected to turn up at the concert) were away at a conference in London, where Hunter had also gone, it appeared for some sort of interview. The village, however, led by Eames, had come along in force.

The last traces of the music vanished from loft, chancel, pews, roof, gallery. Ayscue began to speak in his public tone, the one he hated whenever he caught himself at it. On those occasions he would wish he could sound as if he meant what he was saying. But he knew that that made people uncomfortable. And it could hardly be argued that wanting one's words to be believed was the same as meaning them.

'This will take about three minutes flat,' he said, not too bluffly, he hoped. 'You came here to enjoy yourselves, and if anybody feels like muttering that he doesn't see why he should have to put up with a dose of uplift thrown in, well, I rather sympathize with him. Many of us are in the habit of keeping our pleasures and our more serious thinking in separate compartments, and we wouldn't be human if we didn't tend to resent having our habits disturbed. But just for a moment I'm going to try to disturb this one a little. We've been listening to some music by Thomas Roughead, very finely performed by Mr Townsend and the members of the choir. Not much is known about Roughead's life, very little more than what you see in your programme. But we can learn something of him through his music. Whether he was writing church anthems like the one we've just heard, or whether, as in that song immediately before the anthem, he was celebrating the earthly pleasures that are every human being's birthright' – this was said with a hard look at the vicar – 'Roughead had his eye, his musical eye if you like, on the glory of God. You may think I say this because he was a church composer, because a large part of his music is obviously religious in character, in function. That's true, but I mean more than that. Every piece of music, every work of art, and in fact everything that human beings produce, doesn't come simply from them, from their human minds and hearts. God is with and within us all in everything we do, and never more than when we're doing the best things we're capable of. It's God's glory that we're celebrating at moments like that. It was God's glory that Roughead was celebrating in these compositions of his, God's glory that our musicians have been participating in as they played and sang them, God's glory that's been revealed to the rest of us as we sat here listening to them. This is what happens to us throughout life, even at moments that seem to have nothing of God in them.

'We're in his house this evening. It's only common courtesy to say a few words to him, I think you'll agree.

'Let us pray.'

As he turned and knelt, Ayscue was troubled less by the content, at once hectoring and chummy, of his penultimate sentence – ideas like that seemed to come from nowhere – than by the triteness, obscurity and illogic of what had gone before. He thought to himself he must be getting old. Then, as always on these occasions, he prayed, because here at any rate one got the chance of saying what one meant, even if to nobody.

'Catharine. Don't do it to her. Let her get well and stay well. Please.'

Whenever he had prayed before it had been like talking into an empty room, into a telephone with nobody at the other end. But this time it came upon him with certainty, if certainty could apply to an image, that the room had ceased to be empty, or that somebody was at the other end of the telephone, not saying anything, nowhere near that, but listening.

It frightened him rather. He felt he could believe that this was the first stage of a process, a chain, a series of which the

303

last would be a joy so enormous that it justified everything, or at least an explanation so cogent that human beings would unhesitatingly forgive all the wrongs God had done them.

Without thinking about it he got to his feet, rather sooner than everybody had expected. Then he recollected himself and walked firmly back to the lectern.

'Now we are going to play you,' he said, trying to breathe normally, 'a work by Thomas Roughead that has probably not been heard for a hundred and fifty years. Trio-sonata in B minor for flute, violin and piano.'

Townsend crossed from the stairs leading to the loft and sat down at the piano on Ayscue's right. Pearce came down the aisle, flute in hand, and took up his position behind the music-stand that had been set for him. Ayscue picked up his violin and bow from the top of the piano. With the minimum of delay they began. It was immediately clear that they would do well.

Outside, Ayscue's dog Nancy was secured by her lead to the railings by the gate. She was used to being in this situation, and when he prepared to leave his room to go to the concert she had responded so enthusiastically that he had not had the heart to leave her behind. But music had always had a bad effect on her, even at a distance, and the sounds now coming from the church seemed to strike her as especially intolerable. Squeaking, she tried as never before to slip her collar, and at last succeeded.

She had run through the gateway on to the sunlit pavement and was standing uncertainly there when an agricultural lorry came jolting down the village street. Although devotedly maintained, it was an old vehicle and its driver knew that it was nearing the end of its service. When Nancy, evidently too interested in something across the street to notice the lorry, moved cautiously into its path, he spun the wheel to avoid her. The steering failed to respond.